Baum's Boxing

Fringe

By E.M. Lindsey

Fringe Contender
E.M. Lindsey
Copyright © 2019

All rights reserved. This book or any portion thereof
may not be reproduced or used in any manner whatsoever
without the express written permission of the publisher
except for the use of brief quotations in a book review.

This book is a work of fiction. Any resemblance to persons, places, jobs, or events is purely coincidental.

Fringe Contender

Book Three of Baum's Boxing

A note to my readers,

I try to avoid these author's notes as often as possible, as I want you to get into the story without any sort of influence from me. However, some of the topics in Fringe Contender are sensitive ones, and I feel like a few things need to be addressed before you begin.

Writing transgender characters can be tricky, just as writing any character who experiences life in a way different to yours can be. My main concern was doing Trevor's experience as a gay trans man justice. I'm very fortunate to have many transgender people in my life—most notably my best friend and platonic soulmate who has been my closest confidant for almost twenty years of my life. He's the person who taught me to be myself without apology or regret, and has spent a good deal of time teaching transgender youth, the beauty and power in body acceptance. There's a line in this book where Trevor's explaining to Cole how he can tell other trans people to accept themselves whilst being in the throes of agonizing dysphoria and self-hate. That was given to me by my friend, because, he said, it's one of the most poignant lessons he had to learn being a trans man *and* a trans activist. Sometimes you can give others the advice you can't give to yourself.

Trevor's character was carefully written and supervised by L, and I did my best to listen to every single correction he gave me. The most important point he wanted me to make here, though, was to remind the readers that his experience, and by proxy Trevor's experience, is not the experience of every trans individual. Trevor uses terminology for his body in masculine terms (cock, dick, etc) that might not reflect how other trans people refer to themselves. Each transgender person's experience is unique, and Trevor does not represent that as a whole. He's simply a reflection of someone near and dear to me who was willing to share intimate details of who they are and how they lived in order to bring Trevor to life in a realistic way.

Secondly, I wanted to give a brief warning here that some of the content in this book may be potentially triggering. I have done my best to keep the story realistic, not erasing a trans person's experiences whilst also not making their story *about* oppression, dysphoria, or transphobia. This book does deal with mentions of past-abuse, transphobia, some mild phobic language, and the loss of a pregnancy, so please feel free to skip this volume if those things are too difficult for you. I understand that life doesn't come with trigger warnings, but in my humble opinion, your entertainment should, and hopefully I've been able to provide that for you.

That being said, I hope you enjoy this final instalment of Baum's Boxing, and I look forward to hearing your thoughts.

All my best,

Elaine xx

To love someone is to strive to accept that person exactly the way he or she is, right here and now.

Fred Rogers

1.

Trevor Greene was no stranger to intimidation. He couldn't recall a single period of his own history which wasn't full of it. Starting early with his drugged-out, alcoholic father who would peer over his inflated, purple nose at his child and slur a hundred uncreative insults in some attempt to get him to align better with the person he thought Trevor should be, to his mother who had never had the spine to stand up to the angry man. He recalled with vivid clarity the fear he felt in the face of the DCS agent who showed up to take him by the hand and lead him first to a group home where he slept next to a dozen other kids who cried themselves to sleep, then to some abstract grandmother figure eight months later who had previously only existed in toxic rants from his father's drunken rages. He couldn't help wondering if this woman in a pencil skirt and three-inch heels might put him somewhere else, somewhere less kind, if she knew the truth about him.

Mostly because Trevor was a *him*, but no one knew it. He didn't exactly have the language, at nine years old, to express how he really felt, why all of this was wrong. Why dresses and skirts and pretty baubles and violent beatings from an angry father, who just wanted his daughter to be more girly, wouldn't change the fact that Trevor was…well… *Trevor*.

He expected his grandmother to intimidate him. How could anyone but a monster have raised the man who had given Trevor life, then tormented him for the first nine years of it? Except instead of being a monster at all, she'd sat him down and asked him questions and actually listened when he told her that he was, in fact, a boy. That he didn't like his name, that it wasn't the right one. He hadn't expected a trip to the doctor, to a therapist office, medication that suddenly made him feel more like himself. The day he stood in front of a judge with a new name and the knowledge that he belonged to his gran and not to those angry people who once called themselves his parents, he broke down and cried for half an hour straight.

Then he went about his life, because his grandmother's acceptance wasn't everything. The world outside still existed, still refused to understand who he was. Total strangers still felt it was necessary to impose their opinions, their bias, their anger and bigotry on his identity. He never really felt peace, even as he raced toward his dreams, and dated, and made friends, and continued to see his own identity as a form of resistance. Even after his grandmother died and he felt alone in the world again, he still retained himself as the man he'd grown up to be, thanks to her.

Trevor Greene had always been who he was. Tall, red-haired, freckled, transgender, gay, brave, smart, and too often intimidated.

Those facts followed him into a dark, empty classroom where a vicious man with an ugly smile, who had once pretended to be a friend, now stared at him with cruelty in his eyes. "I know the truth."

Trevor blinked at him. "…Okay? Charlie, I don't…"

"I know that you're actually a *girl*," he spat.

Trevor hadn't been misgendered in so long, it was like a physical blow to the gut. "I'm not a fucking woman," he found himself spitting, refusing to be cowed by some transphobic bigot.

Charlie's grin widened. "I also know what you did at the fertility lab."

At that, Trevor's jaw slammed shut and he felt sick at the look of triumph in Charlie's eyes. "How…?"

"You don't need to worry about that. I have a lot going on right now, and all *you* need to know is that when I turn in my evidence that you were fucking an undergrad, *Professor* Greene, you're going to bow your head and accept your termination without argument."

"I have never fucked an undergrad," Trevor spat.

"Photos of you and a blonde Delta Phi beg to differ," Charlie said with a shrug.

Trever spluttered. "That's…she's my *cousin*. As in biological. You can't use that against me. She'll happily testify to that." In truth, he wasn't entirely sure Amelia would. She was a fourth cousin or something, no one he'd known growing up, and he'd done it as a favor after she tracked him down when she found out what his last name was. He'd helped only because he was starved for biological family members and it seemed foolish to turn her away. Maybe, he realized, that was coming back to bite him in the ass.

"If you want the University and the rest of the fucking world to find out that you bribed one of the specialists to let you into the IVF program against University policy, then sure. I can't."

Trevor felt his stomach twist, his face heating up with panic, even as he realized Amelia probably wasn't involved. The room began to spin, and he groped for one of the desks to keep himself steady. "Why? Why are you doing this? What do you want?"

"From you?" Charlie asked, then let out a disgusted laugh. "Nothing. You've literally never been on my radar. I mean, I've seen you flirt with Noah and I don't love that, but I know he wouldn't give someone like you the time of day. I'm doing this as a favor to a friend."

"Who?" Trevor asked in a faint whisper. He racked his brain, tried to think of anyone he'd pissed off this much. He had a handful of relationships under his belt, and none of them had really worked out, but he didn't think any of them hated him this much. He'd never conflicted with students, his co-workers all seemed to like him.

Charlie shrugged. "I'm not really at liberty to say. All I know is that you've been here under the false pretenses of being a man—"

"I *am* a man," Trevor retorted.

Charlie let out a snort. "Biology begs to differ. And I know that you broke the law to get pregnant, which only backs up my statement, because *men* do not get *pregnant*."

The shock of it was probably what kept him from dissolving into utter panic, and he clenched his hands into fists. "What do you want me to do?"

"I already told you. You're going to be fired, you're not going to fight it, and you're not going to show up here ever again. That's all our mutual acquaintance wants from you." Charlie gave him a slow up-and-down look, then turned on his heel.

As the door slammed, a benediction to the hell that had just descended upon his life, Trevor sank into one of the desk chairs and started to shake.

***

"Oh fuck, Oh god." Rhys squeezed his eyes shut, his hands braced against the wall. The pressure was intense, almost eclipsing the pleasure, even though the guy had the right angle to hit his prostate with every thrust. His whole body shuddered as he let himself think, *I'm being fucked in the ass. A cock is fucking me in the ass.* It had been so long.

"Holy shit, you are so tight. How are you so tight?" the guy behind him gasped. His mouth latched on to the back of Rhys' neck and nipped, giving a good suck, though not hard enough to leave a mark which Rhys appreciated.

He let out a strained laugh as his balls tightened, his hand itching to reach down and grab his dick, but he wasn't ready for it to be over just yet. "It's been a while," he managed through clenched teeth. "A long while."

That wasn't a lie. Not entirely. It had been exactly one year and eighteen months since his divorce was finalized, and exactly two years and three months since the last time he'd fucked anyone. Vanessa hadn't really been interested in sex during the last leg of their marriage, though he later learned it wasn't that she was disinterested in sex, but more she was getting it on the regular with his best friend whom she'd eventually marry.

Also, Rhys hadn't been with a guy since before he and Vanessa tied the knot. They had a short break-up, six months in his last year of law school, during his year-long internship with the ACLU. He, and one of the other interns, had gotten drunk one night after a major loss and decided to comfort each other with a couple of mutual blow-jobs. That had turned into something a little more regular, and after two months, Rhys had even considered something more serious. Serious enough to contemplate coming out, which was huge considering Rhys had been in the closet from the moment he realized he was bisexual. Only Vanessa showed up at his door that weekend, her blonde hair in disarray, no makeup, with a contrite apology and a promise to make it work in the future.

For Rhys, the decision had already been made, because he loved her. Because he had a ring stashed in the back of his freezer inside a box of frozen waffles, just waiting for their anniversary. They'd been together so long, he'd forgotten what it was like to not have her as his guaranteed forever. They'd make it work. Marriage, home, careers. Eventually kids, and someday even grandkids. Vanessa was just part of who he was. A bisexual lawyer who had never come out to his family, but none of that really mattered because he had her.

Until she left, and he didn't anymore. And he was fine with it. Really, he was just fine.

Except that ended up not being entirely true. Except there was a reason Rhys found himself here. In a storage cupboard with his hands braced against the wall, a condom-covered cock pounding into his ass, sending intense sensations through every limb.

"I'm going to come," he blurted. The guy's cock gave a valiant throb, and Rhys managed to get his hand around his dick, stroking once, then twice, and he shot it all over the wall. He let his head drop forward, a ragged gasp bursting from his lungs as the pleasure began to recede. The guy had grabbed his hips and was thrusting without rhythm. The stuttered breaths told Rhys it would be over soon.

The guy cried out softly against the back of his neck, everything on his body going still except the pulsing penis inside of him.

Then it was over. Just like that. No finesse, no promises. The guy just pulled out and threw the condom away, and then they dressed. Making their way back to the bar, neither man asked for a name or number, and neither of them offered one. Rhys picked up the guy's tab because he figured it was the polite thing to do, then he finished his lager and called for his uber.

When he looked back from his place by the door, he saw the barstool was empty and the man was gone. It was just as well, Rhys really didn't have a thing for blondes anymore.

***

Walking into the house, Rhys tried to ignore the pressing silence of his place, the way everything was just too damn loud in the empty room. The crack of the beer bottle top sounded like a gunshot, and he winced at the sound it made when he tossed it into his little bin with all the others. He tried not to look at how full it was, at how much he'd been relying on the slow burn of alcohol to numb the ache deep in his gut. He was close to it becoming a problem, and he stared at the neck of the current brew he held, knowing he was going to have to do something besides this if he really wanted to move on. He was sore in all the right places, but for whatever reason, it felt so wrong.

The frustrating part was that Rhys rarely let himself fall like this. Granted, he'd led a life of privilege, but it hadn't been without trial and tribulation. He'd had a close friend die, he'd failed classes, he'd survived a stupid jet-skiing accident without a single scar or broken bone, had more than one falling out with his brother. Paling in comparison to what many people may have suffered in life, but all the same, he prided himself in how he dealt with emotions in the face of crisis.

And maybe it had everything to do with the fact that he and Vanessa had seemed like the two people who would be together forever which had shaken him. They'd pursued each other, falling in love over a library counter with her behind the desk and him checking out ever-increasing numbers of books he had no intention of reading. He wooed her with fancy coffee and horrible dad jokes, and somehow, they'd become a thing.

They had survived his years in law-school, and taking the bar exam, and the inevitable work hours he had to dedicate to his career because he wanted to make it in a private practice. She'd thrown herself into her anthropology Ph.D. and they'd weathered her semesters abroad and academic travels, and he always thought someday she'd settle down at home. That he'd get a partner or two at the firm, and he'd carve out time in their lives for the thing he wanted.

Like kids. Like family vacations. Like holidays and birthdays and anniversaries that were more than flowers delivered and boxes of chocolates left on tables with hand-written notes of apology for not being able to make dinner.

Swallowing thickly, he stared over at the single remaining picture of their wedding party that sat on the bookshelf to the left of the TV. He told himself he was keeping it because it was the last photo he had of Jake before he died, but in truth it was because he couldn't quite yet bring himself to rid his life of the last, lingering trace of her. She was remarried, and the whole reason he was trying to numb the pain tonight was because his masochistic streak had led him to her Facebook page. To her newly updated cover-photo of herself and her husband, his hand on her flat stomach, a little chalk-board announcing the upcoming due-date of their baby.

She was expecting.

His mind couldn't help but wander back to one of the last fights, right before she packed a bag and walked out. Right before she reached into a folder and pulled out paperwork he knew all-too well. "I'm not a walking incubator, Rhys!"

He'd scrubbed both hands over his face, wondering if he really was in the wrong here. "I'm not...*shit*, Vanessa, you know I don't think of you like that. I just thought we were on the same page. You told me someday you wanted to consider having a family."

"That I'd *think* about it, not that I was contractually obligated to crap out a litter of kids for you," she hissed.

He swallowed thickly. "Okay. Look...*okay*. Kids are off the table. I'll never bring it up again. Just...stop packing, *please*."

She turned to him, her eyes half-lidded and sad, and that told him more than anything it wasn't about kids. "You want them with me, Rhys, and I can't do that. I don't want kids with you—with anyone. And I can't take the idea of having a family away from you."

"I can get a dog," he told her, and he meant it. He had spent his life achieving nearly every single goal he'd set out. He could compromise on this one. "I can get two dogs. There are plenty of couples happy with—"

"There's someone else," she interrupted, her tone flat, matter-of-fact.

Later Rhys would compare the moment to having his heart physically ripped out of his chest. Most people would assume it would hurt, that the pain would bring them to their knees, but that wasn't right. The shock overwhelmed any sense of pain, and all that was left was a sense of numbness and inevitability. He sank into that as he watched her—unable to say another word—throw the last handful of clothes from her drawer into the case lying open on their bed.

His bed, he supposed. Because she was leaving him.

"I didn't mean to tell you like this," she said, a little softer this time.

He couldn't help a bitter laugh. "How the fuck did you mean to tell me?"

Her cheeks went a little pink, and she tucked a lock of blonde hair behind her ear. "Honestly? I *wasn't* planning on telling you. I was hoping we'd just move on and finalize the divorce, and you could maybe assume I got together with him right after I left. But you won't fucking let it go. You gave me no choice."

He clenched his hands into fists. "Seriously? *I'm* the bad guy who forced you to come clean about fucking another man because I wouldn't stop trying to save my marriage?"

She let the lid of the case fall from her hands and she turned to face him fully. "I don't know what you want me to say."

"I want you to tell me why you're not even willing to try with me," he said, his tone begging. God, he felt pathetic. Even after all this, he was willing to try and make it work knowing she had been sleeping with someone else. He swallowed again. "How long?"

Her face fell and he knew. Somehow, he knew. "A while."

"How. Long."

She turned away before she spoke again. "The week after our honeymoon. And…and before too, when we were dating in college."

Rhys took several steps back, collapsing into the desk chair and he felt every ounce of strength drain from him. "The entire time?" he whispered. "The…" Shaking his head, he fought the urge to grab her and shake her until she admitted it was a lie. "Who is it?"

At that, she looked a little terrified, but unwilling to lie. "Mark."

The rug was ripped from under him, and Rhys had no choice but to fall. "Mark. My best friend Mark. My former roommate, and the person I trusted with everything." His tone was flat, dead, like the hollow feeling in the center of his chest.

"Yes," she said. She turned to look at him with hard eyes. "I was in love with both of you, and he wasn't ready to commit, so I thought staying with you was…safer."

He nodded, the pain fading into that overwhelming numbness. "And now *he* is?"

She shrugged. "I wish I had a better answer for you, Rhys, but I don't. You didn't do anything wrong, you just didn't do anything right for me, and I can't live like that."

He said nothing. In fact, he said nothing again directly to her from that moment on. He spoke through attorneys, he managed to have her petition for alimony thrown out, and he found himself momentarily grateful they didn't have kids together, because that would have just led him down another hellish path.

He couldn't help it now, though, to look at that pregnancy announcement and wonder what it was he didn't have. What hadn't he been able to offer that Mark had? What about him was so inferior that she had maintained a long-standing affair with his best friend during the course of their entire marriage, and eventually, in the end, chose him?

Closing his eyes, he let out a shaking breath and took down half the beer in one go. It wasn't enough, but more than that would be dangerous. He had to find his footing again. Traveling had done nothing, and now he had a pile of cases waiting for him to get back to his life. His life without her, in this house they'd started together. Only, had they? Because now that he knew the truth, now that he knew she had only been using him as a placeholder, he realized it had never been theirs. It had always only been his.

The weight of that was crushing, and he wasn't sure he was strong enough to survive it.

2.

"Well, well, well, look who finally decided to grace us with his presence," came a light, admonishing voice from the front desk.

Rhys flushed a little, rubbing the back of his neck as he offered his assistant a sheepish smile. "Come on, Mel, you know you loved it while I wasn't here."

She winked at him, her freckles standing out a shade darker than her light brown skin. "I mean, the office orgies were fun. The yoga studio next door provided some very flexible entertainment, but it is nice to feel like I'm earning my paycheck again."

Rolling his eyes, Rhys walked over to the coffee machine and dropped one of the pods in. "The terrifying thing about you is all of that could be plausible."

She smiled sweetly at him as the scent of fresh coffee wafted up from his cup. "Billie's out of town all month on conferences. She'd murder me if I attended an orgy with yogis without her."

Sighing, Rhys fiddled with an over-gelled clump of hair near his temple. "What's on my agenda today?"

Mel cleared her throat, dipping her head down and impatiently brushing one of her dreads back behind her ear. "You have four potential client meetings today. You have one at eleven, then the rest are back to back starting at two forty-five and going until five-thirty. I think the three later in the afternoon are just in for the consults, but this one coming up sounds," she pursed her lips in thought. "Something about it sounds serious."

Rhys nodded. "Okay, I can deal with that. What's the client requesting?"

"He was really hesitant to say," she confessed. "He indicated it was a possible discrimination suit against his work, but he was reluctant to tell me anything about it."

Rhys frowned as he took his coffee and began to add in cream from the dry packets. "Mel, is there a reason you booked me a meeting with a person who won't tell you anything?"

She bit her lip, then said, "Because I think it's of a sensitive nature that eventually I'll have to learn about, but maybe not until he's an official client."

There was something in her tone that had him both on high alert, and oddly settled. He'd been working with her for three years now, as she finished up her own degree at the University, and he was already considering offering her a job with him once she passed the bar. She was good, and she rarely steered him wrong on clients, which meant he was willing to trust her instincts.

"Fine. What else have I got?"

She rattled off the rest of his to-do list, things he'd been putting off which were mostly follow-ups, and paperwork to finalize since he'd returned just in time to head off to court on three of his cases the following week. It was a slow start, and frankly he should have been focusing on obtaining more clients, but it was hard to want to work when everything felt so heavy and ugly.

He knew it was probably obvious on his face, but he appreciated Mel didn't say a word, and simply handed him off his weekly agenda and went back to things as normal. At the very least, he was grateful to be able to count on that.

Just before he stepped into his office, Mel's voice stopped him. "Oh, and your brother called earlier. He said he'd like your recommendation after all. When I asked him to elaborate, he just said you'd know what he was talking about."

Rhys turned slowly, feeling another heavy weight settle in his gut. Ryan hadn't given much detail about the situation Noah was in, but he'd given enough. "Ah. Yeah, I need you to get me a phone meeting with Carl Sandburg, tell him I'm calling in a personal favor."

Mel's eyes widened. "Seriously? What did Ryan do?"

Rhys couldn't help his laugh in spite of how serious the situation was. "This time it's not his fault, but it's a mutual friend, so I can't take the case. Carl owes me though, from that golf game last month."

Mel smirked. "Got it. Golf game, cashing in favor. I hope it's worth it for whatever this is. That's a big favor."

Rhys' smile was a little tight as he nodded to her. "It's definitely worth it. Let me know what he says." He gave the wall a sharp double pat, then turned and walked into his office.

Helping Noah was *more* than worth it. Rhys had grown close to him back when he and Ryan were dating during their graduate studies. Rhys saw the split coming a mile away—his brother could be a real dipshit about his heart and about letting anything get too close, and Noah had suffered the brunt of that. It was a surprise to nearly everyone when Noah kept Ryan as a close friend, but Rhys couldn't help but be grateful for it. He knew his brother deserved to be happy, if only he could get his head out of his ass and let himself be loved, and Noah wasn't a friendship Ryan should squander.

After Noah's accident, Rhys had spent a decent amount of time with him and Ryan during the recovery, had seen the inner brute strength Noah possessed that Rhys didn't think he could ever have. He watched him go from half-blind and unable to speak to teaching a full semester of lecture classes in less than a year, and he loved the guy for it. He lamented that he'd never call Noah a brother-in-law, but he cherished what they had.

Knowing someone was coming after Noah, knowing someone would want to hurt him, left Rhys with a fury he had a hard time controlling. It was one of the reasons he'd come back a little early. When Ryan called and confessed part of what was going on, Rhys was ready to join up with the guys at Baum's and go full vigilante on this guy. It was by Ryan begging alone that Rhys had backed off, but he was sitting in wait just in case.

This guy could not go unpunished.

Grateful that all of this had a distracting effect, Rhys found the concentration to begin with work, and it felt like no time at all passed before Mel was knocking on his office door. "Your consult is here. Trevor Greene."

Rhys nodded, rising as Mel opened the door further and a tall, broad-shouldered redhead stepped in. The first thing Rhys noticed was how strikingly handsome the guy was. He was about three or four inches shorter than Rhys, lanky but with corded muscles poking out of his short-sleeved button-up shirt. His red hair was rich, full in waves styled short and well groomed, and his beard was manicured to perfection. When he extended his hand, Rhys was startled by how long his fingers were, enticed by the firm grip.

It had been a long while since a man had caught his attention so quickly and Rhys had to pull himself out of it before he became suddenly unprofessional. "Mr. Greene, it's nice to meet you. Why don't you have a seat here. Can I get you anything to drink? Coffee?"

The guy laughed, shaking his head as he moved to the guest chair and sat. "No, thanks. I've had like three espressos already and I feel like I'm about to jump out of my skin." His voice was higher than Rhys expected it to be, and had a grainy, hoarse quality to it that he immediately loved.

Swiping his hands as discretely as possible over the thighs of his trousers, Rhys sat back at his desk and pulled out his legal pad to start notes. "So, Mr. Greene, my assistant said that you were reluctant to talk about why you needed a consultation. Are you able to share details with me?"

Trevor's head looked back at the closed door, then he let out a breath. "Yeah, I can. It's just complicated and I don't…uh. Do attorney-client privileges apply here? Like if I did something that's not exactly on the up and up, are you required by law to report me?" When Rhys looked mildly alarmed, Trevor held up a hand. "I didn't murder anyone or anything like that. I just," he blew out a puff of air instead of finishing his sentence, and looked so scared, Rhys couldn't help but feel for him.

"You're paying for this hour, which means I'm currently under your employ," he assured him. "It means whatever you say here stays between us." That wasn't true in the strictest sense, but he had a feeling whatever this guy was going to say wouldn't leave Rhys feeling morally obligated to call the police.

Trevor swallowed thickly. "I'm being blackmailed."

The coincidence of it rocked him instantly. "Can you elaborate?"

"Yeah," Trevor said with a bitter laugh, "I'm a professor at the University working in the Classics department, and I'm being blackmailed by this other dickhead professor. I was just fired for sleeping with an undergrad."

Rhys tried to control his pounding heart and felt an immediate panic because he couldn't work for this man. It was an immediate conflict of interest. "Is that the part which you're worried about telling me? *Did* you have sex with an undergrad?"

"No," Trevor said, heat in his tone. "This asshole has photos of me dancing at a club with one, but she's my cousin. She was at a party and this guy was messing with her, so she asked me to help her out. I figured intimidating the frat-boy was better than taking him outside and beating his ass, getting fired, and arrested. Only now, that's being used against me."

Rhys frowned, sitting back. "So why not come forward with that information? Clearly a photo of you and another student—especially a blood relative—can't be grounds for termination."

"It isn't," Trevor admitted. "The thing is, the guy knows something else." He hesitated a long while, then said, "It's really, really complicated."

"Try me," Rhys told him. When Trevor hesitated, Rhys leaned over his desk a little and met his gaze directly. "Mr. Greene, I can't begin to know how to help you unless I have actual information."

Trevor nodded, his face paling, making his freckles stand out even more. He scratched at his beard, just under his jawline, then licked his lips. "For any of it to make sense I need to tell you…" He blinked, then said, "How do you feel about LGBT rights?"

Rhys was taken aback by the question, but he cleared his throat and said, "I'm in the business of keeping to the law. I understand a concern over bias, but I can assure you—in a very personal way—the rights and safety of all members of the LGBT community are very, very important to me." He could only hope the sincerity in his voice showed.

When Trevor relaxed a fraction, Rhys hoped that was the case. "I'm trans. I'm a transgender man." He paused a moment to let Rhys absorb that information, which Rhys was grateful for. He wouldn't have guessed, not in a million years.

"Alright," Rhys said, urging him to go on with a soft nod.

Trevor licked his lips. "I went on puberty-blockers when I was nine. My uh…my grandma, she had custody of me after CPS…" He stopped and shook his head. "That part isn't important. I started HRT when I was about thirteen, right around the time I should have had a period, and I've been on testosterone pretty consistently since then. It's not…it's not like a secret or anything, you know? But it's not something I advertise either, for obvious reasons."

"Of course," Rhys said.

"My gender marker changed when I was eighteen, after I had top-surgery since I needed that to comply with the state requirements. My grandma had my name legally changed during the adoption, so I never really had to uhh…to come out. You know, to strangers. I wasn't obligated to disclose that information to the school staff—that I'm trans. By all legal accounts, I'm a man named Trevor Greene. I have a Ph.D. in classical and vulgar Latin, I graduated summa cum laude, I've worked consistently since I received my doctorate."

Rhys nodded, making a couple of notes only to show that he was paying attention.

"I made a friend at the University. He, his wife, and his team were doing research with IVF." Trevor cleared his throat, and his cheeks turned pink as he stared down at his hands. "I've always struggled with the idea of biology—with having biological children," he corrected. "I eventually planned to have a hysterectomy, but my therapist told me to wait, because I was so torn on the idea of never being able to have my own kids. The testosterone over that period of time compromised my fertility, but it didn't necessarily make me infertile. My personal life was a mess, but I had this sudden opportunity to ah…to have a child. With this study. I didn't qualify for the program since I was employed there, but there were ways around that."

"Ah," Rhys said very softly.

"It was against University policy, but I wanted it, and he offered me a place in the study if I could pay for it. I paid him twenty-five thousand dollars, went off testosterone, and I began treatments there. I tested positive for a pregnancy after six months."

Rhys let out a puff of surprised air. "And when was this?"

"A few months ago," Trevor said softly. When Rhys couldn't stop his eyes from darting downward to the guy's midsection, Trevor covered his stomach with a defensive hand. "It didn't stick. I miscarried, and they didn't have any spare anonymous donor sperm for a second round. So, I went back on T and that was that. Or…I thought that was that. Because the person blackmailing me is threatening to out me. To out that I'm trans, and to out that I illegally obtained fertility treatments in an attempt to get pregnant. I didn't speak up when I was fired, and now I'm working at a bar and trying to stay afloat. I just…I don't think I can keep this up, Mr. Anderson."

Rhys let it sink in, let the gravity of the situation hit him, and he felt more rage rising toward Charlie Barnes for the way he was setting fire to people's lives. "You were terminated last month?" Rhys asked. "Along with a handful of other professors?"

Trevor frowned. "I didn't say that, did I? Do you know something about this?"

"I can't take your case," Rhys interrupted, then when Trevor looked like he'd been shot, he hurried to say, "I have a friend in your department who is currently facing the same blackmail."

Trevor blinked, then looked stunned. "Noah."

Rhys bit his lower lip. "I can't confirm who, but I can tell you that you're not the only one facing this."

"Are you taking that case?" Trevor looked almost desperate, and Rhys hated himself for the answer he had to give.

"I can't take any case relating to this situation," Rhys told him. "I'm too close to one of the petitioners. I wish I could. Believe me, there's nothing more I want than to face this piece of shit in court and send him screaming all the way to prison, but my hands are tied. If I get involved, there's likely to be a mistrial and that won't benefit anyone. I can, however, recommend an attorney that might be assisting the second client in this case."

Trevor looked slightly intrigued. "He could help get my job back?"

"Absolutely," Rhys said. "If you and the second client throw in your lot together…"

"Does that mean I have to come out with the information Barnes has on me?" Trevor interrupted in a small, quiet voice.

Rhys sat back in his chair and let out a long breath of air. "I want to say no, but chances are, Barnes will tell his lawyers everything and they'll attempt to discredit you in court using it."

Trevor shook his head, going so pale Rhys thought he might faint. "I…no. I can't. I…"

Holding up his hand, Rhys fought the mad urge to cross around the desk and take this man into his arms. "I'm not asking you to do that. I wouldn't. But it does limit your options."

Trevor took in a trembling breath, then met Rhys' eyes. "Is there anything else I can do that won't involve me coming out?"

Rhys passed a hand down his face, then let it fall to the top of his desk. "I want to tell you yes. I want to tell you that you can fight this without any risk, but that's just not possible."

"Because that's ridiculous," Trevor finished for him, a slightly sardonic smile curving over his mouth. Rhys had another, startling moment at just how attractive the man was, which was wholly inappropriate for both the professional setting and timing. Fuck, he was seriously lonely. "I understand. I think maybe I just needed to hear it."

The little timer Rhys kept on his desk went off, signaling that the time paid for was over, and he felt something uncomfortable twist in his gut. "Listen," he said as Trevor made to stand, "I want you to keep in touch with me."

Trevor blinked at him, his expression confused. "Why?"

"Because you're not alone in this. Even if you can't come forward, you're not alone, and I want to do something to help. This guy isn't going to get away with this forever, and if there's something I can do once it's over, I will. You don't deserve this. Neither of you do." He reached into his desk for a name card, then flipped it to the back. His fountain pen hovered, and he had just a moment of hesitation before jotting down his personal number, then pushed it across. "It's my cell phone. As in my personal, only friends and family have this number. If he starts to threaten you, if anything new comes up, I want you to call me."

Trevor's hands shook just a little as he took the card and slipped it into his pocket. Rhys had to wonder if it was just going to end up in the bin the moment he was out of the office, but he couldn't help hoping that he'd keep it, that maybe he'd call. That maybe, by some miracle, Rhys would figure a way out of this mess for both Trevor and Noah.

Stranger things had happened.

He rose then, along with Trevor, and walked around the desk to shake his hand. Their palms lingered together, and Rhys was desperate to ignore the way touching him made him feel. Too right, too important. He rationalized it away that it was just the ache of knowing Vanessa had gotten married, was now pregnant, was living a life she was supposed to have with him.

"Can I just say thank you?" Trevor asked, his words piercing Rhys' near spiral.

He blinked and frowned at the other man. "Of course, but I didn't really do anything."

Trevor laughed and gently drew his hand away. "You listened to me, you heard the stupid choice I made and maybe you judged me because trust me, I'm still kicking my own ass for being so impulsive, but you didn't treat me the way most people would have when I told them the story."

Rhys' frown deepened. "I think I'm afraid to ask how that would be."

Trevor shrugged but didn't elaborate, instead taking a step back and heading for the door. Rhys wanted to stop him, to offer lunch or something—anything to get that agonizingly lost look off of his face—but he couldn't do that. It wasn't his place and he didn't even know this guy.

So instead he stood in silence as Trevor let himself out. He listened as Mel made pleasant small-talk, then the office door shut, and Rhys caught a glimpse of him passing by the window. His feet were moving before he was really aware of it, and he gripped the door frame and peered around the corner to where Mel looked like she was expecting him.

"Refund him," he said.

He thought maybe she'd balk at it, or snark, but instead she just smiled a little softly and turned to her computer.

"And reschedule my other meetings. I have to go out for a bit."

"You got it," she said with a mock salute, and didn't argue that he was one day back from his trip only to fuck off out of the office for the rest of the day. He wasn't sure what he was going to do, but he figured that asking Ryan might at least point him in the right direction.

***

Trevor groaned, his back aching from the long shift at a job he never thought he'd work again. It was by some miracle that Plato's was still around, let alone hiring, let alone remembered him. Marty had been an uppity assistant manager five years ago when Trevor had first applied there to be a bar-back for some extra cash when he was scrambling for a full-time position, and now he was the GM of the little hole-in-the-wall, wanna-be hipster club which had gone from serving cheap domestics in cans to hand-crushed tomato bloody mary's and truffle fries.

But Marty had hired him on the spot, no questions asked, had started him at a decent rate and had given him both Friday and Saturday night shifts. It meant that his desperately empty savings account from paying Andrew for the treatments had at least two zeroes in it, and it meant he'd probably make his rent if he smiled enough, and looked cute enough, and pretended to take enough numbers from drunk, beardy assholes who were feeling a little bi-curious that night.

But it had been a damn long time since he'd worked on his feet until two in the morning. As a matter of fact, after acquiring nearly a hundred grand in student loan debt to have that shiny Dr. attached to his name, he didn't think he'd be forced behind a bar ever again. At least, not one that he didn't own himself.

Oh, how the mighty fall, he thought with a sardonic laugh. He turned the heat up in his car and curled toward it, letting the rapidly warming air bring some life back into his fingers. As he sat there, he thought about the lawyer guy. Rhys Anderson. The man was probably one of the most attractive humans Trevor had ever seen in his life. He was so symmetrical it actually made him angry. Tall, fit, long, Grecian nose, a sweep of expertly styled brown hair, and green eyes he could have gotten lost in for days.

And he was fairly sure—though things had been rough lately, so his radar was off—but the guy had been staring at him. And not like he was some sort of specimen to be studied. He was damn sure the guy had blushed, and he'd definitely lost track of the conversation more than once.

Reaching into his console, Trevor touched the corner of the name card that had been sitting there for two weeks now, knowing there wasn't anything he could do with it. But there was something comforting about having it. And there was something comforting at how fiercely Rhys Anderson had defended his stance on the LGBT community—not just like he had loved ones in it, but like maybe he was part of it.

Trevor didn't want to hope, mostly because attractive, cis, gay men almost always viewed him as *other*. They never accepted him as a man completely, even if they supported the idea of him, and used his name and proper pronouns. It made dating complicated and exhausting, and almost never worth his time. Still, he appreciated it. He couldn't stop thinking of the way Rhys had stared at him and licked his lips briefly.

Trevor forced himself it sit back and put the car into drive. There was no sense in thinking about this now. What he wanted was his bed, and a long shower, and maybe an herbal tea before he collapsed under his blankets and slept until he had to be back at this hipster hell-hole. He was only grateful the drive was short, and that there was front row parking close to his apartment entrance.

Palming his keys, Trevor dragged himself over the pavement and around the corner to his door. He was only half aware of his surroundings as he approached and spied the little white paper stuck to the front. He assumed it was a menu or some warning about the electric company doing some test, so he ripped it off and curled it into his hand. He shoved his key into the door, turned it, then froze.

Nothing happened.

With a sigh, he jiggled the key again, and still nothing. He pulled it out, put it back in slowly— the lock remained stubbornly tight. Panic started to rise, and he took a step back, squinting at the numbers on his door. It was the same apartment he'd been living in for six years now. The same apartment to he could find blind-drunk—and had, when the need arose.

His stomach sank as he felt the sharp edge of the paper biting into his palm. He stepped under his neighbor's porch light and uncurled the sheet. His eyes scanned the words and it took his brain far too long to sync with what he was reading.

> *Eviction Notice…*
> *In accordance with…*
> *Due to the circumstances…*
> *Five days…*
> *Pick up your belongings at…*

He took a few staggering steps backward, nearly falling over the edge of the pavement before he caught himself. He was being evicted. Apart from everything else going on, now he was being thrown out of his apartment—and not because he hadn't paid his bills. There was no way this was legal, and yet he was cuckholded again by this maniac who seemed bound and determined to see him suffer.

And for what? His brain searched desperately for some idea of who it could be. If it wasn't Barnes, then who wanted him ground into the dirt like he was nothing? His hands were shaking as he realized he had nowhere to go. His bank account was at a few hundred bucks, and he'd made a bill and a half during his shift, but that wasn't enough to cover emergency lodgings. A hotel anywhere in the city would set him back at least eighty bucks for some flea-bitten mattress near the freeway, and that would get him through a night, maybe? Two if he wanted to cut his food bill down to nothing.

Shit. His food. His things. Everything he owed apparently packed up and thrown into a storage locker which he had five days to secure before it was put up for auction. How? How was this his life? For the first time in years he felt the loss of his grandmother so achingly painful his tears began to well up.

Amelia lived in town—but she was at the sorority house and he couldn't stay there. Her father was some random relative of his dad—not a waste like his sperm-donor, but not friendly about him existing, either, and he lived hundreds of miles away. Trevor was well and truly alone. He'd never gotten close to people, and when he'd been fired, any work acquaintances had fizzled into nothing.

His chest ached as he turned back to his car and felt a momentary wash of relief that at least it was paid off. He could find somewhere to park it, maybe? Catch a few hours and then…

And then?

He had no idea what he'd do next.

3.

"I'm sorry, but it looks like your application has been denied," the woman at the desk said, frowning at her computer.

Trevor blinked at her, a little startled by the admission. "I don't understand," he said quietly. "I have a great credit history, I have steady income, my debt to income ratio meets all the criteria."

She gave him a look, and his stomach plummeted to his knees. "I'm sorry, but there's a red flag on the account and there's nothing I can do about it."

Trevor swallowed thickly. "It's going to be the same everywhere, isn't it? Any time I fill one of these out."

Her look was sympathetic, but it didn't reach her eyes and he had to wonder exactly what the report said. "If they use this system, then I'm afraid so. There's always renting from a private owner, and I'm sure somewhere in the city has assistance for people with…complicated pasts."

Complicated pasts. He shook his head, rising and trying not to take his frustration out a woman who really had no control over the situation. "I understand. It's fine. Thank you for your time." Without a further farewell, he turned on his heel and hurried out, walking to his car where he'd spent the last few nights curled up in his back seat. He was surrounded by what little he could fit from the storage shed—some of his prized books his diplomas, his important paperwork, and some of his clothes. The rest was gone now, off to auction and likely the trash because he'd never really owned anything of real value.

It almost made him laugh. If the situation hadn't been so dire, he was pretty sure he wouldn't be able to stop laughing. How the mighty fall had become the most apt motto, and he was contemplating using the last of his cash in savings to have that tattooed across his damn forehead, because nothing else could sum this up better. He'd gone from a University Professor with a nice savings and cushy contract, to homeless, living in his car and taking standing baths in the bathroom of the bar was tending. He was running low in his testosterone, and low on his cash, and low on his syringes, and without the insurance he had counted on, the cost was going to add up to beyond what he could hope to afford.

He felt his stomach twist, the small lunch he'd managed before walking into the apartment office threatening to climb back up his throat. He sat behind the wheel and gripped it so tight his knuckles hurt. Through the front window of his car, he could see the woman peering out at him, and he fought the irrational urge to burst into the office and just unleash everything he'd been through. Maybe then she would find a work-around. Or maybe she'd be one of those types who thought that because of his gender, his sexuality, or his stark lack of religion, he deserved everything he had coming to him.

Closing his eyes, he let out a shuddering breath. When he opened them, he sat back and glanced down at his console where Rhys' card sat. He had too much pride for the moment to tell the guy what was going on, but maybe—just maybe—there had been more information in the case. It had been a while now since he'd first sat in the lawyer's office. There could be an update on the case.

With trembling fingers, he entered the number into his dial pad and pressed the phone to his ear. His breath caught in his chest as he listened to it ring. And ring. And ring. "Fuck," he whispered. He was just about to end the call when it picked up, a scraping noise like the phone was being shuffled around, and then a voice answered.

"Yeah?"

"Mr....Mr. Anderson," Trevor managed.

There was a long pause. "Who is this? How the fuck did you get this number?"

Trevor felt his face turn white-hot with shame and he just barely stopped himself from hanging up. "This is Trevor Greene? You gave me this number on your card, and I was...I just..."

"Shit," Rhys breathed out. "I'm so sorry. Jesus, I didn't mean to come at you like that. I'm just dealing with some stuff right now and," he went quiet a minute. "Are you okay?"

"Fine," Trevor lied, not really caring if Rhys could hear it in his tone. "I just wanted to check and see if maybe there was some progress?"

"There might be, but we don't know a lot right now," Rhys said. "I know that's not what you want to hear but..."

"No, it's fine," Trevor told him. "Might be is better than nothing, right?"

"Mm." Rhys' tone was hesitant, his silence filling the space between them, then he said, "Are you sure you're okay? You don't sound like it."

"It's just been a long day. I want to keep you, you sound really busy..."

"I'm not," Rhys began.

"...so, I'll let you go. Thanks for the update. I'll call when I can." He didn't give Rhys a chance to speak again before he ended the call, threw the phone on silent, then tossed it to the seat. He couldn't stand pity in the guy's tone, couldn't stand the fact that Rhys' warm voice made him want to confess things. He had no doubt Rhys would go out of his way to help, either. Trevor had seen it all over his face during their meeting. He'd seen it in the three-hundred-and-forty-dollar refund that hit his bank account three days after the consultation. He couldn't stomach it. When the world was viciously stripping him of everything that made him feel human, he couldn't let one more thing drag him under.

Jamming his key into the ignition, Trevor pulled out of the parking spot and out onto the street. Something had to give. He had to reach for something else and he had options. There were other universities within driving distance. There were community colleges with demands for people like him in humanities. He wasn't totally devoid of all choices, he wasn't doomed to sleep in his car and tend bar forever.

He found a café not far off and pulled into a free space. Grabbing his laptop and wallet, he hoped he looked like someone with a too busy schedule rather than a homeless man who had just lost everything he'd ever owned apart from six boxes and two suitcases. He hoped to god he didn't smell like a man who hadn't had a real shower in three weeks.

Walking inside, he quickly ordered a large drip and a scone, smiling at the barista who didn't bother looking him in the eye. He handed over a wad of cash, stuffing a few bills into the tip jar in some faint hope that maybe karma wouldn't bite him in the ass for it. Some day he might regret losing that two bucks, but he had a shift tonight, so today was not that day.

Setting up at a small table, Trevor pulled up the job account and typed in his password. He'd always kept his eye on the market, but he hadn't checked in for so long—not since before the incident with Barnes. He had a few alerts and saw that the community college was hiring for a Latin professor, and one for world history. He was qualified to teach both, so he quickly sent off his resume and his pre-written cover-letter, then whispered a small prayer to himself just as his coffee and scone dropped near his elbow. He didn't look up but tried to offer a smile as he perused the rest of the market.

It was Sahara Desert dry, and his entire body went tense with the realization that he had so little in the way of opportunity. It was still mid-semester, and even if he did get called back, it would be months before he'd be allowed to work. He might get lucky with a few late-start online classes, but his hopes were quickly fading.

Fighting back a sob, he curled his hand around his hot mug and let the heat distract him from how much this hurt. He hadn't made the smartest choice when he walked into the research lab and handed over a wad of cash to a man with too little integrity, but he didn't think it made him a bad guy. He'd fought so hard for most of his life, and he thought that for once—for the first time in so long—he'd be able to just live as himself. Now, everything that made him who he was had been systematically stripped to nothing.

***

Rhys hesitated before pulling into the gas station parking lot. It had been a long day, he'd been given endless shit from the judge for his late submissions, and one of his clients was ready to walk. It had gone on too long for Vanessa to be responsible, and he wasn't even really involved in Noah's issue, which meant he had only himself to blame.

Right now, at ten pm, he wanted nothing more than to curl up with a bottle of cheap whiskey, a carton of ice cream, and a stale bag of chips. He had several shitty Netflix shows queued up and he had no problem neglecting a night of paperwork for this imposter version of self-care. Grabbing his wallet from the dash, he strolled in and winced at the bright fluorescent lights. He passed by the candy aisle when the coffee he'd guzzled over the last half hour hit him, and his bladder suddenly tried to explode.

"Bathroom?" he asked the bored attendant playing on her phone.

She waved her hand toward the back near the slushie machine and he saw the little sign hanging above the beer cooler. Walking fast, he pushed the swinging door open and came to a stuttered halt. In front of the sinks stood a familiar redhead, wearing only an undershirt, his locks dripping down his face from a makeshift wash he was clearly doing under the rusted faucet. He had an overnight bag hanging off the side of the other sink, and a dirty towel resting over his arm. Their eyes met and Trevor looked like he wanted to bolt.

Not willing to let that happen, Rhys positioned himself in front of the door and cleared his throat. "I think we need to talk."

Trevor's jaw clenched so hard, his temples throbbed with the rapid pace of his pulse. "No."

"You should have called me," Rhys said. His hands curled into fists, mostly angry at himself for not recognizing this sooner. He knew something was wrong when Trevor had called the week before, but he hadn't realized how bad it was.

"This isn't your business," Trevor all-but snapped.

Rhys snorted. "This is because of blackmail, and thanks to Noah, it *is* sort of my business. What the fuck happened?"

Throwing up his hands, Trevor reached for his shirt and pulled it over his head. "Well," he started, his voice tight and hoarse, "after I got fired, whoever the fuck is behind this made a call to my landlord and got me evicted. When I went to apply for another place to live, my record came up with a red flag—whatever the fuck that means—and that prevented me from getting another apartment, so I've been sleeping in my car."

Rhys let himself absorb the shocking blow of his admission. "You don't have any family you can stay with?"

At the devastated look on Trevor's face, Rhys felt like a complete asshole. "No. The one person who ever gave a shit about me died before I turned twenty. And I was never really close to anyone else. Not here, anyway. My cousin lives at her sorority house, her dad hates me, and my old work colleagues were definitely happy to side with the school when I was fired for fucking a student."

Rhys closed his eyes, took a breath, then opened them. "My car's out front. I have to piss and then pick up some junk food. My place is a ten-minute drive from here, and I have a pretty decent shower so you can…"

"Fuck no," Trevor spat. "I am not a charity case."

Rhys couldn't help a dark laugh as he looked the guy up and down. "I hate to be the bearer of bad news, but yeah, you are. You're the poster-child for charity cases. It's not your fault and believe me, the things I want to do to this bastard who's fucking with your life— I don't even have words for. They're dark and depraved and he would *suffer*. But I can't do any of that. What I *can* do is give you my guest room and continue to help Noah take this piece of shit down so the both of you can get on with living your lives."

Trevor's lower jaw trembled a little and his cheeks went bright pink, making his freckled stand out. "I can't," he whispered.

Rhys took a step forward and leveled the man with his most serious look. "You can. Where else are you going to go? You can't live like this forever, and I'm not offering this to you out of pity. I'm offering this to you because for some reason this guy is shitting on you and you don't even know why."

At that, Trevor's eyes began to well and Rhys felt something in his chest twist painfully. "You don't even know me. What if I actually am some monster who totally deserves it?"

"Then fool me once," Rhys said with a shrug. "I'm willing to take the chance. Now, I really have to piss, so don't leave, okay? If you do, I will hunt you down. I have friends. Cop friends. With license plate scanners."

Letting out a tense laugh, Trevor nodded. "Yeah I…fine. Not for long. Just for a little while."

"For however long it takes," Rhys corrected. He pushed past the other man and went into the stall instead of stopping at the urinal just to make the situation more comfortable for him. As he unzipped and began to relieve himself, he could hear Trevor packing up his things. He felt a sense of urgency, like maybe Trevor was still on the edge of bolting, and Rhys wouldn't be able to live with himself if he let that happen.

He quickly zipped himself up, flushed, and hurried out of the stall, convinced he'd find an empty restroom. Instead, Trevor was there, waiting with his back to the wall, his arms crossed over his chest and staring at his feet. Rhys swallowed and said nothing, instead washing his hands and swiping them dry over the thighs of his trousers.

"Okay," he said as he reached for the door, "I've had the most shit day so I'm loading up on everything bad for me. What do you want?"

He glanced back to see Trevor flushing and glancing away. "Whatever you get is fine."

He was holding something back, Rhys was certain of it, but he decided now was not the time to call him out. Instead he just shrugged and added two of everything he'd planned to buy before, including the whiskey. He paid the bored teen at the register, then led the way to his car before realizing that Trevor had his parked not far from it.

"I'm not sure this is a good idea," Trevor said, hesitating on the side walk.

Rhys turned to him with a sigh. "I already told you—"

"Every time I attempt at getting myself out of this, something shows up. I found this a few days ago tucked under my windshield wiper when I left a coffee shop. I'd spent the afternoon sending out my resume for teaching positions nearby." He pulled a folded bit of paper out of his pocket and handed it over.

Rhys unfolded it and tilted it under the shitty, faded yellow light, squinting at the typed words.

> **Withdraw the applications or the information comes forward. There is no rest for you.**

Nausea roiled in his stomach and he clenched the note so tightly, it crumpled in his fist. "Fuck this, and fuck him," Rhys hissed. He looked up at Trevor with heated eyes. "He's not going to do this to you."

"If he finds my car parked at your place, he'll know," Trevor told him.

"So we won't park it at my place. I have a friend who has spare room in his garage. We put your car there, and you come home with me, because I'm not letting you continue to sleep in a fucking Volvo until you freeze to death!" He immediately reigned his tone in, knowing that coming at Trevor with anger he didn't deserve wasn't going to help the situation.

"Has anyone ever told you that you can be a real asshole?" Trevor asked.

Rhys couldn't help his startled laugh, dragging a hand down his face with a groan. "Yeah, my ex-wife every day for a month when I was able to successfully block her petition for alimony."

Trevor looked startled. "You refused to pay alimony?"

"To the woman who started cheating on me with my best friend right after our honeymoon, then left me for that guy?" He let out a frustrated huff and nodded. "Yeah, I did."

Trevor winced. "Shit. Sorry, that was a dickhead thing to say."

Waving him off, Rhys beckoned toward Trevor's car. "Go grab what you need—grab all your clothes and shit, and anything else important you can't live without. Then we're taking mine and I'll send someone to pick this up."

Trevor looked at him for a long moment, then managed to crack a smile. "What even is your life that you have a guy you can send to pick up my car?"

Rhys was fairly sure that was rhetorical, so he busied himself with putting his food in the back seat as Trevor grabbed what he needed. It turned out to be one box and two suitcases, which fit easily in the back, and then they were buckled in and Rhys was pulling out onto the main road.

The silence between them was awkward, but there was no way around that. He'd picked up an ex-co-worker of Noah's who was presently homeless, who he didn't know at all, who he was still wildly attracted to in spite of the situation being all wrong for it. The guy was beaten down and he definitely did not need some lonely, bisexual divorcee trying to get into his pants. Trevor deserved a hell of a lot better than that.

4.

Pulling into his garage, Rhys killed the engine, then closed the doors before they got out. He grabbed the food as Trevor grabbed his things, and Rhys held his door open with his foot as the other man passed him by. In spite of being homeless and clearly not having had a proper shower in a long time, the smell that invaded his senses was overwhelmingly appealing. It was musky and masculine, a hint of cologne and something else that was uniquely Trevor.

He wanted the feel of his rugged body beneath him, the scratch of his beard, blunt nails digging into his skin. His thoughts were far from appropriate, but he couldn't help himself. He did his best to shove them away as he led the way into the kitchen, setting everything down on the table.

"So, my plan for the night was to get drunk and binge Netflix," he told Trevor as he threw his keys and phone on the counter, then shucked his jacket off. "I'd love you to join me, but if you want to shower and get some sleep, I won't blame you."

Trevor flushed. "I'm sure I look like the world's biggest mess."

Rhys quickly shook his head, unable to stop himself from laying a hand on Trevor's shoulder. "You really don't, that's not what I meant at all. I can't even imagine how you're feeling right now, but you're holding up and that's one of the bravest things I have ever seen in my life. I swear to god, I don't care what it takes, we're going to find a way to fix this."

Trevor's gaze darted away, and he gave a soft shrug. "I'm not sure I can believe that anymore. Not after…not after everything. I know this was my mistake."

"That one mistake should not be costing you. Not like this. You don't deserve any of this bullshit, Trevor. Okay? You do not deserve it." Rhys knew hearing it like that wasn't going to make a damn bit of difference, but he wasn't about to let Trevor's insecurity and fears have the last word. Not tonight. He dropped his hand, hating to pull away, but he knew it was for the best. He beckoned the other man along to the guest room and motioned toward the bed. "Throw your stuff here, and then use my bathroom. I splurged on the shower when we remodeled, and you'll thank me afterward."

Trevor looked a little dubious, but he gathered up his toiletry bag and followed Rhys down the hall to the master bedroom. His en suite bathroom didn't have a door, and he passed under the arch and flicked on the light, displaying the wide expanse of tile and marble under the soft lights. His bathroom really was his pride and joy. The half-circular shower had rotating glass doors, and jets that protruded along the tile to give a full-body spray. The free-standing oval garden tub was next to it, shelves lined up with fragrant soaps and bath oils. He rarely used them, but everyone he knew made an excuse to stay with him whenever he had free time, and he knew it was all for the bathroom.

"Holy shit, are you fucking serious?" Trevor demanded.

Rhys laughed. "My brother calls it the Star Trek shower, and he kind of hates me for it, but not enough that he doesn't use it every time he crashes here."

Trevor smiled softly. "I uh…I don't know how to thank—"

"Don't," Rhys said very softly. "Seriously, just don't. If you deserve anything, it's a nice shower and long sleep, okay? And I don't need to be thanked for it."

Trevor nodded. "Yeah. Okay." His tone told Rhys he clearly didn't believe that, but he was accepting it which was a step at the very least.

"Lock the main bedroom door since I don't have a door in here, and then you can grab something to eat if you want. I'll be in the living room losing myself in some bad reality TV whenever you're done."

Trevor managed a small smile at that, too, and he didn't move as Rhys turned on his heel wand walked out. A moment later, the door closed behind him, and Rhys heard the soft snick of his bedroom lock. It was progress. Not much, but some, and that in itself was a triumph.

He made his way back to the kitchen and pulled one of the whiskey bottles out of the bag. Just an hour before, all he'd wanted was to lose himself in the bottom of that cheap liquor, but now it had very little appeal. He thrummed his fingers on the top of the table, then bit his lip as a thought hit him. Trevor had been living in his car for a while now. Weeks, probably. Which meant it had probably been that long since he'd been near a shower, or a bed, or a fucking kitchen. He realized Trevor's hesitance when he offered him junk food and had a feeling the guy had probably been subsisting on gas station burritos and fast food burgers.

Rhys wasn't a celebrity chef, but he wasn't the worst in the kitchen, either. Maybe whipping up something would bring a smile to Trevor's face, something genuine, something unlike the small, strained thing he'd been sporting since they arrived.

Walking to his fridge, he was dismayed to find almost nothing decent, and definitely nothing that would impress. Eggs, some leftover grilled chicken, a bag of spinach, cheese, mushrooms he was pretty sure hadn't turned. An omelet wasn't exactly impressive, but it was a far cry from gas station food. Taking a breath, hoping that this little gesture might mean something, he set out all the ingredients and got to work.

***

Trevor managed to hold back his tears until the warm water hit him on three sides from the powerful jets set into the wall. Something about the steam, the heat of the water, the thick soap in the palm of his hand made the feeling of so many weeks of sleeping in his car and not feeling like he'd ever have a place to rest his head overwhelm him. He'd done his fair share of crying, late in the night as he shivered under his comforter in the back seat of his car, but this threatened to bring him to his knees. He braced himself on the foggy tiles, bent over at the waist, and let the sobs wrack his body. It was exhausting, but cleansing in a way. He pressed the side of his fist to his lips in order to stifle the sounds, but he realized that even if Rhys could hear him, he didn't think the man would judge.

He allowed himself five minutes of falling apart under the spray before he straightened and began to scrub off completely. Rhys used expensive shampoo and soaps, stuff Trevor hadn't ever bothered with even when he had the funds to do it. It felt almost too decadent, and he felt a strange bit of guilt as he let himself step into this world he wasn't a part of. Barnes—or whoever was behind him—was determined to see Trevor break, determined to see his life fall to ruin in a way he'd never be able to pick back up. But what this faceless, nameless person hadn't counted on was that Trevor was a survivor. He nearly resisted Rhys in the bathroom at that gas station, but the earlier exhaustion of spending another night in his car, another night begging for more shifts and hoping to god he could find someone—anyone—to rent to him was just too much.

When Rhys had barged through that bathroom door and looked him in the eye, he couldn't say no. He'd not only called Trevor a charity case, but told him in so many words that there was no shame in it. Trevor had to remind himself that if he hadn't found his own humility as a young child struggling to find out who he was, struggling to find an ally in the world who would decide for him, he might not have ever gotten to be the man he was today. He knew he had to swallow his pride and accept the help, as much as he hated it.

Mostly, he knew, because Rhys wouldn't expect anything beyond gratitude, and maybe the promise that he wouldn't give up. At the very least, Trevor could offer that.

Though the shower was less than fifteen minutes, it felt like it had gone on for hours, sloughing off the weight of his troubles down the drain with too-expensive suds. He used the fluffy towel hanging on the rack near the shower door, then slipped into his clothes. He was grateful he'd been able to do some laundry at the local laundry mat near Plato's so he could comfortably put himself in Rhys' guest bed without feeling like he'd contaminated the place.

He stepped in front of the mirror and dug out his comb, raking it through his hair and beard which felt clean for the first time in weeks. He shivered, then dug through and saw he was down to four syringes and fourth to last dose of testosterone which was due two days from then. It left him a month at best. And then what?

Taking in a shuddering breath, he zipped up the travel case and headed out. The moment he opened the bedroom door, a heady smell of cooking meat and spices hit him. His stomach twisted with desperation, his body run down with tinned food, meals from paper bags, and gas station microwaves. He hadn't dared risk what little he had in his pocket for a sit-down meal, and his feet took him toward whatever smelled so heavenly without meaning to.

He came to a stuttered halt in the doorway to the kitchen, his eyes immediately fixed on Rhys who was humming to himself as he prod at a large frying pan. He was dressed down—jogging sweats and a white t-shirt which showed off rippling biceps and bare feet. He looked sleepy and soft and relaxed, and Trevor fought down the intense urge to walk to him, put his arms around his waist, and just let himself be held.

But it wasn't his place. Hell, even his assumption that Rhys liked men went down the drain when the guy had mentioned his ex-wife. He didn't want to let himself hope that there could be more, and now wasn't the time. Not when Rhys was offering him so much already.

Realizing standing there made him kind of a creep, he cleared his throat and couldn't help a smile when Rhys jumped and turned, grabbing his chest. "Jesus, you scared me."

Trevor almost laughed. "Sorry, I didn't want to interrupt."

With a sheepish smile, Rhys rolled his eyes and turned back to the pan. "I realized I was hungry for something besides junk food, so I made up a couple omelets. If you don't want one, I can save it for later, but I was hoping you didn't mind sharing."

Trevor's face bloomed red. He knew what Rhys was doing. It had to be painfully obvious he hadn't had anything proper to eat in so long, but he didn't want to make him feel singled out for it. The gratitude he felt was too much, and he felt his eyes begin to well up with tears before he could stop himself.

At his continued silence, Rhys turned, mouth opening to say something. When he saw the tears, however, he froze. "Shit. Did I offend you?"

Trevor swallowed thickly, shaking his head. "No. No, I…" His breath came in shuddering sighs, and he rubbed at the back of his neck. "Thank you."

Rhys looked torn, like he wasn't sure what to say or do. Turning back to the pan, he slid the food onto a waiting plate, then set his spatula down and crossed the distance between them before Trevor could think properly. His hands flew to Trevor's face, cupping his cheeks, brows dipped in a way that made his face look achingly serious. "I'm not going to tell you not to thank me, because I know how shitty it would feel if my gratitude was rejected in a situation like this. But I will tell you that I'm not doing this because I feel sorry for you. I'm doing this because I'm pissed off and it's keeping me from getting in my car, driving over to that dickhead's house, and beating him within an inch of his life. The people he's hurting do not deserve this, and if I can make it feel at least a little better, I'm going to."

Trevor couldn't stop himself from leaning into the touch, even when it scared him. He let his eyes close and let Rhys pull him in to a warm, soft embrace. It had been so long—*so damn long*—since someone had touched him like this. Before his life fell apart, Trevor was the guy who liked hook-ups, liked to spend a weekend with someone he met at a club, but never this. Never basic comfort. He'd never wanted it, never liked the way it made him feel vulnerable and needy.

But right now, it was like heaven, it was like finally being allowed to breathe again. He let his head fall down to rest on Rhys' shoulder, and let the other man drag hands up and down his back as he settled back into his own skin.

"Okay," Rhys said after a moment, "let me feed you and put on some shitty TV, then we can get some decent sleep. Sound good?"

Trevor nodded, sniffing as he rubbed the side of his hand under his nose. "Yeah."

"And tomorrow I'll do some actual grocery shopping because I'm a pretty decent cook, but I haven't had the motivation in a while." He finally released him, stepping back to the stove to grab the waiting plates. As he handed it over, he smiled softly and beckoned Trevor to follow him into the living room. "Do you cook?"

Trevor snorted a laugh, unable to help it. "Uh, that would be a big no. I've never been good at it. I can get by. Like...spaghetti, scrambled eggs, toaster waffles."

"Jesus," Rhys muttered, but he was grinning as he sat and nodded for Trevor to join him on the sofa.

"I was always so busy, it was hard to make time to really learn," he defended. He ignored Rhys' pointed look and immediately dug into the eggs. Normally he wasn't a spinach and mushrooms kind of guy, but the egg dish might have been the best thing he'd ever put in his mouth. He zoned out on it completely, losing himself in the flavors, in the cheese, in the richness of it. His stomach started to protest at the last quarter, but he forced it all down, then laid his head back with a groan.

"I'm taking that as a compliment," Rhys declared.

Rolling his head to the side, Trevor peered at him with one eye and chuckled quietly. "You should. I normally hate spinach and mushrooms, but that was amazing."

Rhys startled him by blushing. "Sorry. I should have actually asked."

Sitting up slightly, Trevor pushed his plate onto the table and then gave Rhys a serious look. "You just cooked me my first actual meal in over a month. Trust me when I say I'm not going to complain."

For a moment, Rhys looked like he wanted to argue, but eventually he gave up and shrugged, setting his own plate alongside Trevor's, then settling back. "Well at least point me in the right direction for the future."

Nodding, Trevor gnawed on his lower lip as he considered this situation. "I can't stay here forever, you know."

Rhys lifted a brow. "I mean, technically that's true, but it's not like you're imposing or anything here. I live alone."

"Since your divorce?" Trevor asked, knowing he might be crossing a line, but he wanted to know the all-but stranger he was suddenly rooming with.

Rhys' eyes flared with a little pain, but it didn't look like heartbreak. It looked more like frustration, like insecurity, which was startling. "It's actually been a while, but yeah. She decided to move in with her lov—with her *husband*. They got married," he clarified, like he was mostly talking to himself. "Right after the divorce was final, they got married and she moved into his place."

Trevor let out a small breath and offered what he hoped looked like a sympathetic smile. "I'm sorry. That *seriously* sucks."

Rhys' laugh was soft but genuine. "Yeah, it *seriously* does. I mean, it sucked slightly less than hearing she'd been fucking him since our wedding, but that's not saying much."

Shaking his head, Trevor pushed himself up a little higher on the cushion to better look at Rhys. "Do you know why she did it?" He realized it was kind of a rude question and he shook his head. "I just mean, I've never been in a serious relationship, so I don't really understand why. Why get married if you're just going to jump into some other dude's bed, you know?"

Rhys looked a little surprised by Trevor's admission. "She couldn't give me a straight answer on that, so I can't tell you. It certainly didn't occur to me." He blinked rapidly a few times, then said, "You've never been in a serious relationship?"

Trevor felt his cheeks heat up and he rolled his eyes up to look at the ceiling. "It's not as easy for me. For any trans guy. Not that trans people can't, but being trans and gay, it gets a little complicated."

"Yeah," Rhys said from behind a sigh. "I guess I can get that. Dick worship is kind of a thing with gay dudes, isn't it?"

Trevor looked at him a long moment. "You know from experience?"

Rhys laughed softly and gave him a knowing smile. "Are you trying to ask me if I have experience with dick-worshipping gay guys?" When Trevor just shrugged, Rhys snuggled back into his cushion and toyed with the hem of his t-shirt. "My brother Ryan is gay. He's the out and proud, one-man-pride-parade sort of guy and has been since we were pretty young. He never felt like he shouldn't over-share his experiences, so I heard a lot."

"So, your brother is one of those guys?" Trevor asked.

Rhys' laugh was a little bitter, and a little sad. "He was, I think, though maybe not so much anymore. Ryan...his life got complicated after his break-up with Noah."

Trevor looked startled. "Wait. Your brother is *that* Ryan? Noah's ex. The guy who fucked the dog-walker?"

Rhys blinked, then threw his head back with a laugh. "Oh god, is that how the whole department knows him?"

Trevor shrugged. "I wasn't around for all that, it was way before my time, but yeah. Noah was a popular guy, and the whole Big Bad Ex who fucked him over for the guy they hired to take care of their dog? Everyone knows that story. I've actually met your brother. Jesus, I flirted with him a little at last year's department holiday party. I mean, nothing serious. I wasn't really into a guy who'd do that to me."

Rhys' smile dimmed a little and he thinned his lips in thought. "He's not that guy anymore. I mean, he did cheat, yeah. It was a massively dick move, and I was angry at him for a long time because Noah is like family to me. But they were both young, and Ryan was scared and stupid, and he learned his lesson. Noah forgave him years ago, but Ryan won't let himself be forgiven. I want him to be happy, but I don't know how to help."

"Maybe he just needs you to talk him through it?" Trevor offered. "If he's all those things you say he is, I don't think he's going to turn away support from someone who clearly loves him unconditionally. And maybe a little solidarity is just the thing."

Rhys raised both brows at him. "Are you sure you're a Latin professor? You're not into that psych 101 shit?"

Trevor started to laugh, but it was interrupted by a huge yawn. "Oh god, sorry. That's only slightly mortifying."

Rhys' face was drawn with sympathy as he reached over and squeezed Trevor's wrist. "You can definitely *not* apologize for that. It's been a long night and you need sleep."

Trevor opened his mouth to protest, but another yawn took him, making his face erupt into a soft, mottled pink. He was profoundly aware that Rhys was still touching him, the skin of his palm warm against his wrist, and he had an absurd urge to just let himself fall into Rhys' embrace and just stay there. "Yeah," he finally conceded, "it's time for me to sleep."

Rhys stood along with him, and before Trevor could tell him not to bother, he gave him a gentle nudge toward the guest room. "Let me just make sure everything's made up in there, okay? Then I can let my own mind relax. Trust me, if I don't, my mother will somehow sense it seven-hundred miles away and just materialize out of nowhere to teach me better manners."

Trevor laughed, but he felt a slightly sharp pang behind his ribs, wondering what it might be like to have a parent like that—a person who gave a shit. His grandmother had been that for him once, but she'd also never been the conventional type. She helped him find his way, become who he was, but she'd never been the PTA parent, the one who whipped up rice squares for bake sales, or made it to school concerts. He certainly never blamed her, but he couldn't help his envy for people like Rhys who clearly grew up loved beyond all reason. The sort of love he'd wanted to give to his own child, though that dream had long-since turned to ash.

He let Rhys enter the bedroom first, lingering near the door as the other man inspected the sheets, the pillows, making sure the bedside lamp was working. When he was satisfied, he turned and gave Trevor a sheepish shrug. "Seems alright."

"Look, not to sound crude, but I've been sleeping in my car for damn-near a month. At this rate, a blow-up mattress on the floor in the corner of a living room is like the goddamn Hilton in comparison." He regretted his words when Rhys' eyes widened and the apples of his cheeks went dark.

"We're going to figure this out," Rhys promised. There was a ferocity in his voice which was startling, but warmed him, and maybe frightened him a little. Probably because he wasn't used to people caring—especially someone who was, for all intents and purposes, a total stranger. Before Trevor could answer, Rhys reached for him and pulled him into a hug.

It had been a damn long time since anyone had touched him like that, either. At least, not without the intent of asking for more. He felt his throat tighten again, but he was damn sick of crying now and managed to swallow back any tightness before Rhys pulled away.

"We'll grab something to eat tomorrow morning before we figure out step one, okay?" Rhys didn't give Trevor any time to protest, and instead walked out, closing the door almost all the way as he left.

Bone-tired and unable to keep his eyes open, Trevor decided all he could do right then was let sleep take him. At least, for those few hours, he didn't have to think.

5.

Rhys: Are you and Ivan still a thing?

Ryan: How is that your business?

Rhys: I might need a favor and was hoping you still had one with him. Nothing's for sure just yet.

Ryan: If this is about what I think this is about, can you hold off for a little while. We might have a lead and I think this asshole is about to get busted. Like in the legal sense.

Rhys: Yes, but I still might need that favor.

Ryan: You realize how much you'll owe me for that, right?

Rhys: '96 Spring Break.

Ryan: I hate you so fucking much. You're really willing to cash out for this guy?

Rhys: I am.

Ryan: Sorry that took me so long. He said he can meet you at The Café on Thursday at six. I'm assuming you know what the fuck that means.

Rhys: I do. Thank you. I owe you.

Ryan: This makes us even. Just remember that.

***

 Tapping his pencil on his desk, Rhys' eyes flickered back up to the man sitting across from him, a wave of guilt hitting him mostly because he'd been caught out. It was times like this he wished he worked with partners. Nothing was more time-consuming and ultimately time-wasting than mediation. Especially over civil bullshit when both parties were clearly at fault. He wouldn't have even bothered, except his client was willing to pay, and because his client's cousin had hired one of his main competitions, Jacob Lister, who was currently giving Rhys a smug, I'm better than you, smirk.

"Listen, I think we can safely say we're done for the afternoon," Lister said, closing his laptop and resting his folded hands over the top. "Unless there was anything else you wanted to add?"

"We remain at an impasse," Rhys said, confident enough that nothing else had changed. Frankly, he knew how this was going to go. His client and Lister's client would come to the agreement that both lawyers had advised them to, but only after weeks of wasting time, of paying court-fees, mediator fees, and constantly refreshing the retainer which Rhys couldn't be too mad about. He wasn't a complete do-gooder. He had bills to pay, and petty rich men like his client helped with that. A lot. Which meant he could do other things—like take the single mom's case, who was working two restaurant jobs and fighting off her ex who had been inconsistent until his new girlfriend mentioned that the ex might be able to qualify for child support if he had more than half of the custody, pro-bono.

Or looking into Trevor's case even deeper because he sure as shit wasn't going to charge him, but he needed to make sure he could afford his mortgage now that more than one person was depending on it. Though he wasn't about to say that to the skittish man who seemed ready to flee the moment Rhys appeared inconvenienced.

Ryan hadn't mentioned anything about Noah's case after the series of texts, but Rhys had Mel look into it that morning and she managed to pull up the public record of Charles Barnes, who had just pled guilty to the charge for stalking and conspiracy to commit battery. The battery thing was what got to Rhys, and he felt a pang of worry, thinking he should probably give his brother a call.

"You wanna grab a drink after this?" a voice asked, interrupting his thoughts.

Rhys blinked up at Jake who was waggling his eyebrows at him. "Seriously?"

Jake shrugged. "Look man, just because I embarrassed you in there…"

Rhys sighed, reaching for his laptop bag, and glanced around to make sure their clients had long gone. "First of all, I'm not going to dignify your bullshit with a response. Second of all, I have places to be." Namely home, to wait for Trevor to get off his early shift so the two of them could finally do some proper grocery shopping. Trevor had been there four days now, and all four days the pair of them had been too busy to get anything done apart from sleep, eating late-night take out, and drive-thru breakfast.

Trevor was using Rhys' Jeep while his car was being stored off the street, and he'd had a series of closing shifts. Until tonight, when he was doing inventory until five and it meant they would have some time together. Rhys was trying not to read anything into it, but he couldn't help the way his heart pounded a little at the thought of getting some alone time with the other man. They hadn't gotten to know each other well just yet, but what he did know, he found he liked more than he thought he would.

Trevor was clever, witty, insightful, and more than a little sarcastic. In short, he was everything Rhys liked in a person. He'd probably have been trying a little harder if the guy wasn't currently depending on him for a place to stay.

"You got a hot date or what?" Jake asked as he held the elevator for Rhys to step in. When Rhys said nothing, Jake laughed. "Damn, it's about time? She hot?"

With a sigh, Rhys shook his head. In truth, he did have a meeting with Ivan later, and under different circumstances, he might have actually considered it a hot date. But with Trevor in his life, it was difficult to think of anyone else. "I don't have a date, not that it's any of your business. I have a friend staying with me for a while and I need to actually find time to pick up provisions so he doesn't think I live like some college freshman."

Jake chuckled, but before they reached the ground floor, his face sobered. "Hey, Rach told me about Vanessa. About the uh…the baby thing."

At that moment, Rhys had never hated more how small their social and career circle was. Vanessa had moved on, and moved, and re-married, and yet he was still being confronted by her personal life.

"It's fine," he said, though he knew everyone around them would understand what a blow it was. Rhys hadn't exactly made it a secret how much he'd wanted a family, and Vanessa hadn't exactly made it a secret how she felt about the idea. Until now. Fucking Facebook. "Trust me, I'm glad it's not me. Not after what she put me through."

Everyone had also known about Mark. Well, everyone but him, apparently. As if his situation wasn't humiliating enough.

"It's just a dick move, and I know we're not best friends, but if you want to grab a drink and talk, I'm here."

As much as he thought Jake was kind of a slime-ball, he was oddly touched. "Thanks, but really, I'm good. She found what she wanted, and it means I'm free to do the same. Once I actually have time."

Jake gave him a clap on the shoulder just when the elevator doors pinged open, and he was grateful for his ability to quickly escape.

***

Rhys arrived home and had just enough time to shower and slip into jeans and a sweater when he heard the garage door open. Trevor was entering the house with less trepidation as more time passed, feeling at home rather than an imposing guest which in itself felt like a triumph. He peered at himself in the mirror, his hair just combed through and his five o'clock shadow in dire need of a shave, but it was good enough for a quick shopping trip.

Walking out of the room, he peered around the corner of the kitchen and saw Trevor leaning over the small table with his hands pressed down, his head bowed, a faint pink flush up the side of his neck. It was a telltale sign things hadn't gone well, and Rhys felt his stomach lurch.

"Do you want to talk about it?"

It was saying something when Trevor didn't startle, instead just shrugging his shoulders without looking up.

Rhys hesitated in the doorway, then walked in and leaned against the breakfast bar. His hand reached out, fiddling with a few unopened bills just to give himself something to do as he regarded the other man. "Charles Barnes has been charged and is awaiting a hearing right now. From public record, it looks like he's back in jail and awaiting the judge," Rhys said quietly.

Trevor stiffened, then he raised his head and let out a bitter laugh. "I guess it confirms he wasn't lying."

Rhys frowned. "What do you mean?"

"Someone was following me today, and then I found this under the Jeep's wiper blade." He dug into his pocket and pulled out a thick bit of paper, folded into fours. With trembling fingers, he handed it off to Rhys.

Rhys looked down at it, such an unassuming bit of nothing—scrap paper folded into a square. Until he opened it and a small, glossy square tumbled out. He barely caught it before it fluttered to the ground, and there was no mistaking the black and white image on the front. It was an ultrasound. Rhys hadn't ever seen one on person, but he'd watched enough movies and recognized the little blob in the center for what it was.

Unable to speak just yet, he glanced at the writing and his stomach twisted.

I'm still watching.

Three little words, something he might have laughed at, something he could hear in the high-pitched whine of a school-yard bully. Only this was a threat. This, with the photo, was just a blatant statement that whoever was doing this had the power. Barnes was in jail, but that didn't matter because in Trevor's world, he hadn't been anything more than a messenger. A pawn in all of it.

Rhys' stomach twisted with rage and he took a few, controlled breaths as he crushed the note in his hand. "Did you see who it was that followed you?"

Trevor's jaw clenched and he shook his head. "No. I had to run a couple of errands, do a bank deposit, and we always turn in our bread requisition to the bakery by hand because it's a little mom and pop shop. I noticed whoever it was there. They were hovering by the Jeep and watching me, but they were too far for me to be able to make them out. Then they were there at the bank, and again when I got back to the bar."

Swallowing thickly, Rhys gave a decided nod. "Look, I've been meaning to call my brother. He's got a couple of friends who owe him favors—people who can be discrete. It may be a dead end, but I think it's our best bet to track down the source."

Trevor's jaw tensed again, like maybe he wanted to refuse, but after a long moment, he just nodded. "Okay."

Rhys' hand twitched, wanting to offer him some comfort. He thought about their shopping trip, but he wasn't sure Trevor was interested in getting out again. "Do me a favor?"

Trevor looked almost startled by the request. "Uh? Sure?"

"Go take a bath. Use the jets, soak for as long as you can stand it. Ryan gave me these ridiculously delicious smelling bubble bars with like chamomile and lavender. I need to go meet a colleague for a few minutes, then I'm going to make a quick stop at the store, I'm going to cook, and we're going to watch some shitty movie and forget about today."

Trevor stared at him a long time, then his shoulders deflated like Rhys had sucked all the air out of him, and he gave a nod. "Yeah. Yeah I...thanks."

Unable to help himself now, Rhys reached for him and took his wrist, giving him a gentle tug. He kept his grip light enough that if Trevor wanted to pull back, wanted to resist him, he could have without trouble. But instead of that, Trevor came willingly, let himself curl against Rhys' slightly larger chest, let Rhys' arms come around him and just hold him.

Dipping his head forward, Rhys' nose touched Trevor's soft locks, breathing in the scent of his own shampoo which sent something almost fierce and possessive shooting down his spine. He tried his best to reign it in—but it wasn't getting any easier. Each day he wanted the man more, each day created new fantasies of what they could be, if their situations hadn't been so complicated.

"Keep your phone on, and call me if you need me," Rhys warned before he reluctantly dropped his arms and took a step back. From the embrace, Trevor looked slightly more rejuvenated, and with any hope, the food and movie would finish the rest of the job for him. "Promise me," he insisted.

Trevor smiled this time, a small but genuine thing. "I promise."

He wanted to say more. He wanted to say a hundred other things that meant, I like you, I'm into you in ways I didn't expect, I'm scared but I want to go further. Instead he reached for his keys and hurried out the door, more than anything just desperate to get back.

6.

It was half six by the time Rhys walked through the café doors. The regular crowd had gone, leaving behind the bearded-hipster artists and the harried students looking for a change of venue to cram their studies.

And then there was Ivan, seated near the back with his hands curled around a large latte mug. He met Rhys' gaze with a smile, and Rhys held up a finger before heading to the counter to order a sandwich and a masala chai. He paid, checked his phone, worried that Trevor might give up on him with how long his day was taking, but he didn't have a choice. There was an opportunity and he needed to seize it.

Taking the chair across from Ivan, Rhys took a long drink of the chai and let some of the day's anxiety fade into background noise. "Sorry, I didn't think it was going to take a hundred goddamn hours for Markus to get tired of listening to me speak."

"How did it go?" Ivan asked, though Rhys knew the question wasn't anything more than polite conversation.

"Ended with a continuance, which is the best I can hope for today." He went quiet as one of the baristas dropped off his sandwich, but he wasn't hungry suddenly. His brain was in a tangled mess, trying to figure out how to bring up Trevor's issue without giving away information Trevor wasn't ready to come out with.

"Okay, you look like you're about to lose it, Rhys," Ivan said quietly. "You want to tell me what's up?"

"Well, I feel a little bit like a dick, asking you for a favor when I know you and Ryan haven't uh…that things have been…"

"Cooled off?" Ivan offered with a faint grin. He shook his head and chuckled as he took a sip of his drink. "Ryan and I haven't been together in a long while, and we both knew what it was. There's no heartbreak. I genuinely like him as a person."

Rhys let out a small breath of air. "Okay."

"Does that help?"

"I don't know," Rhys confessed. "I still feel a little bad, but I don't think I have much choice. I have a client that I can't go forward with right now because he's being blackmailed."

Ivan looked suddenly alert. "This isn't…"

"Noah?" Rhys offered, then shook his head. "No, but the case is related. Sort of. But he isn't," Rhys stopped and let out a sigh, hating how inarticulate he sounded. He was a lawyer, for fuck's sake, the success of his career was rooted in his ability to verbally make a case for those he was advocating for. "He can't come forward with information, but the blackmail didn't stop with Barnes' arrest."

"So there's one more person involved," Ivan said, now sounding interested.

"At least," Rhys conceded. In truth, he wasn't sure Barnes, or this mysterious figure, were working alone, but he could only speculate with so little evidence. "He destroyed my client's career. He lost his job, his house, his savings. He was living in his car with the clothes on his back when I found him."

"You said was," Ivan pointed out.

Rhys blew out a puff of air. "Yeah. I found him taking a standing-bath in a dirty gas station bathroom and made him come home with me. He was reluctant and there's every chance he's not going to stay, but he also has nowhere else to go."

Ivan nodded, giving him a long look before he folded his hands next to his cup. "What is it you need from me?"

"Information, maybe, or help getting it," Rhys said. "I need to convince him to trust you with as much as he can."

"With what? You know I can't protect him if he's done something illegal," Ivan reminded him.

"It isn't that. There's an obvious personal vendetta going on here, and I need to find the connection. I'm thinking about asking the guy who found all that shit on Noah if he can dig around here, but it might not be enough. I wanted to know if you might be willing to ah…"

"Do a little freelance work?" Ivan offered.

Rhys flushed, but he nodded. "Something like that. Just putting out feelers."

Ivan reached for his cup, staring down at the contents before he finally looked up again and offered a soft grin. "I've always liked you. Ryan was always a difficult person to be with. He's drowning in insecurity self-deprecation and I could never get him to see past it to the man worth loving, but you've always done what you could to remind him he's worth it."

Rhys felt guilt grip him by the throat, as startled as he was by the abrupt subject change. "I get a lot of praise for that, but I haven't always been a great brother."

Ivan chuckled quietly. "You wouldn't be a brother if there weren't moments in the past where you were at your worst. The point still stands. I like him a lot, and I think the parts of him I'll always treasure were the parts you helped keep alive. Whoever he ends up with should be grateful for that too."

Rhys wasn't sure what to do with that kind of praise. It was the kind of praise which had caused a rift between him and Ryan in the first place. Their parents had spent the better part of Ryan's teenage life comparing his accomplishments to Rhys', and it hadn't done either of them any favors. "I just…"

Ivan held up a hand and Rhys went quiet. "Of course I'll help you, if you need it."

"More like when I do," Rhys confessed.

"When," Ivan amended with a shrug. "To the best of my abilities, and as long as it won't come back to bite me in the ass."

"I'll do everything I can," Rhys promised, because it was all he could give.

***

Trevor wasn't sure what to do with Rhys' kindness. As he lay back in the tub, the bubbles covering almost all of his chest, tickling at his chin and earlobes, he closed his eyes and breathed in the soft, relaxing herbal scents released by the little bath trinket. The water was almost too hot, but it felt good on his skin. He'd been keyed up since he noticed the strange figure, and seeing the evidence of his failed experiment to give himself a family, he'd been damn-near wrecked. The note he'd shown Rhys had come with his first and only sonogram picture, but at the last second, he'd chosen not to show Rhys.

He hadn't really been pregnant long—he'd miscarried in the first trimester. He hadn't even heard a heartbeat. His body just wasn't ready. Maybe it never would be. He'd been warned before treatment that being on testosterone for years would probably affect the outcome, but there was no way to predict how. And even after the miscarriage, he hadn't been able to find the answer to his question—*was it my HRT?*

"Way too many pregnancies end this early on—not just with IVF, but with these fertility treatments, the risk is even higher," Andrew had told him.

So, Trevor had been forced to accept it, and he remembered the distinct feeling of both visceral grief and absolute and utter relief when he took up his syringe and stabbed himself in the muscle for his first dose of T in so damn long. With that single jab, he had decided he was done trying. The idea of children wasn't impossible, but it wouldn't be the way that the rest of the world would expect him to become a parent. He could live with that, because living with it wasn't taking anything away.

Only now, to see that picture again, to be thrust not only back in that moment—that single picture of proof that he once carried life—but also to have it used against him in the worst way—was too much. If Rhys hadn't been there, hadn't offered that momentary reprieve of arms keeping him close, he probably would have lost it. And instead he'd been comforted, then shuffled off to the bath to soak.

He wasn't sure how long he'd actually been in there, but he came back to the present when he heard the sound of the garage door opening and closing. With a sigh, he inspected his overly-wrinkled fingers, then used his toes to dislodge the drain plug. He let the bubbles drop down into the swirling water, then he reached for a towel and rubbed himself down.

The scent of the bubble bar lingered, his entire person feeling soft and warm and sleepy, comforted in a way he hadn't thought possible. He walked to the sink, throwing on his boxers, then reached for his bag and pulled out his second to last syringe. He'd taken his testosterone from his room and he felt the bottle to make sure it hadn't gotten too warm from the humid water of the bath.

It felt cool to the touch, and he let out a tiny sigh because he was down to three doses. He had money saved from living with Rhys, and could more than afford his refill, but his doctor's appointment for his levels check was coming up, and he hadn't been to therapy in a while. It was all going to add up to at least several hundred bucks, and without that appointment, his doctor wouldn't give him another script. And it would deplete him. His savings had been ravaged, and his life was in tatters, and now this monster was trying to take away what little, poor-paying job he had left.

Where would it end? When would this phantom finally reveal what the fuck they wanted?

Forcing his mind away from it, Trevor grabbed his alcohol swab and cleaned the spot on his thigh which had mostly grown numb to the sting. Filling his syringe, he took a breath, then jabbed it in, almost relishing in the familiar pain and burn. As he depressed the plunger, he startled when the Rhys stuck his head through the door mid-sentence.

"...thought we could..." He froze, and Trevor cursed himself for forgetting to lock the bedroom door when he'd gone in for the bath. Rhys' eyes were wide, his cheeks a little pale at the sight of the jab, and he licked his lips. "Shit. I'm sorry, I didn't realize you were..." His eyes flickered over Trevor's bare chest, at his defined pecs which still bore the thin, obvious scars from his top surgery. The gaze traveled down his stomach, following the happy trail which led to the waist of his boxers before he snapped out of it.

"I'll be out in a minute," Trevor said, his voice tight. He felt the incredible burn of the delayed, half-given jab, and he quickly finished it, pulling his sharps container out to dispose of the needle before swiping the skin with the second wipe and then dropping it into the bin. As he breathed through the ache in his leg, he gripped the counter and stared down at his hands.

It wasn't as though he'd been hiding it—he didn't care if people saw him—but the look on Rhys' face shook him to the core. Mostly because he couldn't read it. Yes, there had been surprise, and some embarrassment, but there was something else too that Trevor couldn't work out. Was it disgust? Discomfort? Trevor had met with and had even had casual relationships with cis guys who were fine with him because he was passing. But then the reality of him being trans started to seep in. Making out over the clothes, topless even with his faint scars was about as edgy as they were comfortable going. Confronted with testosterone, confronted with the fact that he didn't have a cis-male cock hanging between his legs, was too much for them to handle. It was his reality, dealing with the, *penis is what makes a man*, cis-male culture and trying to find his place there.

He wanted to pretend like it didn't matter. He'd been through that kind of rejection by cis men enough times that it stung, but never enough to ruin his night. And yet, the fear of Rhys pulling away from him shook him. It made his skin prickle with worry, made him want to beg off the night and instead lock himself in the bedroom until he could figure out tomorrow's plan.

Whatever Rhys was feeling, though, Trevor didn't think the other man would let him get away with an easy retreat. Rhys was the sort of guy who confronted everything head on, with a pragmatic plan, a back-up plan, and several contingency plans to ensure every possible avenue was covered. It meant Trevor would have to sit and possibly listen to the man tell him that he just couldn't handle the reality of trans people.

He swallowed down his nerves, quickly dressed, and headed out to brave the potential storm.

Rhys was sitting on the sofa with the TV on, a movie paused at the opening credits—a black screen with some faint yellow text he didn't bother reading. There were several white boxes of steaming-hot food—Greek, it looked like, with pita and chicken, some salad and hummus—waiting to be devoured, and two beers already open and on coasters.

The tidy precision of it all nearly made him laugh, if his stomach hadn't been in complete knots from worry over what was supposed to come next. Rhys wasn't looking at him, either. He was sitting forward, his hands hanging loosely between his parted thighs, his cheeks still faintly pink.

Swallowing thickly, Trevor lowered himself to the floor, at the very edge of the coffee table which gave him a view of Rhys without demanding eye-contact. "So," he started.

Rhys lifted a hand, shaking his head. "Just let me…" His voice trailed off, a little strangled at the end, and he cleared his throat. After a beat, he looked up and though Trevor wanted to break the eye-contact between them, he couldn't. "I'm so fucking sorry."

Trevor blinked, a little startled by the fierce tone of his apology. "Uh."

"I knew you were in there, and I guess…I didn't mean to get so comfortable I'd just stroll in, and I feel like the world's biggest asshole." Trevor dragged a hand down his face and let out a breath. "I totally encroached on your privacy, and I understand if you want to just chill in your room tonight."

It took Trevor a minute to catch up with what was going on, and he couldn't help a tense laugh as he rose slightly to his knees, his elbows resting on the table. "I'm not pissed."

Rhys looked uncertain. "Okay, but I just barged in on you and that was really not cool."

Trevor shrugged a little and sat back, fiddling with the edge of one of the boxes. "Shit happens. I mean, I go to the gym, and I go to the beach and walk around shirtless whenever I get the chance. I'm not ashamed of my body, Rhys. And I wouldn't have forgotten to lock your bedroom door if I was terrified you'd see me half-naked."

Rhys' cheeks pinked again, and he blew out a puff of air, glancing away. "I just don't want you to feel unsafe."

At that, Trevor laughed again, and couldn't stop himself from shifting around the table, moving close enough to take the mortified man's limp hand in his. "I don't. I've lived through enough bullshit that I'd rather sleep in my car than be in a place where I feel threatened. And I know we haven't been doing this roommate thing long, but I hope you know by now that if there was some issue, I'd just tell you."

Rhys stared down at their joined hands, then up at Trevor's face with something akin to hope. It was so endearing and sweet, Trevor almost leaned in to kiss him. Almost. Until he remembered that Rhys was his friend, and he was straight. "You're a good person, and more than anything, I want you to have some reprieve from everything going to hell in your life. I didn't want our place to become just another something you had to endure for a roof over your head."

Trevor was almost knocked back at the casual way Rhys said, 'our place'. He hadn't had that in so long. His apartment had been the place he lived, but it had never really felt like a home, and it struck him now just how much life he'd regained in the little guest room Rhys had given him. It was a dangerous way to feel, considering the precarious nature of his circumstances, but he couldn't seem to help it.

He loosened his grip on Rhys' hand, but he didn't let go. "Thank you for caring. It's been a while since anyone really has."

Rhys' face fell a little, but instead of offering him pity or sympathy, he just squeezed his fingers gently. "Are you okay, though? Are you hurting?"

"What?" Trevor asked, momentarily confused. Then he realized what Rhys was asking, and he laughed again, settling back down to the floor to stretch his legs out in front of him. "I'm fine. Honestly, I barely notice the pain anymore."

"Do you," Rhys began, then stopped. Trevor watched as Rhys' eyes flickered down to his thigh, then looked back up at his face. "I read some stuff. It's once a week?"

"For now," Trevor said with a slightly smaller grin. "I've been on once a month for years, but when I...you know," he waved a hand at his stomach, not really wanting to say the words right now for all the devastation that decision had cost him, "I had to go off for a long time. I was on female hormones in an attempt to boost my fertility, and it was almost like hitting the reset button. I'm back on once a week." *And this is my last bottle before I need to renew my script*, he thought to himself.

Rhys clearly picked up on the way his face had crumpled, and he reached for him, touching his shoulder gently. "What is it?"

Dragging a hand down his face, Trevor let out a frustrated sigh. "It's nothing. I'm just dealing with a lot."

Rhys bit his lip, then said, "I have an idea. Wes has been asking me to come over and have dinner with him. I know you're uncomfortable about the gym because of Noah being there, but he's got one in his basement. Maybe after we eat you can check it out, let yourself loose on a couple of the heavy bags. Trust me, there's no better way to work out frustration."

Trevor licked his lips, then gave a nod. "Yeah. Yes. That would be great." He meant it, too, but he didn't want to let himself hope it would make a difference. Still, every time he felt like he was falling into some abyss of uncertainty, Rhys was there to offer him a solution, a way to plant his feet on solid ground without taking away his choices, with letting him maintain some control. His feelings were growing by the minute, and it terrified him. Not just because he wasn't used to feeling like that, but because it was an absurd notion he and Rhys could have anything beyond what they had now. He had to be content with it, and he was, in a way. Whatever the future held, Rhys would always be important to him.

He took a breath, then gave the ground next to him a pat. Rhys raised his eyebrows, then let out a huffing laugh, rolling his eyes slightly as he slid from the sofa to the floor and stretched his legs out alongside Trevor's. "I hope you like this stuff. It's a decent drive from here, but it's worth it. The woman who owns it moved here from Nafplio after her husband died, then three of her grandkids who wanted to go to an American university followed her and they all work there waiting tables."

Trevor stared at him, eyebrows raised, absorbing all these little details Rhys knew about a random restaurant owner. He'd never met a person quite like him before. "I see," he replied, reaching for the little box holding the pita.

Rhys shifted to give him room, his cheeks turning faintly pink. "What?"

Trevor couldn't help his laugh as he began to pile chicken and something that looked vaguely like pickled cabbage onto his bread. "Nothing," he started, but Rhys knocked his thigh with his knee. "It's just...you pick up all these things from people. Life stories from random strangers that there's no reason for you to know. It's kind of cool. No one I know does that."

Rhys rubbed a hand down his face and rolled his eyes up toward the ceiling, looking vaguely embarrassed. "When Vanessa left me, I didn't deal with it super well. I started drinking a lot and fucked over a couple of my clients by not showing up to their hearings, and my brother kicked my ass over it a little bit. I guess I was in denial that she really had torched our life, and re-wrote our past," he stopped then laughed and shrugged. "Or, I guess, she opened my eyes to what was really going on. Either way, it took me a while to come to grips with it, and my big epiphany happened when I was sitting at some rickety little table in a Peloponnesian restaurant with some little old grandma bringing me an iced tea refill."

Trevor blinked at him, a little startled. "Seriously?"

Rhys' cheeks went even pinker. "She dropped off my drink and gave me this cute little old lady smile, and I just burst into tears. She had every right to walk away and pretend like this dude in an expensive suit wasn't sobbing into a plate of hummus, but instead she sat down next to me and gave me a hug. The next thing you know, she's telling me the story of how her late husband stole a boat on the night he proposed to her and hid her ring inside the stomach of a fish."

"Gross," Trevor muttered.

Rhys laughed and shook his head. "I know. But she never forgot a single detail of that night, and she told me that it took her a while for those memories to bring her anything but pain after he died. She told me that every day felt like walking through wet sand, but it didn't last. She started feeling better, started finding joy in cooking again, wanted to travel, to do something new. So, she did. She packed up and moved here and got her green-card, and a loan, and her little bistro. It put things into perspective and the next day, I was able to take a breath without feeling like my lungs were full of broken glass."

Trevor swallowed down his mouthful of food, then turned so he could look at Rhys properly. It was hard to think of this kind, generous man who was always smiling, whose eyes were always crinkled in the corners with laugh lines, mourning the loss of his marriage. It was hard to imagine anyone stupid enough to walk away from him.

Trevor felt himself get warm on the inside, his stomach twisting with feelings he was desperately trying not to feel. But he was drawn to him, wanted him—not just to fuck him, but to just be near him. He shifted closer, and when Rhys didn't pull away, he let their thighs press together under the table.

"You kind of amaze me," Trevor said quietly after a few minutes.

Rhys startled at that, giving him a stunned look. "I haven't done much, you know. And I get it, people are shit so your bar for amazing is set pretty low but…"

"No," Trevor interrupted. "I mean, yeah, my bar is set low, but whose isn't? I imagine in the future if you end up with a woman who isn't fucking one of your friends from the start, you'll probably think they're the world's best girlfriend."

Rhys chuckled softly and shrugged. "You might be right."

"But it's more than that. Yeah, you had a hard time, and yeah, you're still hurt and bitter, but you're still full of life. You still find it in you to see hope at the end of this shit-filled sewer that has become my life. You still think I'll be able to make it out of this standing upright."

"I don't think," Rhys said. He put his food down and brought one hand up to Trevor's shoulder, cupping it gently. His palm was so soft, so warm, Trevor felt his threadbare resolve start to snap. "I know for a fact you will, because you're stronger than these weak, cruel, angry people. And I'm not doing this because I want to make myself feel better or useful. I'm doing this because the man who walked into my office and shared a secret that he was terrified to share, is a man who isn't afraid to ask for help when he needs it. And I admire that. I like that about you. It's why we're friends."

Friends. Right. They were *friends*, and nothing more, and that was fine. Trevor licked his lips, then gently pulled back enough to send the message that Rhys needed to pull back. He needed to, or a line was going to be crossed that Trevor wouldn't be able to uncross, and he was too scared to ruin things.

"Thank you for this," he said after composing himself. "I'm not exactly adventurous in eating, but this is amazing."

It was a pathetic subject change, but Rhys took it with good humor. He winked as he grinned and reached for a box filled with small circles of fried dough, shining with what he was pretty sure was honey.

"Try this," Rhys said, plucking one from the container. "These aren't on the menu. She makes them for her favorites."

"Meaning you," Trevor said with a smile as he accepted the sticky sweet.

Rhys shrugged, grinning a little sheepishly as he broke a piece off for himself. "Me and a few others. She likes to adopt the pathetic and downtrodden. But I'll take it, trust me. My parents live too far away now to properly spoil me when I'm feeling sad. And frankly that's probably a good thing. I get complacent when they're around."

Trevor felt curiosity surge through him, a desire to know this man, to know his roots and the stories that made him the person he was today. It always fascinated him to see how people had been shaped by the relationship of their past. A lot of people like Rhys, who had grown up too spoiled, became monsters. Trevor had met enough of them in his life—the refuse of the privileged—but there were others like Rhys. Those who allowed the love from their past to soften them and give them a desire to do more for others.

Trevor knew his life could have gone one of two ways, in spite of how much his grandmother had loved him. He could have allowed his oppression, his bitterness, his anger to consume him and turn him into a hollow shell of himself. But he didn't. He simply allowed it to motivate him, to shape him into the person he always knew he could be.

He could only hope he didn't lose sight of that in all this mess.

7.

Trevor felt his stomach squirming with nerves as Rhys pulled up to the large house settled mostly in the middle of nowhere. It was close enough to the city to be considered suburban, but he could almost feel the family's desire for privacy. The property was surrounded by a vast, tall fence with no hope of peering over without a ladder, and the driveway was long and covered with gravel that made an unbearably loud crunching noise as Rhys pulled up behind a large truck.

As he followed Rhys to the door, he paused at the start of the porch which didn't have steps, but a long ramp. When Rhys looked back, he laughed and shook his head. "I told you Wes was paralyzed, right?"

Trevor's eyes went wide. "Uh. No? You said he was a boxer and he ran a gym."

"Well, he is that. He was also paralyzed during an explosion when he was deployed. He was able to walk again, but he still uses a wheelchair from time to time. So does his brother-in-law. That was the whole point of the gym."

"Right," Trevor said, remembering the bits and pieces Rhys had shared. "Sorry, it's not like it matters, I just…"

"Didn't expect it?" Rhys offered. He nodded his head toward the door, beckoning Trevor along. "Tonight will be good, I promise. The only thing Wes loves as much as his wife and daughter is his grill, and he's amazing with it. We both need some good food and good conversation."

At the mention of it, Trevor realized he could smell rich, fragrant barbeque smoke in the air, and his stomach rumbled. He had his T shot that morning, and inevitably his appetite always increased for the first day or so after. He quickly followed Rhys up to the door and was surprised when the other man waltzed in instead of ringing the bell.

Trevor might not have had the most conventional upbringing, but he'd still been raised with manners, and just strolling into a stranger's house went against all of them. Rhys seemed unbothered, though, and led the way through a wide hallway, then through a sliding door which opened to a large kitchen.

Now that Rhys had explained Wes' paralysis, he wasn't surprised to see lowered counters and cabinets, along with metal grip bars located throughout. A short woman with long black hair and a figure that was very clearly rounding in the middle was taking obvious advantage of her husband's accommodations, as her short stature was right at home chopping vegetables on the low top.

She turned when Rhys entered, and her face brightened into a huge grin. She dropped the knife with a clatter and walked over, throwing her arms around him. "You're here. I didn't hear you come in."

Rhys hugged her tight, then set her back down on her feet. "Should you be flinging yourself at unsuspecting people in your condition?"

She put a hand over her belly and glared at him. "If one more of you assholes tries to treat me like I'm made of glass, so help me god," she warned. Her words trailed off with the unspoken threat, then she turned to Trevor and smiled again. "And you. This one hasn't shut up about you," she said, jutting her chin at Rhys. "I'm Anna."

She stuck out her hand and he took it, giving her a quick shake. "Trevor. It's really nice to meet you. Thanks for having me."

"God, you're so nice. Way too nice. You shouldn't be hanging around these dickheads any more than you have to."

Trevor couldn't help his laugh when Rhys made a noise of protest. "They're not all bad. And who knows, maybe I'll have a positive influence?"

"I've long-since lost hope, but if anyone can do it, I'd say a cute red-head has the greatest chance." She winked, then turned back to the food. "Wes is outside with his other wife and he'll be irritated if you take too long to go say hi."

Trevor blinked in surprise, then realized she was talking about the grill and he couldn't help a small laugh as he let Rhys seize his wrist and pull him toward the door. They slipped out onto a raised back porch, a ramp leading out to a massive grass area that had to be at least an acre or two. In the distance was a swing set and sand box, all accessible by chair over what looked like a hard rubber path.

The grill was situated at the end of the patio, and standing in front of it was one of the largest guys Trevor had ever seen. He had dark-olive skin, a full head of thick black curls which blew a little wildly in the cold wind. He had several tattoos over both arms, his well-muscled biceps making the black and grey ink ripple with every movement.

When he turned, Trevor was taken aback by how attractive he was. Dark eyes, large nose, full mouth stretched into a grin. He set a massive pair of black tongs down and marched over, arms spread for a hug. Trevor noticed a slight drag in his step, but only because he'd been looking for it. The guy didn't hesitate, taking Rhys into his arms and lifting him slightly off the ground.

"I won't manhandle *you* until I know you a little better," Wes said as he set Rhys down, smiling at Trevor.

Trevor didn't entirely know how to handle the sudden and warm feeling at the idea that he'd be around long enough for this guy to know him better. He gave a sheepish smile and stuck out his hand. "Nice to meet you. Wes, right?"

Wes nodded and shook Trevor's hand in a firm grip. "And you're Trevor. Rhys has told us a lot about you."

Trevor felt a moment of panic before he reminded himself that Rhys had promised to keep everything a secret. He wasn't sure what the lawyer had said, but he trusted that none of it was sensitive information. "Thanks for having me over."

"No worries, man," Wes said, moving back to the grill. "Everyone knows I'll take any excuse to show off Rebecca." He gave the grill lid a fond pat, and Rhys rolled his eyes.

"You disgust me. Where's Maggie?"

"In her room. Adrian bought her a bunch of the new superhero dolls that just came out, so she's been in kid-heaven since yesterday," Wes said. He used his tongs to flip a bunch of well-sauced chicken wings. "She'll be down soon enough so you can spoil her."

Trevor couldn't help a tiny grin. He wasn't used to being part of stuff like this. Even after he'd started his career, started making friends and branched out of his own little bubble, he had ever been part of a family. And maybe it was having been denied that sort of familial normalcy his entire life which made him crave it, but this was stirring something in him he hadn't felt since his failed experiment to create something like this of his own. The feelings were still tinged with bitterness, but not nearly as bad as it had been even a few short months before.

Dinner wasn't long after they arrived, and Trevor soon found himself sitting at a table with Wes at the far end, Anna next to him, and their chatty toddler between Wes and Ryan on the far side. Trevor found himself not saying much, but the conversation was taken up with the small girl's musings anyway, until she finally got bored, let her mom wash her up, then darted off again.

"She's usually more interested in hanging with us when we have guests," Anna told Trevor, "but these stupid fucking dolls have had her entire attention span today."

Trevor laughed. "It's fine. I remember when I was like twelve, they had a new line of Transformers come out, and my grandma got me the entire set. I don't think I left my room for a week, and I was way too old to be stuck on a toy for kids."

Wes shook his head. "Hell no. Are you kidding me? I was super into Power Rangers at that age and I think I had every single toy on the market. I would wage war in my room for hours. Don't ever be embarrassed for letting yourself have a longer childhood."

Trevor smiled, but he felt a slight pang because in spite of all that, he really hadn't had much of a childhood. Before he could spiral lower, however, he felt an ankle brush against his and he glanced up to see Rhys giving him a comforting look. He felt warmed by it, his attraction to this man building by the second. It was both terrifying and nerve-wracking, but he couldn't bring himself to pull away.

"So," Rhys said after some time, "I thought I might show Trevor the gym downstairs. He's not really comfortable coming down to Baum's, but I thought maybe he'd be interested in at least seeing some of what you do."

"Actually," Wes said, setting his fork down, "Evan's stopping by in about half an hour for a private session. I don't think he'll mind if you two want to observe."

Rhys frowned. "Evan?"

"New guy, was just referred by the rehab center," Wes said. "Double amputee, visually impaired. Adrian's been working on a lot of techniques with Cole that I'm hoping will help Evan out."

"Cole?" Rhys said softly, frowning.

Wes laughed. "I forgot how out of the loop you are. Cole's the British guy—blind one. He trains with Adrian, but he's been hanging out with your brother a lot lately, if you know what I mean. He's the one who helped unfuck the situation with Noah."

Trevor felt himself jolt but kept his expression as neutral as he could. It was too close for comfort. However, it didn't scare him as badly as it might have even a week ago. Something about Wes and Anna—something about this place, about these people—made him feel safe. That alone worried him. He didn't want to drop his guard, but after confessing everything to Rhys, the feeling of not being alone in this was a little addicting.

"I'd love to watch," Trevor finally said. "I don't really know anything about fighting. I've always been kind of a book nerd, and people were always really reluctant to do anything physical with me. I was in Taekwondo when I was thirteen, but my teachers refused to let me spar."

Wes frowned. "Why the fuck?"

"Well," Trevor said, weighing his options. If these people were Noah's friends and family, he had a feeling he could trust them, but coming out to strangers was always a risk. He took a slow breath, then decided the risk was worth it. "I'm trans. I've been out since I was a kid, and by thirteen I was already starting hormone therapy." He paused, giving them a minute to absorb.

Wes' frown remained. "Okay, but did they really separate sparring classes for kids by gender?"

Trevor shook his head. "No. I think mostly they were uncomfortable because they didn't know what box to put me in. This was way before it was even remotely acceptable for kids to live openly as transgender, and my teachers tried, but the idea of it freaked them out. So, I was always sidelined. I left after a while."

"Uh, yeah, I probably would have too," Wes said, shaking his head angrily. "That's some bullshit there. I can get you up to scratch if you really want to."

Trevor's eyes widened. "Uh…"

"Maybe let him observe first," Rhys said with a wry grin. "You guys go pretty hard." He turned to smile at Trevor. "They're all a bunch of ex-military beefcakes."

Trevor choked on his drink as Wes flipped Rhys off, and Anna hid her laugh behind her hand. "If they're being this ridiculous downstairs," she told him, "you can come up here with me and watch the Kardashians. I'm binging the first season."

Trevor grinned at her. "I might just."

Wes wouldn't hear of it, though, and quickly dragged both Rhys and Trevor to a door which opened to a set of stairs. On the side was a mechanical ramp, which Trevor figured Wes used for his chair, but it was lifted up and locked against the wall.

"Tell Evan to come down when he gets here," Wes told his wife, then kissed her and led the way into the dark.

Once Wes lit the place up, Trevor was impressed by the set up. It was wide, expansive, a little on the cold side though he figured that was a blessing once people got to working out. There were a handful of practice dummies, two heavy bags, and a small boxing ring which was padded, but not elevated like others he'd seen. It was roped off, and Wes quickly hopped over, landing in the center of the ring with a grin.

"He also likes to show off," Rhys said. He had moved to the wall and was toeing off his shoes.

Trevor's eyebrows shot up. "Are you going to fight him?"

"I wipe the floor with him every time," Wes said with an even bigger grin, "but he's good at helping me warm up."

Rhys shucked his jacket, his arms looking actually impressive, and Trevor realized he hadn't actually seen that much of him until now. Rhys walked to the other side of the ring, then came up with a couple of gloves which he tossed to Wes, and then two large mitt-looking pads which he slipped over his own hands.

"I used to come over and help Wes when he was regaining his balance," he explained, slipping through the ropes. "I'm not actually any good as a trainer, but we work surprisingly well together."

"Not a lie," Wes said. "Didn't help I was wildly attracted to him, but unfortunately, he's the straight brother."

Trevor startled a little, giving Rhys a careful look, whose expression was betraying something Trevor knew intimately: a secret. And Rhys didn't look close to sharing it. Trevor itched to ask him what it was, but knew it wasn't the time. Luckily Wes didn't seem to be paying close attention as he was wrapping his hands and putting his gloves on. Then, before Trevor could ask any more questions, they began the warm ups.

It wasn't nearly as interesting as Trevor thought it might be. It was just a series of moves which all looked mostly the same, though he knew there was probably subtle differences in jabs and footwork and other things he didn't get. *Yet. Maybe.* The idea of working with these guys had some appeal, but only a little. He'd never been a big fan of violence.

When Rhys and Wes moved on to actual sparring, Trevor was quickly distracted by the sound of the door opening and closing. He heard heavy, unsteady footsteps on the stairs, and he couldn't help but watch with some trepidation as a body descended.

The man was Evan, obvious by the glimpse of two intricate prosthetic legs, one of which bent at the knee on an elaborate hinge. The second clue was the white cane he held in his free hand, the other bracing himself on the banister as he carefully took each step.

Trevor got a proper look only a few moments later when Evan reached the bottom of the stairs. He was very tall, his upper body even more broad and fit than Wes' with wide shoulders and bulging arms. He was very dark skinned, his hair worn in a very close crop with sharp edges, and his jawline was cut, his lips full, eyes wide and full of mirth.

Trevor was startled when the guy's gaze seemed to zero in on him, and he was even more startled when Evan made his way over with a grin. "How long have they been at it?"

Trevor shrugged, flushing a little at the man's intense attention. "Uh. About ten minutes. They did a warm up, then started talking shit, now they're putting it to fists."

Evan laughed, then stuck out his free hand. "Nice to meet you, man. I'm Evan."

"Trevor," he returned, enjoying how soft Evan's hand was against his own. It was surprising, considering he was a military guy, but he supposed Evan had a chance for more pampering now that he wasn't serving active duty. "Wes and Anna said you were coming to train, and that Rhys and I could watch."

"Are you one of Wes' new students?" Evan asked, his voice a low, pleasant rumble.

Trevor laughed, shaking his head. "God no. Trust me, I'd be awful in there with him. I'm staying with Rhys for a bit and he wanted to introduce me to the idea."

"You're not scared, are you?" Evan asked. "We can go a round or two if you want. I promise to go easy on you."

For a second, Trevor could have sworn the guy was flirting with him, but he was too nervous to read much more than theory into it. "Yeah, I'll pass on that. I've never done anything like that before and I'd collapse in the first nine seconds."

Evan laughed, elbowing Trevor gently in the side. "Come on now, it can't be all that bad. You seem like a decently sized guy."

"How can you tell?" Trevor blurted, then flushed. "Shit. Sorry, I didn't mean…"

Evan shook his head, his mouth still stretched in a wide grin. "It's no worries. Simple answer, I'm not totally blind." To Trevor's utter surprise, Evan reached up and tapped his fingernail on his left eyeball. "This one's not real. The other one suffered damage to my periphery, but I have some vision in it. I mostly use the cane because I keep tripping over curbs and stuff."

"Ah," Trevor said, rubbing the back of his neck nervously. The guy was still looking at him, still smiling in a way Trevor did recognize and had no idea what to do with. "Cool. Well uh…"

"It's not the legs, is it?" Evan asked after a beat.

Trevor blinked. "The legs?"

"Freaks some people out," Evan told him. He tapped his cane on his left prosthesis and Trevor winced with sympathy. "But I promise, I'm steadier than I look."

"Oh. Dude, no. That's not…I seriously meant it when I said I wouldn't last nine seconds. I've had like a week of Taekwondo lessons when I was thirteen and that was it. I'm an ancient history nerd."

Evan waggled his eyebrows. "I actually work out at the gym with another ancient history nerd who can also kick some decent ass, so not an excuse."

Noah. He meant Noah, and it sent Trevor into another mild panic.

Evan seemed to take notice of the look on his face though, and his own expression fell immediately into something more apologetic. "I'm sorry. I'm being a dick right now."

Trevor shook his head. "You're not. I'm just new at all this and I'm acting like a child about it. Normally I have more chill, but things have been kind of rough lately." He glanced over at Wes and Rhys who had noticed Evan's arrival, but were still circling each other.

When he looked back, Evan was giving him a careful once-over. "Yeah? One of those weeks?"

"More like one of those months. Or two." *Or six*, he added to himself.

Evan let out a small breath. "Any chance you want to let me buy you a coffee some time?"

At that, Trevor nearly choked on his own tongue, his gaze fixing on Evan's. "You want to buy me a coffee?"

"Yes," Evan said firmly. "And full disclosure, I mean that shit romantic as hell, but if you're not into it, I'd also be down for a cup as friends because you look like you could use an afternoon out."

Trevor couldn't help but glance over, and he felt a little startled when he saw that Rhys and Wes had stopped fighting, had climbed out of the ring, and were definitely in earshot. "I uh...can I think about it?"

"Yep. But I'm going to leave you my number so you can text me. That cool?"

Trevor couldn't help but see something like fire in Rhys' eyes, something possessive and maybe even a little hurt. But that couldn't be it. "That's cool," he said after a moment.

Evan beamed. "Right on." He clapped his hands together, then turned toward Rhys to introduce himself. When Rhys' greeting was a fraction cold and stiff, Trevor tried to pretend like it was nothing. The only thing was, he knew there was more than just Rhys' wariness of a stranger. What made it all feel worse was that Rhys was straight, and if he was attracted to Trevor it meant only one thing—he didn't see Trevor as a man.

8.

Rhys could feel his jealousy burning in his gut. He wasn't the sort of guy who hated a stranger on sight, but he found himself wanting to go a few rounds with Evan and knock him on his ass. He might have even considered it, too, if he had any hope of being able to beat the guy. But this was not only a Marine, but a student of Wes', and Rhys was clearly outmatched.

And apart from that, Trevor seemed flattered by Evan's invitation to coffee. Eager, even, to get the guy's number. Rhys knew he couldn't stand in Trevor's way. He was still in the closet, and Trevor was only living with him because he had nowhere else to go. For fuck's sake, it was the biggest recipe for disaster.

What he needed was to get laid. If he could have that sort of distraction, find something to occupy him, maybe he wouldn't be so caught up in wanting Trevor. If only he could turn it off. He found himself a little too quiet on the drive back to theirs, and he felt awful about it. The last thing he wanted was for Trevor to feel punished just because an attractive man was interested in him.

"So, uh…Evan," he said when they were five minutes from home. "Seemed like a nice guy."

He saw Trevor give him a careful look out of the corner of his eye. "Yeah."

"You got his number?"

Trevor licked his lips. "Is that okay? I mean, you seem a little pissed about it."

Rhys wanted to smack himself. Instead, he took a breath and did everything in his power to temper his tone. "Of course it's okay. He's attractive, fit, all the good stuff."

Trevor shrugged one shoulder, still a little cold. "Yeah, he is."

"And I meant what I said. He does seem like a nice guy. I think going out with him would be good for you. He clearly likes you."

Trevor softened at that, looking more fully at Rhys now that he'd managed to control his open jealousy. "I'm not really used to guys that look like him being interested in guys who look like me."

Rhys frowned, glancing over at him. "Seriously?"

Trevor shrugged. "I mean, I'm not exactly a GQ model like you assholes."

Rhys couldn't help the small laugh which bubbled from his chest. "Okay one, I'm definitely not a model. And two, you're really hot, Trevor. Seriously."

For whatever reason, that compliment didn't fall as well as Rhys had hoped. Trevor's face went blank and he turned his gaze out the window. "Thanks," he muttered, but Rhys was pretty sure thanks wasn't the word Trevor had wanted to use at all. He went quiet and didn't look back over at Rhys for the rest of the drive.

Not sure what he'd done wrong, Rhys stayed quiet until they pulled into the garage. Trevor was out of the car and storming inside before Rhys could even begin to ask, and he decided to take his time following the other man in to give him a minute to cool off. When he finally got in, Trevor was nowhere to be found, and Rhys wasn't the kind of guy who could just let shit like this lie.

He shrugged out of his sweater, threw his keys and phone onto the table, then made his way through the house until he found himself at Trevor's door. It was shut, but the light was on and he could hear the other man moving around.

After some hesitation, he knocked. "Can we talk about why you suddenly jumped out of the car and ran away from me like I just kicked your dog?"

There was a long pause, then Trevor said, "It's probably best if I take off."

Rhys felt a sudden wave of panic, and without pretense, he reached for the handle and found the door unlocked. Stepping in, he saw Trevor shoving his clothes into his open case, and he held up his hand. "You're not just taking off like this. Tell me what I did? I swear I meant it when I said Evan seemed like a nice guy."

Trevor's jaw was trembling, and he shook his head, refusing to meet Rhys' gaze. "You just...you don't get it. And it's so stupid because it happens all the fucking time, but I just...I thought maybe...it's...never mind."

Rhys took three steps into the room, within touching distance of Trevor now, but he didn't push himself into the other man's space. "Please tell me what I did. I can't possibly learn to be better if you don't tell me."

Trevor dragged a hand down his face, then let the sweater he was holding fall to the hastily folded pile already in the case. "You like women."

Rhys blinked at him. "...yeah? So?"

"So, you said I was hot," Trevor said. "And I get it. I know it's hard to grasp the idea that I don't have the parts you expect me to, but I am a *guy*, okay? And when straight guys call me hot..."

"I'm not straight," Rhys blurted. The words came out before he could really consider them, and for a brief moment, he was overwhelmed with panic. He'd only come out to a handful of people in his life, nearly all of them strangers. Never anyone he cared about, never anyone whose opinion mattered. He licked his lips and backed up, trying to breathe until the world stopped rocking. "I'm not straight," he said again, his voice low enough to be nearly a whisper. "I'm bisexual."

Trevor looked at him, suspicion written all over his face. "Right. I've heard that one too."

"Have you?" Rhys demanded, starting to feel a little put out now. He'd taken a huge step, and that wasn't the reaction he was expecting.

Trevor shook his head again, letting out a heavy breath. "Straight guys are attracted to me, and it confuses them, so suddenly they think they're bi. And it's safe because they think, oh well he's a guy but he has a pussy and the flat chest kind of sucks, but I know what to do with a pussy."

Rhys laughed. He couldn't help it. Not when he thought back to a handful of weeks before when a guy was fucking him in the ass in a bar storage cupboard. "Yeah. Except I was bisexual, long before I met you, and I've been with both cis men and cis women. I know what the fuck it means to be bi, Trevor. I've actually known about my sexuality since I was a teenager."

That gave Trevor pause. His cheeks darkened a little and he reached for his sweater to fold like he needed something to do with his hands. "So...so why does everyone say you're straight?"

"Because I'm not out," Rhys said. In for a penny, he figured. "I've only ever come out to my ex-wife, and the dudes I fucked. The last one was right before we met, by the way. I was at a bar, he was hot, we snuck into a closet and he fucked me in the ass. Is that bi enough for you?"

Trevor looked very contrite then, his eyes flickering down toward the floor and then back up again. "Sorry. Shit. I didn't mean to...it's just, you have no idea how often I've heard that. No idea."

"You're right," Rhys said, immediately wishing he hadn't let his anger get the best of him. "And I could have handled that better. You had every right to question me, and frankly I shouldn't have said what I did in the car. It's so not my place. You were just...you were down on yourself and I don't want you to think you're not hot enough for a guy like Evan, okay? Because you are. I'd have done the same damn thing he did if we met as strangers."

Trevor blinked like he'd been slapped. His hands dropped the sweater into a heap, and he took a step toward Rhys, and then one back. "You...what?"

"God," Rhys said, hating himself. "I'm being such a dipshit right now. I'm so not trying to make you uncomfortable, okay? I just meant to say that when a guy like Evan wants to take you out, it's because you're every bit as hot, and sweet, and nice as he thinks you are. And I'm going to shut the fuck up because I'm ruining this entire thing. But please don't leave, okay? I really, really don't want you to leave."

"Okay," was all Trevor whispered.

Rhys ran his fingers through his hair, then turned on his heel and walked out. He paced the hall for a few seconds, then stormed to the kitchen and grabbed a beer before snatching up his phone and opening his brother's contact.

Rhys: Why am I such a fuck-up?

Ryan: Because God was saving all the good genes for me. What happened?

Rhys: I'm dealing with a delicate situation and I made it worse because I speak without thinking. How the fuck my court record is so good, I'll never know.

Ryan: Details?

Rhys: Can't right now.

Ryan: Extra bad?

Rhys: Remains to be seen. But I hope not because I'm personally invested in this and I don't want to fuck this up. Unsolicited piece of advice for you, baby brother—don't tell a someone who is literally depending on you to keep them afloat that they're hot to boost their self-esteem no matter how true it is.

Ryan: Wow. God really did give me all the good genes. Jesus, Rhys. What the hell?

Rhys: I wish I knew. I'm going to go drown myself in a tub of beer now. Tell mom I love her.

Ryan: Instead why don't you come out with me next weekend. Noah and Adrian want to do something and I'm going through my own shit. Would be nice to have my brother around.

Rhys: Just text me when and where. Thanks for letting me freak.

He set his phone down and didn't pick it back up, even when it buzzed on the counter. He got halfway through his beer when he heard footsteps, and turned, startled to find Trevor hovering in the doorway.

"Thank you for telling me," Trevor said.

Rhys blinked at him. "Which part?"

"All of it," Trevor told him, smiling a little sheepishly. "But mostly thank you for telling me you were bisexual. And also, I'm really, really sorry for putting you in the position that you sort of had to tell me so I'd understand you don't think I'm a...uh..."

Rhys frowned. "A what?"

"A girl," Trevor admitted in a quiet voice.

"Jesus," Rhys said, passing a hang down his face. "I know it's pointless and stupid, but I kind of want to find every person who ever made you feel like you're not a man and beat the shit out of them. Mostly because I have a lot of pent-up energy and I'd like to use it productively."

That got a small laugh out of Trevor which felt like a superbowl touchdown level triumph right then. "Well, you'd be fighting maybe half the population but... thanks."

Rhys shrugged. "I mean it. But also I didn't feel forced to tell you. I could have diffused the situation a different way, but I uh...I wanted to. I hate being in the closet, and I told you because I do trust you."

"Why are you in the closet?" Trevor asked. He walked into the kitchen and went right for the kettle, flicking it on for tea. "I just mean, half your social circle is some sort of queer, right? Why keep it all in?"

"Well," Rhys said, not sure where to begin. The whys were so damn complicated, and he'd never really been able to voice it before. Not in a way that made sense. "Ryan was in my shadow a lot growing up. I was older and I set the bar really high for a lot of things. School work, activities, goals. Ryan came out when we were young, and being gay—being open and proud and everything—that was his thing, you know? And I felt like if I came out, I'd just take that from him. He was so desperate to have something of his own."

"He has no idea?" Trevor asked softly.

Rhys shook his head. "No. I had a serious boyfriend once, before I married Vanessa, and I almost came out then. But it didn't last. Then Vanessa and I got married and I thought, what's the point? She and I are together and why risk hurting Ryan when I've settled down with a woman. So, I just kept quiet, and it was all fine, except..." He trailed off.

Trevor gave him a soft, sympathetic look as he turned to regard him properly. "Except that being in the closet sucks?"

Rhys felt almost punched with relief at how much Trevor got it. "Yeah. It felt like I was hiding this big piece of me, and it's worse now that Vanessa and I aren't together. I want to feel free to date whoever I want, but I'm also terrified of that big reveal after so damn long."

Twisting his hands, Trevor finally dropped them to his side, but they didn't stay there. He took four huge steps toward Rhys and threw his arms around the other man. The hug was crushing, and it was a little devastating, and Rhys planned to soak up every second of this thing he knew he could never have.

"I'm sorry that I put you in the position to tell me this way," he murmured, his face pressed against Rhys' shoulder. "You may trust me, but I backed you into a corner. I was just scared."

Rhys gently carded his fingers through Trevor's hair, allowing himself these stolen moments. He squeezed his eyes shut against the pain of want and denial, then finally pulled away from Trevor's arms. "I promise it's fine. I get why you're worried, and maybe some other way would have been a better idea, but I still trust you, okay?"

Trevor bit his lip, then nodded. "Do you ever plan to tell your brother?"

Rhys let out a tense laugh, taking another step back as he shrugged. His hip rested against the counter, and he folded his arms over his chest. "I think so. I think it's probably time, because I'd like to start dating again soon, and I'd like to allow myself the chance to explore anyone I connect with without worrying too much about what everyone else is going to think."

"I don't know your brother very well," Trevor told him. "We met a few times at staff parties when Noah didn't have a date, and he was sweet. Flirty, but he didn't seem like a predator, you know?"

Rhys nodded. "Yeah, I know. Ryan is a good guy."

"Well, I'd trust him then, okay? I don't think your brother cares about having a *thing* more than he cares about you being happy."

Logically, Rhys knew Trevor was right, but illogically he couldn't shake the fear of rejection, of losing his relationship with Ryan. He was lonely enough as it was, and the risk was huge. But Trevor wanted the best for him, and as much as it killed him, he opened his mouth and said, "As long as you promise to consider giving Evan a chance."

Trevor looked startled. "Really?"

"He clearly liked you, and after all this bullshit, you deserve a chance to be happy," Rhys said. His entire soul was begging him to stop, to block that path, to curl his hands around Trevor and keep him—selfishly and possessively, because Rhys hadn't wanted someone the way he wanted Trevor in a long, long time. Not since his heart was young and foolishly in love with Vanessa. "Wes wouldn't have him around his family like that unless he was a good guy. A really good guy," he added with emphasis. The worst part? None of that was a lie.

Trevor rubbed at the back of his neck in that sweet, endearing way he always did when he was nervous. "He doesn't know I'm trans."

"How long do you usually wait before you tell someone?" Rhys asked.

"Not long. Like first date, before the guy spends a single dime on me," Trevor admitted. "It's too risky not to."

The genuine fear in his voice was yet another reminder of how little Rhys knew what it was like to navigate the world the way Trevor did. Rhys had grown up profoundly aware of homophobia and the dangers straight men posed to people like his brother, but he'd never know what it would be like to have to confess an intimate detail like that to a total stranger to avoid an obviously dangerous situation.

"Do you want me to come with you?" he blurted, half-regretting just coming out with it like that, but not regretting the offer. "Just in case?"

Trevor's smile was soft, his hands twitching like he wanted to reach out. When he didn't, Rhys ignored the flare of disappointment. "I appreciate it, but I've done this a lot. It's easier now. A lot of gay men tend to expect this—maybe not from *me* necessarily, but at least in their dating lives. Evan doesn't seem like the kind of guy who might lose it."

Rhys hated that he had to agree. Part of him wished Evan seemed potentially volatile, if only to have a legitimate reason for Trevor not to go. But he didn't have that. "Just promise you'll call me if it goes to shit."

Trevor's smile was even softer now, and he gave a slight nod. "I promise. And thanks. This is definitely a friendship I didn't expect."

Well, Rhys couldn't argue there. When he first met Trevor Greene, he most definitely had not expected any of this.

9.

Evan: There's this hella cute little park with a duck pond that has machines you can get birdseed. It follows all your rules, doesn't cost money, and gives us time to get to know each other. Any chance you wanna indulge my childish side and feed some birds?

Trevor: LOL nerd. And yes. Just tell me when and where. There's something I wanted to talk to you about anyway.

Trevor felt himself nearly quaking with nerves as he parked his car and got out. The park wasn't really busy in the middle of the day like this. It was near eleven on a Wednesday, which meant the park goers were either retired folk or parents with small children. It meant less protection for Trevor if the guy wanted to create a scene, but it also meant more protection from people listening in. And, he figured, if he was being followed, a person would have a hard time blending in, giving Trevor every chance to find him.

He hated he had to consider those things right then, and part of him wished he had asked Rhys to come along, though not necessarily to protect him from Evan. The guy seemed to be one of the more genuine people Trevor had met in a while. They hadn't done much more than text and a couple of calls over the past few days, but those bits of communication only pointed out more and more what a good person he was.

But he felt vulnerable out there in the open, and Rhys had been his safe space for a while now. The line between their friendship and everything else was starting to blur, and though Trevor liked Evan, his crush on the lawyer was getting out of hand. It was mainly why he agreed to try this out. In spite of Rhys confessing that he liked men and that he thought Trevor was attractive, Trevor couldn't allow himself to believe he had a chance.

Hell, he didn't think he had much of a chance with Evan either, but he was going to take the opportunity, even if he only got a couple of hot make-out sessions from it. Steeling his nerve, Trevor pocketed his keys and made his way to the stone benches near the bird feeder dispensers.

He saw Evan waiting for him, in jeans this time which covered his prosthetics, and a thick, white hoodie. He wore a soft, forest green beanie pulled low over his forehead, and he was clutching his white cane between both hands looking almost nervous.

Trevor hesitated for a moment, trying to find the courage to do this whole first-date, 'hey by the way, I'm a trans man,' thing he always had to do. It got easier a little with each guy, but he couldn't help the pangs of fear—of both violence and rejection—each time he had to do this little song and dance.

He shoved his hands into his pocket and affected a smile as he got close enough for Evan to see him. "Hey. Sorry I'm late."

Evan shot up, grinning a little as Trevor came to a stop. "You're not late. I was nervous so I got here like half an hour early."

Trevor couldn't help a small laugh. "Really?"

Evan shrugged. "I haven't dated in a while."

Trevor's eyebrows shot up to his hairline. "How long is a while?"

There was some hesitation, then Evan shrugged and looked uncomfortable. "Since before I was discharged." Before his injury, before losing his legs, and one of his eyes, and before the side of his face was scarred. It was a stark reminder that there was more than just Evan's rejection at risk here. Evan was also putting himself on the line—a body he was unfamiliar with and trying to relearn. Trevor had a feeling that guys who were uncomfortable with bodies that had parts like Trevor's were probably also uncomfortable with leg stumps.

"So," Trevor said, attempting to lighten the mood, "no pressure, then?"

Evan's face brightened as he chuckled. "None at all. Do you want to walk?"

Digging into his pocket, Trevor pulled out a handful of quarters. "Uh…well, I brought change to feed the birds since you seemed all excited for that."

Evan's entire face lit up and he laughed, sticking out his hand. "Gimmie."

Trevor felt a wave of affection and hoped right then that even if this didn't work out, he and Evan could stay friends. He liked the guy immensely. He wasn't sure he could see himself being happy with him, but likely that was because his crush on Rhys was eclipsing everything else. He wanted to give it a chance though.

Tipping a few quarters into Evan's palm, the pair of them walked to the machine. Evan used his hands mostly, to navigate putting the quarter into the slot, then he turned the knob and they got a small cup of bird seed in the dispenser. Neither of them said anything as they walked to the edge of the lake, Evan feeling out where the concrete ended with the tip of his cane.

"I can't see any ducks," he said, turning his head from side to side. "Am I missing them?"

Trevor shook his head. "No. They're all out swimming. Maybe throw some bits in and see if they come over?"

Evan did, then sat down on the pavement, stretching his legs over the concrete edge, to wait. "You said you wanted to talk to me. Want to wait, or rip the bandage off?"

Trevor sighed, smiling a little as he hunkered down next to the other man. He hung his feet off the edge, the tips of his shoes just barely skimming the greenish-dark water. A few ducks ventured closer, but not enough to nibble on the seed just yet.

"Bandage ripping would be good, I guess." He licked his lips, his throat feeling dry. "I uh…there's a thing I like to tell guys who are interested in me. It's usually a deal-breaker, so I like to get it out of the way first. And you're a really nice guy, so I need you to know that if it's not your thing and you don't want to keep going forward in a romantic sense, I won't be offended." That last bit was a lie, because it always offended him, and it always hurt. Being rejected for who he was, being told he wasn't a man, or not man enough, never felt good. It made him want to rage and scream and punch shit. But that disclaimer always made the confession easier, and usually did a good job at giving the cis guy an out.

"Not gonna lie, man, you're freaking me out a little. Were you like a hired hit man or some shit?"

Trevor laughed. "Uh no. Nothing that exciting. I actually used to be a professor at the University, teaching Latin."

Evan's eyebrows shot up. "*Used* to be?"

Trevor shook his head quickly, not having any sort of energy to get into it. "Long story, and definitely not important. It's just, I uh…I'm." He swallowed, then just dove in. "I'm a trans man. I've been out since I was a kid and have been on hormone therapy for most of my life. I've had some body modifications, but not a lot, and it's important you know that about me."

"Oh," Evan said, he looked startled. He blinked rapidly, and it was then Trevor could see the slightly uneven movement between his prosthetic and biological eye. After a beat, Evan said, "I wasn't expecting that."

"Yeah, I get that a lot," Trevor confessed. "It's because I've been on treatment for so long, I'm pretty passing. But I learned way early on in my dating history that coming clean before getting started anywhere saves us both a lot of pain during the rejection."

Evan shook his head. "*Rejection*? You think that's automatic rejection?"

"Statistics sets that expectation," Trevor told him, trying to keep bite from his tone. "Statistics taught me to expect rejection as the norm, and acceptance as the anomaly. And I promise I won't be upset about it."

Evan bit his lip. "Okay."

Okay. Well, that wasn't entirely the response he had hoped for. There was nothing worse than ambiguity, but he felt like asking for clarity would seem desperate. So, he sat there, and he waited.

"I think I get it," Evan finally said. "I mean, not entirely. Like I said, I haven't dated since I left the service. I was in rehab for a full year, and then outpatient for another three months before I was stable enough to do shit on my own, so I haven't really had the chance to get rejected. But I know that shit's coming."

Trevor wanted to disagree with him, to insist he wouldn't have to live through any of it because he was too damn good, and too damn nice. But that would be a lie. He knew the world way too well. "Not from me," he finally said. "If we don't work out, it won't be for any other reason than we just don't mesh."

"Then I can say the same," Evan told him.

Trevor couldn't help himself from being startled, and a little wary. Was Evan saying that quid pro quo? Was he just going to take what he could get since Trevor wasn't put off by his disability? He hated how little he trusted, but he also hated how the world had given him every reason to suspect every person's motivations. "Are you sure? Have you ever dated a trans guy before?"

Evan shook his head. "No. But to be fair, I haven't really dated much at all. I wasn't out until after I was discharged, and before that I just stuck to dating women, even if it wasn't what I wanted. I came from the bible belt, so being a gay black man was a lot of strikes against you as a person."

"Oh." Trevor hadn't been expecting that, either. And it caused a slight flare of panic because he wasn't sure he wanted to be this guy's experimentation.

"That doesn't sound like a good oh," Evan pointed out.

A few ducks swam up, and Trevor tossed the seed he had in his hand at them. "It's not a *bad* oh."

"But not a good one," Evan repeated. He threw his own seed, but his gaze was on Trevor.

"I've had some bad experiences," Trevor told him. "Guys who think they're okay with it, but when we get down to it, I'm just not what they can handle. My differences."

"Don't you think it would be hypocritical of me to fixate on the way you're different from me?" Evan pointed out.

"Yes," Trevor told him, "but hypocrisy rarely stops people from feeling the way they feel. Don't you think there are disabled people who reject other disabled people for their differences?"

Evan stared at him, then chuckled, his head shaking. "You should have been a damn lawyer, not a teacher."

The word lawyer made him think of Rhys, which was a mistake in that moment. He shoved the image of the other man deep into the darkest corner of his mind. "Trust me, I needed a lot of debate skills to deal with college kids. And anyway, it's the truth. I'm bitter about it, but I still accept it. And to be frank, I'm not sure I have the emotional strength to be your experiment right now. Things have been really rough for me lately and I don't think I can take the offer of acceptance, only to have it yanked away."

"I think," Evan said slowly, "that in spite of lacking the experience, I still trust myself to know what I want and what I don't. The idea of you not looking the way I thought you might doesn't throw me off. Hell, I can barely see you anyway."

Trevor rolled his eyes, flushing a little. "You know that's not what I meant."

"Yeah, I know," Evan said with a small smile. "The truth is, I just like you. Telling me that you're trans hasn't diminished that at all. I have no idea of this is going to work out, but if it doesn't, it won't be for that reason."

Trevor felt a small measure of fear, but he also wanted to trust him. His only real problem lied in the fact that his heart might belong to someone else. That any hurting which happened might be entirely his fault.

***

Rhys couldn't cease his pacing, even though it was making him sound slightly out of breath. Ivan eventually took notice and asked him quietly, "Are you okay?"

Freezing mid-step, Rhys looked around and then let out a ragged sigh. "No. I mean, mostly yes. Except no."

With a soft chuckle, Ivan said, "How about dinner? You sound like you could use some dinner. My abuela sent over a bunch of food left over from my niece's christening, and there's no way I'm going to be able to eat it all. And trust me, it's to die for."

Rhys opened his mouth to refuse, to insist he had too much going on, but that wasn't an excuse he could use right then. Yes, he had a mountain of work he could be catching up on, and yes, he had court in the morning for a case he was pretty sure he was going to lose, but he wasn't going to be able to concentrate until he got Trevor out from under his skin.

And maybe dinner with Ivan would help. Not that he particularly thought going to dinner at his brother's ex lover's house was the smartest idea, but maybe that's what he needed to shake things up. At any rate, a good meal and a beer or two couldn't hurt.

"Yeah. Yes," he said. "What time?"

"Now would work," Ivan told him, a smile in his voice. "I was just heating up my steamer for the tamales."

Rhys didn't give himself a chance to over-think it. He walked into the kitchen, grabbed up his keys and jacket, then stepped into the garage. "Send me your address and I'll throw it in my GPS. See you soon?"

"Absolutely."

The line went dead, and less than half a minute later, his screen lit up with Ivan's street number. It was only ten minutes away, which made him both relieved and panicked. Not enough time to work himself up to cancel, but also not enough time to find his chill.

Rhys found himself taking the streets a little faster than he should have, and he arrived two minutes ahead of the predicted GPS estimate. Ivan's place was nice, a little one-story house nestled in one of the older neighborhoods mostly occupied by the rich retired community. He pulled through an open set of wrought-iron gates, then parked right next to Ivan's little electric car. He tried not to wonder if maybe Ivan was the one who influenced Ryan's last car purchase because it meant acknowledging what Rhys was stepping into—and that was forcing him to confront that he wasn't there with entirely platonic intentions.

He licked his dry lips, then got out and headed for the front door. It opened before he could ring the bell, and Ivan stood there in casual joggers and a t-shirt, his hair slightly damp and ruffled. Rhys had known the guy a while, but very rarely outside of a professional setting. Seeing him in civvies was almost too real, and his stomach twisted.

He also didn't miss the way Ivan's gaze roamed up and down his body, almost hungry. Ivan wanted him too, this wasn't all in Rhys' head. He felt nerves firing up, the tips of his fingers tingling, and he forced himself to put one foot in front of the other until he was inside. The place smelled amazing, rich with spices from the food, and it was warm and cozy.

Rhys wasn't exactly sure what to expect from the guy, but the minimalist décor worked. It was utilitarian, but also lived in, with a sleek sofa, an afghan draped across the top, and a handful of ink-sketches framed on the walls. He had a few hanging ivy plants near his window, and there was a cat tree which meant he didn't live completely alone.

"Let's get drinks. I have beer and wine, also juice if you'd rather not have alcohol," Ivan said, beckoning Rhys down a small hallway and around a corner which led to a small but comfortable kitchen. There was a breakfast table with enough space for two, and Ivan beckoned to the chairs before walking to the fridge.

"Beer is great," Rhys said after a second. He'd probably need to be a little loose if he was going to find his way out of himself.

Ivan smiled, grabbing a green-bottled lager, then picked up what looked like a half-gone glass of dark red wine. "Food's almost done. I'd offer you some *tacos de cabeza de rez*, but I don't usually offer that to newbies."

Rhys blinked at him. "Head...tacos?" he asked, drawing on his college Spanish.

Ivan laughed, shaking his head as he walked over to the stove and pulled a lid off the steamer pot. "Yep. She also made *chapulines*, but I figured I'd leave those off too and go with chicken enchiladas and tamales."

Rhys bit his lip, then grinned at him. "I'm not entirely unadventurous, but I think tamales and enchiladas sound right up my alley tonight. I could really use some comfort food."

Ivan replaced the lid, then turned to face Rhys with a concerned expression. "I could tell. Do you want to talk about it?"

Rhys gripped his beer tightly, his thumbnail toying with the edge of the label. "It's complicated."

Ivan gave a faint chuckle. "You're a thirty-six-year-old lawyer, what isn't complicated these days?"

"Fair," Rhys said, giving him a return smile, though he knew it didn't reach his eyes. "I've just been in a funk since I found out my ex-wife is pregnant."

"Your baby?" he asked.

Rhys nearly choked on his swallow of beer, swiping his hand across his mouth as he tried to clear his throat. "No. God, no. *No*, just...that was one of the reasons, you know? We didn't work because she didn't want kids, but apparently it was just with me."

"Ah," Ivan said. He turned away, grabbing a couple of plates, and in minutes he had them filled with food which smelled heavenly, even if Rhys' stomach was starting to rebel against the idea of eating anything. Ivan put everything on the table, then moved his chair so he and Rhys were directly next to each other. "Would you change it? If you had the power, would you have kids with her?"

Rhys bit his lip, then shook his head. "I don't think so. I loved her the only way I could, but it wasn't enough, and I think deep down we both knew it. I just…it makes me wonder if I'm defective, you know?"

"Yeah, I do know," Ivan said quietly. "I haven't had the best luck with relationships. I tried with Ryan, but he was very clear he didn't want to risk anything more than a superficial hook-up. It killed me a little. I could have loved him, but he didn't want that."

"You would have deserved better," Rhys said. Before Ivan could get defensive, he said, "I love my brother and he deserves someone amazing, but he has a lot to work through, and you deserve to be with someone who doesn't have a mountain of shit to navigate before they can love themselves, let alone someone else."

Ivan laughed softly as he thumbed the rim of his wine glass. "I'm not going to argue with you. It's why I didn't fight him on it. I only brought it up because I understand."

Rhys lowered his eyes, feeling overwhelmed with the desire to just come out, because now that he'd done it with Trevor, he found the feeling of not hiding, of not being in the closet, overwhelmingly good. Better than any high he'd ever had. "I'm kind of in another, complicated predicament."

"Okay," Ivan said. He reached over and pushed Rhys' plate closer to him. "Take a few bites, then tell me as much as you can."

Rhys obeyed without really thinking, letting his fork sink into the soft, saucy corn tortilla. He put the bite on his tongue and let himself be overwhelmed with the smoky, rich flavor. He wanted to buy Ivan's abuela a hundred muffin baskets for this. The food actually comforted him, in a way he hadn't felt since his own mom's roast chicken and potato dish she made every time he felt sad.

He breathed, ate a little, then dared to look up at Ivan's face. He couldn't entirely read his expression, but he felt safe being honest. "I think I'm ready to come out of the closet."

Ivan blinked. He was visibly startled, and it made Rhys panic for a second, wondering if maybe he should take it back. Then Ivan let out a breath. "To whom?"

"Well, you right now," Rhys said with a tight laugh. "Obviously. Uh, I'm not gay. I'm bisexual, but it's never really been a thing before, since I was with Vanessa for so long."

Ivan cleared his throat, blinking a few more times. "Does your brother…"

"No," Rhys said quickly. "Sorry, I just…no. I never told him. I was always too afraid he'd get pissed off or think I was just trying to encroach on his territory. And like I said, it was never important."

Ivan frowned. "Your sexuality is part of who you are. There's nothing wrong with wanting to stay in the closet, but it doesn't mean who you are isn't important."

Rhys felt his throat go a little tight. He wasn't sure what response he expected, but it wasn't that. "I…right."

Ivan reached for him, taking his hand gently. "I just don't want you to think that staying in the closet means you have to sacrifice that piece of you. It took me forever to come out. Being a cop, being who I was, my big-ass Mexican-Catholic family? Trust me when I say the closet and I are intimate friends."

Rhys was able to muster a genuine smile. "Yeah."

Ivan ran his thumb over Rhys' knuckles. "Have you been with a guy before?"

With a small laugh, Rhys nodded and reached for his beer, taking several long pulls before answering him. "Yeah. I started hooking up with guys in high school, we just always agreed we'd never tell anyone. I was semi-serious with a guy in college when Vanessa and I were split up, but then she came back, and we ended up getting married. If she hadn't, I would have come out then. I really liked him."

Ivan gave him an apologetic look. "Sounds complicated."

Rhys laughed, taking a bite of his food while profoundly aware that Ivan was still holding his hand. "Yeah. It was. I've hooked up once since the divorce. No one I knew—just a guy I met in a bar. But that's not what I want."

"I get that," Ivan said.

Rhys wet his lips, then said, "I'm into someone, but he and I can't be together."

"Because of your brother?" Ivan asked.

Rhys shook his head. "Because the situation is complicated, and he's going through some shit, and it's just completely unethical."

"The guy you asked my help with," Ivan said. He drew his hand away, and Rhys felt the loss profoundly.

"Yeah. I'm not in love with him," possibly a lie, "but I do like him, and I think mostly I'm just really, really lonely." A half-truth, but he could live with it.

Ivan gave him a careful, considering look. "Is that why you're here?"

Rhys bit the inside of his cheek. "I don't know, to be honest. Technically you're off limits. You had a thing with my brother and going there is against at least half a dozen bro-codes."

Ivan snorted a laugh, draining the last of his wine. He hadn't touched his food, but he didn't seem interested in eating what was on the table. The way he was looking at Rhys, however… "Are you really that invested in the bro-code? You don't think you owe it to yourself to be happy? You know Ryan and I were never in love. We weren't dating. We fucked whenever he was feeling antsy or angry. He was fucking Wes too. You know that, right?"

Rhys didn't know that, but he'd always suspected the little comments Wes made had some measure of truth to them. He knew Wes and Anna had an open relationship, so there was no real surprise there. "Yeah," he said. "I mean, *no*, but I'm not surprised."

Ivan reached for him again, and Rhys didn't pull away. "I'm not proposing marriage or a relationship. I confess I'm not entirely sure how comfortable I am starting something with a guy clearly hung up on someone else, but I've always had a thing for you."

In spite of having clearly seen the desire in Ivan's eyes when he first arrived, Rhys found himself stunned by the open admission. "I…you…"

Ivan shrugged, looking a little pleased with himself that he'd managed to render the wordy lawyer into a stuttering mess. "You know you're attractive, and you're a good person. It's kind of the whole package. I'm willing to be patient if you want to give this a try, Rhys. I'm not expecting miracles, but I'm also not really interested in another situation where it's just sex."

"I don't want that either," Rhys said, his voice so quiet it was nearly a whisper. He thought about the last hook up, the cold closet, the wordless goodbye, the empty feeling of having been fucked by a total stranger. It scratched an itch but left him worse off than before.

"How about take some time to think about it?" Ivan proposed.

Rhys licked his lips, then stood up. "I can do that." He glanced over at the little digital clock above the oven and saw he'd been there just over an hour. It felt like almost no time had passed, but also felt like an eternity had crept by. "I should go."

"Yes," Ivan said, acknowledging the charged heat between them. If Rhys stayed, more might happen. He stood up alongside Rhys, and the pair of them stared at each other, neither daring to make a move.

Then, as Rhys' breath caught in his throat, Ivan's hand lifted to touch the side of his face. "I'm not sure I can give you what you want," Rhys murmured, leaning into the caress. It was softer, and so fucking much sweeter than any person he'd been with in so long. It didn't stop Trevor's face from flaring to life behind his closed eyelids every time he blinked, though, and he knew that was a problem.

"I know," Ivan said after a moment. He stepped closer, the distance between them growing smaller and smaller until there was barely a centimeter left. His hand remained on Rhys' face. "Is it terrible that part of me wants to say fuck it? In case you change your mind? Because I can't lie to you, I think I'll regret it for the rest of my life if I can't touch you at least a little."

"Shit," Rhys groaned, because as much as he was falling for another man, he was only human. Ivan was attractive, and Ivan wanted him, and Rhys desperately wanted to be wanted. "I can't make you promises right now, and I know that probably makes you think of my brother…"

"Your brother is the last person on my mind right now," Ivan said, his voice full of purpose. "Believe me." His gaze flickered down, and Rhys knew his erection was obvious, straining against the zip in his jeans.

His mouth dry, Rhys attempted to lick his lips. "If you can accept me for what I am right now," he murmured.

"If it means getting to swallow your cock," Ivan said, "then I'm all in."

That's all Rhys needed for his go-ahead. His hands went to Ivan's waist, and that was the last breath of space between them, gone in a hot press of bodies. Rhys ground himself against the other man's fit chest, feeling the swelling cock pressing to his hip, wanting him—*god*, wanting him so badly.

He let Ivan manhandle him out of the room, down the hallway and into a bedroom. It was dimly lit by a desk lamp, and just as warm and minimal as the rest of the house. He had an unmade bed, a dresser, a closet door hanging half open.

Then the background faded into nothing as Ivan's hands were on him. Rhys fell back against the messy covers, letting Ivan meticulously strip them both, starting from shoes, ending with a slow drag of Rhys' boxers down to his knees. They hooked around his ankles, but before he could kick them off, Ivan was leaning over him, licking a hot stripe at his pubic bone, just a breath away from where Rhys desperately wanted him.

"Fuck," he groaned.

"Yeah. God, yes, I'm going to fuck you. I'm going to do whatever you want. Tell me what you want. Tell me what to do." There was a note of desperation in his voice, begging in a way, wanting to be ordered. It sent Rhys' head for a spin because he'd never been involved in anything like that.

His partners had always wanted sweet, or passionate, but never this. He bit his lip and pushed up on his elbows. His hand reached out, a tentative stroke along Ivan's cheek. "Get a condom." He almost made it a question, but changed his tone at the last second and was rewarded by Ivan's pupils dilating.

He wasn't sure he liked it, but he was curious enough to keep going. He watched Ivan's naked form scramble to his feet, rush to the dresser, returning with a box of condoms and a bottle of lube. "I don't know how far you want to go tonight," Ivan started.

Rhys shook his head, trying to regain his composure. If he was going to be able to make this good—and he wanted that, he wanted Ivan to feel good—they would have to talk first. "You want to be told what to do, don't you?"

Ivan's face went scarlet, his gaze sliding away. "I like...I..."

Rhys reached for him, tugging him close. "I've never done that before, and I don't think I'm really comfortable with going too far."

Ivan shook his head. "I wouldn't ask that of you. Trust me, I know where to look when I need *that*. I just don't like to be in control. I don't want to be a leader here. I just want someone to take charge."

"I can do that. I *think* I can do that," Rhys amended. He'd never participated in anything beyond vanilla sex, but he was still worldly enough he understood how those things worked. "Do you have a...a safe word?"

Ivan looked mildly surprised, but he shrugged. "We can just use red."

"Red," Rhys echoed. "Is there anything else I should know?"

Ivan shook his head. "Just tell me what you want me to do to you, and I'll do it. That's all I want right now."

The problem was, what Rhys wanted right then wasn't Ivan. It was absurd to think about. A gorgeous guy on his knees for Rhys, ready and willing to do whatever he wanted. But he wasn't ready. Jumping in like this wasn't the way he wanted to move on from Vanessa, or from his pointless feelings for Trevor.

Ivan could see it on his face, and in his flagging erection, and he pushed up to his knees, his face drawn and serious. "It's too much."

"No," Rhys said. He pushed up to his elbows and reached for the other man, but Ivan stayed out of his grasp. "It wasn't that, I swear. It's just...you were right before. I don't want a hook-up. I want something with substance, and whatever this is tonight, it'll taint whatever happens in the future."

Ivan looked vaguely surprised. "You think there might be a future here?"

"I don't know," Rhys confessed. "It never occurred to me to think of you as an option."

At that, Ivan laughed, dragging a hand down his face as he collapsed to his side, rolling to face Rhys. "Same here. I meant what I said—I always found you hot, but you were my lover's big brother and at the time, I thought you were straight. You were everything I couldn't have, and it was enticing."

"But unattainable?" Rhys offered.

Ivan nodded. "So now what?"

Rhys shrugged, biting his lip as his head fell back against the pillow. "I don't know. I came over tonight because the guy I like is out on a date with another guy he met at Wes'. A hot, friendly, sweet guy who would probably be perfect for him. I thought maybe food and company would cheer me up, and if I was lucky, maybe a blow-job. But I want more. I want something with possibility."

"And I'd like to have a guy who isn't pining for someone else," Ivan confessed.

Rhys let out a heavy sigh and turned onto his side, reaching for Ivan's face. He stroked the backs of his knuckles along his stubbled cheek. "I'm sorry. Believe me, you have *no idea* how sorry I am. If I hadn't met him first, I'd probably be all in."

Ivan shook his head. "I'm not broken-hearted, you know. And I still like you. And hell, we can make a pact. If we're both single and lonely at forty, we just say fuck it and make it work."

Rhys laughed. "I think I made that deal with my Intro to Bio lab partner my freshman year. But she's probably forgotten, so yeah. If we're forty and still single, lonely losers…"

Ivan pushed up, then crawled into Rhys' space. "Kiss on it? Because we skipped that part with all the grinding, and I don't think I want you to leave before we do that at least once."

Rhys licked his lips, then nodded and moved his hand to curl around the back of Ivan's neck. His fingers dug into the short-clipped hair, feeling the buzzing of it against the sensitive pads. His eyes fluttered closed as Ivan moved in close, then there was a warm, soft press of lips. It was gentle, not entirely chaste when Ivan pushed his tongue into Rhys' mouth in a slow, easy drag, curling around his own making it wet and hot. But it wasn't full of their earlier passion. It really did feel like a goodbye.

Rhys felt something heavy settle in his gut. Mostly because he was going to walk away and go home and have to hear about Trevor's date. He'd have to watch the man he wanted slowly fall in love with a guy he couldn't even hate, because Evan was decent and kind and deserved a good soul like Trevor.

When they broke apart, Ivan was breathing a little heavily, pushing his forehead against Rhys'. "You know I'm still here for you, right? As a friend, as a colleague. If you ever need help…"

"Yeah," Rhys said. He felt a sting of pain when they finally broke apart, a longing to just say fuck it and let himself sink into this. But he knew it would never feel right, and he owed himself a chance to find something that made his heart sing. The way Noah and Adrian felt, the way Wes and Anna had fallen in love.

He gathered his clothes, then Ivan insisted on packing him some food to go. They lingered in the door and shared one final kiss before Rhys made his way back to the car, and he felt like a stone had lodged itself in his gut for the entire drive back.

10.

It had been years since Trevor had felt so innocent leaving a date. After the park, Evan had insisted on buying lunch, so they headed to a little café nearby and had sandwiches on the patio under the heaters. They talked about everything and nothing—who they were, things they liked, but nothing of substance.

Trevor couldn't help but bring it up when he pulled up to Evan's apartment building, and the other man had just laughed. "I figure all that stuff is for the second date. If you're up for it."

In all honesty, Trevor wasn't entirely sure. He liked Evan a lot. More than he expected to, but he couldn't deny his mind and heart were occupied elsewhere. More than once, he'd stopped to wonder what Rhys was doing, had fought off the urge to text him and check in. He had to start trying to move on, and Rhys had all-but shoved him into Evan's arms.

He just wasn't sure it was a great time to be dating. And yet, he was also allowing his situation to dictate every single aspect of his life, and that was part of what he was trying to move on from. He had help now, and friends. He wasn't alone. He had options. Why shouldn't he let himself at least try?

"I'm up for it," he told Evan before the man could climb out of the car.

Evan turned in his seat, grinning, and he reached for him. Trevor had half expected a kiss, but instead, Evan had merely brushed the side of his cheek softly and leaned in to say in his ear, "I can't wait. Text me."

Then he was gone, and Trevor was left a little stunned and very unsatisfied in the driver's seat. It was good though. It was better than good, it was perfect. It meant he hadn't pushed himself into something he was unsure of, but he hadn't burnt that bridge, either. He was letting himself take time. Evan didn't care that he was a bartender. He didn't ask why Trevor had a Ph.D. but was living with another person and slinging drinks for a living. He just seemed to genuinely enjoy his company.

Trevor had been on dates far worse than that one.

When he pulled into the garage, he was a little startled to find Rhys' car gone. And not only that, but no text or note indicating where he'd gone. Trevor realized in the short time he'd been staying there, he'd started to expect that level of communication. In reality, he had no right to Rhys' private time. The man didn't owe him a damn thing apart from the legal aid outlined in their verbal agreement.

But it rankled him. He couldn't help the feeling of being left out, couldn't help his mind wandering. Had he taken the opportunity to meet someone since Trevor was now occupied with his own personal life? Was he seeing someone new?

He hated how jealous it made him feel. Normally he would have gone straight to the kitchen to cook, but the idea had no appeal. Instead, he threw on his pajamas, then grabbed a pear from the fruit basket and plopped on the sofa for a TV binge. He threw on whatever Rhys had been watching last—some docu-series about old Scottish castles—and he zoned out as he lay there.

His life was still in shambles, he was possibly thinking about dating, but didn't know if he even liked the guy, and the one person he'd give up everything to be with made it very clear he wasn't interested. All in all, it was a complete shit-show.

Trevor was almost asleep when he heard the garage door and had just managed to sit upright when Rhys came walking into the living room holding a couple of containers filled with red-sauced food.

"Have you been home long?" Rhys asked.

Trevor scrubbed a hand down his face, then glanced at the wall clock. "Uh. I guess a couple hours. I didn't realize you were going out."

Rhys frowned, and Trevor felt a pang of fear like maybe he'd crossed a line. Instead of answering him, Rhys turned and walked into the kitchen, and Trevor felt suddenly helpless against following him. He watched the other man set everything on the counter, then frown at it like he was trying to solve a complicated equation.

"You okay?"

Rhys looked startled as he glanced over. "Oh uh…yeah. Weird day. How was your date? Did it go alright?"

Trevor shrugged, folding his arms over his chest. "It was fine."

Rhys clearly read something in Trevor's tone, because he turned fully and gave him a careful look. "Was he a dick about it?"

Trevor realized he was letting his jealousy show itself as anger, and he quickly reigned it in. "No. He was really great about it, actually. We got a bite to eat, then I drove him back to his and we planned another date."

Something flashed in Rhys' eyes, and his shoulders tensed a little. "Oh. That's. Yeah. Good, right?"

Trevor shrugged. "Is it?"

At that, Rhys gave a slightly frustrated laugh. "I don't know, Trevor. It was your date. I wasn't there with you."

Trevor swallowed, then glanced at the food. "Where'd all that come from?"

Rhys' gaze flickered over, and Trevor definitely recognized the look on his face. It was shame, or guilt. "A friend. I went to visit a friend."

"Like a sex friend?" he asked. He froze then, horrified at the way the words just erupted out of his mouth like he had no control. His face went flaming hot, and he turned away. "Jesus Christ, I'm sorry. That's so none of my business and I just…"

"Yeah," Rhys said, his voice very soft. "He is. Or well…maybe. I don't know where we're at, exactly." With a long, drawn out sigh, Rhys leaned against the counter, his head bowed. "I want to move on, you know? I feel like I've existed in my little self-imposed, post-divorce isolation for long enough. But when I got there, and we started to…" He trailed off with a self-deprecating laugh, and as much as hearing all this was killing Trevor, he couldn't help but step forward, wanting to comfort the other man who was clearly hurting. "I froze up, like a dipshit."

"Have you ever…you said you've been with men, right?" he said, trying to remember everything Rhys had told him before when he'd come out.

"Yeah," Rhys said. He curled his hands into fists, then released them and turned to face Trevor. "I have, but I realized this wouldn't just be a one-time deal. He wants something more, and I'm tired of these anonymous encounters. I'm," he swallowed thickly, "I'm lonely."

All of Trevor's anger faded, his jealousy simmering in the background, but eclipsed by a wave of sympathy because Rhys was a good guy, and he didn't deserve Trevor's petty mood, or mind-games. Rhys was selfless and kind, and he deserved to be loved. "If you want it," he said carefully, coming to stand beside Rhys at the counter, "and if he wants it, what stopped you?"

"Fear," Rhys said. "And complicated feelings." Trevor had a feeling there was something heavy in that last, but he didn't want to pry. "Mostly I'm afraid that I'm going to fuck it up again, and he's a good guy. He doesn't deserve it."

Trevor licked his lips, then asked, "Do I know him? I mean, is he one of the people you've introduced me to?"

Rhys smiled faintly and shook his head. "No. He's not one of Wes' guys or anything. But he's as good as they are—maybe better. I don't know. I've known him for a while."

"Did he know you were…"

"Bi?" Rhys said, then shook his head, and there was a flare of anxiety in his wide eyes. "Nope. He does now, which is also a little terrifying, but I don't think he's going to sell me out."

Trevor bit his lip, then glanced at the food. "I'm proud of you."

At that, Rhys visibly startled. "What?"

"You came out to him, and you put yourself out there, and that's huge. And I know that sounds patronizing, but sometimes it's easy to forget that even the little things are accomplishments. People like us, we'll probably be spending the rest of our lives coming out in some way or another. We're never going to live a life that's just assumed, you know? And it's always going to be a little terrifying, and we're always going to have to be a little bit brave."

Rhys' face softened and he reached for one of the containers. "His abuela made these, and they're amazing. Do you uh…do you want to binge food and TV on the sofa for a bit?"

Trevor knew that saying yes would only torture him further, but he could tell Rhys needed a friend, and if that's all Trevor got to be, well that would have to be enough. "Yeah, I do."

The smile on Rhys' face made that moment totally worth it.

***

Trevor felt another pang of nervousness, just like he had getting ready for his first date with Evan. Only this time, it was a proper one. This time, it was dinner and drinks, and then hanging out at Evan's for a night-cap. And whatever else he might feel ready for.

Trevor wasn't the kind of guy who fucked on the first date. Mostly because he didn't trust his cis partners not to freak the fuck out every time they got naked and they remembered he wasn't like them. He wanted to trust that Evan knew what he was getting into, but he didn't really know the guy at all.

And if he was really being honest with himself, he was mentally dragging his feet because he wasn't there yet. His mind was still wholly occupied with Rhys, and it was just getting worse as the days went on. In truth, he realized he was going to have to make a change. He'd have to figure out a new living arrangement because the longer he was so close to Rhys, the more impossible it was becoming to move on from him.

He resolved to start asking around, to see if anyone was looking for a roommate. His job at the bar paid an okay wage on the busy nights, and he was sure he could find a second job to help fill in the gaps. Especially since whoever was after him seemed to have backed off. It had been weeks since his last threatening message, and maybe—just maybe—things were starting to go back to the way they were.

If he met with silence for any longer, he might try putting his work feelers out there. The community college was always hiring for history professors, and it wasn't exactly his forte, but he could do it. The very thought of getting his life back was heady, like a drug, and he wanted it more than anything in the world.

Trevor pulled up to the restaurant, snagging a decent spot, and when he walked around to the front, he saw Evan waiting for him on a low bench. He was spotted immediately, Evan's face breaking into a wide smile as he pushed himself to stand. He was leaning on a forearm crutch and wasn't carrying his white cane.

"Hey, you," Evan said when Trevor was close enough.

Trevor grinned. "Hey. How are you?"

Evan laughed and thumped the crutch on the ground. "Oh…the usual. Had a nasty fall and torqued my knee, so I'm stuck with this thing for the next few days."

Trevor frowned. "Shit. If you're in pain, we can just postpone."

"There's no way in hell I'm waiting any longer to romance you," Evan said, making a flush rise to Trevor's cheeks. "And anyway, it just means I look even more awkward than usual."

A protest rose to Trevor's lips, but he bit it back. He didn't think Evan was fishing for reassurance, and Trevor knew how much it irritated him when people tried to contradict him when he complained about not looking man enough. Sometimes it just was. And there was no denying that Evan's gait was altered. His center of balance was different than other people, and with his compromised vision, he was obvious.

"Well, you're in good company," he eventually said, and it was the right thing, he could tell, by the way Evan's smile widened. "Did you put our names in?"

"I did one better. Made a reservation on the top deck." He offered his free hand, and Trevor took it. He liked the way Evan's skin felt against his own. His palm was smooth, save for a few callouses where he bore most of the weight when he lifted, and his hand was so warm.

Evan gripped him tight, and let him take the lead, and Trevor made sure to measure his steps at an even pace. They were taken to a small elevator, which surprised Trevor, but it made sense Evan would know about a place like this. The top deck had only a handful of tables under a glass dome, which looked out over the city. Their table was right at the edge, and it gave Trevor a little vertigo to be up so high, but he adjusted quickly as he leaned back in his chair.

"Great, right?" Evan asked as he reached for his water glass. "I took my mom here last month when she came to visit."

Trevor's eyebrows went up. "Did she love it?"

Evan snorted shaking his head. "My mom's something else. She spent the entire night quietly losing her shit about the menu prices. She tried to get away with ordering a cup of soup to eat with the free bread, and when I ordered her the fish, she almost swooned. But I think she had a good time once her heart palpitations calmed down."

Trevor chuckled, feeling a little warm inside as he pictured Evan wooing his mom. "That's really sweet. Does she live far?"

Evan shrugged. "Two-hour flight. She tried to convince my dad to move down here when I was transferred to the rehab facility, but he put his foot down after I told him I needed space to get back on my feet. She loves me hard, but it can be a little suffocating."

Trevor had no way to understand that, but he smiled anyway. "I'm glad she was there for you though. It must have helped."

"Mostly," Evan said. "What about you? Your parents close enough to annoy the shit out of you?"

At that, Trevor flushed, and he cleared his throat as he glanced back out the window. He tried to make his tongue work, but he had forgotten how awkward it was to tell someone he wanted to be with just how fucked up his early life was.

Evan seemed to pick up on it, because he swore quietly under his breath. "They're dead, aren't they?"

Trevor blinked at him and was unable to help his startled laugh. "Actually, I don't really know. I uh…I was kind of a system kid. My parents were addicts, and DCS took me out of the home when I was about nine. After a couple of group homes, I went to live with my grandma. She's the one who helped me transition, change my name, all that. She died a few years ago, and my parents didn't bother to show up so they're either dead too, or they don't know."

Evan swore again. "*Shit.* I'm sorry. I just…I assumed. I'm sorry."

Trevor shook his head. "Trust me, I actually don't mind when people assume I had a normal childhood. I worked hard to overcome a lot of it, and it just means my hard work shows."

Evan leaned his elbow on the table. "You're definitely not like anyone I have ever dated before."

Trevor met his gaze steadily. "Good thing or bad thing?"

Evan's grin spread wide, bright, warming the room. "Good. Really fucking good. Now, can I ask an awkward as hell question?"

"Go for it," Trevor said, not nearly as nervous as he might have been even minutes before.

"Can you help me read this menu? Because in this light, I can't see shit."

***

After the initial fumbles with their opening conversation, the rest of the date went smoothly. They ordered, had dessert, finished their drinks holding hands beside the empty plate of flourless chocolate cake. Evan's calloused thumb rubbed gentle circles on the inside of Trevor's wrist, and he felt the slow start of tingles up his arm.

It was what he was looking for—proof that this was more than just distracting himself from Rhys. He needed substance and possibility, because Evan deserved better than to be a consolation date. When Evan suggested they take it back to his place, Trevor readily agreed, and offered to get the car since Evan insisted on paying.

Trevor had no problem finding the place again and took up Evan's assigned spot. "I can't drive anymore, so I'm not using it," he said with a grin.

Trevor felt a pang of sympathy for the loss, but it wasn't anything more than that. He couldn't pity a guy who was clearly adjusting to his new life and was making the best of it. Trevor still wasn't sure anything was going to come of this, but he wanted to at least keep a friendship. Evan seemed to brighten any room he was in, and Trevor didn't have a lot of people like that who stuck around.

Inside the apartment, it was nice, with more things than Rhys had, though it was tidy. His sofa was sitting in the middle of the room, an area rug beneath it, and it was facing a large TV mounted on the wall. He had a few bookshelves which were mostly covered in plants and photo frames, and one wall had an entire case dedicated to DVDs and what looked like old vinyl records.

"Your place is really nice," Trevor breathed out. It honestly reminded him of his own—before everything had gone to shit. He'd always been a little messy, a collector of things. His therapist once suggested his attachment was rooted in his trauma from childhood—said people like him tended to either be extreme minimalists or extreme collectors. He was lucky he was toward the middle of the spectrum, but he really did have trouble parting with things. He knew that was likely why he felt so unsettled, even if Rhys had given him a place without any real expectation of him moving out.

"Let me get some drinks," Evan said, propping his crutch against the wall. "Alcohol or non?"

"Non," Trevor said, wanting to keep his head. "I'll just take water."

Evan nodded, then motioned toward the sofa. "Get comfortable and I'll be out in a sec. I'm going to get out of these trousers."

Trevor nodded, staring a little at Evan's ass as he moved down the hall, then he lowered himself to the cushions and sighed as he sank down into the comfortable fabric. The place smelled like Evan as much as it looked like him. Woodsy and warm, comforting without really trying to be. He knew he could like it here, could like Evan. It would have been so much less complicated if he hadn't met Rhys first.

But his heart and his head were both morons.

Evan came out a few minutes later, startling Trevor a little when he appeared in his manual chair, both legs off. He had socks over his stumps, one which hung an inch or two below his knee, and the other a few inches above. They were a little misshapen, though Trevor assumed that was from the blast and the ragged amputation.

Evan looked a little wary as he met Trevor's gaze, and after a beat asked, "Is this okay? I know it kind of freaks people out sometimes, but my legs are still healing, and I'm not supposed to walk around too long in my prosthetics."

Trevor sat up, waving off Evan's nervous question. "I swear, it's totally fine. Can I help with drinks?"

Evan seemed to relax a little, though not entirely, but he shook his head and smiled. "I've kind of become an expert in balancing shit. Just sit back, I'll be with you in a minute." He wheeled himself into the kitchen, and Trevor sat back.

He forced himself to examine whether or not Evan's amputations really did make him uncomfortable. He'd known disabled people—he'd taught wide ranges of disabilities after becoming a professor, but he'd never been close to anyone who wasn't able-bodied. Noah was the first person he'd ever become proper friends with, and Noah's eye wasn't noticeable unless you were truly looking for it.

It was only fair he consider it. If he was going to expect the same thing from Evan, a serious self-examination of prejudices and comfort—he had to put himself through the same.

By the time Evan came back, holding two bottles of water between his thighs, he'd come to the conclusion that it would take some getting used to, but it didn't matter. He wasn't sure Evan would feel the same about him, once he was stripped down and navigating sex and intimacy, but he could only hope.

He shifted over a little as Evan parked his chair near the sofa, then used deft motions to transfer over. He kept a space between them, but Trevor was feeling a little bold, and closed the distance so they were nearly touching.

"Is this okay?" he asked.

Evan's eyes were heavy-lidded, his face serious, but not nervous. "It's damn perfect. I really wasn't expecting this to go so well."

Trevor couldn't help his laugh, covering his face with one hand. "I know what you mean. My life has been a series of total disasters lately, so I was kind of expecting this night to go to hell."

Evan's face fell a little bit, his head cocking to the side. "Do you want to talk about it?"

Trevor licked his lips, desire to just vent everything and a desire to keep it all in so he at least appeared like a normal person, warring inside him. Evan definitely deserved honesty, but Trevor was a little too terrified of bringing anyone else in the loop. "It's...complicated. Let's just say something outside my control cost me my job, my house, drained my savings, and left me at the mercy of someone else's charity to keep from freezing to death on the street."

"Shit," Evan breathed. He shifted to face Trevor, tucking his slightly longer stump of his left leg under his right thigh. "Is there anything I can do?"

Trevor flushed, smiling as he shook his head. "No, and I wouldn't want you to. I'm kind of enjoying that this," he waved his hand between them, "has nothing to do with everything else going on. It's bad enough I have to live with my damn lawyer."

Evan's eyebrows shot up. "Rhys is your lawyer?"

"Uh...sort of," Trevor said, not wanting to explain the full scope of their relationship. "I know it's unconventional, but so is this situation, and I promise it's not like...breaking the code of ethics of anything."

Laughing, Evan shook his head. "No that's not what I...Jesus, no. I just thought he was like the jealous ex or something."

Trevor, who had just taken a sip of his water, choked on the swallow. He coughed a little, staring at Evan wide-eyed. "The jealous ex?"

Evan shrugged, looking a little sheepish, even as he was grinning. "He was staring at me like he wanted me to spontaneously combust when you and I were talking. I assumed it was jealousy."

That hit Trevor like a sack of bricks. He had no idea what to do with that information, because he damn well hadn't picked up on anything like that. "I think he's just feeling protective," he said slowly, trying to process. "He's been helping me get through all this. He uh...he pulled me out of a tough situation and got me back on my feet. Though..." He trailed off, not sure that he was ready to voice the rest of it. He was trying to make a good impression and telling this guy he was a step above homeless and ready to troll the personal ads for empty rooms in dingy apartments wasn't exactly the way to impress.

Evan didn't seem ready to let it go. "Though what? You can talk to me, you know."

Trevor bowed his head. "Yeah. It's just kind of mortifying. I went from middle class University professor, to bartender living off the good graces of others."

"We all got our shit to go through, our paths to walk," Evan told him. "Believe me, I've learned that the hard way."

Trevor felt a little ashamed, and took the gentle chastisement with some grace. "Living with Rhys is making things a little tough. There are lines, and they're starting to blur, and I don't want to compromise his ability to help me with my case."

Evan looked at him carefully. "Was there a scandal or something? I heard Wes talking about his brother's boyfriend and the shit he was going through."

Trevor flushed. "Something like that, yeah. I really can't talk about it, though." Technically a lie, but it was the last thing he wanted to bring up on a damn date.

Instead of pushing the issue, Evan scratched his chin, then said, "What if I could help?"

Trevor blinked at him. "How?"

"I know people. I know a damn lot of people. I'm a charismatic guy," he spread his hands and Trevor chuckled. "Couple guys I know are working on a startup and could use the help if you're looking for work. Couple guys I know are always looking for decent roommates. I could put out an inquiry or two if you think you'd be interested. Maybe getting back on your own would help."

The offer was almost too good to be true. The idea of leaving the safety of Rhys' home was vaguely terrifying, but deep down he knew he would have to someday, and soon. He was getting complacent, dependent, and that wasn't going to do him any favors in the end. Of course, taking up Evans offer would leave him indebted to one more person in his life. And if it didn't work out...then what? Moving in with Evan's friends would be great, but it's not like those strangers would take Trevor's side if things went sour.

"I know what you're thinking," Evan said quietly. He reached over, taking Trevor's hand, and brought his knuckles up for a kiss.

"Not sure you do," Trevor said softly.

"You're thinking it might make things between us complicated. Or it might leave you out on your ass if you and I can't make this work."

Evan was annoyingly perceptive, and Trevor couldn't help a little, irritated sigh. "Okay. I guess I'm obvious."

"You're just thinking exactly what I would be, if our places were switched. But we can leave it strictly business, okay? You and I—like this," he wriggled their joined hands together between them, "that won't factor into this roommate and job thing. All I'm gonna do is get a couple names. The rest will be up to you."

Trevor bit his lip, then he nodded. It was the exact thing he'd been hoping to find, but there was more weight to it when the offer came from Evan. Much like the offer to stay with Rhys had been.

"I get it," Evan said quietly, tugging Trevor in close to him. "Pride gets in the way and..."

"It isn't pride," Trevor said, laughing a little bitterly. "Trust me, these last few months have stripped away all sense of pride. I just...I just want something normal, and this feels about as normal as I've had in a long damn time."

Evan reached out, tracing the edge of Trevor's jaw with the tip of his finger. "Is this okay?"

Trevor smiled, leaning into him. He'd been deprived of touch for so long, he was starved for it. The few and far between embraces between him and Rhys hadn't even begun to take the edge off his need, and he found himself dangerously wanting. "Yeah. It's very good."

Evan shifted again, and Trevor leaned against him more fully. "I like this. I knew you were something else when I first saw you. I didn't get a real good look until I was close enough, but I heard you laugh at something and it just stirred something in me."

"Is it awful that I *did* see you and I basically couldn't talk for thirty seconds because of how hot you were?" Trevor asked.

Evan laughed again and shook his head. "Nah. I'm flattered. Trust me, a body like this, I wasn't sure anyone would think of me like that ever again."

Trevor found himself frowning, reaching without really thinking about it, and laid his hand on Evan's thigh. "Is this okay? I don't want to hurt you or make you feel uncomfortable?"

"I have a lot of learning to do," Evan told him, but he pressed his hand down on top of Trevor's and dragged it lower, toward the end of his stump. "Like I told you, I haven't been with anyone since my accident, and I've been working hard on loving my new body, but it's not easy. I was blown to shit, and I'm grateful to be alive, but the price for that has been pretty high."

Trevor turned to him and made sure he'd captured the gaze of Evan's sighted eye. "If we don't work out, I need you to know now that it has nothing to do with your body, okay? You're literally one of the hottest men I have ever met."

Evan chuckled and leaned in, nosing at Trevor's temple. "Okay. I'll take it. But you say that with a tone like maybe you know something I don't. If I'm making you uncomfortable...if you're having doubts..."

"I like you," Trevor said, then decided there was no point in keeping anything from him, "but I also have feelings for someone else. Big, scary feelings, and it's ridiculous because he is the furthest thing from interested in me, and it's time for me to move on. But it's not as easy as I thought it would be."

To his credit, Evan didn't pull away, though he sat back to regard Trevor more carefully. "Fair enough."

"I'm sorry," Trevor breathed out with a small sigh. "It's probably unfair of me to ask you to give me time."

"Maybe to some people, but not to me. You need it, you got it. We can go slow as you want."

Trevor hadn't realized just how much he needed to hear those words until right then. "Thank you."

Evan nodded, taking his hand. "And if it helps, I like you too. Enough that I'd like to be friends, even if this mystery man and you end up working out."

"We won't," Trevor said with a confidence he wished he didn't have, "but I appreciate it. I'd like that too."

11.

When Rhys stripped the label off his fourth bottle of beer, Anna reached over and snatched it from him, setting it on the empty table next to them. "You're starting to make a fucking hamster nest," she complained.

Rhys flushed, piling up the bits of paper and shoving them off to the side. "Sorry."

She shook her head and glanced at her husband, giving him a pointed look Rhys knew well from having been married. He braced himself for Wes to step in. "Is it Trevor?"

Rhys hadn't expected the immediate gut-punch, and he flinched, giving himself away. "Can we not talk about it?"

"We've been sitting here for forty-five minutes. I'm in a *bar*," Anna stressed, "pregnant with twins, ignoring my doctor-appointed bed-rest because you obviously need friends to talk to, and you haven't said a damn word. So, either spill, or I'm taking my husband and we're going home."

Rhys groaned, letting his head fall forward, boding bending until his forehead thumped onto the edge of the table. "My life is a nightmare."

"Yes," Anna drawled, petting her fingers through his hair. "It must be so hard to be a rich, white lawyer who sets his own hours and can take off on vacation whenever he feels like it."

He turned his head, affecting a glare in her direction, but there was no heat behind it. "I think I'm falling in love."

Anna's eyes widened and she dropped her hand from him. "Seriously?"

Rhys shrugged, feeling the telltale prickle of anxiety climbing up his spine, because admitting this much meant either lying, or coming out, and he wasn't sure he wanted to do either. "Yeah. Seriously."

He watched her gaze flicker across the table, which meant she was trying to assess whether or not Wes knew about all this. When it became obvious he didn't, she reached back over and prod at his shoulder until Rhys lifted his head.

"Are you going to tell us who she is, where you met her, why she's not with you, any of it?" Anna demanded. "Because I know for a fact your assistant is married to another woman, and I don't think either one of us has introduced you to anyone lately."

"You make me sound like such a loser," Rhys groaned, ignoring Wes' barking laughter. "I'm capable of meeting people on my own, you know."

"Clients," Anna said flatly.

He flushed. Hard. His cheeks went white-hot, and he saw the moment Anna realized the truth. "Look, I…"

"You're not. You *didn't*," she insisted.

Wes sucked in his breath and leaned toward him. "Even *I* know that fucking your client is a bad idea."

"I…we haven't fucked," Rhys said, dragging a hand down his face. "And they're not exactly my client. I'm just helping out with stuff. It's complicated and uh…and…" He licked his lips, his gaze flickering between the two of them. "I haven't told anyone about this, okay? I can count how many people know on one hand."

"Who she is?" Anna pressed.

"He," Rhys finally said, swallowing down his nerves. "Who *he* is. But no, I meant...I meant that I'm bisexual, and it's a guy, and yeah...also my not-quite-client."

There was a long, heavy pause, then Anna pushed herself up and off the tall chair. "We need to go right now."

Rhys felt a moment of panic bludgeon him like a physical blow. Logically he knew some people weren't going to accept it—even outright reject him—but he hadn't expected either of those people to be Anna or Wes. Neither one of them were straight, they were in an open marriage, and Wes apparently had been fucking his brother.

And yet, here he sat, openly rejected and shunned at a table inside a dingy bar.

After a moment, when only Wes had moved to stand, Anna reached out and smacked his arm. "What are you waiting for? A written invitation?"

Rhys blinked at her. "You want me to go with you?"

She scoffed, tugging on his sleeve until he slipped down to the floor. "We're not letting your come out happen in some nasty-ass sports bar, Rhys. We're going back to ours. Maggie's with Wes' mom, we have top shelf liquor that isn't going to cost nine bucks for half a shot, and there won't be drunk strangers staring at you if you need to cry a little bit."

He opened his mouth to protest, but Wes' heavy, warm hand against the small of his back had his jaw snapping shut, and his feet following after the very demanding woman. He was momentarily grateful she was the DD. It allowed him to climb into the backseat of her car and quietly freak out until they reached the Baum's front door.

***

"Okay," Wes said, taking over for his wife who had gone to shower and throw up, as she had so eloquently described, "so you're bisexual."

Rhys shrugged. "Yeah."

"Is this a new thing? Like you met a guy and you started having feelings and..."

"I've known since I sucked Chase Masters' dick in the band closet my junior year of high school," Rhys muttered. "He was a flautist in the marching band, and we used to butt heads all the time."

"I'd judge you," Wes said, smiling over the rim of his scotch, "if I didn't have like half a dozen of those same stories." He took a sip, and when his gaze returned to Rhys', his face was serious. "Can I ask why you never told us? I mean, Ryan tells everyone you're straight."

"Because he doesn't know either," Rhys said. He was exhausted having to explain the whys over and over, though he knew it would be his curse. It was his groundhog-day, forced to relive the same coming out again and again and again. *Why didn't you tell your gay brother you were sometimes into dudes? Don't you think he'd understand?*

Wes didn't ask, though. He just nodded. "Okay. So, it's a secret thing?"

Rhys stared into the amber liquid resting in the bottom of his glass. He could see a distorted reflection of his own eye, and it unnerved him enough that he had to look away. "It's more like a thing I might be ready to start telling people. Because I want to date."

"Your client," Wes pointed out.

"Please stop calling him my client. But, yes," Rhys couldn't help but admit. "I'm not going to, but it *has* helped me realize I'm ready to just come out. That I don't need to be actively involved with a guy to be myself. And I think doing it now would take the pressure off doing it in the middle of dating."

Wes shrugged, letting out a slow breath of air. "I get it. I mean, I knew I was bi since...maybe forever? Hell, I wasn't even sure I really liked women until I met Anna. And even now, I," he stopped and cleared his throat.

After some hesitation, Rhys said, "I know about you and Ryan. I mean, no details," he put up his hand as though he might be able to stop Wes from confessing anything about his brother in detail, "but I know you two are a thing."

Wes flushed a little and shrugged. "Not anymore. But yeah, we were. And for the record, I don't think he's going to care if you tell him."

"I know," Rhys breathed out. "It's just a little terrifying coming out after all this time. And he's going to be so pissed that I kept it from him for this many years."

"Maybe," Wes conceded, "but he'll get over it. Besides, he's kind of going through some shit right now, so I'm not sure he even would bother getting pissed. Really, you probably need to focus on the fact that you're into your fucking client and that's a big deal."

Rhys shook his head. "Trust me, I don't plan to act on it." He paused. "Is Ryan okay?"

Wes waved the question off. "Stop trying to deflect my interrogation, asshole. What are you going to do about this guy?"

"What guy?" Anna asked, walking into the room in her pajamas, hair wet and braided down her back. She let Wes drag her against his side, and Rhys felt a pang of jealousy for how much he missed that casual comfort. Mostly because he had something like it with Trevor, but it could never be more than that.

"His client," Wes reminded her. "We established that he's bisexual, that he's known since at least his junior year of high school, and he's got some inappropriate feelings for someone he shouldn't."

Rhys scowled at his friend. "It's not like I caught feelings on purpose. Trust me, if I could stop having them, I fucking would."

"Well," Anna said thoughtfully, "he's a client, so you can't possibly see him all that often, right?"

At that, Rhys blushed, and Wes' eyes immediately went wide. "Oh no. No. *Rhys...*"

Rhys bowed his head and sighed. "Yeah."

Anna gave her husband a pointed look. "Explain."

"The adorable redhead he brought over the other night. The one currently on a date with Evan." Wes crossed his arms over his chest and gave Rhys a hard stare. "Trevor? *Seriously?*"

Rhys sagged against the cushions and put his free hand over his face. "He makes me feel things I haven't felt in...maybe ever? And part of me thinks he might like me back, which is even worse."

Wes blew out a puff of air, and Anna leaned toward Rhys, taking his hand. "You're an idiot."

"Oh, believe me," Rhys said darkly, "I know."

"He's living with you," she said. "You're helping him on a case, and he's living with you, and you're falling in love with him. This is not going to end well."

"I know," Rhys groaned again. "That's why I need a drink. That's why I need all the drinks."

"Yeah," Anna said. "So bottoms up, you have an entire bottle to get through."

12.

Trevor half expected an annoyed Rhys waiting for him in the kitchen or the living room the way he usually did whenever Trevor came in late. He'd planned to be home a lot earlier, but Evan's hands holding him had felt so good, and later, their kisses had sent him reeling, wanting more. It was through sheer force of will he'd made himself leave, and he had smiled the entire drive home.

He had a feeling he could make this work with Evan. If he could get away from Rhys' house, get over this hump of wanting the one person he couldn't have, this thing with Evan could be so good. He was tired of being alone, tired of letting this blackmail shit keep him half-drowning in hell's lake of fire.

He deserved better than that.

Still, when he strolled into the house to find it cold and dark, he couldn't help a tiny pang of disappointment. He hadn't entirely been looking forward to Rhys being able to see the signs of his almost-passionate night with Evan, but he wanted to be seen. He wanted that quiet, vulnerable time where the two of them curled up on the sofa and just existed together like they were meant to be.

A taste of what he couldn't have, and it was torture, but he wasn't ready to give it up yet. Only, maybe Rhys had decided for him. The guy was definitely not the sort to party all night, but when one o'clock that morning rolled around, Trevor realized there was more to Rhys than he expected. He couldn't actually set a clock by him. He didn't know if that made things better or worse. Whatever the case, he forced himself to get to bed and capture a few hours of broken sleep before morning came.

He was halfway through his second cup of coffee, the morning stretching into ten o'clock, when the garage door finally opened, and Rhys stumbled in. He was still wearing his suit from court Friday afternoon, and he looked rumpled like he'd slept on the floor. Or maybe an unfamiliar bed.

His cheeks blazed pink when his bleary eyes fell on Trevor, and he quickly glanced away. "Hey. You're up."

Trevor blinked at him. "Yeah," he said flatly, "it's ten so…"

"Right," Rhys said. He sighed. "Right I uh…I'm…shower. Going to shower." He fumbled through the room, and in the distance, Trevor could hear the bedroom door slam.

Trevor winced at the sound, feeling his stomach drop, wondering if this wasn't a sign that he was on the right path. He had no right whatsoever to be hurt that Rhys had stayed out, and yet he felt betrayed. His stomach hurt with it, legs poised and tense to run after him, and he had to physically force himself to stay put.

Grabbing his phone out of his pocket, he pulled up Evan's number and sent a quick text.

Trevor: Any chance you want to meet up today? Need to get out.

Evan: I was thinking about a hike. Want to come along?

Trevor wasn't exactly the super athletic type, but he thought maybe a romp through the woods was exactly what his day needed.

**

He left without letting Rhys know, as the other man still hadn't come out of the bedroom an hour after he'd gone for his shower. Trevor reminded himself he didn't owe Rhys any explanations regarding his private life. They weren't a couple.

They weren't anything.

He was mostly out of his funk by the time he arrived at Evan's, and the man was waiting for him at the curb holding a small backpack, a tall walking stick, and his cane. He looked as gorgeous as always, his arms covered by a thick Henley, but legs visible under a pair of knee-length shorts. He had a baseball cap pulled low over his brow, and a pair of wrap-around sunglasses tucked up on the brim.

"Do you have GPS?" he asked when he got in. "The company I work for is building this app for blind people and my partner just mapped out a good hiking spot with a wide path I wanted to check out."

Trevor handed over his phone and let Evan put in the address for the trail parking, and they fell into an easy silence for the half hour it took to get out there. Trevor had always been a bit of a homebody, so it was a little bit of a surreal experience to go from the center of the city to a mountain area, lush with green, and a little snow to either side of the road.

The parking area was mostly empty—probably due to the cold, he figured—so they got a good spot and Trevor pulled on his heavy parka as Evan adjusted his backpack, then put his cane out in front of him, balancing against his walking stick with the other.

"This is one of my new challenges," Evan told him as they carefully climbed up a set of stone steps. The path ahead was mostly flat, only the slightest incline for a while, though the turns were winding through the trees. "Learning new balance was the biggest bitch after I got up on my legs, and the whole lack of depth perception thing made it ten times harder."

Trevor winced. "Yeah, a friend of mine lost an eye in an accident some years back, and I didn't know him before, but he was talking about it once after he kept dropping shit at a department meeting. I can't imagine having to deal with that, plus adjusting to new legs."

Evan had his cane tapping in a wide arc on either side of his body, but he kept as close to Trevor as he could. "I've been trying to push myself lately. My legs aren't strong enough for running yet, but that's my goal. I used to do ten miles a day, and my prosthetist was showing some fucking cool tech they have for runners."

Trevor smiled at him. "I'm jealous."

"Of my legs?" Evan asked, a little surprise in his tone.

Unable to help a small laugh, Trevor shook his head. "I mean of having goals like that. When all this shit happened, I just…shut down. I mean, I got by day to day, did what I could to live, but I haven't been able to bring myself out of this funk. At least…not til now."

"The roommate thing?" Evan asked, his tone careful.

"Yeah." Trevor went quiet as they took a huge bend in the road, and the path began a slightly steeper incline. Evan's steps got a little slower, but Trevor didn't mind easing up on their pace. "And considering a new job thing. And trying to regain a sense of independence. Things have been quiet now for a while, and I think I might apply to the community colleges again. They have a couple positions open."

"Yeah?" Evan asked, turning his head toward him with a grin. "To teach what?"

Trevor bit his lip as he felt a small surge of joy at the prospect, though he didn't want to get his hopes up. "Well, there's always history. That was my minor, and it's not something I'd look forward to, but it's something I could do, you know?"

Evan turned his head to properly see him, smiling a little. "What do you want to teach?"

The question created a fresh surge of pain, of loss he had been trying to avoid for a while now, and it took him a minute to answer. "When I started college, I chose a psych major—because I think probably everyone who goes into academics at one point or another decides to be a psych major. But I ended up taking this writing-intensive course about the Roman occupation of Israel. And you know, I think it could have gone either way for me—I might have hated it, but my professor was amazing. She was originally an archaeologist and had spent the first part of her career traveling around to old ancient Roman ruins and battle sites, and she just had such a passion for it. I think midway through my second semester of my freshman year I changed to a Classics major. I started taking Latin along with my French class, and the next thing I knew I was studying abroad in Italy for a semester. Then two. Then I finished the first half of my Ph.D. working in Tunis where there's some ruins of ancient Carthage." He stopped, realizing he'd gone on a tangent. "Sorry. I get a little nerdy."

"Don't," Evan said, weight to his voice. "Don't apologize for that. Do you know how beautiful it is to hear that from you? That kind of passion, Trevor…you can't let it go."

Trevor took in a shaking breath, his steps slowing to a halt with Evan close at his heels. "I'm trying," he said, his voice tight with emotion. "It's…fuck. This person has been fucking with my life—he put me out of a job, put friends of mine at risk because I made one stupid decision, and I…I don't know why."

"Who is it?" Evan asked quietly.

Trevor shook his head. "I don't know. He used an intermediary to threaten me—and what he's got on me would ruin me professionally. At least right now, if I comply, there's a chance I could work again. But if he comes forward…"

"Tell me someone's helping you on this," Evan said, reaching for his hand. "Have you gone to the cops?"

Trevor shook his head, realizing he was offering a little too much information to a man he didn't yet trust to keep his secret. "If I go to the cops, the information has to go public in order to find him. If that happens, I'm screwed either way. But I'm not alone."

"Rhys," Evan said, squeezing his fingers.

Trevor nodded. "Yeah. And he knows some people, and we're working it out slowly. I'm starting to feel stable again, and that means everything. I just…if I can get out of Rhys' house and find my independence, it'll make a world of difference. I know it will."

Evan watched him for a long moment, then let his fingers slowly pull away. "It's Rhys, isn't it? The one you have those big scary feelings for?"

Trevor was so stunned by Evan's ability to pick up on it, he couldn't bring himself to deny it. "I…"

Evan let out a sigh, licking his lips as he took a step back. "I don't think it's a good idea if I wait around for you to get over him."

A little shocked, Trevor blinked at him. "I'm not the kind of guy who pines forever, you know. I don't usually torture myself with men I can't have."

"Oh, I believe you," Evan told him, fiddling with the top of his cane, "but that's the problem. The look on Rhys' face when I showed up wasn't him being protective. It was him burning with jealousy because that dude is into you probably even more than I am."

"No," Trevor started. "No, trust me. He's made it very clear he's not into me."

"Has he?" Evan pushed. "Or has he been trying to prevent something that would be a huge breach of trust?"

Trevor was struck mute for a moment, because for all that he was a clever person—and he truly was—he hadn't considered that was an option. Rhys was unbelievably good looking, and kind, and sweet, and selfless. He was rich and humble, and had opened his home to Trevor without a second thought. He couldn't fathom Rhys had been capable of finding him attractive.

"Look, there's a part of me that wants to fight for you, because I like you a damn lot. But I'm also not the kind of guy who goes after a relationship that's doomed to fail. Before we met, you were already in it with this guy, and I think if you're patient, it'll go somewhere."

Trevor dragged a hand down his face. "It's already so fucking hard."

"I don't doubt it," Evan told him. "And I think you've got the right idea, moving out of there. I still want to help, and I meant what I said—I still want to be your friend, because that's good enough for me."

Trevor felt his stomach sink, even as he understood how much truth and wisdom were in Evan's words. "I'm sorry," he murmured.

Evan reached for him, tugging him into a hug which felt so good, Trevor didn't want to let go. "You deserve a lot better, and I hope you trust me enough to let me be there as a friend."

"I'd like that," Trevor said. He swiped his hand across his face, trying to hide any lingering moisture that betrayed his emotions. "Can we finish the hike? Because I meant what I said about needing to be out today."

Evan chuckled and clapped him on the shoulder. "Hell yes, we got five more miles up to go, and I'm looking forward to a good sweat."

***

Rhys sighed into the phone, feeling the pang of guilt for refusing his brother. "This is really, really not a good time for me to go out and get wasted with you."

"Please," his brother said, and there was a note of desperation in that one word which struck Rhys right in his heart. "I wouldn't ask if I didn't need you. You don't even need to drink. I just...I just need you."

Another refusal was at the tip of his tongue, but Rhys knew he couldn't refuse Ryan when he was like this. He loved his brother too much. "Who's coming out with us?"

"Noah and Adrian," Ryan replied, sounding relieved. "I invited Wes and Anna, but they said they used up their allotted out time doing some other shit and I just...please. I'm hurting and I'm confused and I don't want to be alone right now."

Bowing his head, Rhys sighed into the phone one more time, knowing full well he was going to regret the words coming out of his mouth. "Fine. I'll meet you out, but I'm not drinking, and I'm not taking care of you when you lose all control."

"Yes, you will," Ryan told him, and unfortunately—at least for the second half of Rhys' declaration—he knew Ryan was right.

Rhys puttered around the house for a few hours before finally getting ready. Trevor was out, and though Rhys had no real reason to expect him home at all, let alone at the hour before dinner, it still gutted him a little that he was doing up his shoes and he was still on his own in the too-quiet living room.

He was just about to search for his keys when he heard the garage door open, and his breath caught in his throat, a surge of jealousy rising in him when Trevor walked in. He looked well-fucked, hair a mess, face a little red in the cheeks, eyes half-lidded. Rhys did his best to banish the thought from his head, but he couldn't help picturing Trevor laid spread-out under Evan, his eyes closed, mouth parted, groaning in bliss.

He hated it. He hated the way he was feeling, and hated Evan a little for being someone Trevor could find that happiness with. He squeezed his eyes shut, then rose as Trevor walked into the room.

"Are you leaving?"

Rhys swallowed thickly. "Uh. Yeah. I'm out for the night."

Trevor's cheeks darkened a little. "Oh. Okay. Well…can we talk? Maybe tomorrow? There's something we need to discuss."

Rhys felt his heart ramming against his chest. Evan and Trevor hadn't been dating long, but maybe it was long enough for Trevor to decide it was time to move on. And that was…it was a lot. It was enough to have his lip curl into a sneer. "I'll see if I can pencil you in. Unless you think you'll be busy with your boyfriend."

Trevor blinked like he'd been slapped and took a step back. "Are you angry with me for dating someone?"

Rhys forced himself to calm down. "It's…I'm sorry. It's not you. I just need to…I'll see you later." He brushed past him, knocking Trevor's shoulder slightly as he hurried out of the room and to his car. He jammed the start button and was halfway down the street before the guilt gripped him by the throat and he realized what a complete and total asshole he'd been.

Trevor didn't deserve that. Trevor hadn't done anything wrong, and the man had suffered enough. Rhys was better than that, and he knew it. Checking the time, he decided Ryan could wait on him a little longer, and he pulled the car around, heading straight back to the house.

He didn't bother with the garage, pulling up to the curb, and he hurried inside through the front door. The living room was empty, and as he ventured toward the hall, he could hear sounds in his bedroom. The door was open, cracked part way, so he walked in and moved into the bathroom.

The sight in front of him had him freezing mid-step. There was Trevor, stripped down to his boxer briefs, one leg up on the closed toilet lid. He had a syringe poised above his leg, the needle already imbedded into the skin, and when he looked up with a start, he flinched at what was obvious pain.

"Shit," Rhys stuttered. "I didn't…I'm sorry, I thought you…I'll just…" He backed out, nearly tripping over himself. Part of him wanted to run and deal with this later. Maybe when he was drunk enough to forget what an ass he'd made of himself twice now.

Only, Trevor still deserved better than that. He went back to the living room and collapsed on the sofa, bending over his thighs, resting his elbows there as he covered his face with both hands. He took several breaths, unable to control the shaking, and he hated how he could now picture Trevor actually naked.

It was no longer an abstract concept. It was real, and there, and in his face. Trevor was freckled along his shoulders and partway down his chest. A smattering of red hair decorated down his sternum, and around his dusky nipples. He had thin scars below his pecs, a surprisingly thick happy trail, and every muscle in his body was fit and cut in spite of his only casual physicality.

He was everything Rhys had imagined, only better, and that made his problem ten times worse. He was madly in love, and now he was in lust, and he was so, so screwed.

Rhys looked up when he heard a soft voice say his name, and he found Trevor leaning against the wall, dressed in sweats and a t-shirt with his arms crossed defensively over his chest. His cheeks were still pink, but his jaw was set in a determined scowl.

"I'm really sorry. I came back to apologize, and the door wasn't locked. I should have knocked though. I didn't mean to walk in on you. Again."

"It's fine," Trevor said.

Rhys blinked at him, saying nothing.

"It freaked you out again," Trevor went on.

At that, Rhys rose and shook his head. "No. No, I'm just mortified that I just walked in on you for a second goddamn time. I read," he said, then stopped. In truth, he'd been obsessively consuming blogs, websites, and stories written by trans people since he and Trevor had first discussed his weekly injections. At first, he'd just wanted to understand, to be a good roommate. Then, secretly, he hoped that one day he'd have a chance to be a good partner, to make sure Trevor never felt less of himself because of Rhys.

Trevor took a step forward. "You read?"

Rhys rolled his eyes up to the heavens, praying for a spontaneous death. It was not granted. "I read that for a lot of trans people, taking their hormone treatment is an intensely private thing. Especially around cis people, because it brings to the forefront the stark difference between the genders. I...I don't want to make you feel dysphoric."

Trevor looked surprised for a minute, then his lips twitched like he was holding back a smile. "You read that?"

Rhys gave a helpless shrug. "I was just trying to understand, but I didn't want to force you to be my textbook."

"That's," Trevor started, but he didn't finish his sentence. He simply shook his head and let out a sigh. "Why did you come back?"

That was a question Rhys was happy to answer. "To apologize for being an asshole. I'm dealing with some shit right now, and it wasn't fair of me to come at you like that about Evan. I'm glad you're happy. I'm glad you met someone like him. And if you want to move out of here and be with him, I'm more than willing to see that through and give you whatever you need."

Trevor gave him a look full of something complicated and almost hurt. "If you want me out..."

"God, no," Rhys blurted before he could stop himself. "No, that's not it at all. Believe me, that's the last thing I want. But I don't want my feelings to influence your future happiness. Evan is a good guy."

"Yes," Trevor said, and that one, small admission was like a knife to his heart. "He's absolutely a good guy. And I," he hesitated, biting his lip. "I *do* want to move out."

Rhys bowed his head. "Yeah. I figured."

"But, not to move in with Evan," Trevor carried on, and Rhys' gaze snapped up. "You're not the only one dealing with some shit. Evan told me I'm better off telling you straight out, because apparently there's something here that I'm not seeing—or I wasn't letting myself see." Rhys' mouth went dry as Trevor took a step toward him, and then another. They were nearly touching by the time he stopped. "You like me."

Rhys felt his entire face go white-hot, and a denial sprung up, but he couldn't bring himself to utter it. It would have been a lie, and Trevor deserved the truth as much as he deserved to be happy. "Yes. And I've been trying to not be so obvious."

"I've noticed," Trevor said a little dryly.

Rhys closed his eyes slowly, then opened them. "I understand why it makes you uncomfortable, and why you'd want to leave. But for the record, you have to know I'd never act on my feelings. I'd never, *ever* try to take advantage of you."

"I know that," Trevor said, his voice very soft now. Rhys' entire body went taut—like a too-tight guitar string—when Trevor raised a hand and placed it against the side of his neck. "You haven't made me uncomfortable. I want to move out because I want be with you. I've wanted you since I set foot in your office, and I know damn well you and I can't be anything more while I'm living here and we're navigating this whole mess."

Rhys couldn't help himself. His eyes drifted closed again, his face turned slightly, and he pushed further against Trevor's touch. "I can't give you legal counsel and be this. I know that."

"Right," Trevor said softly.

"Your future is the most important thing to me. I can't risk it, so I understand," Rhys said, though the words were almost impossible to get out. He'd never wanted anyone this much in his life. He didn't think it was possible to need another person the way he needed Trevor.

Trevor's hand moved to Rhys' cheek, his thumb brushing against his faint stubble. "We have to figure something out, because I don't think I'm willing to give up the chance to be with you."

Rhys couldn't stop himself. His hands moved of their own volition, fingers pressing into Trevor's side as he pulled him flush against his own body. He dipped his head in, not kissing, but their mouths were nearly touching. "Tell me what to do."

Trevor laughed softly. "If I start that now, it's going to make things even more complicated."

"I'm trying to remember why I care about that right now," Rhys confessed. "God...god, I want to kiss you."

"Me too," Trevor murmured. His grip on Rhys tightened, and suddenly it seemed like kissing was nothing more than an inevitability. "We need to talk about this rationally."

Rhys nodded, but he knew right then, rational thought was impossible. Just as he opened his mouth to say that, his phone began to buzz in his pocket, and reality hit him once more. Ryan was waiting on him. His brother, who needed him, who was dealing with something and had nearly begged.

"That's my brother," he told Trevor. "I promised him I'd go out. But I'll cancel. I'll tell him we can talk later."

Trevor shook his head. "You should go. It'll give us time to think. I'm going to be here when you get home."

Rhys hadn't realized how desperately he'd needed to hear that until right then. His grip on Trevor's waist tightened and he tugged him even closer. "I want to kiss you before I go."

"I'm okay with that," Trevor breathed out, the words desperate.

It was all the invitation Rhys needed to lean in, to cross that bare centimeter of space between them, and close it. Trevor's lips beneath his were pliant, warm and soft and parted just enough to slot their mouths together like puzzle pieces. Rhys felt a groan bubbling from his gut, past his lips, Trevor catching the noise in his mouth. They opened their lips a little further, just enough for tongues to tease, but not deep enough for their desperation to take over.

Though it was a near thing. Rhys' entire body was burning with want, with need, with the desire to throw all responsibility out the window and drag Trevor to his bed. He was lucky Trevor possessed enough self-restraint to back away, though it was a slow drag of pecking kisses and nuzzling.

"Go," Trevor murmured, finally releasing him completely. "I'll see you when you get home."

Rhys nodded, his mouth opening, then closing when he couldn't find anything of importance to say. "I won't be long," he eventually promised.

Trevor merely smiled, then turned and left the room. Rhys took a moment to gather himself, and wondered if he'd be able to play it off and appear like a brother who gave a shit for the hours he was forced to separate from the man he wanted.

13.

Leaning his forehead against the steering wheel, Rhys pressed his phone to his ear as Trevor's sleepy voice greeted him. "Can you unlock the door?" Rhys asked. "I'm in the driveway and I have my brother with me. He's completely wasted."

Trevor chuckled. "Yeah, no worries. Give me a second. Do you need a hand with him?"

Rhys glanced over to see Ryan with his face plastered against the window, lips parted in a drunken snore, drooling a little out of the corner of his mouth. "You know, I might?"

Trevor laughed again. "Be right out."

The line went dead, and Rhys shoved his phone back into his pocket, getting out and coming around to the passenger side. The front door opened a minute later, and Trevor walked out, looking soft and sleepy, his red hair mussed and his feet bare. Rhys felt a wave of affection course through him, an echo of some nights before as they sat on the living room floor with Greek food and palpable tension in the air.

He wanted him, wanted this man, more than he'd wanted anyone in a long damn time. Trevor had made it a point to pull away, and Rhys wasn't about to push the issue, but it was getting harder and harder to ignore it. He wasn't sure it would ever happen, but now that it was, he wanted this to start out right. He wanted to make Trevor feel safe, and wanted, and above all, he wanted Trevor to know Rhys saw him as the man he was. No caveats, no compromises.

"Wow," Trevor said, staring at Ryan's smooshed face against the glass, "I can see the resemblance."

Rhys gave him a flat look and felt his cheeks heat up when Trevor laughed. "Hilarious. Now help me get him inside. He can crash on the couch, and I'll take him home in the morning."

Trevor frowned as he prepared to catch Ryan's body when Rhys opened the door. "Oof," he said, catching the limp arm. Ryan was dead weight, though he gave a slight moan to show he was still alive. "He's really fucked up."

Rhys snorted a laugh. "I think he tried to drink the bar dry, and I'm not sure he had food today. He's having a rough time right now."

"Then give him my room," Trevor said. Together, they managed to drag him up the walkway and through the door. Luckily Trevor's room was closest, but Rhys hesitated.

"I'm not putting you out because my brother acted like a moron," he insisted.

Trevor sighed, smiling just a little, and he tugged Ryan's body in the direction of his room. "You're not. He's your brother, he's already going to be in a world of hurt tomorrow, just let him take a bed."

"Then it can be mine," Rhys started, but Trevor made an annoyed sound.

"This isn't some competition of martyrdom. I used to sleep on the couch all the time marking papers. I was also a college student, okay? I basically lived on the couch all seven years." He gave Rhys a pleading look, one Rhys found he couldn't deny, and he gave in.

"Fine, your room it is." They made the short walk over, and Rhys carefully deposited his brother on top of the duvet. He moved the bin near the edge of the bed to catch any potential evacuation of his stomach, then backed up toward the door. "I would be angry with him, except that would mean I have to admit I haven't bothered to call in a while and had no idea he was even in a relationship."

Trevor pulled a face as Rhys shut the bedroom door. "Break-up binge drinking?"

Moving to the kitchen to grab a bottle of water, Rhys shook his head. "I don't think that was exactly it. We all met up and I thought this was going to be about Barnes, but it turns out that Ryan's been kind of involved with the guy who helped Noah get out of the blackmail mess. He said he and Cole started out casual, but I could tell Ryan was having some serious feelings, and apparently Cole has been hiding shit. I didn't really get the full story out of him, but he looks pretty wrecked about it. I figure I can make him a greasy breakfast in the morning and see if I can help."

Trevor gave him a soft look, a little too full of affection. "That's nice of you."

Rhys shrugged. "We have a complicated relationship, but he's important to me. It would have been easier if I could have done my own drinking tonight, but at least I got him home."

Hesitating, Trevor moved over to the cabinet beside the fridge and pulled out a bottle of scotch. It was mostly gone, just enough for two glasses each, and he waved it. "Well, you're home safe now, and if I have some with you, it's still social drinking."

Rhys couldn't help his laugh, and reached past Trevor for the glasses. "Deal. But can we take this into my room?" He felt shame rip through him, and his cheeks heated. "I just…he still doesn't know I'm into guys and if he sees us…" He realized what he was implying, and he quickly opened his mouth to insist that he didn't mean he and Trevor were involved, but Trevor just shrugged and grabbed a box of crackers.

"Your room it is. You have the big TV in there anyway, and I was halfway into that new show with Jane Fonda which I'm completely in love with."

Rhys felt another wave of affection as he rummaged in the fridge for some carrot sticks, then followed Trevor into the master bedroom. He felt strange, having someone else in there. He was fine with sharing the master bath and even letting people rummage around in his closet, but he'd never hung out there with another person. Not since Vanessa left.

He had to admit, it felt strangely nice. He was used to being alone in his bed, but he couldn't deny how much he missed those late nights with her, curled up under a couple of blankets, the window letting in cold air, the heat blasting, bad TV playing in the background. He loved her so much then, in those soft moments which sometimes led to her riding him, or him pressing into her with her legs up over his shoulders, and sometimes they ended with him giving her a foot rub or her falling asleep on his chest.

In those moments, he would have never been able to contemplate her leaving him, her having that with someone else. But it was the other moments that made her choices a reality. Like how often she slept in the guest room, or how often she was home late, or how often he woke up on the couch because he hadn't wanted to disturb her. How often they never really spoke, and how he went weeks without kissing her and hadn't even really thought about it until she threw it in his face during the divorce.

He wanted to hang on to the good parts, though. He wanted to make more of them.

"You look really sad right now," Trevor told him, his voice low and soft. "Is this a bad idea? Me in here?"

Rhys blinked, then smiled and shook his head. "No. It's just been a while. Not that I'm saying…I mean, I'm not implying that…"

Trevor sighed and snatched the glasses from his hands, setting them on the nightstand as he began to pour. "You need a drink, because you're thinking way too hard and drinksies night is about not thinking."

That was what Rhys was afraid of, though. Not thinking. Not thinking led to making decisions he couldn't take back. It led to lowered inhibitions, and right now he wanted a lot, and he didn't want to lose Trevor. But he also had to trust that Trevor was a grown man who was capable of saying what he wanted, and what he didn't. And Rhys would never, ever push him. Just because they had kissed before he left didn't mean Rhys expected anything more.

"Bottom's up," Trevor said, clinking his glass to Rhys'. They both took a long gulp of the burning liquid, then Trevor leapt onto the bed and snuggled down. He fumbled for the remote, then fired up the TV app, starting the show from where he'd clearly been watching it.

Rhys hesitated a long moment, then finally lowered himself down to the bed. They reclined halfway on the pillows, drinks in hand, the crackers and carrots between them. The characters on TV carried away in the background, but Rhys couldn't focus on that. Not when Trevor's foot snaked over and touched the top of Rhys' socked one. Not when it stayed there, a gentle pressure making him want more.

He took another drink of the scotch and felt the heady sensation of a buzz coming on. His tongue disconnected from the roof of his mouth, and somewhere in the back of his mind, he warned himself not to feel too comfortable.

Trevor reached over him to refill their glass, the last of the liquor, and Rhys took another drink. When Trevor settled back down, he turned his body to face Rhys', though his gaze was still on the screen. His arm lay pliant between them, his fingertips brushing gently against the waistband of Rhys' sweats.

"This feels like it might be flirting," Rhys heard himself say. He felt hot all over, but he couldn't seem to stop himself. "It's been so long for me, I don't actually know."

Trevor didn't look up, but the pressure of his touch on Rhys' waist increased. "Would it be a bad thing?"

Rhys swallowed thickly. "I don't...maybe," he conceded. "Not because I don't want you, because holy hell you *know* I want you. But this situation is..."

"Damn complicated," Trevor finished for him. He threw back the last of his scotch, then reached over Rhys to set his cup down. When he returned to his spot, he let his hand rest on Rhys' sternum and dug his fingertips into the soft cotton of his t-shirt. "It's damn complicated, and I don't want to ruin the good thing we have going, but I also want you so fucking bad I can taste it."

Rhys' eyes fell shut and he groaned. "Jesus. You have no idea what you do to me. I've been reciting baseball statistics to try and stop myself from picturing the way you looked the other night with your naked leg up on the counter as you took your shot. You are so fucking hot."

"Rhys," Trevor whispered.

Rhys forced his eyes open, turned his head to find Trevor just outside of kissing distance. It would only take a slight motion to change it. He licked his lips, unable to take his eyes off three distinct freckles which sat on the very edge of Trevor's bottom lip. He wanted to lick them, taste them, bite them. "Are you drunk? I don't want to do this if you're drunk. I don't want regrets, I don't want you to feel unsafe. I want you here more than I want to change things between us."

Trevor's hand slowly drifted up, his blunt nails scratching along the edge of Rhys' jaw, then moved up to the hair at his temples, tugging gently. "I'm not drunk. I'm horny, and I'm lonely, and I like you so much I don't really know what to do with these feelings. I know that not sleeping with you isn't going to make any of this go away."

Rhys couldn't stop himself from moving, from setting his glass down, from kicking the food away, and pressing his body right up against Trevor's. His dick was rock hard, throbbing, pressed against the other man's hip. "It's probably not going to make it better, either."

Trevor nodded, his eyes fluttering closed for a minute, then he opened them and shrugged. "Ask me if I give a fuck."

"Do you give a—"

Rhys couldn't finish his sentence. Not when a hungry, hot, demanding mouth closed over his own. Trevor kissed like he was never going to be allowed to kiss again, like he was starving for it. His hands dug into Rhys' hair, pulling him in, tongue soft and wet-hot, brushing against his own. A moan tore from Rhys' chest, his hands flailing before they fell to Trevor's hips, and he slotted their bodies together at a more perfect angle. His erection pressed in the gap between Trevor's legs, and he couldn't stop himself from thrusting.

"This is going to get out of hand fast," Rhys groaned, peppering biting kisses across Trevor's lips. The freckles tasted even better than he imagined they would. "Tell me to stop."

"Fuck that, fuck no," Trevor moaned, then kissed him harder.

Rhys was certain he would drown in the sensations, sure that everything about him would just become consumed by Trevor, and he'd never wake from this. He was okay with it, he would accept that fate. Then, as he gave another, hard thrust, Trevor broke their kiss and pulled back, panting.

"Wait."

Rhys immediately froze. "Shit. Did I…"

"You're fine. You're perfect," Trevor said. "I just…there are logistics to this that you might not feel…normal about."

Rhys licked his lips, shoving one hand up the back of Trevor's shirt because in that moment, if he couldn't touch skin, he felt like he might die. "Would you think I'm the world's creepiest man if I told you that I read some sex stuff?"

Trevor blinked at him. "Read some sex stuff?" he parroted.

Rhys' sigh felt punched out of his chest, but he had to tell Trevor the truth. "I've wanted you for a while, that wasn't a lie. Even before I saw you all half naked and burning hot in my bathroom. I never wanted to pressure you, but I thought maybe you liked me, so I did some research. I looked up all these trans people run blogs, joined some forums. I want this to be good for you. I mean if we ever…" He swallowed thickly, then boldly reached between them, but he didn't touch, just hovered his hand over Trevor's crotch. "I know your dick isn't like mine, but I think I could make you feel good."

Trevor's eyes fluttered closed, then he thrust his hips forward and let himself make contact with Rhys' hand. He was warm and pulsing beneath Rhys' fingers, even through the fabric of his sweats. "You amaze me," Trevor muttered softly.

The echo of those words before sent Rhys' head spinning. "Just tell me what you want, what you like. I want to make you feel good."

As though unable to stop himself, Trevor gave Rhys a shove backward, hovering over him. He straddled Rhys' hips and ground his crotch into Rhys' throbbing cock. "I like a lot of things, and it's been years since I felt any shame in my body's differences. And right now, I can think of a hundred things I want to do to you," he leaned in and pressed their lips together in a deep, hot kiss, and finished speaking against Rhys' mouth, "but the most important thing is that so far, everything you've done has made me feel good."

Rhys felt his body burst into white-hot heat and desire, his hands flying to Trevor's hips, grinding up against him. Trevor's own face was flushed pink, his freckles standing out against the stark color, his mouth parted on a breathy sigh. He rubbed himself back, thrusting along the length of Rhys' still-clothed cock, his eyes half-lidded with the pleasure of it.

"I want to suck you," Rhys said, his eyes drifting downward to where their bodies were pressed together. "Can I?"

Trevor needed no further asking, rolling over onto his back. Rhys scrambled up to his elbows, reaching hands out to help pull at Trevor's shirt, as his sweats, leaving him there panting and clothed only in a pair of tight boxer-briefs. Rhys ran a flat hand up Trevor's hairy thigh, letting his bunt nails scrape along the insides, watching as his skin broke out into gooseflesh, watching him shudder.

His mouth went dry with want, his tone all-but tingling at the anticipation of tasting him, of letting Trevor spend right there against his lips. He felt a prickle of fear, not sure he would get this right, but he'd be damned if he didn't try.

"Let me?" he asked, curling his fingers into the elastic of Trevor's pants.

Trevor, now wordless with anticipation, nodded and closed his hands around Rhys' wrists, giving them a tug downward. In one swift motion, the barrier between them was gone. He was red there, too, a thatch of thick, bright curls which faded into a trail up toward his belly button. Rhys couldn't resist kneeling between Trevor's parted legs, couldn't resist nosing along that happy trail, tasting his first bit of salty flesh at the juncture of Trevor's hip.

"Fuck," Rhys whispered. His hand moved down, urging Trevor's legs apart a little more, fingers pressing his folds aside to fully reveal his cock. Rhys had read enough to know what he might see there, but nothing could have prepared him for the throb of desire it caused in the swollen bit of flesh. His tongue felt heavy with need to lay it there, to suck and lave him until he cried out and came. "Where can I touch you?" Rhys murmured.

"Everywhere," was Trevor's instant reply, which made Rhys feel like he was flying. Tacit permission to do everything in his power to make this man tremble with pleasure.

Breathing in, Rhys lowered his hand and gave his first, long lick of the cock. It was thick against his tongue, heady and musky in the scent, and the way Trevor bucked against him nearly threw him over the edge. He dug his fingers into the fleshy bits of Trevor's thighs as he opened his mouth a little more, taking him in as best as he was able, tuned in to every twitch, every groan, every hiss of pleasure to make sure his lover was enjoying this.

And Trevor was not a passive receiver. He got his hands right into Rhys' hair, directing his head exactly where he wanted it, pushing up against him, thumb stroking along the side of Rhys' mouth as he coaxed him to open wider, to lick with his tongue over and over and over.

"Put a finger inside me," Trevor asked, breathy and stuttered. "Just the tip of your finger, I need to feel it."

Rhys groaned, his hand moving, finding the hole, letting himself sink in just to the first knuckle. Trevor clenched tight around him, his hips undulating, driving himself closer and closer to the edge. He moaned with Trevor's cock on his tongue, feeling him pulsing, feeling him nearly there.

"God, yes, suck me, *god* suck me," Trevor gasped, and then in a rush, he came. Rhys felt the wetness surge over the tip of his fingers, felt Trevor's inner walls spasm and draw his finger in deeper as he let the passion rock him.

When it was over, Rhys kissed a soft trail down his thigh, letting his cheek rest as his own body started to relax. He was still hard enough to cut glass, and he wanted, but he was sated in a way he hadn't expected, and in a way he never had been before.

"Jesus," Trevor said, once he'd regained his ability to speak. He dragged a hand down his face, then looked down and laughed. "I had a feeling you'd be good, but I didn't realize it would be *that* good."

Rhys smirked, then turned his head to kiss Trevor's thigh once more. "I don't know what to say. Except you're welcome, maybe?"

Trevor rolled his eyes. "Ass. But I guess I like that about you." He reached down, letting his fingertips trail along Rhys' jawline, over his lips. Rhys parted them to suck on the digits, reveling in the way it still made Trevor moan. "I want more," he said after drawing his hand away from Rhys' mouth. "I want to feel you."

Rhys gave a small groan, turning his head to the side. "Yeah?"

"I want my ass in the air, I want you fucking me until you can't see straight," Trevor demanded.

Rhys felt dizzy with the unexpected rush of desire, and he was nearly on his knees before he'd even realized he'd moved. "Condom," was all he managed to say.

"And lube," Trevor told him.

Rhys nodded, fumbling in his drawer for the box of condoms and the small bottle which was nearly full. He dropped them to the side as he became aware he was still dressed, and it took him less than a minute to shed his clothes to the side of the bed. He caught Trevor's hungry look, the way his gaze raked up and down his form, the way he licked his lips at the hard cock which was swollen and desperate to be touched.

Rhys' head fell back on his shoulders as Trevor's long fingers curled around him and gave a few experimental strokes. Having someone else's hand on his dick after this long was so good, it nearly ended right there. He reached down to curl his fingers around Trevor's wrist, staying his motions.

"If you keep at it…"

Trevor's eyes fell into a half-squint, a grin on his lips, but he stilled his stroking. "We don't want that."

"No," Rhys said, breathy as he reached for the box. "No, we really don't. Turn over. Hands and knees." He put a slight command in his voice, one that made Trevor go a little pink in the cheeks, his eyes dilating with want. His hands trembled a little as he hurried to obey, his face tipped down toward the pillow, ass jutting up into the air. From that vantage point, Rhys could see all of him, his small pucker, leading down to a swollen hole, his folds still parted to show his engorged dick. He couldn't help but reach out, draw the line with the tip of his cock from Trevor's ass to his front, taking it all in. The way Trevor shuddered, the way his breath stuttered in his chest, the way he arched back, seeking more.

Rhys hurried to get the condom on before it was too late. He drew his hand away, only to fill his palm with lube, slicking himself. It was only then he hesitated as he poised his erection behind Trevor and wondered what was next. What would make him feel good? What did he want?

He didn't want to kill the mood, didn't want anything to sound like some psych 101, trans guy textbook, but he also wanted to get this right. He cleared his throat, then touched the back of Trevor's elbow. "Put me where you want me."

Trevor looked back, a startled smile on his face, warring with the intense desire in his eyes. "Who knew you were so bossy?"

Rhys couldn't help his laugh. "Are you okay with it?"

"Bossy sex," Trevor said with a tiny smirk, "fuck yes, I am." With that, he lifted onto his knees, reaching back for Rhys' hips, then plunged the head of Rhys' cock right into his hole. It was a tight fit, the lube slicking the way, but unexpected and so, so perfect. Rhys bit the inside of his cheek, curling his hands into fists for a second to control his desire to just let go and fuck him into the mattress.

He let Trevor adjust around him, moving his hand to the back of Trevor's neck and holding it with a firm pressure. He gave his hips an experimental thrust, burying himself just a little deeper, letting himself hear and feel the moan ripped from Trevor's throat.

"You like that." It wasn't a question. Trevor didn't answer, either, not with words. He dropped down to his elbows, his ass still in the air, full to the brim with Rhys' cock. Licking his lips, Rhys pushed the pad of his thumb against Trevor's exposed asshole and he reveled in the rippling shudder that passed through Trevor's body. He thrust again, letting his thumb increase the pressure, though never dipping all the way inside. "You ready for me to fuck you properly, or do you need another minute?"

"I need you to fuck me," Trevor gasped, resting his forehead on his bent forearms. "Right now, fuck me."

Rhys needed no further instruction. He grabbed Trevor by the hips, hauling his ass even higher, pressing more snuggly against the perfect, round globes, then did exactly that. The only sound after that was flesh slapping flesh, was the wet suction of lube as Rhys rammed his cock in and out of the other man's body, the punched-out groans coming from both of them as they careened toward orgasm.

Rhys felt himself build as Trevor began to spasm around him, and when Trevor gasped out, "Shit, fuck, I'm coming, *I'm coming*," that was all it took. His hips stuttered in slow, abrupt thrusts, then he threw his head back and felt his cock swell, filling the condom with his hot seed.

His body felt made of jelly as the pleasure began to ebb and fade, and it was all he could do to roll over, pinching the condom and tying it off. He lobbed it toward the bin, not sure if he made it, but he'd worry about it later.

For now, he just wanted to look at this other man, to be near him. They had no understanding between them, no promises to make or break, just this moment. Trevor rolled onto his side to face Rhys, and Rhys traced a finger down his profile. "You're gorgeous."

Trevor smiled, turning his head to kiss the tip of Rhys' finger. "Not so bad yourself. I haven't been fucked like that in a while."

"Glad I could help." Rhys worried his bottom lip, then said, "This is the first time I've slept with someone whose name I knew since Vanessa."

Blinking in surprise, Trevor pulled back just a little. "Seriously?"

Rhys couldn't help his blush, glancing away, feeling an odd sense of shame come over him. "I...I just...I was so angry, and so insecure. I spent so many months wondering what it was about me that drove her to do that. There had to be something fundamentally broken with who I was that I couldn't make her want to stay faithful." Before Trevor could open his mouth to protest, Rhys sighed and said, "I eventually got over that. My therapist helped me work through all the bullshit, but I just never felt ready for a real connection."

Trevor looked mortified. "Oh god, did I just pressure you into this?"

"No," Rhys said, reaching for him, drawing him in close. "Oh my god, Trevor, no. I didn't feel ready until you walked into my office and my entire body tingled with the desire to make you mine."

Trevor calmed a little, reaching out to draw the tip of one finger down the center of Rhys' chest. "I'm not sure this was the best idea, to be honest. I mean, we're in a weird position, and there's so much up in the air. But," he said before Rhys could panic, "I feel the same way. I took one look at you and I just...wanted. God, I wanted, and I don't regret this. I don't regret this, and all I can think about how much I'm not going to regret doing this again."

Rhys groaned, pulling Trevor into him, their lips meeting in a firm, furious kiss. He wasn't kind about it, nipping at Trevor's bottom lip, sucking on his tongue, fingers digging into his hips. He wasn't twenty anymore, he couldn't get himself up again that fast, but a faint thrum of pleasure still raced up his spine.

"I want to fuck you," Trevor murmured.

Rhys pulled back and quirked a brow. "Yeah?"

"I have a strap on," Trevor clarified. "I love topping, and Jesus, seeing you bent over for me..."

Rhys' dick gave a valiant effort at getting hard again, a pulse at the base, though nothing much else happened. All the same, he rocked his hips, rubbing his soft cock against Trevor's naked thigh. "I want that."

Trevor grinned at him, reaching for his face. He dragged his thumb over Rhys' bottom lip, sucking in his breath when Rhys couldn't stop himself from licking at it. "We should get some sleep."

Rhys wanted to argue, wanted to stay up all night and do everything his mind could conjure up in case the sunrise brought with it the reality of their circumstances. But he was also exhausted. It had been a long night, his brother was sleeping it off in the other room, and he had a feeling there was more on the way.

"Stay," Rhys found himself saying as he kicked at the sheets and blankets to dislodge them from beneath their bodies. "I mean... if you want, I'd like you to stay in here with me."

Trevor looked torn for a moment, then reached down and pulled the covers up to their waist. He laid back with his hands beneath his head, and Rhys propped up on his elbow, staring down at him. He had a gorgeous profile, all sharp angles, just a hint of softness under his beard. He couldn't stop himself from reaching out and letting his fingers brush along the coarse strands.

"Beard guy?" Trevor asked.

Rhys chuckled and shrugged. "Never really thought about it, but I'm pretty sure most of the men I've slept with have been clean-shaven."

Trevor scratched under his chin, then turned toward Rhys. "I was on HRT for almost five years before I was able to get anything of substance. I'd pretty much given up at that point, but then it started to grow in thick and fast."

Rhys dragged his finger along Trevor's jawline. "It suits you."

Trevor huffed a small laugh. "Yeah. When I was thinking about stopping T for the hormone treatments, I had this panic attack that I was going to lose all my progress. But apparently the hair growth is permanent. I think that was the thing that cinched my decision to go through with it."

Rhys' eyes twinkled with his grin. "Your beard?"

"It's stupid, I know, but I hadn't been misgendered in a really long time, and the thought of going through all that again was too much."

"It isn't stupid," Rhys said, leaning in for a soft kiss. "I'll never understand what that struggle is like, but I think I can safely say that there's not some rule about what is and isn't allowed to make you feel like a man."

"You'd be a pretty good therapist if you ever wanted to change careers," Trevor said with a grin. He rolled to his side and grabbed Rhys' hand, pressing it to the center of his chest. His pecs were well defined, and Rhys could see the faint, half-moon scars from his surgery in the faded light from the window. "There was this chunk of time when I was about sixteen where my body started freaking out, and I had a period for like six months. It wasn't heavy or significant, but it was enough for dysphoria to kick me in the ass really hard. My therapist told me that I was a man, no matter what my body did or what it looked like, but that didn't mean I wasn't allowed to have things that made me *feel* like a man."

Rhys glanced down between them, at the flat belly below his navel, peppered with a smattering of red hair. He couldn't help but drag his fingers through it. "It would be worse with a baby, wouldn't it?"

Trevor let out a slow breath of air. "I don't know. Maybe. There would probably be moments it would get bad. But I also talked to some trans guys who went through it before I decided to give it a shot. There's not a lot of them, but there are enough. Some of them had an easy time, some of them regretted their decision."

"So what helped?" Rhys asked.

Trevor was silent a moment, then said quietly, "None of them regretted their children."

Rhys felt his heart twist, a yearning and jealousy hot in his belly for something he wasn't sure he'd get the chance to have. "If you had the chance again, would you," he stopped himself and blushed. "God, don't answer that. That is so none of my business. I'm sorry."

Trevor pinched Rhys' chin and lifted his gaze up with gentle pressure. "You were just inside me, you were just sucking my cock like it was the best thing you've ever had in your mouth. I'm cool with an inappropriate question or two."

Rhys couldn't help a smile, even if he still felt like shit. "I don't ever want to assume with you."

Trevor shrugged. "There are people I forgive for insensitivity, and right now you're one of them. And to answer that, I don't know. Right now, it's a resounding hell no. That one decision fucking tanked my life and I'm not exactly in a hurry to repeat that." He went quiet, studying Rhys, and when he asked his next question, it hit like a punch to the gut. "Kids are important to you, aren't they?"

Rhys blinked rapidly, collecting himself. "Not in the way you're thinking. Vanessa and fought so much about it. When I thought maybe she just didn't want to put her body through it, I offered adoption, or surrogacy, whatever would make it easier. I don't care how I get kids, I'd just like to have them. Someday."

Trevor licked his lips, nodded, but said nothing. He snuggled in deeper, put his arm around Rhys' waist, and that was when Rhys knew the topic was over. It was too deep for them anyway, too close to something intimate they couldn't touch. Not yet.

So, he closed his eyes and did his damndest not to think of what life might be like if their circumstances were different.

14.

Rhys: Sorry, some shit went down and I'm with my brother right now. I have no idea when I'm coming home, but I'll be there as soon as I can. Let me know if you need anything while I'm out.

The text was so domestic, Trevor actually had to set his phone down and walk away from it. He knew that fucking Rhys the night before was going to change things, and sleeping with him after—wrapped up in his arms like he never wanted to leave—was going to cement that change into something permanent. There was no going back after post-coitus snuggles. He'd either stepped into the best thing in the world, or he'd doomed what might have been an amazing, lifelong friendship.

Either way, there wasn't much he could do about it. He'd woken up nearly an hour before Rhys and had started coffee and breakfast before the other man woke. He had intended on having something cheap and greasy ready for Ryan's inevitable hang-over as a way of showing both sympathy and maybe easing the guy into the idea of his brother being bisexual.

Rhys had woken not long after, and the two of them had shared a few heated kisses over coffee, right up against the counter. Then all hell had broken loose. Or well, Trevor imagined it did. Ryan stumbled into the room, half-dressed and frantic, mumbling something about Cole and a crisis at his house. Rhys promised to explain when he got back, then he'd taken off, and that was the last Trevor had seen of him.

He had a shift early in the afternoon to prep for the night rush since Thursdays came with discounts and happy hour food, and he was always happy to lend a hand. The threat in the folded up note still loomed, but he wasn't ready to give up just yet. A few more shifts and he could at least afford the doctor's appointment and his next month's dose of his hormone and syringes. The lab would bill him, and he'd worry about the mounting debt later.

He managed to laze around for as long as he could afford it, then quickly showered and dressed. The drive to the bar was quick, and as he slipped through the employee entrance, he saw one of the early afternoon servers waiting for him. She was a short, young girl named Tamara who headed toward him with a look of confused purpose on her face. He hovered near his cubby, shoving his coat inside, watching her out of his periphery.

"So uh," she said, fidgeting with the front pocket of her apron, "some guy came by and told me I had to give this to you. I thought maybe he was like a process server or some shit, but he didn't have me sign for anything." She withdrew a thin envelope from her apron and held it out gingerly, like it might explode if she didn't handle it carefully.

Trevor felt his throat go a little tight, but he managed to affect a smile as he plucked it from her fingers. "Thanks."

She nodded, took a step back, then hesitated. "Are you okay, Trevor? I mean, are you in some kind of trouble or..."

He shook his head quickly, stopping her words. "No, I promise. It's all good." Before she walked away, his hand darted out and he seized her shoulder. "What did he look like, though?"

Her face scrunched up in thought. "I don't know. Older, I guess. Like maybe late forties, early fifties? He was wearing a blue ball cap and I didn't get a good look at his face, but he seemed normal."

Trevor bit his lip, then nodded. "Okay. If he shows up again, will you let me know."

Her eyes narrowed with suspicion, clearly reading the lie in his earlier admission that everything was fine, but she didn't call him on it. "No worries."

He let her go this time, and as soon as she walked back into the main lounge, he slipped into the break room and tore the envelope open. Inside was a page printed off a computer with a single sentence right in the center.

It doesn't matter who you know, or who your connections are, this isn't over.

His entire body went cold, and for whatever reason, that vague threat felt like someone had grabbed him by the throat and started to squeeze. It took him several long moments to catch his breath, and he realized then he was going to be completely useless on shift. The last thing he needed in the world was to miss a day, but he also didn't need to be getting fired because he couldn't concentrate on drink orders or managing small-talk with their regulars.

Heading down the hall in a slight fog, he found Andreas, in the office, going over an accounting sheet on the computer. He looked up when Trevor poked his head in and grinned. "Hey man. You okay? You look a little pale."

"I think I need to go home," Trevor said, and he wasn't faking the tremor in his voice. "I'm really sorry, and I can make up my shift whenever, but…"

"No, it's fine," Andreas said, waving Trevor off. "If you caught something, we don't need it spreading around here. It's flu season and I can't afford to be at half my night staff."

Trevor let out a grateful breath. "I don't think it's the flu, but I'll keep you posted. Thanks." He didn't wait for a response, or for Andreas to change his mind as he grabbed his things back out of his cubby and hurried back to his car. His hands were trembling as he went for his keys, half afraid there would be someone waiting for him there, or maybe another threat waiting under his wiper-blades. There was nothing, but Trevor was struck by the realization that whoever it was had been close. Had missed him by less than an hour, and very likely the person had been watching him.

The thought made him sick, his stomach churning, and he braced himself on the side of his car as he tried to regain his composure. He wasn't foolish enough to think it was over. Even when he could have something good, like finally—*finally*—crossing a line into something more with Rhys, there was always a price to pay. He had to refocus, had to take back as much control as he could.

As he reached for the key fob, his phone began to buzz again, and he nearly ignored it. It was probably Andreas calling back to offer him a make-up shift, but when he glanced at the caller ID, he saw Rhys' name sitting there, bold and demanding.

He struggled a moment to answer it, but eventually put the phone to his ear as he collapsed into the driver's seat. "Hey."

"Hey," Rhys said, sounding out of breath. "I'm *so* sorry everything was crazy this morning. I wanted you to meet Ryan. I was so ready to…"

"Hey, can we talk when I get home?" Trevor interrupted.

Rhys immediately stopped his flow of words. "What happened?"

Trevor swallowed thickly. "Our little friend came by the bar this morning and left me a note with one of the servers."

"*What?*" Rhys demanded.

Trevor let out a slightly hysterical laugh. "Yeah. He might have still been there, too. I told Andreas I couldn't work today, and I didn't see anyone lurking by my car, but he could be watching. Shit, Rhys, he could follow me home and…"

"Trevor," Rhys interrupted, almost a growl.

"Yeah, yeah, I know. You'd never let anything happen to me, blah blah. I'm a fucking doctor of classical language and literature and I can't even keep safe at my fucking job tending bar at some bullshit hipster place where they serve happy hour French fries in old shoe boxes!"

Rhys was silent, and Trevor was half sure he was trying not to laugh. "Come home," he said.

Home. There was a strange warmth to the word, but it warred with how much Trevor didn't want it. Because it wasn't his choice, because it was that or live in his damn car. He hadn't been given the chance to explore this thing with Rhys with any sort of freedom or autonomy over his situation, and that filled him with anger.

"I'm going to," he started, then stopped. He was going to what? Grab a coffee? Get some lunch? Go on a self-care shopping spree at Target? The answer to any potential anything was no, because every single penny he had saved he needed for whatever bleak future he had in front of him. He couldn't live with Rhys forever, not without being able to contribute something, and right now he was being cut down at every turn.

"Please," Rhys said softly.

Trevor sighed, realizing he wasn't actually going to be able to deny this man, and he pressed his forehead to the steering wheel. "Yeah, okay. I'm on my way." He ended the call without allowing for some sweet goodbye or a promise of anything more. He wanted—god how he wanted—but he couldn't let the night before repeat. Not until he had some way of being self-sufficient. He knew Rhys would never expect anything out of him for what he was doing, but he was so turned around, so confused and unsure, he was doubting everything.

Maybe it was a test of Rhys, and maybe it was unfair, but it was all he had.

***

Trevor pulled up beside Rhys' car and walked in, trying to affect a look of nonchalance. Rhys was waiting for him on the couch, and Trevor appreciated that he didn't leap to his feet or make a dramatic show of concern. He had a couple of sandwiches wrapped in butcher paper on the table—nothing out of the ordinary—but the sight of them made his gut twist.

He could have afforded to treat Rhys to something like that today, but only today. Maybe tomorrow, but not much beyond that, not unless he had a couple of really good nights at work. Biting his lip, he lowered himself to the sofa, keeping a cushion of space between them. "Is Ryan okay?" he asked eventually.

Rhys dragged a hand down his face and groaned. "It's complicated. He's in something deep, and I don't even know where to begin helping him."

"What, like drugs?" Trevor asked with a frown. That wouldn't go along with anything Trevor knew about Ryan, but he couldn't think of anything else Rhys would be talking about.

It gave him some measure of relief when Rhys shook his head. "No, something else. Something weird. Last night he told me a little more about Cole—he's an ex-Marine, I guess, from the UK. He was blinded during his service and he's here because…" he paused and frowned.

"I'm not actually sure why he's here. But Ryan's theory the guy's keeping secrets... well, after this morning, I think my brother might be on to something."

"Vague, but okay," Trevor said.

Rhys pinked, and Trevor felt a rush of guilt for making the guy feel bad. "When we got to his place, it was trashed. Not like a party got out of hand trashed, but like someone had gone through his shit and they were clearly looking for something. And they definitely didn't care what kind of mess they left behind. Ryan got things sorted while I looked for the guy's guide dog, and when I got back, Ryan just left with me. He wouldn't talk about it, but whatever happened with him wasn't good."

The sheer level of worry in Rhys' voice sent Trevor's problems retreating into the shadows. They would be there, no matter what he did, but he didn't mind tucking things away to offer someone else comfort. It was the absolute least he could do. Shifting a little closer, he reached out and took Rhys' hand. "That sounds fucked."

Rhys let out a strangled laugh. "Something like that, yeah. Maybe it's not as bad as I think it is. We don't live in some conspiracy theory political thriller movie, so I'm probably overreacting. But Ryan's been through a lot. He's been punishing himself for cheating on Noah for a goddamn decade and even Noah's moved on. The guy deserves to be happy, and last night—for just a minute—I thought maybe he was letting himself. But if this guy is involved in some shit..."

Trevor heard the warning in the silence that followed, and he couldn't help but appreciate the protective nature of this man. "Look, it might suck right now, but you're good at being there for people when they need you. He'll get through it, whatever it is."

Rhys rubbed his thumb along Trevor's, the warmth between them soft and sweet. "Thanks."

Trevor shook his head. "Just telling the truth."

The pair of them sat back, the lunch untouched by either man, and Rhys distracted himself by playing with the tips of Trevor's fingers. After a beat, he sighed and asked, "So this afternoon..."

Trevor squeezed his hand to quiet him. "I really, really don't want to talk about that right now. I don't even know how to process all of this. They're systematically destroying my life, bit by bit, and I don't know where it's going to end. I don't even fucking know why the person's doing it!"

Rhys licked his lips, then said, "According to Ryan, Cole's some sort of hacker genius, and I think I'm going to see about asking him to help."

Trevor blinked, a little startled at the reality of Rhys' offer. "Seriously?"

"The worst he can do is say no, right? But he was able to track the guy who beat the shit out of Noah and find a paper trail. Barnes is going to jail because of that information. We don't know for sure what's out there about your mysterious blackmailer, but I'm willing to bet there's something, especially since he's connected to Barnes."

Trevor bit down on his lip, not sure he should get his hopes up. The person doing this had always left his trail in physical copies, never anything electronic—nothing that could be traced. "We don't really have anything except the letters he sent."

"Yeah," Rhys breathed out. "Well, if Cole can't help, I still want to ask Ivan about it. Thanks to his position, he might be able to come up with something we can't."

"Ivan," Trevor said flatly.

"He's the cop, the one Ryan used to hook up with," Rhys hedged.

"Why would he be willing to help you if he's Ryan's ex hook-up?" Trevor asked.

Rhys licked his lips, then stared down at his feet. "The failed date I had? Where I couldn't..." he trailed off and cleared his throat. "That was Ivan. We parted on good terms though, and he told me he's willing to help with whatever I need."

Trevor blinked at him in surprise. "You told a cop about my situation?"

"No," Rhys said in a rush. "No, of course not. I just laid the foundation, told him I had a friend who might need help finding information. He has no idea who you are."

Trevor felt an irrational surge of jealousy, even knowing that it was for the best Rhys hadn't told Ivan the truth. He also wanted to tell him no, because the more he tried to get ahead of his blackmailer, the worse it would get. But he also couldn't keep going like this. It was only a matter of time before the mysterious person came after Rhys, and Trevor wouldn't be able to live with himself if that was the case.

"I," he started, but instead of words, a shattered sob erupted from his throat. Trevor felt a rush of irritation at his own weakness, but it was quickly overcome when Rhys pulled him into an embrace. The emotions he'd been repressing since leaving the employee parking lot bubbled up, then over. He closed his eyes against the flood of tears and shoved his face into the front of Rhys' shirt. He felt a little foolish, behaving the way toddlers did—covering their eyes with the innocent belief that if they couldn't see, no one could see them. But it felt safe that way, a little less mortifying that he was heaving great, shuddering sobs into the soft, expensive cotton of Rhys' t-shirt.

It didn't last long, though the few minutes felt eternal, but he was eventually able to suck in a full breath of air, and his eyes began to dry. Swiping his hand under his nose, he hesitated in pulling away, knowing he looked a hot mess.

"I wonder how long you've needed to do that," Rhys murmured quietly, his fingers gently running through Trevor's hair. "I get the feeling you've been holding that one in for a while."

Trevor huffed a small, shuddering laugh and shrugged one shoulder as he breathed in Rhys' calming, woodsy scent. "I had a good cry the first night you brought me here, but nothing since then."

Rhys made a noise of surprise. "If it was me, I'd be doing this every damn day." He reached one hand up, slow and tentative, and used the pads of his fingers to swipe Trevor's cheeks clear.

Trevor licked his lips and glanced away, finding it a little too overwhelming to keep staring him in the eyes. "If I let myself, I'd never be able to pull myself back together, and I can't let that happen. I keep telling myself this has to end sometime. This person can't keep it up forever."

"We could always flee the country," Rhys said with a tiny smile. His hand dropped to Trevor's shoulder, and he gently traced a path along his neck with the edge of his thumb. "Find some cozy little spot off the coast of Santorini? You could teach locals archaic Latin and I could represent them in court over fishing disputes."

Trevor rolled his eyes, though he was smiling. "Santorini is nothing but tourists anymore. We need something obscure. Like...Sikinos. We can go stay in the ruins and live off the land."

Rhys laughed softly, easing a little closer, his arm still firmly tucked around Trevor's middle. "Sikinos it is. I used to fish with my dad when I was little, I'm pretty sure I could keep us fed."

Trevor stared at him, opened his mouth to say something, but another instinct took over. He leaned in and took Rhys' mouth with his own, his hands immediately diving into his hair, curling the thick locks around the tips of his fingers. Rhys opened to him without question, without hesitation, letting Trevor push him back to the cushions. His legs spread slightly, and he shifted his hips when Trevor lifted one leg over to straddle him. He could feel Rhys' bulge beneath him, throbbing, wanting more than just rubbing off, and Trevor felt it too. He felt heavy and wanting, empty in a way where all he could think about right then was being filled.

His resolve to keep things at a distance was broken in the face of so much rejection. But Rhys wasn't part of that. He was holding on to Trevor with a white-knuckled grip and Trevor—for the first time in so long—felt properly anchored.

"Fuck me," he murmured against Rhys' lips.

Rhys groaned, thrusting up against him, his dick pushing through his folds to where Trevor's own center was throbbing and desperate for friction. "I thought you wanted to…would you like to top?"

Trevor couldn't help his smile, even as he shook his head. "It's not what I want right now, and to be honest, I don't know where I stored it and I'm in no mood to wait. I want it hard, I want it rough. I want you to pin me against the wall and fuck me until I can't think. Please," he begged, then leaned in and kissed Rhys without any of the previous softness.

Rhys' fingers scrabbled to curl into Trevor's hips, his own moving without any real rhythm. Each drag of his dick through Trevor's jeans was sweet torture, and he knew he wasn't far from his completion. "Go into the bedroom and take all your fucking clothes off," Rhys said, a low growl in his voice that went straight to Trevor's middle. "I want you to get the lube out of the drawer, get a condom, and start fingering yourself wherever you want me to put this." He punctuated his sentence by dragging Trevor's hand down to his bulge.

Trevor gulped, letting his hand curl around it, and he nodded. "I can do that." He stood up from Rhys' lap, his legs shaking, but he managed a steady gait all the way to the master bedroom. His mind went wild with curiosity as he began to methodically shed his clothes. Was Rhys disrobing out there? Was he sitting on the couch and stroking his cock as he thought of Trevor naked, covered in lube, fingering himself?

That alone got him too close, and he buried his face in the mattress, ass up in the air as his fingers circled around hole. He wanted it this way right now. He needed the sting of it, the rarely used piece of him that didn't bring him the same pleasure as other things, but he had a feeling it would be exactly what he needed. Rhys was possessive in an unobtrusive way, in a way that allowed Trevor to retain his freedom and autonomy, but still told him that Rhys had staked his claim and wasn't letting go.

Trevor should have been terrified, but instead all he could think of was Rhys' dick filling his ass. His cock throbbed and he pushed a finger between his folds to stroke it, feeling the engorged flesh pulse against him. A sharp wave of pleasure hit at the first drag, and then settled into a low simmer as his fingers breeched his ass. The warring sensations was almost too much. His orgasm was just beyond his grasp, and he'd only need a tiny push.

But he wasn't about to do that before Rhys got in. He removed his hand from his dick and concentrated on stretching the rest of him. He added two rounds of lube and was up to three fingers before he heard footsteps and the door gently swinging open. He started to move his head, but the sharp tone of Rhys voice stopped him.

"Don't look up. Fuck, don't move any other muscle but the ones you need to keep fucking those fingers in your ass." His voice was strangled, and Trevor knew he was just as close to losing it. He groaned, thrusting his ass against his hand and he could hear the faint sound of Rhys sucking in his breath.

It felt like a hundred years before a warm hand landed on his back, but he was grateful for it. The lengthy prep gave him time to compose himself, to allow the moment to draw out so he could truly enjoy it. With the feeling of Rhys' hand on his skin came that familiarity and security he'd been so uncertain about, but so desperate for. And there was more to it. Not just desperation, but a genuine want. He would have done this—would have wanted to keep doing this—even if he'd met Rhys in a more traditional way.

It was the one tiny thread keeping him going forward.

Trevor didn't stop fingering himself when Rhys stepped up behind him, and his whole body flushed hotter when he heard Rhys groan and press one finger alongside his. His ass felt full—so full he wanted to cry, or laugh, or moan—and then a gentle hand pulled his away. Before he could complain, he felt the blunt pressure of a cock against his opening, and Trevor clenched his fists in the blanket, his knees buckling slightly as he was pushed toward the mattress. He let out a gruff sound as the head breeched him, then he felt Rhys' strong hands lift him toward a better angle, sliding in completely.

"Shit," Trevor gasped. "Shit, that's so good." Pain-pleasure rippled up his spine as he was tugged further upward, his back now pressed to Rhys' firm chest. Rhys' hands on him were an anchor, a ballast, one hand on his hip, one arm stretched over his chest to keep him pinned. There wasn't room for more than shallow nudging, the pressure and girth of Rhys' cock stretching him beyond what he was used to from his toys.

Then Rhys' hand moved from his hip to his front, parting his folds to get at his dick, and that…*god*, that made his head spin with waves of pleasure as Rhys' slicked fingers began to stroke up and down the engorged flesh.

For the short burst of time, nothing else mattered but that. Everything else in the world ceased to exist except the thrusting cock in his ass, and the clever fingers working him up, and up, and up. His head fell back against Rhys' shoulder, and he felt Rhys bow his head, nipping at his ear, tonguing the shell. "Can I," Rhys asked, his fingers drifting lower, asking for permission to push inside.

"Yes," Trevor murmured. His hips arched a little, his body begging for it.

Rhys was so good, so perfect, reading Trevor's body like he was made to do it. His arm moved away from Trevor's chest, dipping down to stroke at his dick with two fingers of his other hand shallowly thrusting in time with the dick in his ass, no deeper than the first knuckle.

It was the most full, the most consumed Trevor had ever been. His eyes filled with tears again, but this time from sheer, overwhelming euphoria. He was going to come, and a part of him wondered if he'd ever be able to stop. No one had ever possessed him like this, no one had ever tried to know him, to give him anything close to this. A vicious piece of him wanted to cling to it, to say fuck the rest because more than anything in the world, he wanted to keep this. He wanted this all the time, any time he asked for it, didn't want Rhys to even consider looking at another man.

His orgasm hit when Rhys changed angles, bending him over slightly though his hands didn't cease their movements, and then a second hit moments later, when he felt Rhys start to swell inside him. It became too much after that, and he gently nudged Rhys' hands back up to his hips.

With tacit permission, Rhys grabbed Trevor hard, then began to fuck him in earnest, bending him over the mattress and pushing into his ass with long, slow thrusts. The pleasure zinged up and down, his knees bashing the mattress with every one of Rhys' grunts, and then he felt it. He felt the way Rhys stuttered, the way he lost rhythm and spilled.

A faint echo of a third orgasm hit, making his insides quiver and pulse. A gush of wetness escaped between his legs, and then warmth filled his limbs. He felt made of jelly, far worse than he'd been before, and he managed to plant his hands on the bed and crawl forward just as Rhys pulled out. It was by miracle alone he managed to make it up to the pillows and bury his face there, grinning when Rhys curled around him a moment later.

"Holy hell," he murmured, letting himself fall back into that warm chest once again.

Rhys chuckled, kissing along the back of his shoulder. "Yeah."

"It's never been like that for me," Trevor admitted. He felt almost punch-drunk, head still spinning, body still in that almost-numb space as he came down from his high. "Like, never."

"Me too," Rhys said, his voice nearly at a whisper. He closed one hand around Trevor's hip and held him tight.

The surprising honesty in Rhys' tone momentarily shocked Trevor out of his euphoria. "Really? Not even with your ex?"

Trevor snorted. "No. Not even close. This was the best sex I've ever had."

"What was the second best?" Trevor asked, stroking his fingers up and down Rhys' arm.

He hummed, nibbling on the side of Trevor's neck as he thought. "Probably my first hook-up at University. I was away from home for the first time, and I was so far from it, no one knew me. I had this idea that I could reinvent myself, or at least live the life of a guy who didn't exist under assumptions. I could be openly bisexual, and people wouldn't start pointing fingers at me because of my brother. I went to a party with some friends and this guy who—well in retrospect wasn't even that attractive, but he was my first uninhibited hook-up. He was fucking gorgeous—he asked me to dance, and I was tipsy and a little stoned, and he had a key for one of the upstairs rooms. He covered my thighs in lube and fucked them while he jerked me off, and it was just the taboo of the whole thing, the...the, I don't know..."

"Freedom?" Trevor offered.

Rhys chuckled and kissed him again. "Yeah. It made it so much better than it rightfully should have been."

"Did you date?" Trevor asked.

He could feel Rhys shake his head, his hand moving to draw absent lines across Trevor's stomach. "Nah. We passed out in that bed, and I woke up at like three am and stumbled home. I didn't even realize I hadn't gotten his number, but then I saw him like two weeks later walking hand-in-hand with some guy and it definitely didn't seem new."

"Shit," Trevor whispered with a breath.

Rhys shrugged. "I figure, if you're going to be immature and shitty, college is the time to do it, you know? You're not likely to fuck up something that has the potential to be good. *Actually* good, not just the idea of good," he clarified.

Trevor could hear the experience in his tone, the faint bitterness and regret, and it wasn't like Trevor could blame him. He understood, even if he hadn't exactly experienced anything like a divorce, or even a steady relationship. But with Rhys wrapped around him like this, he couldn't help but wonder what it might be like. Could they make it work? Could it be *actually* good?

The potential terrified him and excited him in equal measure. But as amazing as it was, as it could be, he couldn't let himself open up to it. Not until he was steady on his feet.

15.

Rhys knew he lost Trevor somewhere around, 'college is the time to be immature and shitty,' but he didn't regret saying it. Mostly because he knew Trevor understood everything else he was saying. That they were better people now, that there was the potential for something here that couldn't be ignored. Not anymore.

He wasn't going to push it, of course, but he wasn't going to let go without a fight, either. He was falling in love with this man, as much as he'd tried to keep his emotional distance. But he knew his heart, knew it was a fool, and it was going to want anyway.

He took heart in the fact that Trevor let his guard down enough to fall asleep right there in his arms, and Rhys was happy to hold him and bring him some measure of peace while he could. He had plans to do more than that, too. He had plans to wake up gently, hours later, and fix some late dinner, and maybe suggest a movie or ice cream.

Then his phone rang, and all hell broke loose.

An hour later he found himself with Wes, sitting outside on Ryan's terrace with a cigarette and a stiff glass of whiskey—one of which he'd avoided since his younger days of being an idiot to his body. But once the coughing had subsided, the ritual of drawing in smoke and letting it out was oddly calming. Especially since his brother was lying in the other room beat to hell, on the other side of some movie-level military conspiracy theory which ended with Ryan's kidnapping and near-death.

Just thinking about it sent him into fresh waves of panic, and he took a long drink of the alcohol to calm the shaking in his hands.

"He's going to be fine," Wes told him softly.

Rhys huffed a laugh. "Oh, I know. I mean, if anyone can get himself into a situation like that and come out fine, it's Ryan."

Wes' lips twitched up at the corners. "I know, but it would be nice if he didn't constantly keep us on edge like that."

"Thank you for being there. For getting him out," Rhys told him after a moment, his voice shaking a little. "I don't know what I'd do if…" His voice cracked and he had to stop.

After some hesitation, Wes put his drink down and reached over, lacing his hand with Rhys'. "Look, I need you to know that regardless of what our physical relationship is like, your brother is one of my best friends. Hell, he's family. I would do anything for him, and I sure as shit wasn't about to let someone take him out."

Rhys bowed his head. "Except you know as well as I do that sometimes it isn't that easy."

Wes' fingers spasmed against his, but he didn't draw away. "I'd die trying."

Rhys felt a profound wave of gratitude sweep through him and he wasn't sure what to do with it. Luckily, the moment was interrupted by the door opening, and Rhys turned his head to find Noah there, leaning against the doorframe looking haggard but smiling.

"Hey, you," Noah said.

Rhys was immediately on his feet, drawing Noah to his chest. The one thing he was grateful for was not losing his friendship with Noah when his relationship with Ryan went up in flames.

He felt better than he had since he arrived the moment Noah melted against him. "Are you okay?" he asked.

Noah pulled back and rubbed a hand down his face. "I've been better, but I think Ryan's going to be okay. Though he's definitely going to need therapy after this."

"We'll all stay on his ass about it," Wes said.

Noah gave a faint nod and leaned against Rhys. "I don't know how the fuck things keep getting so upside down."

"Yeah," Rhys said from behind a laugh. "First your shit, now this? Has anyone heard form that Cole guy?"

"They whisked him off to some safe-house when the British Commandos showed up," Wes said, a little irritated. "Ryan tried to call him, but the number was disconnected."

"Jesus," Rhys murmured. "So what? That's that? We just move on and never hear from the guy again?"

Noah shrugged. "I...wouldn't entirely count on that. Cole was crazy about Ryan. I don't think he'd let him just walk away."

Rhys might have been inclined to argue out of sheer bitterness toward the loyalty of others, except he immediately thought of Trevor and realized the same would hold true for him. Nothing would be able to keep him away.

"He deserves to be happy," Rhys finally said. It killed him a little that this Cole guy wasn't here to help with Trevor, but more than that, it killed him that Cole's disappearance would hurt his brother.

Noah sighed. "I'm going to use the bathroom and grab a drink. Either of you need anything?"

Both Wes and Rhys shook their heads, and Rhys sat down, leaning back in the chair. "I swear to god, one of those two is going to end up giving me an early coronary."

Wes chuckled. "Sounds about right. Either they will or my kid will, but my money's on Ryan."

Rhys wanted to argue, but his brother had always been on the reckless side. Rhys knew why, knew he'd set a high bar when it came to success in the family, and he'd grown up self-centered enough it had taken him a long while to realize what Ryan was going through. By the time he did, Ryan had already tanked his relationship with Noah and had embarked on a path of self-destruction when it came to letting other people care for him.

"Rhys?" Wes' voice interrupted his internal monologue, and he glanced over at the other man. "Are you okay?"

Rhys couldn't help a laugh, scrubbing at his eyes with the heels of his palms. "You know, I've been better. I want to pretend like it's all this chaos which has me fucked up."

"But it's not?" Wes offered.

Rhys rubbed at the back of his neck as he leaned over his thighs. "It's not." He glanced at the door, seeing of Noah was anywhere nearby. "It's a personal thing, and it's complicated, and there's not a goddamn thing I can do."

"Can I help?" Wes asked. "Is it about Trevor?"

Rhys almost laughed, because it was just like the guy to put himself out there for a near stranger who he'd only just met. "I don't...maybe," he said. "I can't really talk about it though. Not with Noah and Ryan here."

Wes bit his lip, then pushed himself up to a shaky stand. His legs looked a little unsteady, and Rhys had to assume it was from all the strain of the day, but he had a pair of crutches to help him toward the door. "Let's go for a drive. I'm craving a burger right now and I know Ryan doesn't have shit in the way of food in this hole."

Rhys grinned, mostly at the idea of anyone calling Ryan's expensive condo a hole, but also at the sudden and very unexpected offer of help. "Yeah, okay. Let me drive, though. You look beat."

They walked into the condo just as Noah was coming out of the bathroom, and Rhys motioned him over. "Wes and I are going to get some junk food. You want anything?"

Noah shook his head. "I don't think I could eat if I wanted to. I'm going to stay here with Ryan, and Adrian said he'd get me in the morning, so don't hurry back."

Rhys nodded, then grabbed Noah and pulled him into a firm embrace. "Thank you for being here. Thank you for loving him even after everything."

Noah pulled back and stared hard at Rhys. "He deserves to be loved."

Rhys nodded, not really able to say anything else, but luckily, he had Wes to keep him occupied. He followed the other man out the door, then led the way to his car which was parked in Ryan's spot. They didn't say much of anything as he pulled onto the main road, so Rhys headed toward the little cluster of fast food places just off the main freeway.

"Anywhere is fine," Wes said when Rhys gave him a quirked brow.

He picked one of the little mom and pop places that had good onion rings, grabbing himself a shake along with it, and then Wes' burger. Instead of heading back to the road, he pulled onto a parking spot at the far end of the tarmac and leaned back in his seat.

"Okay, so do I need to play twenty-questions with you too, or can you just spill?" Wes asked.

Rhys' eyebrows flew up. "Me too?" he repeated.

Wes chuckled through a mouthful of burger. "Yeah uh...so Cole came to me right before shit hit the fan, and I had to play a guessing game because his involvement in some government shit meant he couldn't outright tell me. Ended up being way more complicated, but he didn't know it at the time."

Rhys blinked rapidly, then laughed. "That sounds like a story I need to hear at some point."

"Just let me know when you're ready for a migraine," Wes said. "But we're talking about Trevor."

"Yeah." He took a breath, then said, "He was one of the professors fired around the same time Noah was being blackmailed."

Wes looked startled. "One of the ones caught fucking students?"

Rhys took a swallow of his milkshake, grimacing at the too-sweet chocolate. "Yeah, except he wasn't doing anything like that. Turns out Barnes was being instructed by some...I don't know what or who...but he got Barnes to threaten him, and he continued to get threats even after Barnes was arrested. He's got something on Trevor that..." He trailed off, shaking his head, because he wasn't about to give explicit details regarding Trevor's situation. "That's what I can't say, but it's enough that he couldn't join Noah's case against Barnes."

"And it hasn't stopped since that dipshit was arrested?" Wes asked.

Rhys shook his head. "No. I was hoping Cole might be able to look into it, but that guy's now out in the wind, and I'm not exactly flush in super-secret hacker tech guys who operate under the law."

Wes snorted. "Yeah."

"The biggest issue he's got right now is that he can't work in his field. This person has destroyed his credit, his job history, his personal life. He came to my office to see if there was anything I could do without going public, and my hands were tied. Especially because of Noah." Rhys closed his eyes, taking in a breath. "I found him a few weeks later living in his car."

"Shit," Wes breathed out.

Rhys opened his eyes, looking at the other man. "Yeah. Shit is about right. He's staying with me now, and yesterday he just threatened at his bartending job. There was a note left for him telling him to quit his job, and one later telling him this wasn't over. He can't keep living like this."

Wes scratched at his scruff, his mouth thinning as he considered Rhys' words. "How can I help?"

"I don't know," Rhys said miserably. "Maybe you can't. I mean, he likes being able to work out with you, but self-defense is only going to get him so far." He scrubbed a hand down his face. "In all honesty, I think I need to involve Ivan, but he's not going to like that."

"Ivan," Wes repeated. "Like Ryan's Ivan?"

Rhys flushed. "Yeah."

"Right," Wes said.

Rhys bit his lower lip, then said, "He's mostly freaked out because Ivan's in law enforcement."

"Did he do something illegal?" Wes asked, his tone honest and careful. "You know if he did, there might not be a way for him to get out of this without facing those consequences."

"What he did was against the University policy, but not necessarily against the law," Rhys said, knowing he was toeing the line with this much information. "He's just scared."

"I get it," Wes said. He chewed on his burger for a few minutes, then said, "I think you're right. I don't know that I can help, but I can at least be there. If boxing lessons are helping his confidence, keep bringing him. It'll at least keep him distracted until you can make some real progress."

"Yeah," Rhys breathed out. "The guys can't find out about this until we get ahead of this either, okay?"

Wes smiled at him. "You know me."

"Yeah," Rhys said dryly, barely holding back a smile. "I do."

"Isn't he dating Evan right now, though?" Wes said after a beat. "I haven't seen Evan in a few days, but last time we talked he was pretty thrilled about how their date went."

Rhys flushed. "I uh...I don't think they're together anymore." He gave a nervous cough, looking away.

Wes stared, then his lips spread into a grin. "Oh damn. Oh *damn*. Does Ryan know you and Trevor are a thing now?"

Rhys felt his entire face burst into white-hot heat and he couldn't meet the other man's eyes. "Uh, no."

"Sorry," Wes said after a beat. "I didn't mean to..."

"No," Rhys said, holding up his hand. He sat up and breathed through the last vestiges of his panic. "It's fine. I haven't told Ryan, but if this is going the way I think it's going, I'll have to soon."

"He's not going to care," Wes told him, repeating the words from the night at the bar, reaching out to touch his knee. "Of all people, Ryan's not going to care."

Logically Rhys knew that, but illogically he was still afraid. "There's just a lot right now."

Wes nodded. "I get it. Look, let's get back to my truck and you can drop me off. I'll talk to the guys tomorrow, then give you a call if I can come up with anything. Fair?"

Rhys nodded, letting some of the tension ease from the center of his chest. "Thanks. I don't know how to repay you for this."

Wes shook his head. "When are you going to realize you're my family too, dumbass? Whether you like it or not?"

***

Trevor ceased his pacing the moment the door opened and Rhys walked in. It was near one in the morning, but he hadn't been able to calm down, even with the updates Rhys had been texting him. He didn't know Ryan well, but getting the truncated version of the events, he could only imagine how he felt, and it was only because he didn't want to force Rhys to answer awkward questions that he declined Rhys' offer to go.

He had his arms open for Rhys the moment he walked in, and let out a small noise of satisfaction when Rhys collapsed gently against him. They shuffled their way to the sofa and eased down, Rhys snuffling his face in the front of Trevor's threadbare t-shirt.

"God, I didn't expect to come home to this, and I definitely didn't realize how much I needed it," he murmured.

Trevor dug his fingers into the tousled locks of dark hair and stroked along his scalp. "How is he?"

"Sleeping. Drugged out of his mind," Rhys said. He shifted to the side so he could look up at Trevor's face. "Terrified. I think everyone's going to have to be on him about making sure he starts up therapy again. He's not badly injured, but he's definitely going to have some trauma to work through."

Trevor smiled down at him and dragged a finger along his jaw. "I have a feeling you'll be able to persuade him."

"You clearly don't know what a stubborn asshole he can be, but he's also been trying to be better," Rhys said. He yawned, then shifted so his head pillowed on Trevor's lap. He wrapped one arm around him, nuzzling into his stomach, and Trevor tried to ignore the intense warmth shooting through his limbs. He wanted, *god* he wanted, but he had to put the brakes on for now.

"It's just nice to know that he has support. Family, you know, to get him through stuff like this." He tried to cover the bitterness in his tone, but he didn't think he was successful. Not when Rhys' eyes opened and he propped himself up.

"Trevor…"

He shook his head quickly. "I didn't mean for it to come out like that. I know I have support here."

"More than that," Rhys said.

16.

Trevor bounced his leg so hard, it was shaking the car as they sat at the stop light, heading away from Baum's Boxing Studio. After a minute, Rhys reached over and pressed his hand down on Trevor's thigh, squeezing gently. "Do you want to talk about it?"

Trevor groaned, pressing his forehead to the glass. "I shouldn't have lied."

Rhys' eyebrows went up. "Lied about what?"

"Everything," he said. "How long the blackmail's been going on. I should have just told Noah all the details. I trust him."

They were on their way to Adrian and Noah's place now, following behind them, but Rhys quickly threw on his indicator and pulled into a gas station parking lot. He found a spot near the back, only a faint, hazy yellow light above them, and he put the car into park and twisted to face Trevor.

"First of all, you don't owe anyone anything you're not ready to give. Secondly, had you come out to Noah before?"

Trevor bit his lip, shaking his head. "He knew I was gay, and chances are he at least suspected I'm trans, but he'd never asked."

"He's not the kind of guy who would," Rhys said confidently.

Trevor licked his lips. "We used to hang out, we always got along, and I trust him. I do. It just…it just all slipped out. I've been hiding this shit for so long now, and I was tired of hiding. It felt so good when we were at Wes', and I just wanted to feel that way again."

Rhys took his hand, pressing a kiss to his palm to calm him down. "If you want to tell everyone else now, you can. They'll get it, okay? No one is going to judge you."

Trevor dragged a hand down his face. "Okay."

Rhys rubbed his thumb over Trevor's knuckles. "If you don't want to do the boxing thing either, you don't have to. Or you can keep up the private lessons at Wes' house."

At that, Trevor's face softened into a grin, and his eyes got a little brighter. "I actually liked it there, and I liked Adrian. I wasn't sure I'd be into the whole, getting punched in the face thing, but I felt good when I was done."

Rhys chuckled. "Yeah. Adrian kind of does that for you. I'm used to it, training with Wes, but he's not as good as Adrian."

"I'm glad Noah met him. Love looks so good on that guy," Trevor said.

Rhys chuckled. "Yeah. You're not the only one who thinks so. And those two fought hard for each other."

"Reminds me of a few other people I know," Trevor murmured.

Rhys cupped his cheek, pulling him in for a slow kiss. "Trust me, I'm not done fighting. I won't be done fighting. Not for you."

After a few minutes, once he was sure Trevor was calm, he pulled back out onto the road and made his way to Adrian's. Noah had been staying there more often than not. It was close to the freeway so Noah could catch his ride to work which was over an hour and a half away, and close enough for Adrian to get to his motorcycle repair shop which was just getting off the ground. Neither of them seemed eager to stay near campus, and after everything they'd been through, Rhys couldn't blame them.

Rhys hadn't been by yet, though he'd been invited, and it felt a little thrilling to walk up the stairs with Trevor's hand in his. He'd come out to Ryan first, in the quiet of the office before confessing everything else going on. Then he decided he might as well rip the bandage off and came clean once he returned to the others. He was welcomed and accepted, just like the logical side of his brain knew he would be. The other part—the one who was terrified he'd be dismissed for being bi, or for others who might think he'd finally 'gone gay'—was quieted with their soft eyes and gentle smiles, and genuine joy at seeing Rhys happy.

It didn't hurt that they all seemed to love Trevor, and Noah was even more thrilled to have his friend back in the fold, even if things were still complicated.

Not an hour into Trevor's first session with Adrian, Ryan had returned, and he was walking with the man Rhys knew had to be Cole. Since Rhys hadn't met the guy, he wasn't sure what to expect, but Cole was nothing like Rhys had pictured. He wasn't Ryan's typical type—his brother had always gone for the sort of frat-boy look drenched in too much axe body spray, and this guy wasn't it. He had very visible scars on his face, a sharp nose, full lips, a head of soft brown hair. His blindness was obvious by the soft, pinched eyelids, and he walked with one hand on Ryan's arm, and the other holding a tall white cane.

Rhys wasn't sure how to feel about the return of Cole. Elated because it meant they might have some extra help, and a little bitter for the heartbreak Ryan had gone through when Cole disappeared on him. Yet, the absolute and utter euphoria on his brother's face had chased any bad feelings away. Now, as he and Trevor walked up to Adrian and Noah's front door, he merely felt content.

The get-together was small, as late as it was in the night. Someone had picked up Indian food, and Rhys' stomach gave a loud growl as he followed the smell of rich spices into the kitchen. Trevor had been immediately accosted by Noah who wanted to talk about his situation more, and Rhys gave his hand a supportive squeeze before letting him go to handle this on his own.

Adrian was in the kitchen handing out plates, and he grinned at Rhys as he offered a beer. "I have something stronger if you prefer?"

Rhys shook his head. "Nah, driving tonight, and I'd like Trevor to get a little tipsy if he feels up for it. It's been a damn long day."

Adrian grimaced in sympathy. "Yeah. But you know, I think training at the studio will be good for him. It might not make any real difference, but helping him feel safer will boost his confidence."

"He needs it," Rhys said. "He's been beaten down for a while now and I just…" He trailed off and shook his head.

"We'll figure it out. With Cole back, probably a lot faster than we would without him."

Rhys nodded, peering around the corner, but he didn't see his brother or Cole anywhere. "Did he and Ryan show up yet?"

"They made a pit-stop, but they'll be here," Adrian said. He began to fill his own plate, then leaned against the counter to eat. "How you holding up?"

"Uh, well…sometimes better, sometimes worse. I can't really do anything about Trevor's situation and it's making me feel a little," he trailed off, trying to find the words. Before he could, something cold and wet bumped against him, and he glanced down to see Lemon looking at him with her big eyes.

Adrian chuckled. "It's either the chicken on your plate, or an offer of comfort. Knowing how perceptive she is, I'd go with the second."

Rhys put his plate down, then knelt beside the dog who quickly nestled into his arms. It was instant comfort, and he let out a heavy breath, understanding at least on some level why these dogs were so damn necessary for people like Adrian. "Thanks, Lemon," he muttered.

The dog licked his face, then promptly trotted away.

Rhys stood up and reached for his plate again, feeling oddly lighter. "Is it like that for you every time?"

Adrian laughed again and shook his head. "Not even a little bit. I mean, sometimes on the less-bad days it's that simple. Some of the time it's her lying on me as I shake apart. But she's good at getting to me before I get that bad, and usually she distracts me which is what I need more often than not."

"I'm glad you have her," Rhys said quietly. He picked at his naan, dipping a little into his saag and nibbling the end of it. "This is such a shit-show. I don't know what the fuck to do."

"Unfortunately, I know how you feel," Adrian told him. He set his plate down, then shuffled to a barstool and sat. "When Noah was in it, I was ready to just find this guy and end him. Has whoever this is come after you yet?"

Rhys bit his lower lip and shook his head. "No. I've been waiting, but I think it's possible he won't try since I have connections. I work too closely with law enforcement that anything he tries, he's putting his identity at risk."

Adrian's brow furrowed. "You'd think he'd stop fucking with Trevor if he knew the two of you were together."

"Yeah," Rhys said with a sigh. "That's what worries me. Either he's as awful at this as Barnes was, or he's got another plan."

"The last part terrifies me a bit," Adrian admitted. "Before all this with Cole, I'd say it was just paranoia talking, but now I don't think I trust anyone."

Rhys couldn't help his tired laugh. "You and me both." He finished up his food, then filled his plate again. "I'm going to bring this to Trevor. You want to bother them with me?"

Adrian shook his head. "I have a couple of email fires to put out from my suppliers, but tell Noah I'll be there in a bit."

Rhys tipped him a short salute of acknowledgment, then grabbed his plate and a fresh beer for Trevor. He wandered into the living room and found Trevor and Noah locked in a tight embrace, Trevor's eyes puffy and red, but his cheeks dry. Rhys softened all over to see it, to see the support and comfort he was getting, and it made him want to cry himself.

"Am I interrupting?" he asked.

Trevor pulled back and rolled his eyes. "Food is never interrupting. Like literally never."

Noah pouted a little as Rhys handed off the plate. "You get couch-side service, and meanwhile my boyfriend is suspiciously absent."

"Is putting out email fires regarding some suppliers. His words," Rhys said with his hands up in surrender.

Noah sighed, but grinned. "Oh fine, I guess I have to let him have this one." He went quiet as Rhys took his seat, then cleared his throat. "So, Trevor filled me in on the details. All the details," he clarified.

Rhys nodded, glancing at Trevor who resolutely stared down at his plate which told Rhys he'd talked about his miscarriage in detail. "Okay."

"First of all, I want to track down this fucker and t-take him out m-myself." The presence of his stutter told Rhys that Noah was still a little raw about the situation, and Rhys felt a pang of guilt for bringing this up all over again.

"Look, if it's too much for you, you know we've got this," Rhys stepped in. "I know you just went through hell with Barnes, and no one is expecting you to get involved."

Noah held up his hand, shaking his head as he took a few breaths. "It's not," he said, slow and measured. "It isn't too much, even if it is a lot. After what Charlie put me and Adrian through, then when Ryan was almost," he stopped abruptly and took a breath, obviously unable to finish his thought. "Now hearing this," he said and gestured toward Trevor, "I'm not about to sit quietly and do nothing."

"Yeah," Rhys said from behind a tense laugh. "Believe me, I get it."

"We're good though," Trevor said softly, reaching for Rhys' hand.

Noah nodded, then looked hesitant as he asked, "What about you, Trev? Not just mentally, but you lost your insurance."

Rhys frowned in confusion as he watched Trevor's face fall a little. "Oh. It's fine."

"I know how expensive that can get. If you need help, please just let us take care of some stuff," Noah pressed on.

Rhys' confusion only increased. "What are you talking about? What's expensive?"

"The appointments," Noah said as Trevor turned pink and looked slightly mortified. "All the testing, the doctor's visits, the meds."

Rhys felt like he'd been hit in the face with a sack of bricks. He knew Trevor was using hormones—hell, he'd accidentally walked in on him giving himself a jab twice, but the rest? "Appointments?"

Trevor shifted, pulling his hand away. "It's not a big deal, okay?"

"Have you been to the doctor?" Rhys pushed. "Since you've been living with me, have you been skipping appointments or tests or anything?"

"Can you drop it?" Trevor all-but shouted. He jumped up and ran his hand through his hair. "That's my business, okay? Just..." He clenched his hands into fists, then turned and stormed out.

A second later, they heard the back door slam, and Noah slumped back in his seat. "Fuck. I just made that worse."

"It wasn't you," Rhys said in a quiet tone. "I haven't been the best at navigating this whole thing. I've done as much research as I can, but I didn't realize," his words stopped, and he ran a hand down his face. "I can't imagine how much he resents this entire situation. He's broke, and he has no way to make up for what he lost, and right now there doesn't seem to be any hope of getting his life back."

Noah frowned, leaning forward over his legs. "Can I ask...why is he so broke? I know this isn't the highest paying job in the world, but the benefits were good, and he was full time. He shouldn't be destitute."

Rhys blinked, startled to death because he'd been so sure Trevor had told him everything. "He didn't tell you about that? About why he...fuck," he breathed out, shaking his head.

Noah's frown deepened into a scowl. "There's more going on here, isn't there."

"Yes, there is," came Trevor's voice in the doorway. They hadn't heard him come back in, and frankly Rhys hadn't been expecting him at all, let alone seconds after he'd stormed out. Trevor looked at them both, then chose a seat in the armchair, and Rhys did his best to pretend like the dismissal didn't sting. "Did you ever know Andrew and Mia Smith? They worked in the research labs, running that fertility study?"

Noah frowned. "It sounds familiar. I'm not sure why, but I think maybe? Esther might know them, she was friends with a lot of those guys down in STEM."

Trevor rubbed the back of his neck. "Well, I ended up getting involved in that. I." He cleared his throat and licked his lips, his gaze fixing at a point on the floor instead of at either of the other two men. "I was lonely, and my dating life was shit, and I asked Andrew if I could participate in the study. So I went off testosterone and I paid him nearly every dime I had in my savings, and I was impregnated."

Noah made a small noise, then leaned forward. "You're pregnant?"

Trevor winced, and Rhys felt his stomach twist with sympathy. "No, I'm not. It wasn't successful, and I didn't have the cash to try again. I figured it was fine, no harm no foul since no one was aware of it and I wasn't really out at work. But this person—whoever the fuck it is—they know. They sent me a copy of my first ultrasound with a threatening letter. They have access to all the information on the study, and they haven't said what they want, but this is what they have on me."

Noah swallowed thickly. "Is it illegal? What you did?"

"It's definitely the sort of thing that would keep me from ever working at a University ever again. It went against pretty much every code of ethics in the research labs, and if I get outed, so will Andrew. He and Mia will lose all their funding, and I'll never work again."

Noah rubbed at his prosthetic eye, blinking rapidly. "What can we do?"

"I don't know," Trevor said helplessly. "Even if we can find who this person is, he can still expose me—he can expose the entire project."

"Maybe," Noah said, and Rhys gave him a careful look. "Charlie had shit on me too, but when Cole got into the accounts to track down evidence, he managed to erase all traces of proof that I had committed any wrongdoing. Even though Adrian wasn't my student, he still was one, and there was plenty of evidence on my phone that he and I were more than just casually acquainted. Cole took care of it all."

Trevor's eyes went wide. "He's that good?"

Noah laughed. "He's that good. He's better, I think. It's complicated now, with all the shit that came out about him, so I'm not sure how much help he'd be without access to those systems. But if he can get access, he can protect you."

"I might know a guy who can help," Rhys said very softly, hoping Trevor wouldn't get upset again at the thought of Ivan helping them.

Right in that moment, the front door opened and Ryan walked in, Cole a step behind holding his shoulder. They looked blissful, euphoric, but also a little terrified, and as much as Rhys wanted to jump up and demand they get to work, he knew it wasn't the time. He gave Noah a significant look, and Noah gave a nod in return. They'd ask. Eventually. Just not now.

17.

The tension between them on the drive home was palpable. Trevor was reeling from Rhys' discovery of his situation with the testosterone, and the way he'd been too forceful in his questions. But he also understood Rhys was coming from a place of love, and he had to make allowances for that. He couldn't do anything but admit his reluctance was out of pride, and out of shame that his situation had fallen so far off his path, he couldn't find his way back.

As they got inside the house, Trevor hesitated in the living room while Rhys put his keys and wallet on the side table. When he turned, he saw Rhys watching him with hooded eyes, his face unreadable.

"I'm sorry," Trevor said after a moment. "I shouldn't have gotten so angry."

Rhys looked startled, and he quickly closed the distance between them. "You are not apologizing because I was an insensitive ass. I was just…I was angry at myself because I hadn't realized how much more you were suffering, and I didn't know how to handle it." He lifted his hand, then hesitated, so Trevor pushed his cheek against Rhys' warm palm and sighed. Rhys' shoulders drained of some tension, and he used his other hand to drag him closer. "Please don't be sorry, but also please let me help."

Trevor shook his head. "Look, I'm a little behind, but my doctor gave me an extra month's supply, and if I have to skip in for a little while until I can afford the appointment…"

"If you had an illness which required treatment—MS, diabetes, anything—would you be saying the same thing?" Rhys pushed.

Trevor clenched his jaw. "That's not the same."

"It is," Rhys insisted. "It *is* the same. I know being transgender isn't a disease, but it *is* something that requires medical treatment, which you're denying yourself, and that's exactly what this fucker wants. He's trying to ruin you, to force you into a place where you don't belong. I know it sucks to think about how much more I have than you, how much more freedom in my own body, in my bank account, in my life. I can't imagine how much that fucking sucks, but one thing I do know is that if the situation was reversed, you wouldn't hesitate in offering it to me."

Trevor bowed his head and didn't argue because it was true. It was all completely, achingly, absolutely true. He wouldn't have even given Rhys the option. "I just hate this so much," he said, his voice barely above a whisper.

Rhys dug his hand into Trevor's hair, holding it firm, though not painfully tight. "I know," he said fiercely. "And someday that situation is going to change, and it won't be like this anymore. But right now it is, and I'm not going to stand here while you suffer even more. So let me help. For the love of god, call the doctor, let me write a fucking check, and you get what you need. Okay?"

Trevor felt his throat get tight, but he nodded and forced himself to look into Rhys' pleading eyes. "Okay."

Rhys' entire body deflated at the concession, and as though he couldn't help himself, he dragged Trevor in for a kiss deeper, more passionate than it had been in weeks. It was full of relief, and need, and want, and Trevor gave himself over to it completely.

"I want you," he murmured against Rhys' mouth. "I want..."

"Anything," Rhys insisted, kissing him again, then again, and again. "Anything you want, it's yours."

"I want to be inside you, I want to fuck you."

Rhys groaned, shoving his face into Trevor's neck and gently biting down. "Yes," he murmured against Trevor's flush-warm skin. "Yes. Do you have...do you need to..."

"My room," Trevor said, then dragged his hands down to meet Rhys', tangling their fingers together in a tight hold. He took several steps backward, Rhys following without losing contact, and after a short eternity of fumbling along, they made it to the bedroom.

Trevor would be the worst liar if he tried to say he hadn't planned for that moment right there. Maybe not then, maybe not right away, but there was a reason he'd dug up that specific box and had it within easy reach of the bed. He nudged Rhys to the mattress, and the two of them collapsed on the unmade duvet, hands roaming, pulling at shirts, unbuttoning jeans, grasping at bare skin, and nipping at exposed necklines.

When Trevor's hand went for the front of Rhys' pants, Rhys' fingers stopped him with a gentle squeeze. "Before we do this," he said, his words strained faintly with his obvious effort to put a pause on their actions, "I need to know that you're sure about this. Because you said before you wanted to wait."

Trevor bit the inside of his cheek, cursing himself for denying the thing he wanted most. "I know I did, but I do want this."

Rhys cupped Trevor's face between both hands and looked him in the eyes. "I don't want you to regret anything with me, Trevor. You know how I feel about you, and I don't want to live with knowing you would take back this moment if you could."

Trevor swallowed thickly, leaning in to take the kiss he desperately needed before he could form the words to put Rhys' mind at ease. "I won't regret this. The only regret I'll ever have is denying myself being with you. I've wanted it since the moment I set foot in your office, but I was afraid. Maybe I was punishing myself," he shrugged as he kissed Rhys quickly once more. "But I'm done. Tonight, watching Ryan and Cole together, it made me realize that I have no idea what the future will be like, and I'm not about to waste another minute. I...I love you, okay? I do."

Rhys' eyes squeezed shut, like hearing the words were painful, but before Trevor could try to take them back, Rhys leaned in and kissed him. Hard. For all that he was worth. "I love you too. *So* much."

It made Trevor's head spin, made him feel more wanted than he ever had before that moment, and he clutched at Rhys' hips, his own seeking some sort of friction for the throbbing between his legs. With one hand out, he grappled for the lube which was in the bedside table, and he pressed the mostly-full bottle into Rhys' palm.

"Can you start getting yourself ready while I..." He trailed off, his eyes darting to the side of the bed.

Rhys bit his lower lip, nodding as he rolled onto his side, pouring a generous amount of the clear gel on his fingers. Trevor started to get up, but he found himself captivated by the sight of Rhys reaching behind himself. He couldn't see it, but the way his arm moved, the way his eyes closed, head tipped back, the soft groan from his lips, Trevor knew Rhys had breached himself with at least one finger. Maybe two. He could hear a soft noise of friction, and he knew that once he strapped the cock on, that would be him there instead of Rhys' hand, and it was enough to make his own dick throb between his folds. He squeezed his thighs together as he swung his legs over the bed, then took a moment to collect himself as he searched for the box.

It wasn't far, just behind one of books, and he quickly pulled the top off. The thing nestled inside had been cleaned and sterilized—used only once and then never again. It was rare he found cis lovers who were in any way interested in being fucked like this, and he knew it meant something that Rhys was so damn eager. Something about Rhys made him feel good, made him feel strong and manly, and his therapist would probably have him unpack that later, but for now, he was just going to enjoy.

He glanced over at Rhys who was working himself hard, his hips thrusting back against his own hand, and Trevor had to bite down on his cheek again to keep himself away from the edge. *One of these days*, he thought, *I want to bring myself off while watching him. I want to feel myself pulse and come all over my hand as Rhys fucks himself.*

He shuddered with need, then quickly reached for the harness. It slipped on easily, belting into place with a tight fit, and he turned himself side to side to make sure it was snug. The vibrator, which would stimulate him, was wedged between his folds against his own dick, and he gave it a quick test. He grunted as a wave of pleasure hit him, and he glanced back over to see Rhys watching him with dark, desperate eyes.

"You like this?" Trevor asked. He reached for the silicone dick and held it out for his inspection. It was the same color as his own flesh, veiny and circumcised, and he thumbed the tip as Rhys' cheeks went faintly pink. "This is what's going in you."

"Can I stroke it?" Rhys asked. His hand was still working himself, but he stretched the other out and Trevor let it press against his palm. He felt another wave of erotic pleasure wash over him just by watching Rhys treat it like it was flesh, like it was part of him. Trevor had been with several men, and none had showed any of his toys reverence in that way.

He swallowed back feelings that he wasn't in the mood to examine just yet, and he quickly pulled away to ready himself. As he got the cock situated, Rhys turned himself onto his stomach, grasping a pillow for his midsection. His hand had finally pulled away, but with his ass exposed, Trevor could see his hole slick and slightly open, waiting for him.

"Fuck," he gasped, bucking his hips into the air a little. "God, fuck, you're so hot."

Rhys smiled a little as he turned his head to look at Trevor. "So are you. And I'm ready."

Trevor swallowed thickly, nerves suddenly hitting him because he was so in love with Rhys, and he wanted this to be good. He wanted Rhys to lose his mind, to be taken somewhere he would never, ever forget. He wanted Rhys to look back and know that Trevor had been able to give him something no one else had.

He wanted Rhys, and he meant to keep him. With shaking fingers, he took the lube, pouring a generous amount in his palm. He warmed it between both hands, then slicked up the cock and put one knee on the bed. His hand reached for Rhys' hip, and Rhys fucked his hips into the pillow propping him up.

"Hurry. Please just...hurry."

Trevor wasn't entirely capable of words, so he used his hands to push Rhys' legs together slightly, then reached up to part his cheeks. With one hand, he took the tip of the cock and rubbed it up and down the crack, and when Rhys let out a desperate moan, he pushed himself against Rhys' hole and sank down until the tip was just inside.

"Shit, shit, god, I can feel you," Rhys babbled, his face down, hands curled into fists in the sheets. "I've wanted you for so long, and I can finally feel you. *Trevor*," he whispered.

Trevor turned the vibrator on, and the shock of it traveled down the cock and straight into Rhys' ass. Rhys bucked wildly, pushing back, desperate for friction, and Trevor had to steady him with two firm hands.

"Let me take the lead," he said softly, though what he wanted more than anything was to just pound him into the mattress until they were both screaming each other's name, coming. But more than that, he wanted to take his time. He gave another nudge forward, and then another. It was a sweet, aching agony of shallow thrusts which carried on and on before he was fully sheathed. He was seconds from his first orgasm, he could feel it. He wasn't sure how close Rhys was, but he didn't think the other man would last long.

"I need you to move," Rhys finally managed. He gave a tiny thrust backward. "Please. I feel like I'm going to rip in half if you don't move."

It was all Trevor needed to get going, to pick up a firm, steady pace. He relished the sound of his hips slapping against Rhys', threw his head back as his orgasm hit, crying Rhys' name into the dim light of the room.

"I'm," Rhys managed to say. He was fucking his hips wildly into the pillow, and Trevor let himself imagine the beading precome smearing all over the pillow case, the cock throbbing against what couldn't have been nearly enough pressure. But Rhys didn't ask for more, he just kept pushing back, seeking more friction that way. Then one hand flew back, reaching for Trevor's ass to hold him in place, and Trevor could feel the way Rhys' entire body started to shudder. "Coming," he gasped. "I'm coming."

Trevor reached his second orgasm just as Rhys spilled all over the pillow, and the pair of them collapsed forward, Trevor barely holding himself up as he pressed his forehead to the center of Rhys' back.

"Jesus," Rhys said, his voice breathless and hoarse. "Jesus. That...I've never felt like that before."

Trevor had, but not with anyone who wasn't Rhys. Each of their love-making had been better than the last, and he could only imagine how better it would be once they'd learned each other's bodies without hesitation or restraint.

And god, how he wanted that. God, how he *needed* it.

He pulled out carefully, unbuckling the straps and carefully dropping everything into the box to get cleaned later. Right now, wild dogs couldn't have dragged him from the bed, or from Rhys' arms which pulled him tight, and close. The soiled pillow was flung to the end of the bed, and the pair of them curled up on the one remaining between them.

As the room began to chill his sweat-soaked skin, Trevor dared to open his eyes and found Rhys looking back at him. Rhys' hand lifted, brushing a few damp locks from his forehead, a gentle smile playing at the corners of his mouth.

"Did you mean what you said earlier? That you want to keep going forward with me?" Rhys asked after a long silence. "Because I respect why you wanted to wait, but I don't know if I have the strength to keep walking away."

Trevor felt his heart twist, knowing that so much of Rhys' distrust in him was his own fault. He'd pulled him in, pushed him away, then pulled him in again—and though Rhys understood, it only made sense he would be cautious. He curled his fingers in toward his palm, then dragged his knuckles along Rhys' jaw as he took in the sight of him—sweaty, pink in the cheeks, eyes bright and intense. He well and truly loved this man.

"I meant it," he said, and he felt Rhys relax a little. "I am falling in love with you, and I do want to be with you. I'm done living in fear and done denying myself happiness where I can find it. I'm also grateful you went out on a limb for me—with letting me stay here, with Cole, giving me a group of people who treat me like family. If I'm going to put my life back together, I need to start somewhere, and...and I don't know what I would have done if you hadn't been patient."

Rhys chuckled, pinching Trevor's chin between his fingers, and gave him a stern look. "You're worth it, babe. Okay? I'd wait forever if I have to."

"Well you don't need to wait that long," Trevor said, and pulled Rhys into his arms. "You have me now."

***

Trevor felt a little apprehensive about accepting Noah's invitation to breakfast, but Rhys insisted he go. "It'll be good for you to reconnect with him. You have more than just me in your corner here, and Noah is a good reminder of that."

He didn't exactly have a come-back to that, so he got dressed and headed to the little café not far from Rhys'. Noah was already there waiting for him with a cup of coffee, and the moment he sat down, the server arrived to get his order.

There were a few moments of awkward silence, then Noah chuckled. "It didn't used to be this difficult to talk to each other, did it?"

Trevor grinned at him. "No, but I used to hit on you a little, and that feels really weird now."

Noah shook his head, hiding his smile in his cup. "I always kind of liked it. I think mostly because I knew you weren't really interested in me, but you made me feel attractive and worth it when things were shitty."

Trevor wasn't expecting that, and he felt a burst of warm affection toward his old friend. "I'm glad I could help. I liked having that with you. You were one of the few people in the department who made me feel safe."

Noah's expression turned serious, and he set his cup down, reaching over to put his hand over Trevor's. "I'm sorry the others didn't. And you know I'm here for you now, right? For whatever you need?"

Trevor licked his lips, letting out a small sigh. "I do. Part of me just feels like it's never going to be over. Like whoever the hell this is will never be caught, and I'm going to spend the rest of my life looking over my shoulder."

"I do know," Noah said, and Trevor was profoundly aware Noah had experienced those exact same feelings. "But it will end. Actually, one of the reasons I wanted you to come out today was to tell you that Cole wants to meet up with you and talk."

Trevor's eyes widened with slight surprise. "Seriously? Why? I mean, we haven't even spoken to him yet."

"I think Wes might have," Noah said, a little caution in his tone. "I don't think Wes told him everything, but he probably told him enough. Cole told me thinks he can help. He thought you could pop by his work today and you can chat for a bit. He knows how hard it is to spill your secrets to a total stranger, so he thought it might be a good neutral place to go over everything. Only what you're comfortable with," Noah added, holding up his hands in surrender.

Trevor wasn't really sure how he felt. He hadn't exactly given tacit permission for everyone to talk amongst themselves, but there was a small measurer of relief in knowing he didn't have to break the ice with Cole. Trevor was in a position where he was being forced to deal with people he didn't know well, and he'd take these moments where he could get them. "Do you think he'll really be able to find anything?"

"He did for me," Noah said. "I owe him…*god*, I owe him so much. He might not have the same resources as he did before, but he has the skills, and I think it's worth a shot. I don't want you to keep suffering like this, Trev. When I found out you were going through all this…"

"Better than thinking I was fucking my students, right?" Trevor cut in, and he let a hint of bitterness creep into his tone. He didn't want to make Noah feel bad, but he couldn't deny how badly it had stung when everyone he'd been working with had so readily believed he was capable of taking advantage of his students.

For his part, Noah flushed and looked down. "I never," he stopped and met Trevor's eyes steadily. "I don't think I ever believed it," he finished, measuring his words carefully. "I knew you. I couldn't imagine it was this, but I could never let myself believe what they said about you was true. The only reason I didn't try to find you was because Barnes had me by the throat. The last thing in the world I wanted was to turn his attention onto someone else. But if I had known what was really happening, I wouldn't have left you out there alone. I swear."

There was such sincerity in Noah's tone, Trevor was almost bowled over with a sense of relief. "Thank you," he muttered.

Noah shook his head. "It's only fair that I trusted and believed you. You stood up for me when a lot of people refused to. But more than that," he said, leaning forward, "you don't deserve anything that's happening to you right now. And if I can help, then I'm going to."

18.

Trevor was a little surprised to find himself pulling into the parking lot of an old elementary school. The place looked pretty deserted, a few of the windows knocked out and boarded up, but there were a handful of cars parked around him, so he assumed it was the place. Noah had assured him Cole was expecting him, so Trevor got out and slowly made his way to the front doors.

Taped next to the window was a weathered bit of paper with the words, **AbleTech Inc**, printed in the center, and beyond that he could make out a person sitting behind a desk in the lobby. He pulled the door open, and the woman looked up, smiling at him as he approached.

"Can I help you?" she asked, her voice soft.

Trevor rubbed at the back of his neck. "Yeah uh, I'm here to meet Cole Price?"

"Trevor, hey," came a voice to his right. Trevor turned to see Cole coming down the hallway, his hand holding the harness of his guide dog, and he was smiling. "Noah texted and said you were on your way."

Trevor smiled at the receptionist, then walked to meet Cole halfway. "Yeah. He said now as a good time."

"Absolutely," Cole said, coming to a stop. "You alright?"

Trevor shrugged. "It's been a day, but not all bad. Are you sure I'm not interrupting?"

Cole chuckled, motioning for him to follow as he turned to walk back down the hallway. "Not at all. Nate—one of the guys who started the place—he and I are going to be testing the new software on the smartcane, so it's a perfect time for us to chat."

Trevor had no idea what any of that meant, but he was happy to follow Cole along the small maze of hallways until they reached a door which led to a courtyard. He could tell once upon a time it had been a playground, but it was gutted and emptied of children's equipment, replaced with grass, a winding stretch of pavement, and a lot of orange cones set up in various places.

"This is the obstacle course," Cole explained as he led the way to a bench which held a couple of white canes. "We're testing a product that a person will connect to Bluetooth through an earbud and alert the user to things in their path. Stuff a normal cane can't."

Trevor's eyebrows went up. "Wow, that's pretty badass."

Cole chuckled. "It is. It's been fairly buggy so far, but we're hoping by the end of the quarter, we have something we can present at a couple of tech conferences. We're hoping to get a little more grant money this year since there are about seven other products we want to get to market along with it." With that, Cole bent down and unhooked Kevin from the harness and commanded him to run off. The dog didn't need telling twice, his tongue lolling out as he took off at a loping gallop.

"Likes to be free?" Trevor asked.

Cole snorted a laugh. "He likes having most of the yard to fuck off in." He put his hand on the table, then felt out for one of the canes. "I think he likes this place a lot better than my old office."

Trevor bit his lip, having heard the story about what Cole had been through, how a man had faked Cole's enlistment in order to con him into helping recover some classified information. It had resulted in Cole's daughter and Ryan being kidnapped and nearly killed, and Trevor wasn't sure how Cole was so okay after that ordeal.

"Do you," he started, then hesitated for a breath. "Do you like this? This new job? I mean, it's totally different to what you were doing before, right?"

Cole shrugged as he leaned against the table and fiddle with the small white box on the handle of the cane. "When I joined with the Marines, all I knew was that I was good at computers. I had no idea what I was going to do once I was out. Honestly, I hadn't planned on ever leaving, not until I was too old to serve. Then I was blinded and…well, you know the rest, don't you?"

"Yeah," Trevor said.

Cole dragged a hand through his hair. "After that, I felt a bit lost. Then Wes introduced me to Evan and Nate, and all of this fell in my lap. I was a little bitter at first. I felt like I wasn't being allowed to escape the identity of being a *blind* man, and then I realized it was stupid to think that way. This could make my life loads easier, and the lives of so many other people. And I'm good at it. I've not been given this job out of pity, I've been given it out of skill, and that meant everything."

Trevor licked his lips, his shoulders sagging a little. "I don't know if I'll ever find something like that. If I can't find my way out of this mess," he stopped when his voice cracked, then went on at a whisper, "I don't want to work behind a bar for the rest of my life."

Cole set the cane down and reached for him, taking his wrist and squeezing it gently. "That's not going to happen."

"I've never really been good at a trade," Trevor told him. "I had a weird talent for archaic languages, and ancient history was something I understood in ways I didn't understand anything else. But that's good for exactly one thing, and right now that's so far out of reach, I don't know if I'll ever get there again."

"And that's why you're here with me," Cole told him firmly. "I don't know how much help I can be, but I'm going to try absolutely everything in my power to find out whatever I can. It's not over and you're not giving up."

"No," Trevor told him. "I swear I'm not."

Cole grinned and released his arm. "Good. Now, Nate's going to be out here in a minute and we're going to spend a little while testing this stuff, then you and I can talk a little more. Sound okay?"

Trevor couldn't help smiling back. "Sounds perfect."

***

Trevor grinned at the sound of Cole's laughter, and the startled tone in his voice. "I can't believe you got it to work that efficiently. Bloody hell, mate, that's amazing."

"Did you get the numbers on that one?" Nate asked Trevor, who had volunteered to take down the distances between obstacles the cane's software had alerted the user to.

"I did," Trevor answered after giving a nod, then remembering neither man could see him. "Do you want me to enter them?"

"Not yet," Nate said. He touched Cole's arm, then replaced the sonic cane with his previous one. "I need to call Evan and have him adjust a couple of things in the system, then send me a refresh signal. Give me ten minutes."

"I'll give you twenty," Cole said, swiping a hand across his brow. "I need a little sit down."

Trevor tucked his notepad under his arm and walked up to Cole's side. "Need directions to the bench?"

Cole gave him a grateful smile and extended his hand to take Trevor's shoulder. "Ta, mate. Adrian had me flat on my arse nearly half the night last night, and my brain is exhausted. I'm amazed I was able to get here today without collapsing."

Trevor chuckled as he led Cole over to the table, and grinned wider at Cole's grateful sigh as he eased down onto the bench. "He's a little terrifying, I'm not gonna lie. I've only been working with him for a little while, but my future looks kind of painful."

Cole snorted a laugh as he felt for his water, then uncapped it and took a long drink. "I know that feeling. When I first started down at Baum's, I wasn't sure I would ever get through the initial training. Now I'm prepping for an actual fight."

"Are you nervous to do it?" Trevor asked, sitting down next to him.

"Fighting in general, or fighting blind?" Cole asked.

Trevor appreciated the way he didn't beat around the bush when it came to his disability. "Both, I guess. I mean, were you a fighter before?"

"I had skills from basic training, and I worked out a lot, but I'd never done anything like this before. Not for fun or sport. In the Marines, I was the tech guy and spent most of my time in a tiny, cold room monitoring transmissions and code. But Adrian's made me feel..." He hesitated, then shrugged as he rubbed the back of his neck. "Training with him made me feel freer than anything else my occupational therapists have given me. Not that I don't appreciate being able to make eggs or a cuppa without scalding myself, but this is more. And Wes' place has a way of letting you feel like a person, rather than a condition first, and person second."

"I get that," Trevor said quietly. And he did. Not in the same way, but he knew once people found out he was trans, he lost manhood in their eyes. Even the strongest allies who never misused his pronouns still saw him as something *other*. But training with Wes, then starting with Adrian, hadn't felt like that at all. He just felt like himself—welcomed, and brave, and willing. He'd gotten a few knocks to the face by Adrian during their short sparring sessions, and it shouldn't have left him elated, but it did.

"May I ask you something?" Cole ventured after a beat of silence.

Trevor couldn't help his small laugh, and when Cole frowned, he waved him off and said, "Every time someone asks me that, it's usually about either about me being trans, or the whole blackmail thing."

Cole's lip quirked to the side, and he shrugged. "Do you want to go back to work exactly where you were before all this happened? Or do you want your name cleared so you can start over somewhere new?"

Trevor felt a small push of surprise. "I...shit. I don't know. I think in the back of my mind I just wanted things to go back to the way they were, but I'm not sure if that's possible now."

"It can be," Cole told him. "If you want it to."

Trevor startled a little. "You sound so sure of that."

"I am," Cole told him frankly. "It'll take some work, but trust me, it's possible. It's really about what you want, in the end."

"I wish it was an easier question to answer," Trevor admitted. "I don't know what I want right now."

"You have some time," Cole reminded him. "I'm here to help you however you need me."

Trevor flushed a little and bowed his head. "I seriously don't know how to thank you for that. I would have come to you sooner, but I didn't want to unload a ton of work on you while you and Ryan were still trying to get your shit back together."

Cole laughed, his head shaking a little. "I appreciate that, believe me. It's...been interesting, settling into an actual civilian life and trying to navigate a new, proper relationship. But being able to work here with Nate, and having something that's just mine, it's helped me get back on my feet. Did Noah mention that I won't have the same access to systems I had before, though? I still have quite a bit of hacking skills, but there are places I just won't be able to get into without someone who has some sort of access already."

"Yeah," Trevor said. "Rhys and I talked about it, and he said he has a friend in law enforcement who could help with that."

Cole surprised Trevor by scowling. "I think I know who you mean. Ivan Perez?"

"Yeah." Trevor said carefully.

"Chief of police, good looking, used to shag my boyfriend?" There was some humor and some tension in Cole's tone, and it made Trevor laugh.

"Yeah, that's the one. Right before I met you, Rhys went out to dinner with the guy, to see if he'd be able to dig some shit up for me," Trevor said, still smiling, "and they sort of...hooked up a little bit."

Cole's eyebrows shot straight up. "You're having me on."

"Nope. To be fair," Trevor added, "it didn't last, and Rhys only went on the date because he didn't think he and I would ever be together. But I almost went insane from jealousy."

"I would have," Cole said fiercely. "If I thought I was on the verge of losing Ryan..."

Trevor shook his head. "See, that's the thing, he wasn't into the guy. But I was the idiot who kept pushing him away. We worked it out, obviously, but that was kind of the catalyst. I knew then I didn't want anyone to have the freedom to kiss Rhys who wasn't me."

Cole's mouth softened into a little grin. "Fair enough. I still don't look forward to working with the man who used to shove it up my boyfriend's arse. But if he's helping you, I think I can handle it."

Trevor chuckled. "And from what Rhys says, Ivan and Ryan have been over for a long while. And anyone can see how crazy Ryan is for you."

Cole's smile widened. "Oh, I know. Even I can, and I'm a man with no eyes."

Trevor choked a little, then shook his head with a wide grin. "Thank you though, for helping out. This has been a total nightmare and I'm just...I'm ready to wake up."

Cole reached out and gave his fingers a squeeze. "I'll do everything in my power to find something. It might not be much, but..."

"But it'll be a place to start," Trevor said, and he knew that's all he could really ask for.

19.

Rhys could see Trevor's knee bouncing up and down, and he reached over, laying his hand down firmly on his thigh. When Trevor's motions calmed, Rhys smiled at him, though he was pretty sure his next suggestion was going to kick up Trevor's anxiety all over again.

"I need you to consider something," he said carefully.

Trevor was quiet a long moment. "Okay."

Licking his lips, Rhys dared a glance over before looking back at the traffic in front of him. "You need to consider getting in touch with the people who ran that fertility test."

He heard Trevor's sharp intake of air and felt his thigh tense. "Why? Why would I do that?"

"Because the person going after you has access to your files," Rhys said. "I don't mean this to sound harsh, I really don't, but it should have been the first place we looked."

Trevor groaned, passing a hand down his face, then he leaned his head against the window with a thump. "I know," he breathed out. "I know, and it's been in the back of my head this entire time, but I've been afraid."

"Of what?" Rhys pushed gently, wanting to see where Trevor's head was at. He had some theories, but he didn't want to assume.

"I let myself get close to them, trusted them, and if somehow they've been part of it," Trevor admitted trailing off.

Rhys nodded, because that was the first place his own mind had gone. "But if it is them, we can take care of this problem."

"But if it isn't?" Trevor asked.

"If it isn't, maybe he knows something. Maybe he was targeted too," Rhys suggested. "Weren't more people fired along with you for the same thing?"

Trevor made a soft, curious noise. "Yeah, though I never did get to find out who else. But…" He trailed off a moment, looking thoughtful. "Is Noah going to be here tonight?"

Rhys lifted a brow at the topic change, but he nodded his head. "Yeah, Ryan and Cole invited pretty much everyone. Why?"

"Because Noah was working at the University way before me, and he has a friend there who works in admin. She might not be able to tell me, but I bet she'd be willing to tell Noah who was let go. At the very least, if anyone in his building was fired."

"You mean Esther," he said, half smiling. He had known Esther and Sabrina for years. "It's worth a shot, and I know she'll be willing to help. She loves Noah." He felt a small surge of happiness that Trevor was willing to go forward, even when it didn't involve Cole's hacking skills or Ivan' database access. He was starting to worry that Trevor was getting complacent, accepting this as his fate because it was easier than fighting, and he didn't want Trevor to give up. He'd take him, no matter how their lives looked, but Trevor deserved better.

Cole's place wasn't too far from Rhys', and they found a parking spot at the curb not far from the front door. There was a ramp set up over the front stoop which led to the door, and it was cracked open. A few cars were already parked, and Rhys was glad they wouldn't be the first there since they would be the last to leave. Cole promised to do some minor research to get started as Rhys was waiting for Ivan to get back to him, and Trevor had agreed to get started right away.

"I think that's Adrian's bike," Rhys said, nodding to the motorcycle parked off to the side of the garage. "Why don't you go ask Noah about Esther right now and get it over with, then we can relax and enjoy the rest of the evening."

Trevor nodded, though he looked a little hesitant as he pushed his door open and stepped out. He waited for Rhys to take his hand, which was a good sign he wasn't shutting down. They made their way in and found Adrian and Ryan in the living room with drinks in their hands.

"Hey," Ryan said, standing up. "Glad you could make it."

"Hey man," Trevor said, nodding. "Is uh…is Noah here?"

"Kitchen with Cole," Adrian said. "Wes has the kids and the dogs outside, and I think Cole and Noah are putting together the stuff to grill."

Trevor gave Rhys a pointed look, then nodded firmly and walked into the other room. Rhys felt something tight in his chest, an urge to follow and hold him and make sure he was going to get through this okay, but he forced himself to take a seat instead. He was profoundly aware of the way Ryan and Adrian were staring at him, but he ignored it.

Unfortunately, Ryan wasn't the kind of guy willing to let things go. "Are you two fighting?"

Rhys rolled his eyes. "No, asshole. We're not fighting. He needs to ask Noah something. About the whole mass firing of people from the University."

Both Ryan and Adrian looked startled. "Is there something new?" Adrian asked, worry in his voice.

"No, but we may have tracked down a possible lead on the person going after him, and Noah's kind of the interim." When they looked confused, Rhys sighed. "Esther and Sabrina. They always know everything about everyone, and we need to see if the team in the research lab was fired."

Adrian looked relaxed again, and he chuckled. "Yeah, if there's anything to know, those two will be able to find it. And they'll tell Noah anything he wants."

"No one ever tells that asshole no," Ryan said, but he said it with a grin. "So, everything else is okay?"

"Better every day. Especially since he started working out. I owe you and Wes free legal representation for life," he said to Adrian who laughed. "Seriously, man. It's not exactly Trevor's dream anything, but he's been handling shit a lot better since he's been able to work out his frustrations."

Adrian shrugged, leaning back against the sofa cushion. "Wes does that. He's like everyone's pseudo-dad. And honestly, Trevor has a lot of talent. He'll be good at this if he wants to be."

Rhys smiled softly at him. "I think he might be changing his mind on how he really feels about boxing. And that's entirely your fault."

Adrian shrugged. "I'll gladly take the blame."

"Is Anna here?" Rhys asked after a minute, slightly eager to change the topic for a little while.

Adrian's face fell a little. "No. This pregnancy is kicking her ass. Because it's twins, her bedrest has been extended to pretty much until she gives birth. She is not happy."

"Yeah, I've been avoiding their place like the plague," Ryan said with a slight shudder. "I think Wes is using every chance he can get to stay out of the house."

Rhys laughed softly. "That's great though. Twins."

"I think they're both scared as hell," Adrian said, but he was smiling like the proud uncle he was. "I'm excited, though. I get two new babies to spoil *and* I get to give them back when they're being little shits."

Rhys felt a little pang in his chest, a momentary mourning of what he had so desperately wanted. In hindsight, he was grateful it hadn't been with Vanessa, but he considered his future with Trevor and wasn't sure his new lover would be interested in attempting that road again. Rhys could be happy without kids. If he was in love, if he was content in his relationship, it was a compromise he was willing to make.

And maybe the universe was telling him it just wasn't in the cards.

"You okay?" Adrian asked.

Rhys realized he'd gone very quiet, and he offered a smile, shrugging. "Yeah. I'm hoping to play the fun uncle one day since I don't think there are kids in my future." He gave his brother a significant look who pointedly looked away.

Adrian opened his mouth, maybe to argue, or to offer some sort of condolence, but his words were cut off when Noah and Trevor walked back into the room. Adrian's face immediately went soft, his arm coming around Noah's waist and tucking him in close. "Hey, you."

Trevor approached Rhys with far more hesitation than a familiar lover, but Rhys didn't mind it too much. He wasn't entirely sure how to act in public since it was so new, and the last thing he wanted was for Trevor to feel uncomfortable.

"Everything good?" Rhys asked quietly.

Trevor nodded. "Noah said he'd make a couple calls."

"And Cole said he's ready to look into a few things after everyone else heads out," Ryan told him. "He was able to check into a couple of the old tracking systems he used, and he thinks he can at least get a path back to whoever was sending Barnes instructions. *If* they happened by email," he added.

Trevor bit his lip. "The only thing that worries me is the person has only ever used hard copies. He might actually know better than to keep evidence on his computer the way Charlie did."

Rhys reached for his hand and squeezed his fingers. "That might be the case, but it can't hurt to try."

***

Wes didn't hang out long past dinner. Maggie was getting cranky, and Claire wasn't thrilled about a fussy playmate, so she didn't fight them leaving too hard. Adrian and Noah left not long after, likely knowing that they were eager to get started on the investigation.

"I'm going to take this one to bed," Ryan said, grabbing Claire's hand and spinning her in a circle.

Claire giggled, attaching herself to Ryan's leg, and Rhys was struck by a moment of wonder at his brother falling so effortlessly into a father-like role. Of all the people in the world Rhys could have pictured as a parent, Ryan wasn't one of them. He was happy for his brother, and so envious he could taste it.

"When's mummy coming home?" Claire asked as Ryan started to lead her away.

"Tuesday, sweetheart." Ryan's voice fell into a faint murmur, and Rhys looked over at Cole who was leaning against the counter, his face resting in a soft smile.

After a beat, Cole reached for the dog dish on the counter and felt around for the little stool. "Alright, let me get Kevin set up, then we can head to my office and we can start."

Trevor gave Rhys a slightly panicked look, but he cleared his throat and nodded. "Yeah, cool. I mean, I don't think we'll be able to find anything but…"

"I wouldn't give up hope just yet," Cole said before Trevor could spiral. He filled his dog's dish with water and food, then put his hand against the wall, leading himself to the doorway.

"There's a lot to find that people don't even realize is there. Every time you access someone's records, it leaves a footprint. We just look for the odd-one out, and that'll give us some clue as to who or what we're looking for."

Trevor blinked in surprise, reaching for Rhys' hand as they followed Cole to the office where his computer was set up on an L-shaped desk. There were two office chairs off to the side, and then the rolling chair Cole eased into in front of the monitor.

Reaching for a set of earbuds, Cole put one into his left ear, then pushed a long, silver mechanism to the front of the keyboard. "You said all your threats were through written letters and through Barnes, right?"

"Yeah," Trevor breathed out. Rhys saw the way his knee was bouncing, and he reached over, gently pressing his hand over Trevor's thigh. He gave Rhys a grateful smile before he went on. "Mostly letters. Charlie only came to see me once, and he didn't say much about how he'd been contacted, but my guess would be that it was also in person."

Cole hummed in thought, then reached for his computer. Rhys could hear it turn on, but the monitor remained dark. There was a faint shuffling noise, and Rhys saw little dots appear on the silver and black bit, and Cole's fingers ran over it, reading the braille. "I can't guarantee I'll be able to access Barnes' email address without being found out, and my contacts can only cover up so much. Especially since there's still active charges pending against him. You've never been contacted online at all?"

Trevor shook his head. "No."

"What about personal accounts? Has the person tried to hack into your credit cards, bank, email, anything like that?"

Trevor started to shake his head, then his eyes widened. "Actually...I mean, I think they were able to get into my rental history, if that counts?"

"What do you mean?" Cole asked, his brows dipping in a frown.

"I don't know if it's the same in England, but when you rent here, they run your name through this database. It's sort of like your credit, only it checks your rental history and background. After I got evicted, I tried to rent a few places, but whatever they pulled up on the report caused them to deny me. Is that something?"

Cole's lips twitched up into a grin. "That's something. That's absolutely something. If someone's messed with your background check, I'll be able to trace it."

"What do you need from me?" Trevor asked, and Rhys felt a sudden wave of gratitude because for the first time in a long while, Trevor sounded hopeful.

20.

When Cole said it was going to take most of the night, Rhys insisted they head home and come back in the morning to see how it went. Esther and Samantha were still looking into the history of the other people who had been fired during the whole sweep, and there was always the option of Ivan if all of those things turned into a dead end.

Still, Trevor couldn't help but feel like the night had been a total wash. Yes, it had been nice to get together with everyone, and yes there was a level of safety and comfort with being accepted into this strange little family Rhys had brought with him when he took Trevor in. But Trevor was tired of feeling like he was making no progress. In spite of the way things were going between the two of them, he hadn't changed his mind. Not about starting to look for a new job, and not about finding a new place to live.

He knew if he and Rhys couldn't find some semblance of normal between them, their relationship was dead in the water, and he didn't want that. The thought of it ending before it truly got started terrified him. Trevor hadn't liked anyone this way possibly ever in his life, and he needed this to go right. He'd already lost too much.

When Rhys pulled into the garage, he turned to look at Trevor, his face pensive. "Tell me what you're thinking."

Trevor dragged a hand down his face with a sigh. "A lot of things right now. I'm frustrated that we have to wait until morning for answers. And I wanted to be further along by now."

"With what?" Rhys asked softly.

"With moving on from this fucking disaster. I'm tired of being in this stasis—having no idea whether or not I'm going to be allowed to get on with my life. I don't know if I'll ever get to be Dr. Greene again. Maybe I'm going to spend the rest of my life tending bar or working retail and barely scraping by—and maybe not, but I don't know, and the not knowing is killing me."

Rhys frowned, then gave him a careful look when he asked, "Would you really be okay with that?"

"With what?"

"With never being Dr. Greene again. With working retail the rest of your life. Would you actually settle for something like that?"

Trevor bit his lip, considering the questions. It irked him, rubbed him the wrong way, like Rhys was pressuring him to take action against something he couldn't fight. He knew it wasn't really the case, but he couldn't help the instant tension rising in his shoulders. "I don't fucking know, do I? I never imagined being in a situation where I'd lose all my credentials, where I'd be drowning in student loan debt for the rest of my life because one stupid mistake cost me everything."

"I'm sorry," Rhys said very softly. "That was really unfair of me. I'm just scared. I'm scared you're giving up, and I don't want you to. I'm not going to stop fighting."

Trevor's shoulders sank down a little and he leaned his head back against the headrest. "Can we go in? I want to not think right now. I want to be somewhere that I can forget about all this mess. Just for a little while."

"I can do that," Rhys said, then reached for his hand, pressing a wet, hot kiss to the inside of his wrist. "If you'll let me, I think I can make you forget for a while."

Trevor went hot all over. Maybe there was something wrong with him that in spite of his life falling apart, in spite of the mess he was in, he could be so goddamn turned on. But right now, he was willing to overlook it. He didn't care. All he wanted in the world was to get inside and let Rhys put his hands and mouth *everywhere*.

He didn't give Rhys a verbal answer, but he pushed the door open with purpose and stepped out. He caught Rhys' grin out of the corner of his eye and suppressed his own as he led the way through the garage door and into the kitchen.

Rhys was at his back almost immediately, hands going to his waist, a warm press of lips against the back of his neck. Trevor stopped walking, letting Rhys take control for that moment. He wanted that—needed that—needed someone he trusted enough to just let go. "I don't want to think," he murmured.

Rhys ran a hand up and down his side, kissing his neck again. "I've got you. I want you to do something for me." His hand slowly made its way down his front, pressure over his sternum, his belly, then fingers digging into his crotch in a gentle rub. "Can you do something for me?"

"Yes," Trevor said, his eyes fluttering closed at all the sensations. "Anything."

"I want you to go to my room, take all your clothes off, then get on the bed. I'm going to be there in a few minutes, but while you're waiting, I want you to put your fingers inside yourself."

Trevor gave a full-body shudder, barely choking back his moan. "Fingers where?" he just managed to ask.

"Anywhere you want them. Just make it good, get yourself all worked up and ready for me. But don't come. Promise me." Rhys punctuated his command with a nip to Trevor's ear lobe, and Trevor had to bite the inside of his cheek to keep from making a completely embarrassing noise.

"I promise," he finally managed. He peeled himself away from Rhys' hands, feeling a little desperate to obey, but also desperate to stay in Rhys' firm, safe grip. Still, he knew that doing what Rhys asked was only going to benefit him in the end. He trusted Rhys to take care of him, to give him what he wanted.

One foot in front of the other, he made his way to the master bedroom. He wasted no time in stripping down to nothing, almost enjoying the way the cool air and the stiff sheets felt against his over-sensitive skin. He pushed up against the pillows, half up with his feet crooked, and he let his hand drift between his pecs, fingers twisting in his coarse hair as he made his way lower, lower. His hands parted his folds, feeling his dick throbbing, engorged and wanting as he dragged a finger up. It wasn't wet enough—not yet. There was lube within reach, but he wanted to toy with himself a little first.

His hand ventured lower, feeling his hole pulsing with need when he thought about Rhys pushing his cock there. He went lower still, between his cheeks, his ass almost begging for intrusion. Licking his lips, he rolled to the side and dragged the lube out of the drawer, fumbling with one hand to get the lid open. He drizzled it down from the top of his pubic bone, letting the cool gel run a path to the sheets below him.

After a beat, he touched. He took his dick between his thumb and forefinger and stroked. The sensation was almost overwhelming, and he felt his stomach clench, the hot press of orgasm building behind his naval. But Rhys' words came back to him. *Don't come. Promise me.* Trevor meant to honor his word.

He let his hand drift lower, then finally pushed two fingers inside himself and let his head loll a back against the headboard. As he fucked himself with his fingers, his hips met his own rhythm, the sensation more dulled than when he was touching his cock, but no less pleasurable. The orgasm seemed further away now. His body relaxed into the motion. His eyes stayed closed until he heard the sharp intake of breath and he realized Rhys had come in.

He hadn't heard the door, too into fingering himself, and he peered over at Rhys who was almost completely naked save for his boxer-briefs. His eyes were half-lidded and gaze fixed on where Trevor was pushing his fingers in and out of his body.

"Jesus. You look so…" Rhys didn't finish his sentence and Trevor didn't ask him to. He kept at what he was doing, jolting only a little when he felt Rhys' warm palm brush up his calf, over his knee, then along the inside of his thigh. Two fingers joined Trevor's, and Rhys groaned as his other hand began to fumble with the waistband of the last bit of fabric covering his body. "Is this where you want me? Like this?"

"Yes, but…only…" Trevor wasn't beyond words yet, but close. He turned onto his belly, lifting himself to his knees, bracing himself on his forearms. He had discovered years ago he liked it better this way, it kept his dysphoria at bay, and he didn't have to try to find pleasure where it was a struggle to feel it. He liked the feeling of being claimed, possessed sometimes, and right now he needed it.

Rhys didn't need more direction than that. He fitted himself behind Trevor like a perfect puzzle piece. Somewhere between pulling his boxers off and sliding onto the bed, he'd managed to roll on a condom and drizzle lube over himself, because the press of his penis inside of Trevor was slick and ready to take him to the edge.

The first thrust was everything. It sent zinging pleasure through Trevor's limbs, and he felt a gasping moan rip from his throat as his fingers curled into the sheets. He wasn't allowed to stay in that position long, though. Rhys had him by the torso, lifting him up so they were upright, Trevor's back against Rhys' hot chest. Trevor's legs were spread, hips canting backward at an angle so Rhys couldn't slip out, and he could hear the wet slapping of their bodies as Rhys continued his relentless pace.

"Fuck. God, I love it like this," Trevor babbled. He began to thrust back against Rhys harder, pushing himself backward until Rhys was sitting on his heels, Trevor spread out over his thighs and began to bounce on Rhys' cock.

"Oh god," Rhys said, his hands flying to Trevor's hips to guide his rhythm. "Yes, babe. Yeah, fuck my cock."

Trevor's head lolled back as he lost himself to it, the pleasure, the rhythm. Then Rhys' hand slipped over his hip, his fingers spreading him, then stroking over his cock and his orgasm hit him like a powerful wave. He felt himself come with a force he wasn't expecting, collapsing backward and saved only by Rhys' strong arms as he thrust into Trevor once, twice, a third time before he groaned and pulsed inside the condom.

It felt like a small eternity as Trevor's breath finally returned to normal, and eventually Rhys rolled them onto their sides, facing each other. Rhys had removed the condom, and he lay flaccid and slightly sticky against Trevor's thigh, but the feeling of so much touching was a comfort in a way Trevor hadn't expected.

His hand was a little shaky as he lifted it to brush a little fringe away from Rhys' forehead. "I really needed that."

"So did I," Rhys said. He closed his eyes, leaning into the pressure of Trevor's fingers, and Trevor felt important and powerful in that quiet moment, like he meant everything to this man. The thought was a little terrifying and a little thrilling all at the same time. Rhys took a breath, then opened his eyes. "Ivan wanted that from me."

Trevor felt something ugly twist in his chest only for a moment. "Sex?"

"To give up control. Or...something like it," he amended. "I couldn't do it. Mainly because I was so in love with you, the thought of sleeping with someone else made me feel like I was cheating. But also because the idea of taking control of someone terrified me. I don't trust myself a lot."

"Did we just do something that upset you?" Trevor asked, feeling a little panic like maybe he'd pushed Rhys too far.

Rhys only smiled though, and gently cupped Trevor's cheek. "When you asked, I wasn't afraid at all. This felt right. Giving you what you needed ended up being what I needed. I understand we can't keep this up. You need to get out and figure your shit out and find your footing again. And I want that for you—as long as it doesn't mean I'm losing you."

"You're not," Trevor said. "You couldn't." He was fairly sure he hadn't meant anything that much in a long, long time.

21.

Rhys felt like the worst attorney in the world. His attention span was garbage, and he found himself checking his phone so often his current client had asked him if he was late to something. He finally forced himself to put it in his desk and focus on his meetings, but by the time his last one was over, he all-but ripped the drawer off the track in an effort to check his messages.

He had exactly two.

> **Cole: I have some information that might be helpful. I texted Trevor and he said we can meet at the gym tonight. Six work for you?**

> *Trevor: Cole texted, he knows some stuff. Will you be able to make it to Wes' gym? He said six.*

He hurried to type his reply, knowing he'd be there come hell or high water. Not only would he not let Trevor face that alone, but he needed to be in the know for his own peace of mind. If they had enough of a case that they could come forward without Trevor giving push-back, he'd be ready to move. Immediately. If it meant getting Trevor his life back, he'd be willing to sacrifice anything.

Rhys bid a hasty goodbye to Mel, promising to be in early the next day to go over the case files she'd prepared, then he jumped in his car and sped over to Baum's. It was a quarter to six, so he pulled into the employee parking spaces and went through the side entrance.

He could hear the sounds of gym life, the faint music of a class being held in the side room, the clink of weight machines, low thrum of conversation. The smell of sweat and cleaner and the faint tang of the air conditioning in spite of the cold winter air just outside. He came around the corner to find Wes at the front desk, and he gave Rhys a knowing smile.

"Long day?" He eyed the suit, and Rhys gave a sigh as he tugged at the knot in his tie.

"Something like that. Is anyone else here?"

"Cole and Adrian are finishing up their session, and I think your boy's in there waiting. He went a couple rounds with Adrian earlier. Adrian really likes working with him."

Rhys felt a pang of pride shoot through him, and he couldn't help his grin. "Yeah?"

Wes gave a nod. "Evan suggested he join in on a couple of his sessions too."

At the sound of Evan's name, Rhys tensed up immediately. "I don't know if..."

"Relax," Wes interrupted, pushing up and bracing himself on the side of the desk. "He's over it. He just happens to think the same way I do. Trevor has potential and could benefit. It's not like Evan would be trying to seduce him."

Rhys realized that a little late, then flushed. "Right. Sorry."

Wes chuckled and shook his head. "We all want to see you happy." He gave Rhys a once-over, then sighed. "You should change before you head in. You look like an idiot in that suit."

Rhys flipped him off good naturedly, then headed into the locker room where he had a spare set of work-out clothes in his locker. He didn't waste further time, hurrying into his sweats, t-shirt, and trainers, then made his way to the boxing room. Adrian and Cole were in the ring, the pair circling each other, and Rhys' eyes immediately found Trevor who was sitting in a chair off to the side with Cole's guide dog at his feet.

He looked up at the sound of the door opening, and Trevor's face fell into a gentle smile as Rhys made his way over. "You're early," he said once Rhys reached him.

Leaning down, he brushed a kiss across Trevor's lips. "Yeah. Did you get a chance to talk with Cole about anything?"

Trevor shook his head. "He was anxious to get into his session with Adrian, and I didn't want to interrupt. I'm…kind of freaking out a little bit, though," he confessed quietly.

Rhys glanced around, then found a chair and dragged it over, taking Trevor's hand the moment he sat. "I get it. I mean, it could be everything and it could be nothing. Just remember you're not alone."

Trevor bowed his head a little, but there was a faint smile playing at his lips. "I know. That's why I wanted to meet here." The admission was a little shy, but completely genuine, and it made Rhys' heart thud hard in his chest.

He couldn't find words to reply, so instead he just held Trevor's hand a little tighter and turned to watch the rest of Adrian and Cole's lesson. It was less of a fight and mostly orientation training, with Cole chasing the sound of Adrian around the ring. They were both sweating though, and Cole was sporting a red mark on his left cheek which meant Adrian got one of his famous left hooks, though Rhys didn't think Cole minded much.

When they finished, the pair of them slipped past the ropes and went for their towels and water, tidying up a little before walking over. Cole had his hand on Adrian's shoulder, but let it slip off when they came to a stop, and both Rhys and Trevor shot to their feet.

"Hey, man," Trevor said. "That was pretty amazing. Wes keeps telling me I should think about training to compete, but I don't know if I'd ever be able to hold my own like that."

Cole chuckled. "Trust me, I thought the same thing, but Adrian changed my mind."

Trevor bit his lip, then let out a breath and said, "Can I think about it?"

Adrian chuckled and shook his head. "Man, it's not like a requirement to hang out with us. Rhys rarely lets me knock him around the ring, and I don't hate seeing his face."

Rhys rolled his eyes and Adrian laughed. "Whatever. I'm only here because I was summoned."

"Right," Cole said, and made a clicking noise with his mouth. His dog took that as his cue and rose, walking to his side as Cole felt down for the harness. "Wes said we could use his office. I brought my laptop and it's set up in there. I found a couple of things you might consider suspicious, so I thought we'd go over some names if you're keen?"

"Yes," Trevor said, sounding a little too eager, but Rhys could hardly blame him.

They quickly followed Cole out of the boxing room, down the small corridor, and into Wes' office. It was pitch black, so Rhys got the lights as Cole made his way over to the desk and felt for the chair before sitting. His laptop was set up in front of him with his braille display in the front, and a pair of earbuds attached to the side.

"Like I said before, I don't have access to the same systems I had when I was active duty, but I have access to enough. I spent most of the weekend scouring your accounts and making notes of footprints by their addresses, and who had been in multiple unrelated accounts."

"What do you mean multiple unrelated accounts?" Trevor asked as he took the chair that was near the side of Wes' desk.

"I mean, someone who's accessing your medical records shouldn't also be accessing your rental history. There might be some reason for occasional cross-over—say if it was for medical treatment and you were applying for a line of credit, but it's not something you'd normally see." Cole's fingers moved over the keyboard, clacking away, pausing only to brush over the braille at the bottom occasionally. "There are three addresses—two of them were registered to the University, and Noah is fairly certain one of them is Esther since it was more recent, so we'll rule that out. The other is suspicious though, and we were able to trace it back to one of the research lab portals."

"Okay," Trevor said softly. "But…I mean, I participated in one of their research programs, and they had to go into my medical history and all of that. Wouldn't that be normal? To see him in there?"

Cole's brows dipped. "I suppose, but I don't imagine he had any business in your credit, or your rental history report, and we found that address in both. We also found footprints in some of your online accounts—employment profiles for job hunting websites and LinkedIn. Far more recent than the experiment you participated in."

Trevor's face went white. Rhys had never seen color drain from anyone's skin like that before, and he was stepping forward, afraid Trevor would collapse. "Oh," he said softly. There was a pause, then he asked in a small voice, "The third address?"

"A home computer registered to someone called Shane McCafferty. I asked Noah about the name and he said as far as he's unfamiliar with it. He's checking with Esther this evening, but as the address registers somewhere in Bakersfield, California…"

Trevor, if possible, looked more pale. "I…I was born there. In Bakersfield," he said. He dragged a hand down his face.

Rhys stepped closer to him and touched his shoulder. "Is the name familiar to you?"

"I don't know," Trevor confessed. "It's triggering something, like trying to remember the flavor of a discontinued candy from when you were a kid, you know? Or maybe I think I've heard it before because I want to know it—I want to know who the hell is behind this."

"The more concerning bit is the research department," Cole said. "Esther got back to us last night and informed us that the program you were part of was shut down and everyone was let go due to lack of funding."

Trevor's eyes went wide. "When did that happen?"

"The week after the scandal went wide," Cole told him, sitting back. "Someone called Mia Smith is still technically employed there, and her address is still current, but her husband Andrew isn't. If those two are who I think they are…"

"They are," Trevor said, his voice hoarse now.

"You really should consider they're part of this," Cole said. "I wasn't able to access the system and get into the email address the way I'd been able to do for Noah, and I am sorry about that."

Trevor shook his head. "It's fine. It's…"

"Ivan," Rhys blurted, and didn't miss the way Trevor's face suddenly went pink. "He said he'd help, and that's a way to help. I don't know if he can get around it legally, but we can at least ask."

"There may be correspondence between Mia Smith and this McCafferty person," Cole said. "Or possibly between one of them and Barnes. That'll be the link you're searching for."

Trevor swallowed thickly. "Thank you."

Cole turned his face toward Trevor, his expression grim and sorry. "I hate that I can't do more for you."

With a slightly disbelieving laugh, Trevor stood and approached the desk, putting his hands on the top. "You were able to give me more information than I've had in what feels like forever. Please, *god*, don't apologize for that. I owe you."

"I'm just glad I could help," Cole said, and he stuck out his hand for Trevor to take. "Keep me up to date if you're able to get more on this guy. I might not have what I used to, but there's probably more I can do once we get a firm ID."

"Why don't you and Ryan come over this weekend for dinner," Rhys cut in, and Cole looked pleasantly startled. "We should know more by then, and even if we don't, it'll be good to have the company."

Trevor brightened at that. "Yes. Please, I'd really like that."

Cole smiled at them both. "I think you can count us in."

***

"Do you want to talk about it?" Rhys asked as they got home. Trevor's arms were full of their dinner—a Thai take-away which he planned on eating too much of, but from the look on Trevor's face, he wasn't sure the other man had much appetite.

Kicking the door open with one foot, Trevor edged his way into the kitchen and set everything down as Rhys put his case and file folder on the table. "Not really."

"Okay, but we do need to talk about it at some point. Soon," Rhys added, shrugging out of his jacket. "And not just as your boyfriend, but as the person providing you legal help. Cole's obviously onto something, and if we can get Ivan involved…"

Trevor spun, fixing him with a hard stare. "Woah okay, I did *not* okay involving the cops."

"He's not a," Rhys started, then breathed out a sigh. "He won't be *acting* in the capacity of a cop. But he's got connections we might be able to use."

Sinking into a chair, Trevor bowed his head, heaving a sigh which deflated his entire body. "I don't know how helpful any of this is going to be. I mean, so we track down the person doing this, and then what?"

Rhys frowned, walking over to the table. "What did you anticipate was going to happen when you walked into my office, Trev? What if I had said, yes? That I would take you on as a client, help you find out who it was. What did you plan on doing with that information? You keep talking about getting your life back—and believe me, I want that for you more than anything—but how are you going to make that happen?"

"I don't fucking know," Trevor said, his voice full of barely restrained tension. He finally looked up, his eyes blazing, his cheeks pink which made his freckles stand out. "I don't have any fucking answers, but I know we have to start somewhere."

"And we need some sort of end game," Rhys pointed out, trying not to feel too irritated. "Chances are, you're not going to end this without coming forward about what you did." He tried to soften the blow of the statement by curbing his tone, but the way Trevor winced, he didn't think he was successful at it. "In all honesty, you won't be any worse off than you are now."

Trevor snorted. "Right. And I plan to be content living like this for the rest of my fucking life."

Rhys did his best not to take it personally. "We need a game plan at the very least. First, we find out what's happening."

"I don't know how we can even start," Trevor began.

"We can use intimidation tactics," Rhys offered. "Our little self-made family is a giant gym full of ex-veteran, body-building boxers just itching to put their fists into someone's face who deserves it. We have that on our side."

Trevor chuckled like he couldn't help the sound, managing to look Rhys in the eyes for a moment. "Do you really think that's a deterrent? Charlie went after *Adrian* for fuck's sake. That dude terrifies me, and he likes me."

Rhys let himself smile a little. "Fair enough, but apart from going the legal route, vigilante is our only other option. Unless you want to try to reason with them," he added, his tone growing with horror when he realized from the look on his face, that might actually be Trevor's plan. He splayed his hands flat on the table and rose, leaning toward his boyfriend. "Trevor, you can't be serious. This person has ruined your entire life simply for the sake of seeing you suffer, and you think you can what? Appeal to their merciful side?"

The smile on Trevor's face faded into something akin to hurt. "I can at least try."

"If they're getting off on seeing you suffer, trust me, there's not going to be a lot of humanity there. I've dealt with some of the worst scum humans can offer, babe. I'm not saying this because I don't think you're worth changing for, I'm saying this because sometimes people are just bad."

Trevor's hands curled into fists. "Last time I checked, it was still up to me to decide."

"I'm not going to force you to do anything—or force you not to," Rhys said, trying to keep his voice level. "But it is my job—as both someone who cares for you and as someone invested in our future—to tell you when I see you heading toward a mistake. I have a lot of experience in this area."

"And I have a lot of experience in what it's like to live in a world where people get sick pleasure from seeing people like me suffer," Trevor spat. He rose, the chair scraping across the tile. "You don't know better than me."

"Maybe I do," Rhys said, his voice rising a little. He wouldn't understand what it was like to exist as trans, but he had far more experience in his own field where this situation was concerned. Trevor was so blinded by his desire to get out of this without any information coming out, he wasn't able to see there might not be another way. "Right now, I think I do. Right now, you need to stop and realize that you might not be the expert in this."

Trevor's entire face was bright red with fury. "We're done."

Rhys blinked. "No. You're angry and emotional and not thinking clearly…"

"Don't you fucking patronize me," Trevor hissed, taking a step back from him. "I'm not a goddamn child!"

"Which is just as well since I'm not interested in fucking, or falling in love with, or making a future together with a child. But you are emotionally compromised and you're not thinking clearly," he reiterated. "So you're not going to tell me we're done because you need support, and where else are you going to get that."

Trevor's eyes flared wide. "I can't…I need to leave. I can't do this with you." He brushed past Rhys, rushing to his room, though Rhys didn't let him get too far.

In Trevor's doorway, Rhys tried to maintain his calm as he watched Trevor shove clothes into his travel bag. "Where are you going to go?"

"Somewhere else. *Clearly*," he said, his tone mocking Rhys' earlier words, "you and I need some space. And *clearly* fucking my roommate was a bad idea. Which we both knew."

"You can't just leave. You don't have anywhere to go," Rhys pointed out softly. "I'll head to my brother's and you can stay here. We can take some time apart and…"

"No," Trevor said. He looked at Rhys then, his face pained and conflicted, then he said, "I'm going to Evan's."

That hit like a physical blow, Rhys taking a few steps back like he wasn't able to keep his balance. "Are you coming back?"

"Don't ask me that right now," Trevor said. "I'm…I'm so angry I can't begin to…" His words were stuttered, sentences unfinished. "I need some space from all of this. There's too much happening, and you were right—you and I, it's compromised my emotional state and I can't think anymore. I just…I need to go."

Rhys knew the smart thing to do was stop him—was to do anything to prevent him from throwing himself out of the house without any promise of coming back. But he didn't. He knew if he did that, if he forced his hand, he'd lose Trevor for good, and he wasn't willing to risk it.

He only had one option now.

Rhys: Hi, it's Rhys. Trevor is on his way to you right now, and he really needs someone to support him. But if anything comes up, if anyone comes after him, if he seems like he's in any danger, call me. I don't care what time. Please.

Evan: I got his call, and don't worry, I've got him.

The words were enough to gut him, but Rhys decided it was a just punishment for the way he'd pushed. He didn't regret it—he couldn't regret it. Trevor wasn't letting himself think clearly, and he hadn't been wrong about the two of them. Crossing that line had been a mistake, and their feelings were making it impossible for them to see what needed to be done.

All Rhys could do now was wait. They had time, he just wasn't sure how much.

22.

Swiping the clean spot on the bar for the fifth time, Trevor realized what he was doing and quickly put the towel down. The bar was all-but dead for the night, which was bad for his cash-flow, but good for his state of mind. He'd been in no place to deal with customer service, but a freak snow-storm had hit and they hadn't seen anyone come through the doors since six.

Everyone but Trevor was sent home, and Trevor volunteered to close up before he headed back to Evan's. It wasn't the worst situation he'd been in, but sleeping on Evan's sofa left him feeling empty and bereft. It felt wrong, simply put. He hadn't felt that way with Rhys, even as complicated as the situation had been.

In truth, ten minutes out the door and down the road, he'd come to realize that most of what Rhys had been saying was right. Trevor's emotional state did compromise his ability to think clearly, and he didn't entirely have an end-game. He had no idea what he was going to do with any information Cole dug up, and he wasn't sure how he was going to be able to stop the blackmail and keep himself from getting exposed.

He would have to choose one or the other. He just didn't know which option he'd be able to survive. He'd been consumed with finding out who, and why, but he had completely forgotten to consider what he would do once that happened.

He wanted to go back, but his pride kept his foot on the gas of the car which belonged to Rhys, and kept one foot moving in front of the other until he was sitting with Evan next to him, pouring his heart out about how very much it felt like it was breaking.

Evan assured him that Rhys wasn't the kind of guy to give up easy. "I don't know him," Evan said, toying with the rim of his water glass, "but I know people like him. And I know the man who texted me to make sure that you got here safe and you were protected isn't the sort of man who won't take you back the minute you're ready."

"I just don't know how I can ever be good enough for him. Not after all this," Trevor had said in a quiet voice. "And I know me being here is unfair to you, so I'm sorry for that too."

It was a testament to Evan's ability to read people that he didn't offer any platitudes. Trevor hadn't been fishing, he'd been simply venting his insecurities. Deep down he knew that it wasn't about being good enough—and deep down he knew none of this was his own fault. Whatever decisions he made in the past, he hadn't deserved any of this. But he couldn't help the irrational thoughts which told him Rhys deserved so much more.

It had been three days now. Three days of silence on his end, and on Rhys'. He went to work, stayed as long as he could, then crashed on Evan's sofa only to rinse and repeat, over and over. *Ad nauseum.* He missed his old life desperately, but not nearly as much as he missed Rhys' quiet, calming, strong presence.

Reaching under the bar, he pulled his book out. He was reading one of his older copies of Metamorphosis, the Latin flowing seamlessly even after having been away from it for the long weeks. It was soothing in a way most literature wasn't, though it wasn't bringing him the same amount of comfort as it had done in the past. His hand brushed over the page, turning it slowly, and he didn't look up again until he heard the bar door open.

He gave a small groan under his breath before glancing up, and he was startled to find Cole there. Cole's hand was holding tight to his dog's harness and was giving him quiet directions toward the bar. The dog trotted effortlessly around tables and chairs, and then came to a stop at the edge of the bar top.

Cautiously, Cole reached out, brow furrowed, and felt for the cool marble. "Hello?" he asked.

"Hey," Trevor said.

"I was wondering if Trevor Greene was working tonight?"

Trevor flushed a little. "I…yeah. Yes, it's me. Hey."

Cole's mouth twitched into a grin. "Oh, good. I was hoping I'd catch you before your shift was over."

Trevor frowned, a little worried by Cole's sudden presence. "You doing okay? Is there something wrong?"

"I spoke with Rhys," Cole said, and there was weight to his words.

"Ah. Uh…yeah…"

"He said he hadn't spoken with you in a few days, but I didn't want to wait until you two had reconciled to give you this." Reaching down into the satchel he had hanging across his body, he pulled out a folder. "I had Ryan check these over before printing them. I was able to pinpoint the exact dates and times your accounts were accessed, and with Esther's help, I was able to get into some emails. It looks like the first point of contact was made by Mia Smith's address. I couldn't access the email itself, but I *was* able to find out hers arrived first. It was sent to Shane McCafferty, and emails were exchanged for over two weeks. I decided I should do a little digging on him as well."

Trevor bit his lip, feeling nerves cresting. "Okay."

"He's your uncle," Cole said bluntly. "He's the brother of Julia Greene, who was at one-point Julia McCafferty. Before she married your father. I got an address, but everything I found about it, the place is abandoned. At this point, you might want to turn this into someone with more authority. McCafferty and Smith were the ones who accessed all your accounts, including a few of your job-oriented social media sites as recently as yesterday."

Trevor let the shock hit him, unable to stop it even if he'd wanted to. He took a staggering step backward, his backside hitting the cold cabinet they kept the imported beer bottles. "I…what?" he murmured.

Cole immediately looked apologetic. "It's a blow, I realize that, and I'm sorry. But I thought since he's your uncle, you might know him and there might be a way to get answers."

"I've never met him," Trevor managed to say. That was also the truth. He hadn't met any of his extended family, though his far-reaching memory conjured a foggy dream-like conversation between his parents, an argument regarding his mom's brother. "What the hell could he have to do with this?"

Cole's face fell a little, and his shoulders slumped. "I don't know. I'm sorry. If I had access to the emails…"

"No," Trevor said quickly, shaking himself out of his sudden shock. "No, this is more than enough. Thank you. You didn't have to do even this much."

"I did," Cole said. His hand ventured across the bar, stopping when it touched the book, and Trevor offered his own, letting Cole squeeze his fingers. "No one deserves this. I wished I could have done more for Noah when it was all happening—I wish I had been round earlier for you. I know what it's like to lose all control over what's happening, and this is the least I can do."

Trevor closed his eyes a minute and just let himself breathe. "Rhys says we should involve Ivan."

"It might be a wise choice," Cole said. He let his hand drop back down, and his fingers touched the cover of the book. "What are you reading?"

Startled by the change in subject, Trevor blinked and said, "Uh...Ovid. Metamorphosis. It's the Latin version. Have you read it?"

Cole laughed. "No, I haven't. I wasn't much for literature when I was at school, and I joined up with the Marines the moment I was able. I didn't have a lot of time for reading, and when I did, it most definitely wasn't something in Latin. Do you like it?"

Trevor's lips twitched into a half-smile. "It's one of my favorites. Not because it's the best thing I've ever read, but it was the first book in Latin that I was able to read fluently without my dictionary or translation apps. It was this huge thing—this massive accomplishment. It made me feel like a real scholar, you know? Like I wasn't just pretending anymore." He realized he'd gone back to that now, a life of pretend.

It was a state that haunted him far too often. Pretending to be a girl before he was fully out—only to protect himself. Pretending to be intelligent for so many years at school until the semesters of education finally caught up with his brain and he actually retained the information. Pretending to know what the fuck he was doing the first time he stood up to give a 301 lecture to an auditorium of undergrads. Pretending to be okay with the turns his life had taken simply because he was afraid of what the alternative was.

Pretending like he could walk away from Rhys and not look back.

"Trevor?" Cole asked softly. "Are you alright?"

"I don't think so," Trevor said from behind a bitter laugh. "I really don't think so. Rhys and I fought because he decided to make me face reality, and I wasn't interested in doing that. Now we have to call this guy in on my fucked-up issues—an apparently attractive, nice, talented guy with all his shit together who actually wants to be with Rhys."

Cole's lips twitched into a proper smile and he drew his hand away from the book. "He used to shag my boyfriend too, remember?"

Trevor stopped, then chuckled. "God, you're right. And that's kind of weird, isn't it?"

"I think it might be weird on his part. Two brothers," Cole said with a shake of his head. "But Ryan assured me that Ivan is a person who deserves respect. He also assured me that he doesn't hold a candle to me, and I have a feeling Rhys thinks the same way about you."

Trevor dragged a hand down his face. "So long as I haven't fucked it up beyond repair. I mean I just...left, you know?"

Cole laughed. "Oh, I do know. He's had dinner at mine three nights in a row because he can't stand to be at his with it so empty now."

Trevor felt a rush of guilt, his stomach twisting with it. "I should have left a while ago. Not because I don't want to be with him..."

"But because you do?" Cole pressed. "I get it, believe me. It wasn't easy for me or for Ryan when we first started out. I was bound and determined to keep it casual, physical. I didn't think I was ready for anything more than that. I was still trying to figure out my life being blind, finding my place in the world where I was still useful. Then he happened, and neither one of us were prepared for it. But once we stopped fighting, it all fell into place."

"I just wish it wasn't so damn complicated," Trevor said.

"I know, but it is. So, you just have to find a way to navigate it. For now, just know that I'm here for whatever I can do. And listen to his advice. If he thinks bringing Ivan in on this is a good idea, trust him. He's not going to put you in a situation worse than it already is."

"I hate how right you are about this," Trevor grumbled.

Cole chuckled again. "I also don't think you're wrong about getting some distance. Though, maybe staying with the guy you nearly chose over him isn't the best idea."

Trevor slumped forward, letting his head fall onto his book, and he let out a bone-deep groan. "The truth is, Evan never stood a chance. I didn't almost choose him over Rhys, because there was never a choice to make."

"Then maybe it's time to let him know that," Cole said. "Whenever you're ready, he'll be waiting."

"You're not the first person to say that to me," Trevor said, but in the end, he knew simply that just made those words more true.

23.

Rhys nearly jumped out of his skin when he looked up from his desk to find Trevor hovering in the doorway. The other man looked contrite, unsure, like maybe Rhys wouldn't want him there, and that was the last impression he wanted to give. Rising to his feet, he crossed the distance between them in four huge strides, yanked Trevor inside, and all-but slammed the door.

"Did something happen?" Rhys asked immediately.

Trevor bit his lip, then shook his head. "Nothing new. Well…something new. Nothing's wrong," he finished, adding to Rhys' confusion. Clearing his throat, he sighed and slumped against the closed door. "Cole came by my work last night told me he located that third unknown."

"McCafferty," Rhys repeated.

Trevor's cheeks flushed. "Yeah. He's my uncle."

Rhys absorbed it, blinking with the shock, and he took a step back. "Your uncle?"

"Mom's brother," Trevor clarified. His first step forward was a little wobbly, but he'd regained full strength by the time he made it to Rhys' desk and sank down into the chair there. "I never knew him, but once Cole told me who he was, I had a foggy memory of my parents talking about him before I was taken away."

Licking his lips, Rhys tried to process it as he moved back around his desk and sat. "Okay," he said slowly.

Trevor looked up and Rhys could see the conflict in his eyes. There was a long pause, then he said, "I need you to tell me what to do next. The way I was fighting you—it was so stupid, and I'm sorry."

"Trevor, you don't have to—"

"Yeah, I do," Trevor cut in. "What I said, none of that was fair or true. You've been there for me the way no one else in my life ever has been, and I'm…" He let out a choked laugh. "I'm so scared, Rhys. I'm petrified that I'm going to die alone and destitute—like some sort of shade of the man I once was all because I let myself get complacent."

"Living your life comfortably, not being on constant watch for people like this—that's not complacent, Trevor," Rhys said, his frustration boiling over. "You, just as much as anyone else in the world, deserve to have everything you earned. Everyone behind this—they deserve to be stopped. What's happening to you is not some sort of price you have to pay for being who you are."

Trevor dragged a hand down his face, let out a lungful of air, then nodded. "I know. Logically I know. I guess it just felt like too many good things had happened over the years that the universe was trying to balance out or something. Which I know is nuts. My therapist will have a lot to say about it once we can sit down together again, but I'm working on it. And I really need help. I don't want to keep living like this. I want my life back and I need you to tell me what we do next."

Rhys nodded, trying to force his brain into work mode rather than protect his lover mode, and that wasn't an easy feat to accomplish. "I think we should bring in Ivan. We need to consider that we may need to bring legal charges against the people behind this, and it might mean you taking the hit on your record. And it might mean your friends taking a hit, too."

Trevor drew his bottom lip between his teeth, then said, "Yeah. I mean, they knew what they were doing just as much as I did. And whatever this does to me, it can't be worse than how I'm already living."

Leaning over the desk, Rhys reached for Trevor, and Trevor reached back. Their fingers tangled, and Rhys felt a profound set or rightness in the center of his chest. "I'll call Ivan right now. We'll have him look at everything Cole found, and maybe together, the two of them can get a lock on how this all started."

Trevor nodded, letting out a small breath, squeezing Rhys' hand back. "Thanks."

Rhys' thumb rubbed over Trevor's knuckles, and he knew that pulling away would feel like losing a part of himself. "How are you doing, though? Are you okay at Evan's? Is that where you're staying?"

Trevor looked at him, his eyes bright but almost hesitant. "I'm fine. He really is a nice guy, but you have to know I'm not interested in him. He just told me if I ever needed a place to crash, I could call him."

"Okay," Rhys said, because there was nothing else to say. "But you don't have to...I mean, if you want to come home..." He stopped when Trevor winced, and he dragged his free hand down his face. "I want you to get your own place, Trevor. I want you to regain everything you lost, and I'm not in a hurry to rush what we have. But whenever you're ready—however long that might be, that house is yours too. It's home."

Trevor's jaw twinged with how tight he was clenching his teeth, then all at once he relaxed, letting his hand soften in Rhys' grip, leaning against the desk a little harder. "Thank you. I wasn't sure you really got it."

"Of course I get it. I *do* listen when you talk," Rhys said with a small laugh, enjoying the way it made Trevor flush. "And I promise to do everything in my power to understand. I know I'll never have the same experiences, but it doesn't mean I won't try my damndest."

"Thank you," Trevor replied again. He gently tugged his hand away, and by then it didn't leave Rhys feeling so empty without it. "I was wondering if uh...if maybe we could swing by the gym tonight? Cole will be there, and I thought maybe we could talk to him about it all. And then then I could work out."

Rhys nodded. "I'll text Wes now and let him know to set something up with Adrian for you. Come by here around four—I'll be done with my last meeting. We can get a work out, then some dinner, then I can take you back to my place—"

"Home," Trevor interrupted, his voice strong with purpose, and it made Rhys' heart beat wildly in his chest. "Then we can go home."

Rhys smiled so huge, he swore his face would split, but he couldn't bring himself to care. "Then we can go home."

***

Ten minutes into Trevor's lesson with Adrian, Rhys excused himself to Wes' office to call Ivan. Cole agreed to meeting with him, and Trevor had finally let go of his determination to see this through, regardless of having to come forward about his participation in the fertility study.

The office was dark and empty, though Kevin was curled up on Lemon's puppy bed in the corner, snoring away and didn't stir when Rhys entered. Bypassing the slumbering pup, Rhys lowered himself into Wes' chair, took a breath, then found Ivan's number on his list.

It rang four times before he picked up, and there was a tension in his voice Rhys wasn't expecting. "Hey, I don't have long to talk."

"Are you on shift?" Rhys asked. "I can call back later?"

"No, no it's not...there's just something," Ivan said. He swore under his breath, then sighed. "Sorry, shit's kind of hitting the fan right now and I'm trying to keep it all together. What's going on?"

"I was wondering if that offer was still on the table?" Rhys said, diving right in.

Ivan was silent a moment, then chuckled, "You mean to help your boyfriend?"

Rhys groaned. "How much of an *I told you so* am I going to get if I say yes?"

"Not much," Ivan said, his tone warm and without any hard feelings. "I knew you'd get there eventually. I'm more than happy to help, though things are a little tight right now."

Rhys bit his lip, then said, "We have someone else who has the skills to get the information we need, we just can't get into the system. We need access to a couple of email accounts."

Ivan made a humming noise, then said, "I have a friend who can do this under the table. Why don't I meet your friend—the one who helped out Noah, right?"

"Yeah," Rhys said.

"I'll be the interim, because my guy is a little paranoid. But between all of us, I think we can get shit done. Where can we meet?"

Rhys frowned, trying to put together his schedule. "Mine would be best, I think. You can meet Trevor and he can explain the situation, and then Cole can tell you what he needs besides access to the accounts. We can go from there."

"Tomorrow, then," Ivan said. There was a muffled noise, then he groaned. "I have to go, but I'll text you what time I'm free and let me know if it works."

"I'll make it work," Rhys vowed. "He's ready to move on, and so am I." Rhys felt a pang of guilt, knowing Ivan deserved better than his brush-off, but he couldn't deny what his heart wanted then, just as he couldn't deny it now.

But Ivan didn't seem upset. There was a smile in his voice when he answered, "I'll do everything I can, okay?"

They ended the call without making any real small talk, and Rhys sagged back against Wes' chair, his eyes closing. After a moment, he heard the faint jingle of a harness, then felt a wet dog nose press against his arm. He shifted, glancing down to see Kevin looking at him expectantly. Just as Adrian's dog often did, Kevin pushed his way between Rhys' knees and gave him a snuggle. It was oddly comforting in a way he hadn't expected, and briefly he considered the idea of getting a dog.

The thought led down the path of fantasy—picturing himself and Trevor making his house a home. A dog, maybe a cat, a little spice garden in the kitchen window, a patio set on the back porch. They'd have guests over, they'd plan double date nights with Cole and Ryan, they'd go on vacation together. Someday, Rhys might get down on one knee and slip a ring on Trevor's finger. Trevor might say yes.

He dragged himself away from those images, too afraid to let himself sink any deeper. He was falling a little too hard too fast, and the situation was precarious. There was no telling what would happen in the future, and he didn't want to let himself hope for something that would stay forever outside of his grasp.

With a sigh, he gave the dog a final scratch, then rose and made his way back to the boxing room. Adrian was nowhere to be found, but Cole was at the heavy bag with Trevor, giving him a few last minute pointers. They were both sweaty, and they had lost their gloves, though Trevor's wrapped fists remained at punching height. Rhys couldn't hear what Cole was saying, but he watched him take a step back, and Trevor started pounding on the bag.

His technique was better than Rhys' had been when he first started. There was a natural grace to the way he let himself loose, and Rhys had a moment of realization that Trevor could be good at this. Very good at this, if he let himself. His mouth went a little dry at just how sexy it was, and he had to control himself to keep from tenting the front of his trousers as he walked over.

"How'd you like it?" he asked when Trevor dropped his arms.

Cole chuckled as he passed over a water bottle. "He's going to tell you he loved it—which is a lie. It's always bloody awful right at the start."

Trevor shrugged, swiping the back of his hand across his brow before taking a long drink. "It wasn't as bad as I thought, but I think I'm going to hurt in really weird places tomorrow."

"That's a good sign," Cole insisted, reaching back to grab the chair where his gloves were sitting. "It gets easier with each one. I think Adrian's still impressed."

Trevor flushed a little, shrugging. "I liked it. I mean, Cole's right, it totally sucked. Adrian got me in the face twice and that didn't feel great. But there's kind of...I don't know..."

"Power?" Cole offered.

"Yeah," Trevor breathed out. "There's a power to it—like if you keep reaching, one day it'll be yours, and you won't feel so weak."

Rhys wasn't the sort of guy who understood that. He worked out at the gym to keep fit and he enjoyed being strong enough to hold his own for a few minutes against some of the other guys, but he didn't feel it the way Wes did, the way Adrian did. There was something in Cole's voice, and something in Trevor's, that Rhys would never understand. And yet, he could appreciate it. He wanted it for Trevor, wanted him to have a way to feel like he'd never lose control again.

"When we're done, let's talk to Wes about getting you on Adrian's permanent schedule," Rhys told him,

Trevor's eyebrows shot up. "There's no way I could afford his fulltime fee."

Both Cole and Rhys laughed. "Adrian doesn't train for cash," Rhys told him. "That's definitely not his thing. It's also why he only takes students he sees potential in."

Trevor looked stunned, enough that he didn't say anything when the aforementioned man walked back into the room with Lemon at his side. He looked tired but as happy as he'd looked in a long while, and Rhys attributed that to things with Noah being calm and hitting their stride. It was a good look on him.

"What'd I miss?" Adrian asked as he stopped at Cole's elbow.

"Trevor's a little surprised you'd take him on as a student," Rhys said carefully. "And that you don't charge."

Trevor flushed. "I just... I don't have any experience. And I don't know that I particularly like getting hit. Plus, you should be compensated for your time, man."

"First of all," Adrian said, a small smile playing at his lips, "the point is to *avoid* getting hit when you can and knowing how to take them when you can't. And experience don't mean shit against someone who's naturally inclined. I think you are. Secondly, this isn't my job. I'm opening up a motorcycle garage and that's my money. But it's no pressure, man. If you're not interested..."

"I am," Trevor blurted, then grinned. "Yeah, I think I am."

Adrian smiled back. "Sweet. Then let's get something set up."

"After I'm finished with them," Cole insisted.

Adrian rolled his eyes. "Right. Can't forget the spy shit. Meet me at the front desk when y'all are finished."

As he left, Cole turned to gather his cane, then led the way to Wes' office where he took the chair behind the desk. His face had gone from open and casual to a little tense, and he fired up his laptop as Trevor and Rhys got settled across from him.

"I don't have any new information," he started.

Rhys cleared his throat. "No, I know that. I uh…so I have this friend, Ivan."

Cole's mouth twitched into a wry grin. "I know of him."

Rhys felt his cheeks burn. "Right. Okay I know that might be weird as hell, considering."

Shaking his head, Cole sat back and crossed his arms. "It's fine. Trust me, your brother and I are secure. Trevor and I spoke about him briefly, so I knew this was coming. He's our best link to getting the information we really need."

"The problem is deciding what to do with it once we have it," Trevor added. "And as long as Ivan's willing to work with us."

"He is," Rhys said. "I gave him a call while you were working, and he said he'd be happy to meet up at mine tomorrow. He's not sure what time, and I wasn't sure about your schedule," he said to Cole.

Biting his lip in thought, Cole shrugged. "I'm working, but I can leave whenever. I'm going to assume Ivan wants to work during the evening."

"Probably," Rhys said. He glanced over at Trevor. "Think you can get time off?"

"For this, yeah," Trevor said, his voice a little tight. "Just let me know and I'll be there."

Rhys nodded, feeling better about the entire thing. "Once we have a lead, we'll know what to do with it. My opinion on the matter is to come forward. If they're doing this to you, who the hell else is suffering the same fate? Barnes is going to be serving a decent sentence for what he did, especially after having Noah attacked. If we can prove that this has been one long conspiracy to commit blackmail, it'll only increase the judge's desire to go for maximum sentence."

Trevor was biting the inside of his cheek, making his face look hollowed out for a second. Then he released it and a fresh blush bloomed over his skin. "You're right. It might fuck me over a little, but it can't be any worse than what I'm going through right now. I have to be ready to start over."

"You won't be alone," Cole told him, leaning toward the desk a little. "Whatever happens, you won't be alone."

Trevor let himself smile, though from the tension, Rhys could see what it was costing him. Still, when he answered Cole, his tone was genuine. "Thank you. And I do know. It's time to move past this. I'm done letting someone rule my life."

24.

Rhys wasn't unaware something was wrong when they got to the house, but he let it simmer quietly as Trevor went back to his room and he walked into the kitchen to throw something together for dinner. The rhythm of cooking helped keep his head on straight, helped keep him from following Trevor through the house and pushing.

He had fish and veg ready by the time Trevor reappeared, and they ate in a quiet but comfortable silence at the table. Trevor helped with the dishes when they were done, and then declined Rhys' offer to sit on the sofa and watch a little TV.

"I think I just need some quiet," he admitted.

"Space or just quiet?" Rhys asked.

Trevor bit his bottom lip, staring down at his feet. "Just quiet. I don't know if I," he stopped and didn't finish his thought, but he didn't tense up when Rhys followed him to the bedroom and took up residence on top of his duvet. They both sat propped against the headboard, Rhys holding one leg crooked up, the other stretched along Trevor's thigh. His hand lay pliant, and he just barely managed to hide his smile when Trevor's fingers finally, cautiously, curled around his.

"Do you want to talk about it?" Rhys asked after a few minutes of just being with each other.

Trevor looked over at Rhys, but said nothing for a good, long while. "Ivan," he finally admitted.

Rhys' eyebrows shot up. "Because he and I had a date?"

"Because he's probably a better choice for you than I am," Trevor corrected.

Rhys felt his heart stutter at the thought of choosing Ivan over Trevor. His first instinct was frustration, even a little anger, because listening to Trevor imply that anyone was a better choice was almost like an insult to Rhys' ability to know what was good for him. But deep down, he understood that wasn't what Trevor was saying. "I disagree," he said. "And honestly I don't understand why you'd think that."

Trevor swallowed thickly. He released Rhys' hand, but only to crook his leg up so he could turn and look at him properly. "He's stable, and you deserve that. You deserve someone who has his shit together, and I don't know how long it'll take before that happens for me."

Rhys couldn't help a small chuckle, even as he turned his own body, reaching out to cup the side of Trevor's neck. "Look, stability is an illusion." When Trevor's mouth dropped open to argue, he shook his head. "Stability is what you make it to be. I had all that—all the things you think Ivan could give me. I had a good life, I graduated valedictorian, went to college, went to law school. I started a successful career and married my college sweetheart. We bought a house, and each got shiny new cars. We had a dog together, and two fish. But she was still fucking my best friend for as long as I can remember us being together, and she chose him in the end. We had everything that was supposed to make our marriage stable, and it still failed."

"I know but," Trevor started.

Rhys shook his head. "Just because you hit a stumbling block in your life doesn't mean that this," he gestured between the two of them, "isn't stable. Just because the world undervalues careers they depend on—like food service workers, like bartenders, like janitors and house keepers and trash collectors—doesn't mean *I* don't find value in what you contribute right now. Whether it ends up being temporary or permanent, it doesn't matter. I'm fighting to help you get your life back because it's what you want. All I want is right here, and whatever else comes with it, I'm happy to take."

Trevor's eyes were wide, a little shiny, his jaw tense with barely restrained emotion. "Okay," he whispered.

Rhys moved his hand, cupping Trevor's cheek. "I like Ivan. He's a good guy and he deserves to be happy—but I can't give him that because I'm in love with you. The few minutes we spent together felt wrong, and they'll always feel wrong because he's not you."

Trevor closed his eyes, breathing out a long, shaking sigh, then looked up and nodded. "Okay." This time there was purpose behind the word. Strong, actual belief. When Rhys gathered him close, when Rhys kissed him, he felt Trevor's surrender to it, and it finally felt like he'd won.

***

Tapping his fingers on Wes' kitchen table, Trevor tried not to fidget in irritation. His mug of too-hot tea was at his elbow and Cole was sitting across from him, but all Trevor could see were the figures of Rhys and Ivan bent over a stack of file folders spread out on the coffee table.

The pair of them were currently sorting what they thought was necessary, and Trevor agreed to excuse himself so he wouldn't be taking part in sorting documents that weren't public. The night before, Trevor had finally come to the wholehearted belief that Rhys wanted him and wasn't interested in anyone else, but he couldn't help the small, flickering flame of insecurity once he set eyes on Ivan.

The man really was good looking, kind eyes and a soft smile, and Trevor couldn't bring himself to hate the guy. He wanted to, but it was impossible, and it made the insecurity that much worse.

"May I ask you a favor?" Cole's quiet voice interrupted Trevor's swirling thoughts, and he managed to tear his gaze away from the pair, looking over at his friend.

"Anything," Trevor said. He was just short of desperate for a distraction from all this.

Cole's lip twitched into a half smile. "Can you tell me what he looks like?"

Trevor blinked at him in a little surprise. "You mean Ivan?"

Cole inclined his head in a short nod. "This is the longest I've spent with him, and he sounds different than what I expected. I'm curious, but I don't want to ask Ryan."

Trevor wanted to refuse him, partly because he really didn't want to sing the guy's praises. Part of him wanted to lie to Cole because it meant he could prevent the other man from feeling like this. Only he knew it wasn't fair, and maybe it would be nice to commiserate with someone who understood. "He's attractive. Tall, really tanned—but I think that's his natural skin color. Dark hair, full, a little bit of a curl to it. Really dark brown eyes, nice smile. Long fingers."

Cole chuckled softly. "Long fingers?"

Trevor flushed, feeling a little defensive. "I have a thing for hands, I guess. He's got nice ones. He's wearing a suit, but I think that's because he came straight from work. Looks good on him."

After a few moments, Cole took a long drink of his tea, then set the mug down and folded his hands. "It's what I expected."

"Are you disappointed?"

Cole chuckled again. "No. Ryan was more on the superficial side when he and I first met. I was a little surprised he was interested in someone like me, if we're being honest."

Trevor was startled a little by that. "Because you're blind?"

"Not…necessarily, no," Cole said slowly. "Mostly because I know I look a bit of a horror."

Trevor's brow dipped and he forced himself to really look at the other man, trying to see what he was talking about. It was obvious Cole didn't have eyes. His lids were sunken a little, almost like he was squinting, and there were scars around his forehead and along the bridge of his nose. A larger scar marred his temple, but the rest of his face was smooth, clean shaven, attractive. He's someone Trevor most definitely would have noticed had he not met Rhys first.

"Did someone tell you that?" he finally asked. "That you looked horrible?"

Cole tensed a little, then shrugged. "My daughter's mother. She prevented me from seeing Claire for a time, insisting I would traumatize her."

Trevor was half out of his seat before he realized what he was doing and sat back down heavily. "Are you fucking serious?"

Cole's lips twitched up. "It was a complicated situation which involved the man who kidnapped Ryan and my daughter. She's getting better with it, now that he's gone. It's not second nature to accept disability as readily as Ryan did."

"Being uncomfortable is one thing. I mean, shit, I get that. It happens to me with people all the time. But to stand in the way of your kid seeing you? That's fucked up."

"Are you disabled?" Cole asked, surprise coloring his tone.

Trevor blinked, then realized that he might have come out to some of their friends, but not all of them. His neck felt a little hot and the all-too familiar bubble of come-out panic started to rise in his gut. Still, he liked Cole and he wanted to be honest. "Uh…no. No. I'm actually transgender."

Cole looked surprised a moment, then shook his head as he grinned. "So you do understand."

Trevor felt himself immediately relax, grateful but exhausted at his fear every time he had to do this. "Yeah. It took me a while to really trust that Rhys not only wanted me, but wanted me as a man."

Cole reached for his mug, though he didn't drink from it. His finger traced the rim, his shoulders a little hunched. "I thought maybe Ryan was interested out of pity, or out of curiosity to see what it was like to shag a blind man. It took ages for me to accept that he just…wanted me for me."

Trevor couldn't help a small laugh, and when Cole frowned, he shook his head. "It's nice to be understood. It's getting easier, but I'm not quite there yet."

"You will be," Cole said, and there was such absolute and complete confidence in his voice, Trevor couldn't help but believe him.

25.

It took another half an hour before Ivan and Rhys were ready to include the other two, and then after twenty minutes of still being useless, Trevor excused himself to the basement room where all the gym equipment was set up. He knew he'd be useful eventually, but without any of the computer or hacking skills, he was only getting in the way. Though he wanted to be included, more than that he just wanted the information. If he had to bide his time by bashing into a heavy bag for a while, he could do that.

He changed into one of the outfits from the standing wardrobe Wes kept for his guests, then wrapped his hands the way Adrian had showed him so he could box without gloves and walked over to the hanging bag. He stretched, trying to follow all the rules he'd been given during his lessons, then he began to pound his frustrations out.

Minutes started to bleed into one another, until time became an abstract concept. His arms burned, his knuckles ached, but there was a sort of euphoria that came with the sweat and sting of letting it all out. It was only when he stepped back to find water that he realized he wasn't alone.

Wes was there, leaning against the wall with his arms crossed, a small grin on his face. "Adrian said you were getting better."

"That?" Trevor asked, his neck burning with embarrassment. "That was probably a hot mess."

"*That* looked very familiar," Wes countered. "Believe me, I need to unload like that more than I care to admit." He walked over, his gait a little slower than it usually was, and he steadied the bag which was still swinging. "Will it help to wail on a person instead of a bag?"

"I don't think so," Trevor admitted. "I'm not angry, I'm just feeling a little useless. And I know I'm not," he added before Wes could jump in and defend him, "but I don't have the skills to help at this stage and I hate feeling relegated to the sidelines."

Wes gave him a long look, then walked past him to the mini-fridge. He pulled out a bottle of water and handed it over before beckoning to the small sofa in the corner. "It's comfortable," he promised as he lowered himself down. "Specially designed for days when my legs are acting up."

It was then Trevor noticed a slight spasm in both of Wes' legs, though he tried not to stare. "Does it hurt?"

Wes laughed. "More than I care to admit. I'm due for another surgery soon, and they're a little worried it might exacerbate my paralysis."

"Then why do it?" Trevor asked.

"To alleviate the pain," Wes told him. "I'm trying to weigh the pros and cons right now of trading my ability to walk and fight standing up for being able to get through the day without having to manage this level of pain. If we didn't have twins coming, it would be an easier choice."

Trevor wanted to ask what the choice was, but he didn't think it was his place. "Sounds like shit."

Wes threw his head back with a loud laugh. "That pretty much sums it up, man. It's complete shit. Anna's kind of pissed at me right now for taking my time, and I get it. The longer I wait, the closer she gets to having the babies, and I don't want to be totally laid up after they're born."

"You think you're choosing surgery?" Trevor asked.

Wes sighed, nodding. "In truth, I'm eventually going to lose my ability to walk no matter what I do. My injury was severe and complicated, and there's more pressure on my damaged spine than there would be if I wasn't fighting. I just…wasn't ready to give it up yet."

"Do you have to? Can't wheelchair users box?" Trevor asked, the question genuine.

Wes brightened. "Fuck yes they can. I have at least four of them at the gym now. But…it was a matter of pride, and of vanity. I wanted to be the asshole who beat all the odds while at the same time telling other people the odds didn't exist. I'm basically a giant hypocrite."

Trevor snorted a laugh. "I feel that. I can't tell you how many times I've told some trans kid to love and accept their body while in the throes of overwhelming dysphoria and self-hatred. But it's easier to tell people how to live than live it yourself, right?"

Wes gave him a look, then grinned. "I fucking knew I was going to like you. And I know you feel all worked up because this is taking forever, but I can tell you for damn sure—you're in good hands here. The best hands. Trust them."

Trevor found himself relaxing a little. "I do. I might not feel good about it, but that doesn't change the fact that I know I'm right where I should be." And he felt deep down, he meant every word.

***

They called out for delivery when they hit a snag in being able to hack into the email server. Ivan was convinced his friend—who was working anonymously with them over the phone—could get through to everything, but it was going at a snail's pace.

Once Trevor got over his initial frustration, he changed back into his clothes and joined the others in the office. Cole and Ivan were working side-by-side at the desk, and Rhys was on his tablet trying to get a little work done while they waited.

Trevor eventually joined him on the sofa, and he smiled when Rhys didn't pause, just shifted so they could tuck into each other. He was content to just exist there, watching Rhys work, listen to Cole and Ivan talk quietly about what they needed to find and how to organize it. Wes came in a few times, and Anna brought Maggie in to say hi to them for a bit before she was sent back to the confines of her bed-rest.

By the time the food arrived, the hacker friend had gotten into the emails and was promising to have a huge file sent over by the time they finished eating. That news alone promptly killed Trevor's appetite, replacing it with humming anxiety.

Rhys immediately picked up on the fact that Trevor wasn't eating, and he set his plate aside, rising and tugging Trevor with him. "We'll be back in a few." He didn't look around as he led Trevor out of the office, through the empty kitchen, and to the back porch. It was cold, the wind a little strong with a fierce, icy bite, but the chill seemed to snap him out of his head.

"Sorry," he muttered as Rhys crowded him up against the porch railing.

Rhys shook his head, cupping his cheek as he pulled him in for a slow, lingering kiss. "Don't be sorry. I'm anxious too."

Trevor closed his eyes and took in a lungful of the cold air. "It's ridiculous that I'm afraid. This means we're finally going to have some answers, and we're going to act on those answers, and I don't know if I can handle what comes next."

Rhys reached down, tangling their fingers together, squeezing him in a tight grip. "Yes, you can. Because you've got support, and no one is going to let you sink. It's almost over, and when it is…"

He didn't finish his sentence, but Trevor didn't need him to. Neither one of them could see the future, but they both knew it was more than just Trevor picking up where he left off. Even if he could get a job teaching again, even if he could resume his life where it had been unceremoniously cut away, things would never be the same again. He'd been rebirthed in a way, not as a new person, but an evolved one. He wasn't sure if he was prepared to accept the responsibility that came with it.

Though having his hand pressed in Rhys', knowing the man would always be as close as Trevor allowed him to be, he felt stronger. "I'm not used to this," he admitted. "I was still so young when my grandma died, and I never really got the chance to know anyone before that. People from high school all fell away, no one from college stuck around. It's taking some getting used to."

Rhys chuckled softly and kissed him again. "We're all willing to be as patient as you need us to be. Okay? But first things first, you need to eat. Then we're going to look at these emails, and then…"

And then…

And then the rest would fall into place. Somehow.

26.

Cole had gone home, and Ivan had left to finish out his late shift, leaving Rhys and Trevor in Wes' office with the stack of printed emails spread out in front of them. The puzzle had clicked into place, neat and succinct, and though Rhys could tell Trevor wasn't surprised, he could see the hurt and confusion blooming on his face.

His uncle had been part of it—they had promised him access to some property which had been left from Trevor's grandmother's estate if he cooperated. "Which doesn't make sense," Trevor said, staring down at the email. "I sold that years ago. There's nothing of her estate left now."

The rest of it, though, had been a bigger emotional blow. Andrew Smith had initiated the first email, from his wife's address though from what Rhys could tell, Mia Smith had no idea what her husband was doing.

Andrew had recruited Barnes by promising him help in taking Noah so far down in the process, Noah would have no other choice but to want to be with him. It was sick—twisted in a way Rhys rarely saw, but the worst part about it was there was no reason why Andrew had done this. He hadn't given any of them an explanation for his actions, only vague promises that their participation would benefit them.

That, Rhys supposed, was what was gutting Trevor the most.

They sat side by side, each of them pouring over the emails in hopes of finding something they'd missed, but there was nothing. No secret code, no evidence. Just a vindictive, cruel man who didn't care who he hurt in order to get what he wanted.

"I don't understand," Trevor said after what felt like an eternity. His voice was strained, barely above a whisper, his hands trembling faintly as he clutched the printed emails. "I don't know why he'd do this. In all this time, he never asked me for anything. He just wanted to see me hurt."

Rhys set his papers down, folding his hands together as he let them hang between his spread knees. "How long were you friends?"

Trevor shrugged, dragging a hand over the back of his neck and squeezing. "We met the semester I started working there. He was nice enough, and I liked his wife. They had me over for holidays when they realized I was alone, took me out for my birthday, we had occasional movie weekends. We got close. I thought…" His voice cracked and he cleared his throat. "I thought he broke the rules for me because he cared."

"When was the last time you two talked?"

"After the miscarriage," Trevor admitted quietly. "He was disturbed by it, but I just assumed he thought I was hurting. And I was. But things got busy again and I was recovering. I didn't really think twice about our lack of communication. Then I got fired and when neither one of them called, I just assumed they believed what everyone else was saying."

Rhys frowned. It didn't add up, and now that they knew Smith was behind it, there had to be motive. Rhys just had to find it. "We need to locate him, and I know Noah has Esther and Sabrina the job."

Trevor nodded, his fingers twisting together in his lap. "We'll have to call him soon."

Rhys felt something unpleasant twisting in his gut, because he also knew what was next, and it was the last thing he wanted to do. "We may be able to get more information out of Barnes."

At that, Trevor's gaze snapped up and fixed on him. "I can arrange a meeting with the prosecutors and see if they'd be willing to offer Barnes a lighter sentence if he cooperates with information."

Trevor's eyes went wide. "He stalked and blackmailed Noah. He had him *beaten*." Trevor's voice shook. "He can't get off light just for this."

"They may offer it to him anyway," Rhys said, knowing that once this all came to light, it's something the defense and prosecution would agree on. Getting Barnes a lighter sentence meant bringing in one extra offender and more information. It was just how the system worked.

Trevor took in a breath, closing his eyes as he let his head fall back against the couch cushion. "And if we say nothing?"

"We can't say nothing. Not now," Rhys told him. He reached for his arm, curling his fingers around his wrist with a gentle pressure. "He's not going to stop. He promised your uncle property which he has no means of delivering, and now Barnes is in jail and Noah is happily with Adrian. Hell, at this point, Barnes may already be singing like a damn canary. What we need to focus on here is Smith's motive. My guess is he was going to make you so destitute that you'd be willing to give up any and everything in order to get some of your life back. What I don't understand is why, and what he hoped to gain."

"Then we need to track him down," Trevor said. "Before we come forward, we need to track Andrew down and figure out why he's doing all this, and what he wants. If we can find out before the lawyers get their hands on the information, they won't need bargaining chips."

It was a risky ploy, but Rhys knew it was an option.

***

It took less than twenty-four hours for Esther to come through. She said the Smiths were still technically in town, and still living at their same address. Rhys took the opportunity to talk to Noah and let him know the potential of Barnes' lighter sentence when Noah visited his office that Thursday afternoon.

"I figured," Noah said after Rhys gave his practiced speech. He sank into the chair and looked a little dejected, but not devastated. "Once Ryan told me Cole uncovered the link between whoever this was and Charlie, I knew it would be a bargaining chip. I might not be educated in law, but I've known you and Ryan long enough to know what the next step was going to be."

Rhys' lip tugged up into a half smile. "We're going to do everything in our power to make sure it doesn't come to that. If we can track Smith down, Trevor plans to confront him and figure out why he's doing all this. He's the source."

Noah let out a small, almost bitter laugh as he shook his head. "It's strange to think how much we've all suffered because of these people."

Rhys' face fell. "I'm so sorry."

Noah's eyes widened and he shook his head. "Hell no, don't you apologize for these bastards. I hope Trevor isn't beating himself up over this, either."

"I think right now he's confused," Rhys admitted. "I can't promise he won't feel that way later, once we get to the bottom of why Smith decided to target him, though."

"Do you think it's a hate-crime thing? Some sort of transphobic attack?" Noah asked quietly.

Rhys shrugged, leaning back in his chair. In truth, the possibility had occurred to him, but he didn't want to let himself speculate until they had real answers. There were far too many variables. "I don't know, but as soon as he does, he'll call."

"Trevor's not going alone, is he?" Noah asked suddenly, eyes going wide.

Rhys shook his head. "Not completely. But he pointed out last night that if Smith thinks he's got back up, he's not going to say anything. He has to think Trevor's on his own."

"He has to know by now Trevor found support," Noah pointed out.

Rhys bowed his head a little. "Yeah. There's no way to avoid it, and we don't have the time to stage anything. We're just going to have to make do."

***

Rhys was a hot mess. There was no other way to describe the way he felt sitting in the car a few blocks away from Andrew and Mia Smith's house. He could see Trevor approaching the front door from where he was sat, but he was too far away to do anything about it if things got violent.

Trevor seemed mostly at ease, however, trusting his gut that this wasn't going to end bloody or terrifying. Rhys had to trust him too, but he couldn't let go of the tension in his body as he waited. In truth, he wasn't entirely sure anything was going to come of this. Esther reported back that although Mia was still employed at the University, she had taken six months of personal leave. The activity on her email account had stopped around the time Trevor had been given his first anonymous letter, and then there had been no communication at all.

Ivan assured Rhys that when Trevor was ready to press charges, getting a warrant for the emails wouldn't be a problem. Since Barnes' computer was already in evidence from his previous case with Noah, even if Smith tried to wipe his, there was no way to erase the evidence completely. It meant they had something. They just had to find out how much Mia Smith knew, and how much she'd be willing to testify against her husband if it came down to it.

The second task was locating Trevor's uncle, who had all-but disappeared. Apart from an old apartment address, the man had a couple of employers who said they hadn't heard from him in months, and no other relatives to speak of. As a shot in the dark, Rhys had asked Ivan to locate Trevor's parents, but he'd come up empty-handed. He supposed it was just as well. Trevor didn't need the added stress of the people who had made his early years hell, but Rhys couldn't help wanting to know.

Drumming his fingers on the steering wheel, Rhys nearly jumped out of his skin when Trevor was back on the pavement and heading right toward him. His heart began to hammer in his chest. Trevor looked fine, if not a little pale, but his steps were steady. He'd been gone less than five minutes and Rhys didn't know if that meant good or bad news. He held his breath as Trevor opened the passenger door and slid in.

After a tense moment of silence Rhys released his lungful of air. "Was she there?"

"She was," Trevor said. Licking his lips, he leaned back and sighed with his eyes squeezed shut. "She said Andrew's on business in Portland right now and will be back next month. She cussed me out and said I'm responsible for getting him fired because I went to the ER during the miscarriage."

"She *what*?" Rhys asked, his tone filled with venom.

Eyes still closed, he shook his head. "Neither of those things are true, obviously. When I started to lose the pregnancy, I called Andrew and he came over and helped me through it. I saw the study's doctor shortly after to make sure I didn't need any additional procedures, but it was so early, it was a clean loss. And that was it. I didn't talk to Andrew or Mia again after that. I don't think she knows what he's up to, but if she believes I'm responsible for him losing his job, she might not be looking very hard at his current *activities*."

Rhys clenched his jaw, then released it. "Okay. So where do we go from here?"

"I don't know," Trevor admitted. "She wouldn't give me an address, obviously. My uncle lives in Bakersfield most of the time so we could check out his last-known addresses, but I don't think they're there."

"You'd been receiving notes in person from someone," Rhys confirmed. "One of them is probably here."

"I have a feeling they both are. I just need to make myself vulnerable. There's every chance they know I'm here now. Mia will probably call Andrew and let him know." Trevor scrubbed a hand down his face, then looked over at Rhys. "I need to draw him out. Threaten him. Alone."

"No. *Fuck* no," he added for emphasis. "You're not doing this on your own."

"Then he's going to slither back into the shadows and wait until I'm more vulnerable," Trevor said. "This is never going to end if we can't get him to confess."

Rhys gave him a flat look. "You know that's not true. Ivan said we could easily file charges with the evidence we have now. I won't risk your safety over this." Rhys felt a stubborn wave of protectiveness rising in him.

"I don't know that I'm giving you a choice," Trevor replied back. His tone was soft, but there was a determination in it that terrified him a little. "We could file charges, but that won't guarantee that he'll tell anyone why he's doing this, and I think it was more than just a desire to be cruel. Besides, I think I have a plan."

"What is it?" Rhys demanded.

Trevor shook his head. "I can't tell you. You'll hate it and try to stop me, and I'm pretty sure this is the only way."

"Please," Rhys whispered, feeling suffocated by helplessness. "Trevor…"

Trevor looked over at him, his expression pained. "Just give me a few days to work through things, okay?"

Rhys wanted to tell him no, wanted to cocoon him up in a blanket and refuse to let him leave the house. Wanted to beg him to just accept things as they were, file the charges now, with a promise that they'd just make it work. But he knew he couldn't condemn Trevor to that life. He was being controlled already, by this total unknown, and all Rhys could do was stand by him.

"Okay," he finally said. He wanted to beg for more—for a promise that Trevor would stay safe, that he wouldn't do anything stupid, but he didn't want Trevor to make a vow he would have to break.

So, that was the best he could do. *Okay.*

27.

Trevor wasn't foolish enough to think Rhys would let well enough alone. In fact, he was counting on it. When Rhys excused himself to make a 'work call' after they got home, Trevor had a feeling Rhys was calling in a favor or two. Exactly what he needed, because he was about to take a big risk.

The night went off as it usually did. He and Rhys puttered around the house, Trevor fussed with his resume in hopes he'd be able to use it soon, and Rhys did some work and made a few client phone calls. They made dinner together, watched an episode of their baking show, then climbed in the shower where Rhys got down on his knees and sucked Trevor until he came so hard, he was shaking.

Then they went to bed like it was any other night. Only this time, Trevor lay awake, his body primed and ready for what he had to do. He waited until Rhys' breathing had evened out, and then as quietly as he could, he slipped away. He wasn't sure Rhys remained asleep, but he managed to leave the house without being followed by Rhys, and he was taking that as a victory of sorts.

The drive back to Mia's wasn't long enough for him to really get his head on straight, but he knew it would take more than a few minutes for him to accept what he had to do in order to draw Andrew out. There was no way Andrew was far from his wife, and he was certain his uncle was just as close. Mia was the weak link now, and Trevor intended to exploit it.

He pulled the car to a stop a few houses down from Mia's, then strapped his phone to the inside of his thigh with some duct tape he'd stolen out of Rhys' garage. He set his recorder app to start recording, and then he made his way to the door. It was well past midnight, but he could see the faint glow of the TV on through the living room window. He shoved one hand into his pocket, the other giving a steady rhythm of knocking until the door swung open and Mia stood there, looking furious.

She also looked exhausted. He had noticed before she'd lost weight, her cheeks a little sunken and shallow, her blue eyes red-rimmed, but it was more pronounced in the sallow light of the porch lamp. She scowled at Trevor, her jaw twitching with irritation before she addressed him. "What the hell are you doing back here?"

"I'm going to come inside and wait for your husband," he said.

She opened her mouth to refuse him, but he wasn't going to let her. Grabbing her by the arm, he pushed her inside and tried to ignore the surge of guilt because this wasn't him. He wasn't violent, he didn't intimidate women to get what he wanted, but he had to draw Andrew out somehow.

"I'm fucking calling the cops," she said. She tried to break away from him, but his grip was strong, especially since he'd been working out more.

"You're going to call Andrew," he corrected. "I know he's not out of town, and I don't know if you know what he's up to, but we're both about to find out." He kept his voice low as he took her other arm and frog-marched her to the sofa.

Her jaw was tight again, and she looked ready to spit in his face, but he remained as calm as he could when he reached onto the table and picked up her phone. He considered handing it to her, but he knew he couldn't trust her. Luckily it wasn't locked, so he found her contacts, Andrew being at the top of the list, and he hit call.

It rang and rang, nearly five times before a tired voice picked up. "I told you to stop bothering me about…"

"Andrew," Trevor said.

The line went silent, then Andrew cleared his throat. "Why do you have my wife's phone?"

"Because I broke into your house and I'm holding her until you get the fuck over here and tell me what you want."

There was another pause, then Andrew laughed. "No. I don't think so."

Trevor took a breath, then said, "You're the one who wanted me desperate. Well let me fucking tell you, Andrew, I'm desperate. Desperate enough to be really stupid and reckless if it means ending this now. So show up, or you won't like what you come home to. And I know you love your wife." He hoped to god Andrew couldn't read his lie, because Trevor was fairly sure he'd never in his life be desperate enough to carry out that threat. But he ended the call, then dropped the phone to the floor and smashed it with the heel of his shoe.

Mia jumped in her seat as she watched him, her eyes wide and now a little afraid. "You're not actually going to hurt me. I know you."

"You do," Trevor said carefully. "But you don't know what your sadistic fuck of a husband has put me through over the last few months."

"What *he* put *you* through?" she spat, leaning back with a bitter laugh. "Seriously?"

"He's going to show up and you'll know right from his own lips what he's capable of. Having me fired, left destitute, living in my fucking car and nearly freezing to death. And I have no idea why. He's systematically destroyed every avenue in my life—well before he lost his job, so whatever he told you about that was a lie. I didn't seek emergency care when I lost the baby, Mia. I laid in my empty bathtub with Andrew by my side, and I never once saw the inside of a hospital room."

There was something shining in her eyes—a shimmer of doubt, maybe, which told Trevor she might have been suspecting her husband all along. He understood her willing ignorance. She loved him. They were mad for each other, had been for the years he'd known them.

"He wouldn't," she finally said, her tone soft.

Trevor dragged a hand down his face, pacing a little, though not going far in case she decided to run. "I wish that were true. Before I knew it was him, before we traced all the emails to your address," she gasped at that, and he paused in his step, "I never would have considered him as a suspect. I thought…I don't know what I thought." He let out a bitter, pained laugh. "I don't know who could have hated me that much they'd go to these lengths to see me ruined."

"What are you doing to do?" she asked softly.

Trevor shook his head. "I'm going to make him tell me the truth. I want to know what I did that made him do this to me."

Mia bit down on her thumbnail, then her entire body went tense as headlights flooded the front window. Trevor braced himself, moving around to the back of the sofa and hauling Mia up to hold in front of him. He wasn't sure if Andrew had a weapon, if he'd be alone or with his uncle, but he couldn't take any chances.

He wasn't sure he'd get out of this alive, but at least there would be a way for him to know. For everyone to know, if he didn't get through. The recording would be enough. The moment his phone turned off, the recording would hit his cloud drive and be preserved. It was the only way.

The door flew open and Andrew stormed in, slamming it behind him. Trevor let out a momentary breath of relief when he realized that Andrew was alone, and if he was armed, he wasn't showing it.

"Let her go before I end you right here," he snarled.

Trevor shook his head. "Why not tell me what the fuck this is about first, Andrew," he countered. "What could I have possibly done to have deserved this?"

"You were *faulty*," Andrew hissed. He walked all the way into the living room, coming to a stop a few feet from Mia. His hands were curled into fists, and he looked like he was about to pounce. "It was our one chance. Our *one* chance, and your piece of shit body couldn't handle it!"

Trevor blinked. "What?"

Andrew made a wounded noise, his eyes rolling up to the ceiling for a brief moment. "You were a prime candidate. You're young, your levels were good—even with you poisoning your body with hormones for so fucking long, you were good. You were supposed to go full term…but you didn't. And you killed my child!"

Trevor took an involuntary step back, a wave of panic hitting him sudden and intense. "*What?*" he whispered.

In a flash, Andrew had Mia by the arm, whipping her behind him as his glare fixed on Trevor's face. "Our baby," he clarified, and Trevor knew then he wasn't talking about him. He was talking about Mia.

Mia picked up on it too, because she ripped herself from Andrew's grasp. "What the hell are you talking about?" she demanded.

Andrew ran a hand through his hair, making it stand up in wild spikes as his attention was divided between Trevor and his wife. "I couldn't…I didn't want to tell you. When the test said you couldn't carry, I had to find someone. The experiments were so closely monitored, I couldn't find anyone. Then he walked in and he was…I didn't think it would be possible, but we went through all those tests and he was an ideal candidate."

"You put my eggs in him?" Mia asked in a broken whisper.

"All of them," Andrew said, his eyes whipping back over to Trevor as though he was the devil himself. "It was the best shot at conceiving and it…it worked. It would have been fine, and our baby would have been born, and you…" He licked his lips and shook his head.

Mia was trembling so hard, Trevor worried she might collapse, and it was the distraction he needed to keep himself together through this onslaught of information. "I had surgery after that," she said numbly. "I can't…they took *everything* out."

"I know," Andrew replied. His voice was shattered, and for a brief, insane moment, Trevor felt a surge of pity for him. It was quickly dismissed when he realized what Andrew's plan had been.

"You were going to take my baby," Trevor said.

"*My* baby!" Andrew roared. He rushed forward, but he was too crazed and wild, and Trevor dodged him easily. "It was my baby, and you couldn't fucking do the one thing I needed you to do. You robbed us of this, of ever having a family!"

"You ruined my life for something I couldn't control!" Trevor bellowed. His hands curled into fists, and he was seconds from lunging. "You blackmailed me, you had me fired, stole my home, ruined my life! You used my one remaining family member against me! For this? You wanted me face down in the mud for this?"

Andrew let out a vicious laugh. "I wanted you dead. I wanted you miserable and alone and no longer breathing! Only you won't fucking die. You keep…you keep *surviving*," he stuttered.

Trevor meant to respond, or attack him, or something. Anything to get him to shut up and to end it, only he didn't get the chance. In a whirlwind of action, the front door was kicked open and three uniformed officers, and one suited man stormed in with guns drawn.

Trevor's hands shot up, and when the police shouted for everyone to get on their knees, terror made him the first to comply. It was only when he realized the familiar face of Ivan was reaching for him, drawing him back up with a soft, comforting touch, that he let himself believe it was over.

"I want this fucker arrested!" Andrew screamed, even as one of the uniformed officers was putting handcuffs on him. "He broke into my house, threatened my wife, was about to attack me!"

"Get him outside," Ivan ordered. He was silent as Andrew was dragged away, and then he turned to Mia who wasn't cuffed, but was being closely watched by the woman officer who had come in second. "Mrs. Smith," Ivan said, walking over. "I'm Captain Perez. I'd like to hear from you about the events of the night, and what you might know about an ongoing investigation regarding your husband and Trevor Greene."

Mia swallowed thickly, then looked over at Trevor and he knew right then, she wasn't going to lie. That hit him, like a physical blow and he stumbled back, just barely managing to collapse into a chair. The third officer walked up and started to take his statement, and in a numb voice, Trevor began to talk.

28.

Rhys showed up at the station half panicked, his hands shaking as he held his phone with Ivan's message that Trevor had been detained. There were no charges being filed, however, as Mia Smith had insisted Trevor hadn't forced his way into her home, and the aggressor was her husband.

> **Ivan: She's willing to fully cooperate, which means we get her emails. We're still looking for Trevor's uncle, but he can't hide forever. I've alerted Bakersfield PD to put out an APB, but I'm not too worried about it. I'm not sure if the recording will be admissible, but it's enough to help with a warrant to obtain his computer and files from the University.**

Rhys wasn't worried either. Shane McCafferty might have been greedy, but he was simply acting on an offer he believed to be real. The true danger to Trevor was now being booked, and there was enough evidence to bring about as many, if not more charges than had been brought against Barnes. It was so much and still not enough, because Rhys had done his duty by having Ivan put a tail on Trevor, but he was still painfully ignorant of why Andrew Smith had gone this far.

Trevor was waiting for him in Ivan's office when Rhys was finally allowed back, and before either of them spoke, they stood in a long, tight embrace, just breathing each other in. When Rhys finally pulled away, he could see faint tear tracks down Trevor's cheeks, and he ached to wipe them away.

"Are you okay? Did he hurt you?" he asked.

Trevor laughed. "He didn't get the chance, and I would have wiped the floor with him. I might have only had a few weeks with Wes and Adrian, but the training stuck."

Rhys couldn't help his slightly sardonic smile. "Well, good. Ivan said they're booking Smith in on charges of stalking, but he expects a few more to be added before he sees the judge about bail."

Trevor bit his lip. "I don't think Mia's going to stand with him, but the reason why he did this is directly tied to my participation in the research program."

Rhys had suspected as much, but he didn't say that right now. "It's okay. Whatever happens, it'll be okay."

Trevor let out a tense laugh. "Weirdly enough, I believe you. I mean, I'm probably not going to sleep for a week, but it finally feels over." He released Rhys' waist, only to grab his hand and press their palms together. "I want to go home."

Rhys felt warmed by that, and tugged Trevor toward the door. "Then let's go. There's nothing keeping us here. And when you're ready, you can tell me everything."

"Yeah. I will. Soon," Trevor said. "Just…not tonight."

Rhys could live with that.

***

Neither of them slept much, though Rhys spent the entire night with his arms around Trevor, spooning him in a tight hold to remind him that it was over, that he made it out and it was fine. Tomorrow would bring a host of issues—there was still a chance Trevor would be charged for forcing his way into Mia's home and holding her there, and there was no telling if or when Andrew would be able to post bail.

The first thing Rhys wanted to ensure was that Trevor had an order of protection, though he knew damn well a piece of paper wouldn't stop someone with determination and purpose. Luckily Trevor was protected. He had a community—a family—who wouldn't leave him on his own. All the same, Rhys could only imagine what Trevor was going through, and he had no real way to make it better.

"You should talk to Noah," he said, speaking quiet in the faded, early light of dawn. He knew Trevor was awake, though the other man had yet to turn around and face him. "He's been where you are."

Trevor took a long breath in through his nose, out through his mouth, then nodded against Rhys' arm. "That's probably a good idea. I'm just not up for it right now."

Pressing his nose to the back of Trevor's neck, Rhys tightened his arms a fraction. "How are you?"

Trevor took his time answering, taking a few deep breaths first. "I don't really know, to be honest. I mean, I feel fine, which I think is freaking me out more than anything." He gently pulled out of Rhys' arms, then rolled onto his back to look at the other man. "I don't feel good or bad. I just…feel fine."

"Okay," Rhys said softly.

Trevor shook his head against the pillow, mussing his hair. The light from the window caught it and made it shimmer—copper and beautiful. "I know it's going to hit me at some point, and I think I'm afraid it's going to break me, knowing it's finally over."

Rhys nodded, reaching out to brush his curled knuckles over the edge of Trevor's jaw. "You're surrounded by people who've been there. Noah and Adrian got through with Barnes. Cole and Ryan went through hell just weeks ago. Even Wes knows what it's like to try and put your life back together after everything was upended. They can help."

"And you?" Trevor asked, a little hesitation in his voice.

"I've been privileged. I know what it's like for everything to change. After Vanessa left, I wasn't sure how to be by myself, how to exist as just Rhys Anderson, and it took a lot of time. I was still reeling a little the day I met you. But I don't know what to tell you other than it gets easier. And things stop feeling so cloudy. And that I'm going to be here through all of it."

"Even after I move out?" Trevor asked, his tone a little daring then.

Rhys felt it in his gut, the idea of Trevor's absence, and it hurt. However, he knew why it was necessary. "I'm not going anywhere," he told him firmly. "You not sleeping in my bed every night changes nothing. I didn't fall in love with you just because you were here."

Trevor's eyes closed, and he let out a shuddering breath that shook his whole body. When he opened them again, his eyes swam with tears, though they didn't fall. "Thank you."

Rhys shook his head from side to side, but he didn't counter Trevor's thanks. It wasn't necessary, but he understood why Trevor needed to say it. Instead, he reached his hand over Trevor's middle and linked their fingers together. "We have a ways to go."

"Yeah," Trevor sighed out. He didn't need to say more, that one word was enough.

29.

Trevor hovered in the entry way of Rhys' office, a little hesitant. His assistant was on the phone, having a tense conversation with someone about a bill, and she held a finger at him, signaling for him to wait. Trevor had sent a text after Ivan called him to let him know that his uncle had been arrested twenty miles out of town, but he hadn't gotten a response and he figured Rhys was either in meetings or court all day.

He told himself to wait, but the weight of knowing one of his blood-kin was in jail after helping to destroy his life was a lot to bear. His gaze flickered down to the assistant's desk and he took in her shiny name plate with **Mel** written in bold letters. Beside that, a photograph of Mel and who Trevor assumed to be her wife or girlfriend. There were a few Avengers knick-knacks scattered around, and a succulent that looked like it was only half alive.

It told him there was history here, there was so much that went on before he'd come along to be part of Rhys' life, and it felt strange. It felt strange to think of a time he existed before any of this. In truth, he'd always been six degrees of separation from Rhys, at least since he started working with Noah. There was every chance they would have met at some point, but he couldn't imagine Rhys giving him the time of day if it hadn't been for all this.

He should be bitter about it, but instead he found himself strangely thankful that Andrew had decided to upend his life. He was getting his resume together, and Ryan had put him in touch with a lawyer who promised to have his employment record and rental past cleared from whatever Andrew had done to it. There was a light at the end of the tunnel, and he was desperate to know Rhys would still be waiting for him when he crossed through.

"Hey," Mel said once she cradled the phone. "Sorry about that, today is the day for assholes, apparently."

Trevor gave a soft laugh. "It's fine. I'm kind of dropping in unannounced."

Mel's gaze flickered over to Rhys' closed office door, then back to him. "He has forty-five minutes for lunch coming up, and this meeting has another thirty to go. Wanna go with me to grab sandwiches and surprise the fuck out of him. It's been a hell of a day and I think seeing you and food is going to make him ugly-sob happy tears."

Trevor couldn't hide his grin. "Yes."

Mel shot up from her desk, grabbing her keys, then led the way out the front door. She locked up behind her, but instead of heading for her parked car, she motioned him through the lot and to the next shopping center over where a hole-in-the-wall sandwich shop sat between a dry cleaners and an accountant's office. "This is our go-to for when we need comfort food," she explained as she held the door for him.

Trevor was immediately overwhelmed with the smell of fresh bread and herbs, his stomach growling when it reminded him he hadn't eaten all day.

Mel clearly heard the noise, because she looked over at him with a smirk. "Okay, if you eat meat and dairy, get the chicken and bacon with gouda on their homemade sourdough. It'll change your life."

"Noted," Trevor said. He snagged one of the paper menus from the bin on the wall and perused their selection. It was small, but all of it was homemade, and he had a feeling this was one of the places who understood true comfort food. "What are you getting Rhys?"

Mel gave him a long look, then said, "I'm going to leave that one to you."

Trevor nearly choked on his own tongue. "Uh…no? I mean, you get his lunch all the time, and it's been a long day. I don't want to fuck up and get him something he hates."

She gave him a soft smile and walked up to the counter where a young teen was waiting to take their order. "I trust you," was all she said.

Feeling somewhat panicked, yet strangely empowered, he stared at the menu until the Italian sub glared out at him. "With extra balsamic," he told the teen. "And feta instead of the provolone." When he ordered, he pretended like he couldn't see Mel's smile growing as she handed over the card.

They gathered their drink cups, filling them at the fountain station, then waited at one of the high tables for their name to be called. She drummed her short nails beside her cup, then cocked her head at him. "So, when's the wedding?"

Trevor choked again, this time on a mouthful of fizzy drink. "Uh…"

Waving her hand, she laughed off his reaction. "Okay, I'm not being serious. I know you two just met, but that boy is more than in love with you. I hope this doesn't freak you out, but he's obsessed, and I think you are too."

Biting his lip, Trevor fussed with the straw, then decided there was no point in hiding how he felt. "He's probably the best thing that ever happened to me, and it's a little terrifying."

"I get it," Mel said. "I felt that way when I met Billie. It's been nine years now and if possible, I love her more today than when I first fell for her. When it's right, you just know."

"I've just never *not* known," Trevor told her. "I've never really done the whole relationship thing, and life has been kind of a shit-show lately. I'm afraid I'm making more out of this than it is."

"I don't think love waits for opportune moments, dude," she told him. "It always arrives when everything's upside down, and it's up to you to make it work. Or not. But for the record, I've known Rhys a long time and I've never seen him smile like this."

Trevor felt his entire body heat up with both pleasure and a little fear because that was a lot of responsibility. Yet, he also wanted it. He wanted to be the one who made Rhys light up, who gave him that secret smile no one else could. He wanted to be the one he thought of first thing in the morning, and last thing at night.

It had never really mattered before now.

Trevor had written off the idea of spouse and family, but after meeting Rhys, he was craving it. He was willing to try again, and that meant everything. "I'm not going to fuck it up," he told her.

She smiled at him, soft and a little fierce. "See that you don't."

They gathered their food shortly after, and Mel spent the rest of the time talking about her new puppy on the walk back. The front door was still locked, but as they walked in, Trevor saw Rhys' door was cracked open.

"Is that food? I swear to god Mel, if you weren't married and I weren't madly in love with someone else, I'd probably propose to you right now."

She gave Trevor a sly grin, and he stepped forward and called out, "Good thing you're taken then."

He nearly laughed when he heard the frantic sound of Rhys scrambling from his desk, and his harried face appeared through the doorway a minute later. His eyes went wide at the sight of Trevor, and his mouth stretched into a grin. "Holy shit. What are you doing here?"

"I texted you," Trevor told him.

Rhys turned and rushed back into the office, appearing a second later with his phone in his hand. "God, sorry, I'm such a jack-ass today. It's been non-stop bullshit. Are you okay? You know you can come see me any time."

"I think he knows," Mel pointed out dryly as she started to unwrap her sandwich. "On account of him just showing up and all."

Rhys gave her a dark glare, then looked at the paper bag of food. "Please tell me some of that's for me."

Mel shoved the bag toward the end of the desk. "I let your boy here pick out your food, so you better hope he has good taste."

"I love it," Rhys said dutifully.

Trevor laughed. "You don't even know what it is."

"I don't care. I'd eat eggplant right now if it was sitting in front of me. I'm starving, and you're here. It's good enough."

Trevor wanted to sigh, to melt a little, to cuff him upside the head for being such a romantic asshole. Instead, he grabbed the food and motioned for Rhys to head back into the office. The moment the door was shut, Trevor was backed against it, Rhys' hands on his cheeks, pulling him down for a slow, deep kiss. His eyes fluttered shut and he allowed himself to sink into the feel of Rhys' tongue brushing along his, the hot pulse of want shooting up his spine.

This was no place for it, but he still let himself fantasize about what it would be like to back Rhys up to his office chair, straddle him, and sink down on his cock. The very thought of riding him until they were both sobbing with pleasure into each other's mouths sent a gush of wet into his boxers, and he could feel his dick throb a little.

"Fuck," Rhys said, pulling away with a series of biting pecks, "fuck, if I keep this up…"

"I know," Trevor said. His hand crushed into the paper food bag, and it took him a full half minute to compose himself. "I wasn't expecting that."

"It's been the longest day and the only thing I wanted was to see you," Rhys told him. He took the bag from Trevor, then motioned to his little love seat which sat under the window. The pair of them eased down, facing each other with knees touching, and Rhys dug into the bag, pulling out each sandwich. When he opened his own and saw what Trevor had gotten him, he looked up with suspiciously shiny eyes. "Did Mel tell you what I wanted?"

Trevor rolled his eyes, cheeks flushing. "No," he said with a huff. "She left my ass out in the wind. I just…I tried to remember what you liked. If you hate it, you can have mine. She said the chicken-bacon sandwich is to die for so…" His words were interrupted when Rhys curled a hand into the front of his shirt and dragged him in for another kiss.

"It's perfect."

"It's just a sandwich," Trevor breathed out, cheeks getting hotter.

Rhys kissed him again. "It isn't. It's not *just* anything when it comes to you." He let Trevor go with a slow drag of his fingers, then picked up his food and tucked in. Mouth full, he managed to ask around his huge bite, "How is your day going? What was it you wanted to talk to me about?"

Trevor remembered just then about Ivan's call, and he let his sandwich fall back to the paper. "Apparently my uncle was found and arrested today, about twenty miles outside of town. Ivan couldn't tell me what he was charged with, but he said he expected him to have a pretty high bail set considering the evidence they have."

Though Trevor wasn't entirely sure what evidence the detectives on the case had managed to gather in just a few days, he knew it was enough to press more than misdemeanor charges against both Andrew and his uncle. Mia was still being investigated, but Trevor was pretty sure she hadn't been in on it.

"Are you okay?" Rhys asked. His words interrupted Trevor's spiraling thoughts, and he reached for his sandwich, taking a bite. "Is there anything I can do?"

Trevor shook his head, swallowing before he answered him. "Ivan said to just hang tight. Obviously, all of us are going to be subpoenaed, and he's pretty sure Andrew didn't get the chance to erase the communication between him and my uncle."

"Even if he erased emails and files, there will be phone records, and I doubt he was clever enough to find a way to hack those," Rhys said. He finished his food before he spoke again. "Honestly, I don't think Andrew really knew what he was doing. He had a little skill and some charisma, but that was it. A person who had done this before would know how to cover his tracks. Andrew left a long trail of evidence in his wake. When I first heard about it—after Barnes was arrested and Noah told me what they found on him—I was sure it was some sort of ploy. When you came to me, I thought it confirmed that, but it looks like I was wrong."

"I think I'm a little too scared to believe it was this easy," Trevor admitted.

Rhys took their trash and set it to the side, shifting so he could tuck Trevor into his embrace. He brought Trevor's hand to his lips, kissing it, sending warmth shooting up Trevor's arm and settling right against his heart. "Sometimes it *is* that easy. Sometimes it isn't some big conspiracy. More often than not, actually, it's just some asshole with a half-baked idea, who just wants to make people hurt. Those guys always get caught. They always pay."

Trevor nodded, but he wasn't sure the thought comforted him. Yes, he felt strangely compelled to thank Andrew because it brought Rhys into his life, but there was the underlying bitterness of what he'd been through. A fool would tell him it was just proof that he was strong enough to get through anything, but Trevor lived his life as a gay trans man, partly raised by addicts, taken by the state, and the one woman who really and truly loved him unconditionally died when he was far too young to lose her. He already knew he was strong. He didn't need to keep taking more beatings to prove it further.

It occurred to him right there, however, that Rhys wasn't the fool saying it. Rhys wasn't trying to make excuses or look for the bright side. He simply pointed out that some people were monsters, and eventually they would pay. The simplicity of it all made him love Rhys even more.

"Do you have plans tonight?" Rhys asked softly.

Trevor shrugged. "Adrian called and asked if I wanted another lesson, and I thought it might be a good way to work out some of this energy I haven't been able to get rid of."

Rhys smiled. "I think that's a good idea. Why don't I pick you up from the gym and we can go out to celebrate?"

"Compromise?" Trevor offered. "We pick food up and take it home, then eat in bed?"

Rhys smiled even wider. "Deal."

"Kiss on it?" Trevor suggested.

Rhys reached up and touched his cheek. "You never need to ask."

Epilogue

Trevor's head snapped back, more with surprise than with the force of the blow, but it still messed with his senses a little. He stumbled, shuffling back three steps before Cole came at him again, only this time he was able to block the right hook. Cole got in a rib-shot, and then mislanded an uppercut before Adrian called the match over.

"Not bad," Cole said, his words slurred from his mouth guard. He reached for Trevor who stepped up to his glove and let Cole pat him twice on the shoulder. "You're going to be good at this."

Trevor shook his head. "I'm a disaster."

"You're a fringe contender," Adrian said, walking forward with one crutch cuff hooked around his left arm. "That's not a bad place to be in."

"Doesn't that mean the guy most likely to lose?" Trevor asked, spitting his mouthguard into his hand and reaching for his water.

Cole laughed. "It means the one they'll always underestimate. Don't worry, I get it more than not, and I wear the badge proudly."

"Well, your trophies are starting to add up," Adrian pointed out, and Trevor laughed at the flush rising in Cole's cheeks. "You held your own against a man who has won four of his last six matches, Trevor. That means something."

The thought of fighting a proper opponent still terrified him a little, but the sincerity in Adrian's voice, and in Cole's, gave him a courage he didn't think he'd ever have. "I'll think about it. Lectures start in six weeks and the last thing I need after this whole mess is to show up on my first day with a shiner."

Cole grinned at him as he started to unwind his wraps, leaning back in the chair which was propped against the side of the ring. "Fair enough, but I think it might give you a little bit of a bad-ass edge. If you look like you can take a beating, no one's going to fuck with you."

Trevor couldn't help a laugh. "I'm a Latin teacher, dude. The Classics department is just a bunch of eighteen-year-old nerds from artsy high schools who spent their free time translating passages of the Vulgate for fun."

"So...*you*?" Adrian asked, waggling his brows.

"I want to make some sort of comment about how trying to insult me also insults your boyfriend," Trevor said pointedly, making Adrian's expression fall for just a second, "but I can't. Because it's super not wrong."

Swiping the sweat from his brow, Trevor followed Adrian and Cole out into the main area where he could see Rhys and Ryan chatting to Anna who was balancing a bowl of yogurt and granola on her swelling stomach. She still wasn't technically off bedrest, but her doctor okayed a few hours at the gym per week so long as she stayed in the seat behind the desk. The twins were close to their delivery date, and though Trevor had been so busy putting his life back together he hadn't gotten the chance to stay on top of gossip, he knew things were about to change for them.

He also didn't miss the way Rhys gave her belly longing looks, and how he never missed the chance to press his hand there and feel them kick. He'd already offered almost all his free time to babysitting Maggie whenever they needed him, and Trevor wasn't exactly putting his foot down about it. Because watching that was giving him feelings. Watching that was stirring to life something he thought had died with his former pregnancy.

"Hey you," Rhys said, rising when he saw Trevor walking over. He held out his arms, and Trevor leaned in to kiss him without getting him too sweaty. When he pulled back, Rhys touched the side of his jaw. "Took a nice one there."

"Cole has a mean left-hook, but it wasn't as bad as it could have been. Adrian wants me to consider competing, but I don't know if I have it in me right now when the semester's about to start."

Rhys brushed his fingers along the start of the bruise, then pulled back. "You know I'm here for you, whatever you decide. I think a few matches on the weekends could be fun."

Trevor shrugged. "Maybe. I also like just this, you know? Just being here with everyone I give a shit about. It's enough for me."

Rhys bit his lip, then said, "Go change. I want to get food and go back to yours."

"Mine?" Trevor asked with a slightly smug grin.

"Yes. Yours, with the superior sofa and the better lighting. Now hurry up, I'm starving and we can get kababs before the rush if we hurry."

Trevor leaned in and kissed him one more time before rushing off to do just that.

***

Rhys could feel Trevor's strange, nervous energy as they sat. He was always a little more amped after his training nights, but there was something more to it, like a buzzing under his skin. At first Rhys assumed it was the fact that he was finally getting back to work. It had taken more than seven months to get Trevor's record cleared, and they were still going through hearing after hearing for Smith and Barnes. Trevor's uncle had pled guilty, had been offered a deal, and was now serving the first of his three years behind bars.

Rhys hadn't waited long to tell Trevor about looking for his birth parents, and though he expected Trevor to be upset with him over it, he took the news in stride.

"If they want to find me, they can, and I'll worry about it then," he said one night, hours after he was sweat-soaked and sated from their love-making. "But I don't want to ruin something that might be good, you know? I was given to my grandma and because of that, I had a good life. Maybe I wouldn't have gone through all that shit with Andrew if I'd been adopted by a regular family and had the sort of support you had growing up, but I'm happy where I am."

Rhys had reached over, gently brushing his fingers through Trevor's locks. "Do you wish you'd been given that chance?"

"I don't know," Trevor had started, trailing off in thought. "Sometimes. Mostly after my grandma died and I was alone, I found myself wishing I hadn't met her at all, but it was just my grief talking. I don't think I could ever regret that I was given to someone who not only accepted me, but who did everything to help me live as my true self. And if it hadn't happened the way it did, I wouldn't have met you, and I don't want to imagine my life without you in it."

Now, though, the soft tenderness between them was missing. Trevor's foot was tapping on the carpet under the coffee table, and when Rhys reached over to touch his knee, he stilled with a guilty smile.

"Sorry."

"Do you want to talk about it?" Rhys asked, trying to convey through his tone that he'd be fine with a yes or a no.

Trevor bit the inside of his cheek, making his face look hollow, his cheekbone protruding, then he released it and sighed. "My lease is up in two months."

"Right," Rhys said, trying to pretend like he hadn't been thinking about that constantly, especially since Trevor had only signed one for six months. Six months had to mean something, didn't it? Whether it was to consider moving in with Rhys, or moving away to be closer to his new University post, it was obvious he wasn't thinking of his apartment as permanent.

Trevor's smile was a little tense, thin-lipped, unusual which was setting Rhys on edge. "So, I…it's only…I was thinking, uh…"

"Are you moving?" Rhys blurted.

Trevor's eyes went wide. "Maybe? You said the offer to be with you would always be open, but I didn't want to assume after all these months that—"

Rhys couldn't help but cut those words off with a kiss. He pressed Trevor back against the cushions, straddling his legs and grinding down because he'd been wanting him since they got to the gym hours ago, and he'd been patient long enough. "*Always* assume," he murmured against Trevor's mouth. "When it comes to me loving you, me wanting to be with you, *always* assume it's a yes."

Trevor gasped, arching his pelvis up, grabbing Rhys by the hips and pulling him down. "Okay," he groaned.

Rhys wasted no time in getting their bottoms off, palming Trevor right where he wanted it most. He loved the feel of the coarse hair against the pads of his fingers, the way he could spread Trevor open and stroke two fingers along either side of his cock. Since first making love to Trevor, Rhys had been startled by how well they fit, how different Trevor was to anyone he'd ever slept with, but not because his body was. No, it was because it was right. It was better than it had ever been before, and ever would be, though Rhys didn't want to consider a future where he'd be able to compare.

No, he wanted this forever.

Sinking between Trevor's thighs, he decided the night called for a thorough blow-job because Trevor had all-but just announced they were moving back in together, and it was everything Rhys had wanted since the day he helped Trevor move his last piece of furniture into his new apartment. And in truth, he was grateful Trevor had this—some time to gather himself, to feel independent and safe again—but he was lonely without him.

Laving between his folds, Rhys pushed his tongue in a slow rhythm against Trevor's dick, then slipped two fingers into his entrance, just to the first knuckle. He wasn't very wet, but he was clenching around him, almost pulsing with how close he was, and Rhys knew it wouldn't take long.

Just a few swipes of his tongue and a push of his fingers, and there was a gush of moisture against his hand, running down to his wrist. Rhys lapped it up before kissing his way back to Trevor's mouth, then got his own hand between his legs to reach that edge. He was close enough it only took a few pulls, then he collapsed against his boyfriend's side and they shuffled until they could comfortably lay across the sofa.

"I needed that," Trevor said, his voice still a little breathy.

Rhys smiled into the crook of Trevor's neck, kissing the soft skin there. "Me too. And for the record, I think the idea of you living with me will always get me that hot."

Trevor chuckled and pulled Rhys a little tighter against his body. "Good to know." His hand began to trail a line up and down Rhys' arm, and then he cleared his throat. The nervous energy was back again, and Rhys wondered what more he had to say. But he didn't want to push. He always wanted Trevor to feel safe opening up to him in his own time. "I want to have kids," he finally said.

Rhys was expecting anything but those words, and it shocked him so badly he was halfway to sitting up before he realized he'd moved. Trevor looked a little terrified, so Rhys forced himself to relax. "Okay," he said carefully. "Can I ask what brought that on? Because you said you didn't want go through all that again, and you know I'm okay with that."

"Yeah," Trevor replied. He didn't entirely meet Rhys' gaze, but Rhys knew it wasn't because he was being dishonest. "I didn't. Then I met you and I realized that if I was going to do this with anyone in the world, I want it to be you." He finally looked at Rhys properly. "No, wait, I don't *want*—I *need*. I *need* it to be you. It's just..." He licked his lips and looked a little afraid again. "I don't think I could handle doing it myself. Carrying the pregnancy. It's too much."

Rhys all-but deflated against him, almost too afraid to hope that this was real, but wanting Trevor to understand that he didn't have any expectations about how they created a family. However it happened, it wouldn't matter, because it would be theirs. "Okay," was all he could bring himself to say.

Trevor looked at him a little suspiciously. "Really? Okay? Because you know I am *capable* of it being me."

"I know," Rhys said. He leaned down, resting his elbow on the cushion, keeping himself slightly propped up to look down at the man he loved so desperately. "But I told you before that I don't care how I have a family. However they come to us isn't the point. The point is us doing this together. Because we will love the shit out of them, as much as I love you, and that's a difficult concept to wrap my mind around when I think about just how fiercely I feel for you."

Trevor's cheeks pinked and he reached for Rhys' hand, twisting their fingers together. "We can talk about it? Later, I mean. When we feel ready."

"Yes," Rhys said, then he pulled his hand away to cup Trevor's cheek. "But always assume that I want it, always assume my answer is yes," he repeated, "because it's not just living together, okay? It's all of it. And I want it with you."

Trevor closed his eyes, and leaned in, and smiled.

The End.

Works by E.M. Lindsey

Baum's Boxing Series:

Book One: Below the Belt
Book Two: Fortune and Fate

Irons and Works:

Free Hand

Magnum Opus Series:

Verismo
Tremolo
Serenata

Love in History Series:

Time and Tide
Monsters and Men

Stand-Alone Novels:

Endless Forever

In Secret, In Silence

Absolution

Time to Wake Up

Like Water Catching Fire

Forget-Me-Not

About the Author

E.M. Lindsey lives in the SW United States where she's currently on the Ph.D. track. Her life is family, thesis research, and writing in that order. In what precious little time she has to herself, she reads cheesy romances and binges GBBO and terrible 90s romcoms on Netflix.

Now that Baum's Boxing has ended, check out E.M. Lindsey's new, #1 best selling series, Irons and Works, and follow the lives and romances of five tattoo artists working in a little shop in small town, Colorado.

Irons and Works, book one: Free Hand

Derek Osbourne's life is mostly quiet. A routine that keeps him functioning, a job as a tattoo artist that keeps his rent paid and food in his belly, and if he's alone through it well, there are worse things to be. With his complicated past, Derek is sure no one would ever want to deal with the struggle that comes along with loving someone who has severe PTSD. Especially since the man who spent years abusing him is now in hospice, and Derek has taken over his end-of-life care. Derek's resigned himself to living and dying alone, and maybe that's okay. Then one night, during a raging storm, Derek finds himself stuck in an ATM vestibule with a quiet stranger, and it's in that moment his world begins to change.

Basil Shevach is new to Fairfield, taking over his dead aunt's florist shop. He's also Deaf in a small town, where he and his sister are the only ones not hearing. It's not to say he hates it there, but he's not sure Fairfield is the place for him. At least, not until one night, when a storm leaves him trapped inside the bank with a man quietly panicking against the glass door. He's immediately intrigued by this unbelievably attractive stranger with bright tattoos covering his arms and haunted eyes, but he's also bitter because he's dated a hearing man before and it ended as badly as it could go for him. He had resolved years ago to never make that mistake again, but somehow, the frightened man trapped with him in that little room, crawls under his skin and no matter what he tries, he can't seem to shake him.

Will the two of them be able to find their way together, or will their pasts prevent them from being able to find happiness and contentment when they need it most?